ABOUT THE AUTHOR

Chrissie Bellbrae's dual narratives transport readers from past to present and are inspired by her combined love of history and fascination with genealogy. Chrissie often draws on the lives of her forebears and depicts women during times of social and emotional change. The result is characters who live far more remarkable lives than any of her ancestors experienced.

A Fiona McIntosh Commercial Fiction Masterclass pushed Chrissie to complete her first manuscript and she hasn't stopped writing since. She enjoys an open fire, an oaky chardonnay and a great book—typically anything historical. When not reading, writing, ocean swimming, or watching her beloved magpies, Chrissie looks forward to visits from her children and grandchildren and to sharing her stories with them.

Chrissie acknowledges that she lives and writes by salt water on the coast of Wadawurrung Country.

The Romanov Secret is her second novel.

www.chrissiebellbrae.com

PRAISE FOR CHRISSIE BELLBRAE'S BOOKS

ADVANCE PRAISE FOR *THE ROMANOV SECRET*

'From the opulence of Imperial Russia to the fashion scene of 1980s Melbourne, this sweeping family saga will entrance readers and keep them guessing until the very last page.'
Lisa Ireland, author of *The Studio Girls*

PRAISE FOR *THE FLORENTINE QUILT*

'Breath-taking settings, strong female characters, mystery, intrigue and romance ... *The Florentine Quilt* has it all, and will keep you up turning the pages long after your usual bedtime.'
Pamela Cook, author, writing coach and podcaster

'What an enchanting debut novel by Australian author Chrissie Bellbrae, a perfect read for historical fiction lovers. The Florentine Quilt is set in Italy, Cornwall and Melbourne.'
Gloria, Mrs G's Bookshelf

'An element of mythicism, a serve of history, three unique and well written timelines and a story that allows visual translation to adorn the imagination as the reader connects the dots.'
Craig and Phil, Happy Valley Books Read

'A really lovely book to get lost in.'
Kaye Baillie, author

'There are some books that sweep you away with the storytelling, some are plot-driven, and others are beautifully written on a line by line basis. The Florentine Quilt does all three.'
Emma Babbington, author

'What an astonishing debut! Could not put it down and read the last half when I should have been writing my own manuscript.'
Susan Mackie, author

'An intricately written story with three interweaving timelines. I loved the folklore and mystical elements.'
Pauline Wilson, author

'Great historic novel with a good dose of redemptive romance for the heroine.'
Lynette Steer, GoodReads

'If you're looking for love, mysticism, impeccably researched history and a triple timeline, this enchanting story is for you! The story is written with fairytale feels and lyrical flair and combines current day issues with mysticism, magical realism and historical fact.'
Tania, GoodReads

THE ROMANOV SECRET

CHRISSIE BELLBRAE

SILVER MAGPIE PRESS

The Romanov Secret by Chrissie Bellbrae
Silver Magpie Press, Australia
First published 2025
Paperback ISBN: 978-0-6483969-8-7
Ebook ISBN: 978-0-6483969-9-4
© 2025 by Chrissie Bellbrae
Except for use in any review, the reproduction or utilisation of this work in whole or in part in any form by any electronic, mechanical or other means, now known or hereafter invented, including xerography, photocopying and recording, or in any information storage or retrieval situation, is forbidden without the permission of the publisher.
This book is sold subject to the condition that it shall not, by way of trade or otherwise, be lent, resold, hired out or otherwise circulated without the prior consent of the publisher in any form of binding or cover other than that in which it is published and without a similar condition being imposed on the subsequent purchaser.
All rights reserved, including the right of reproduction in whole or in part in any form. No part of this book may be reproduced, published, performed in public or communicated to the public in any existing form without prior written permission from the author, with the exception of quotes used in reviews. Any use of this publication to 'train' generative artificial intelligence (AI) technologies to generate text is expressly prohibited.
This is a work of fiction. Names, characters, places, and incidents are either the product of the author's imagination or are used fictitiously, and any resemblance to actual persons, living or dead, business establishments, events, or locales is entirely coincidental.

To mothers
who give of themselves selflessly, and without hesitation.
Thanks for your unconditional love and guidance.
Especially you Mum.
Love you always.

Ladybird, ladybird, fly away home,
Your house is on fire and your children all gone,
All except one and that's little Anne,
And she's crept under the warming pan.

JEAN

1

Sydney 1982

This isn't the time to have a run in her stockings. At ten dollars a packet the designer legwear should last at least one night. Jean fluffs out the taffeta peplum of her cocktail dress to cover the run, then recoils as management's three wise monkeys, decked out in tartan waistcoats and flashy bow ties, bounce past like rambunctious schoolboys. Hasn't anyone told them that combing wispy hair over balding scalps is a futile exercise? Nothing disguises the rapid march of middle age.

'Good luck,' Wilkinson raises his eyebrows, 'or should I say, break a leg?'

Ross Milton swaggers a little too close for comfort. 'This is your big chance, love. Don't blow it...'

He's gone before she can offer a suitably acerbic reply.

Jean Campain is perfectly aware it's her vision under the microscope, with the fashion parade to launch the season the culmination of her efforts. Tonight, there are more important considerations than stroking the egos of the trio of peacocks tasked with driving David Jones' margins skyward; the team she's fought every step of the way in her quest to transform the store's conservative stock. She's not about to let anything—or anyone—bring her undone.

It was Jean who had introduced some of the finest Australian talent to the Ladies Fashions floor, including Jenny Kee—a contact from her old partying days. And when photographers snapped *that* photo of Lady Diana, wearing Jenny's Blinky Bill jumper at Prince Charles' polo match, Jean pounced to secure exclusive rights to the designer's Australiana line. They had sold like proverbial hotcakes.

The new season's trend is bold and spirited. Jean's buying direction positions flirty, punk rock inspired pieces by Jenny Bannister alongside the feminine three-piece ensembles of Sally Browne. She trawls Paddington markets for new labels too, and has acquired burgeoning talents Studibaker Hawk, known for their outrageously edgy evening wear. Early sales figures reflect how keen customers are to embrace the fresh juxtaposition of romantic whimsy and androgynous military vibe. She's never felt more confident of her instincts.

With fifteen minutes to go and a last look at the crowd, Jean heads to the dressing room with a satisfied smile. The seats are almost full. This is it. Coaxing glamorous international supermodel Summer Harrington out of retirement for a one-off store appearance was a genius move—and might just be the leverage required to place her in line for the Head of Department role. A tingle of excitement thrums through her.

This evening, stockholders and company directors will rub shoulders with the moneyed elite, the indulged wives of well-heeled property moguls, investment bankers, politicians, and the corporate businessmen of Sydney. Society's upper echelons gifted with deep pockets and stained with the stale whiff of haughty self-importance. Jean can smell entitlement a mile away.

'Ready for the big night, Miss Campain?' Susie from Lingerie blocks her path. Heavy earrings bounce under the tight curls of a voluminous perm as a waft of hairspray assaults Jean's senses. 'I bet you're nervous! Half of Sydney must be here. I'm *dying* to see Summer strut her stuff—we went to the same school in Melbourne.'

'You *know* her?' Considering the reclusive model had been out of the country for the last decade, Jean can't imagine how she managed it.

'Oh no, she finished *ages* before I started. But isn't she gorgeous? She was *always* on the cover of *Dolly*. You've heard of *Dolly* magazine, haven't you?'

Jean resists rolling her eyes.

'What a life!' Susie continues, 'A villa in Tuscany...sailing the French Riviera. A shame she lost everything in that nasty court battle with her playboy boyfriend, but gosh, what a spunk!'

Jean breathes out a sigh. How difficult it is to protect your privacy when the public wants to devour every titbit they hear.

'I reckon she'd still have tons of guys after her, lucky devil!' Susie giggles, mistaking Jean's compassionate expression for envy. 'Anyway, I better get back and man the counter. Good luck.'

Jean prefers not to know the details of the model's private life, but in truth, it was an article in a well-thumbed magazine in her psychologist's waiting room that first prompted Jean to approach her. It hinted that at thirty Summer Harrington's career was finished and reported her return home to nurse her ailing mother.

Backstage, a buzz is circulating. Jean is delighted to see sales assistants mastering roles as dressers and models in their first outfits for the evening. The level of chatter (and far too much giggling) is astounding.

Her heart gallops like a horse on a steeplechase—she can't imagine managing an event like this more than once or twice a year. Jean's stomach churns. She hadn't finished her salad roll at lunch and by the time her hair and makeup were done it was too late. Now she's starving, dry-mouthed and extremely nervous. And she'd kill for a cigarette. Among other things.

The Master of Ceremonies, popular television personality Pete Smith, pokes his head through the curtain. With a voice like honeyed chocolate, he asks if Jean is ready to begin.

Jean takes a deep breath and turns to the girls. 'Rightio, ladies. Let's get this show off and running. Now heads up and don't forget to enjoy yourselves!'

Three sharp chords from an electric guitar spark the girls into action as Duran Duran surges from the sound system. With a curt nod, Summer Harrington leads them into the spotlight, her Nordic-blonde hair lacquered within an inch of its life and shining like a glorious crown. Jean marvels at her grace.

The models systematically shuffle forward like cars on the Holden factory production line and then vanish between the curtains. How she'd love to view the spectacle from the seats instead of peeking through the gap. Jean pecks at her flock as the night rolls on, securing buttons or easing zippers closed like a mother hen.

A dropped bottle shatters behind her, splashing a fine spray of perfume over the sleeve of a blouse hanging on the rack. Without a word Jean whisks it away while her assistant, Tracy, cleans up the broken shards of glass. Using a white cloth, Jean gently sponges the silk and then dries the fabric with a hairdryer before re-shuffling the models' order from the back of the room. When Tracy signals a thumbs-up, Jean ticks another outfit off her running sheet.

Each time Summer takes to the catwalk, effusive applause echoes backstage. A decade ago, Summer Harrington was hot property—her face and name a brand as recognisable as Coca Cola or McDonalds. When Jean suggested the store engage the supermodel to head the parade, pompous Ross Milton vehemently opposed her, insisting on a willowy young starlet instead. Jean argued that they needed a professional catwalk model—one who appealed to their older demographic and someone the customers would relate to. While Summer's international profile made her perfect for the store's upmarket image, it was her bottom line that finally tipped the scales in Jean's favour. Due to circumstances she chose not to speculate on, Summer was willing to accept a substantial reduction in her fee.

Tonight, the obstacles to secure the star are all but forgotten. Forty outfits are displayed, admired and lauded, and the parade is almost over. As Summer glides through the curtain and into the spotlight in her last outfit, Jean smiles and slips out into the crowd. Summer stands with her arms outstretched, sheathed in shimmering silk that slides over her form and hugs her hips. The glorious evening gown is backless to the waist and held in place by a criss-cross maze of fine metallic straps like a golden orb spider's web.

It sparks a memory from childhood. Jean swallows the sting in her throat; Aurora, dressed in a glamorous evening gown, preparing for a rare night away from the family's apple orchard in Red Hill. Jean is at her feet, smiling through fluffy layers of tulle that she has draped over her face like a bridal veil; *I want to be just like you when I grow up, Mummy.*

Sadly, Jean's attempt to attend her mother's recent funeral was a full-blown disaster.

'That dress is stunning!' Tracy appears by her side. 'What a perfect finish.'

Jean nods, unable to reply. Judging by the enthusiastic applause, it's clear Summer Harrington has stolen the show.

The curtains close, and models and dressers gather backstage. 'Three cheers for Jean Campain! Hip hip, hooray…'

I did it. Excitement courses through her body, teasing her to seek more of the same. No. Encouraging any such addictive sensations are dangerous. She takes a deep breath and refocuses on the tidy-up.

Garments are replaced on racks and a hum of satisfaction fills the room; voices resume a more relaxed tone. Summer is packing belongings into her tote bag when Jean approaches and holds out her hand.

'Thank you, Miss Harrington, you were fabulous. I'm delighted I could rely on you and your experience to carry the team.'

'Please, it's Summer,' she touches Jean's arm, 'and it was my pleasure, Miss Campain. It went well, didn't it?'

'Jean,' she corrects. A flush of menopausal heat floods her face. 'And yes—I hope so.'

'Your backstage girls were terrific. Better than some of the professionals I've worked with,' Summer grins. 'Well done all round!'

Tracy appears with a tray of champagne balanced expertly on an extended palm.

Jean's mouth waters, immediately reacting to the astringent aroma. *No one would mind.* The glasses are so close, a mere finger breadth away. She could easily whisk one from the tray. Celebrate. Her lips ache as she purses them tighter; her longing for the taste drains every bit of moisture from her mouth. The tart, fruity scent and fizzy aerated bubbles taunt her from light-filled flutes. It will calm her excitement; take the edge off her nerves and numb her from the attention. She needs it. *Just one.*

Summer smiles and accepts a flute. 'Delicious. Thank you.'

Jean swallows. Her tongue feels heavy, too big for her mouth. She imagines taking a sip; the taste of that first mouthful of heavenly gold, the way the cool liquid swirls into a bliss and tickle of bubbles that slides down her throat and warms her insides. *Take it. You deserve it....*

She avoids Tracy's beaming smile. *No. Not tonight.* She shakes her head, and the tray moves out of reach. Tracy moves on, offering drinks to the others.

The mail arrives early for a Monday.

Jean re-reads the solicitor's letter regarding the details of her mother's estate and places it aside to study the accompanying photo. Of all Aurora's paintings, how distressing to be the beneficiary of this one.

Aurora is seated front-on to the viewer in the surrealism style of Frida Kahlo. Objects of significance surround her, attached to various points of her body with coiled pastel ribbons. While her steely spirit radiates from the canvas, Aurora's rosewood-tinted lips are slightly parted, hinting at a playful sense of humour. But Jean avoids further study of an image in the foreground; the blatant reminder of all she has lost and where the cracks first started.

Reaching for her cigarettes, Jean draws the nicotine deep into her lungs and tries to digest the details of her mother's bequest. Highly regarded in artistic circles, no doubt Aurora Champion's sole self-portrait will be even more valuable posthumously—in monetary terms, at least.

But Jean is confused by the solicitor's statement: '*My client was clear you would interpret the elements within the portrait...,*' and the remark, '*depicted for your knowledge,*' is particularly obscure. Then: '*There are reasons the information is presented in this form; attesting to the truth compromises your family's safety.*' The statement seems entirely bizarre.

I'm too exhausted for riddles today. Middle age is a curse. She woke at precisely three o'clock with the red digits on the clock radio glowing like the old Nylex sign in Richmond. As a child Jean was fascinated by the sight of the neon time and temperature flashing on top of the silos when helping her father deliver crates of Champion apples to the Melbourne markets.

She sips her Nescafé and considers Aurora's veiled reference to the object of irritation in the painting. Why include it? She has no idea. Why, when its very reappearance had torn them apart?

More distressing was how had her mother had waited until her death to dredge up the rift between them. A parting shot from the grave.

Tears prick Jean's eyelids. Though elusive in life, it appeared that no one intended to be excluded from Aurora Champion's funeral. A sea of people Jean had either never met or no longer recalled had filled the church. Journalists and photographers in ill-fitting ties with press lanyards dangling over leather bomber jackets were dotted amongst the mourners. In the south transept, a choir of schoolgirls fidgeted in full dress uniform with socks pulled up to their knees. Emblazoned on the breast pockets of air force-blue blazers, in varying degrees of shapelessness, was her old school motto. Jean knew it well. *Not for ourselves alone.*

She made a beeline for the back of the church and slipped into a pew while her twin sister Evie—and Rick—welcomed artists of note from their places in the front. Jean couldn't face them. Not after disappearing the way she had.

But the sight her family openly mourning Aurora's loss was all too much. She fled from the church before the service had even begun.

Jean replaces the letter in the envelope. That last summer at the orchard, Aurora was working on her portrait of Harriet Sorokin for the Archibald Prize. There was another canvas in her studio at the time. It may have been this one. *But why leave it to me?*

It's too late now to confront Aurora; too late to mend the mistakes of the past. Too late to ask why she robbed Jean of everyone and everything she ever loved. Perhaps the painting will provide some answers.

One thing is certain: Jean's dreams were quashed that last summer. And from the moment Michael Golding came into her life, her path was changed forever.

2

Red Hill, December 1950

The ancient elm in the top paddock had stood in the Champion Orchard for more generations than fifteen-year-old Jeanie ever knew.

She rests against its creviced grey bark, shaded from the rising sun by the tree's viridian canopy. Then, with her sketchbook tucked under one arm and a graphite pencil between her teeth, she hooks practised fingers into the knots and whorls, and clambers up the thick trunk with stems of lavender from her mother's cottage garden secure in her pocket. Beneath branches heavily laden with oval-shaped leaves, Jeanie snuggles into a fork in the boughs and surveys the lines of apple trees that reach to the creek.

Her attention turns to her mother's studio. Aurora is standing in the centre of the full-length windows staring out towards the orchard. It's a look Jeanie well recognises; the artist lost in her subject, with thoughts locked away in a private compartment of her creative mind. *But why isn't she painting yet?* She should be finishing her entry for the Archibald Prize.

The summer holidays are almost over. Jeanie heaves a sigh, dreading the monotony of the year ahead. The return to routine and the rigidity of identical uniforms and standing in line; the long days and cold nights bickering with her sisters and the boarders in close quarters. Beaulieu Ladies' College is almost as old as the Champion homestead, but far less cosy. Sometimes the sisters bunk in together just to stave off the chill. At the orchard they have oodles of space; she and Evie don't share a room, much less a bed.

Jeanie loves the practical layout of the homestead, built of handmade bricks and honey-coloured timber by her settler ancestors. From the vantage of the verandah, it's not unusual to spot the odd kangaroo hopping across the lawn to nibble Aurora's roses, or be spied upon by a family of koalas in a nearby gum, while she's seated in Gran's old rocking chair nursing a cuppa.

Jeanie's almost finished her sketch of the orchard. If only she could find a way to express the true sense of the countryside. The apple trees are starting to bud, with foliage at its fullest and identical to the paint shade, Scheele's Green. How does she capture the sweet scent of the dusty, purple-hued buds of lavender in her sketches, and the way it intensifies when a warm breeze whispers the threat of a northerly? How to illustrate the feel and heartbeat of the earth when she sifts soil through her fingers?

'You're up early, love! Come and give us a hand, will you?' Her father's call breaks her thoughts. Jack Champion's rolling gait picks up speed as he strides downhill. At the base of the tree, he holds up a hand.

Jeanie shimmies down and a gush of squidgy warmth oozes between her legs. The dreaded curse—in equal amounts momentous and hideous—has finally paid her a visit. As the last in her form to get it, the mucky mess in her undies is a relief—she had started to think there was something wrong with her. Her twin, Evie, has been on the rags for months.

If this is what it's like to be a woman, I'm not sure I'm looking forward to growing up. Unlike Evie. This summer, her sister is far more interested in trailing the new farmhand and making goo-goo eyes at him than climbing trees with her twin.

'Be back in a tick...'

'Bring a bucket with you, Jeanie—and don't forget your gumboots.'

Aurora is still gazing out to nowhere when Jeanie rejoins her father. 'What's wrong with Mummy today?'

'It's a huge undertaking to enter the Archibald. She's worked hard to get to this point. Miss Sorokin is coming again this afternoon so your mum can make the final touches. Just make sure you and your sisters steer clear of them; she doesn't need any of us under her feet. You know how she gets.' He winks.

Jeanie's heart does a little flip. Her father is a quiet and gentle man; he rarely speaks in anger, and his dark eyes glisten whenever he speaks of his three daughters. But like a moth to the flame, he loves his wife most of all. It's terribly sweet; they still hold hands across the dinner table.

'I'll miss this when I'm at school.' Jeanie pouts.

'Well, before you can say "Bob's your uncle", you'll be home for Easter holidays.' He grins and heads towards the tractor. 'The orchard will still be here, love; these old trees aren't going anywhere.'

Jeanie is only too eager to show Miss Sorokin into the studio. She loves the smell of paint and turpentine and the grime and dust in the crevices that Aurora fails to notice. The essence of creativity everywhere...

When they enter, Aurora is standing with her arms crossed before a half-finished portrait painted in her classic style.

'Oh, Mummy. I love it...'

Aurora turns, flustered, and takes a few seconds to focus.

'Jeanie? Can you make Harriet comfortable while I go back to the house? I have to check on something and need my sketchbook. Won't be long...'

While Harriet admires her portrait, Jeanie hangs her hat and gloves on the old hallstand and pops the kettle on the camp stove. She's surprised to notice Aurora's office door unlocked and ajar. 'Tea won't be long,' she calls out, and sneaks inside.

A crocheted blanket, all colours of the rainbow, is at odds with the neat stack of canvases leaning against the wall. It covers a small easel in the corner.

Jeanie can't resist a peek. When she lifts the edges, Aurora's face stares back at her from the centre on the canvas. The objects around her are sketched in, but unfinished.

'Jeanie Champion. What are you doing?' The voice behind her is stern. 'You know you're not allowed in here.'

'Sorry, Mummy—but the door was open. I just had to have a squiz. It's lovely...'

A flash of pain shows on her mother's face and swiftly disappears. 'It's nothing at the moment, just an idea.' She closes the door and turns the key, nudging Jeanie towards the exit. 'I'll probably paint over it. Now off you go.' She picks up a clean paintbrush and points it at her. 'Milk and two sugars for Harriet.'

Jeanie nods. True artistic expression evolves when an artist continues to practise and create. Often, the initial inspiration never quite comes to fruition the way first intended.

'Let's have a picnic,' Jeanie encourages on the last day of holidays. 'Come and help me make the sandwiches, Shirley.'

'You're such a bossy-britches, Jeanie! Why can't we just eat lunch here?' Shirley pouts and sags into the sofa.

'Don't be silly! It's a beautiful day. We're going to the creek—you can swim if you like.'

Her little sister claps her hands.

'Well, *I'm* certainly not swimming. I've just done my hair,' Evie smooths a hand over her dark locks, painstakingly set in soft curls. 'But I'd like a bit of sun—the *Women's Weekly* says that a suntan makes you look slimmer. And more attractive to the opposite sex.'

Jeanie rolls her eyes and throws in a tube of sun cream. Although she enjoys school and is keen to do well, Evie's clandestine activities suggest there's more to life than dog-eared textbooks and musty classrooms. Jeanie just wants to be an artist.

She consumes any information she can about the art world, and was fascinated to overhear her parents discussing the lifestyle of popular modernist artist, Sidney Nolan. There was currently a maelstrom of disharmony between him and his Melbourne art patrons, John and Sunday Reed, regarding his series of Ned Kelly paintings.

The artist lived with the Reeds alongside a collective of artists including talented contemporaries, Tucker and Boyd. Aurora would never choose that kind of bohemian lifestyle—she values her privacy. And while she explained to Jeanie the importance of having a patron, Jeanie can't imagine how frightening it must be to expose your work to the criticisms of an entire community.

While Evie decides what to wear and Shirley dances around gathering Bessemer cups and plates, Jeanie cuts the loaf of bread into slices.

'Can one of you pass me the waxed paper if it's not too much trouble?' She slathers homemade crab-apple jam over knobs of butter, and then cuts a wedge from the fruitcake left over from Christmas. Lastly, as a special treat, she fills the thermos with Aurora's fruity iced tea from the new fridge next to the cool storeroom.

Donning matching straw sunhats trimmed in spiky tangerine raffia, the sisters wander down to the creek. Shirley finds the energy to run ahead and scrounge the shallows for tadpoles from its banks.

Evie's eyes are wide and sparkling with excitement. 'I've got a secret.' She swings Jeanie's hand, 'Looks like *I* won't be sweet sixteen and never been kissed!'

'Oh, Evie!' Jeanie's stomach twists uncomfortably. Things are more serious than she thought. Fred seems nice enough, and she has noticed his long-lashed cow-eyes following Evie anytime she moves, but her parents won't encourage the relationship. The last thing Daddy will want is his farmhand mooching after his daughter.

'Too bad we're back at Beaulieu tomorrow.' The pronouncement comes out harsher than she intends. 'Did you tell him?'

'I thought *you'd* understand,' sulks Evie. 'I'd be happy if it were you…'

Jeanie isn't quite so sure. Lately, everything between them seems a competition. The sisters were born five minutes apart, yet are nothing alike. While Evie is dark-haired and prone to impetuousness, Jeanie's wild coppery-blonde locks belie a more measured temperament.

From the orchard gates all the way to the creek, a continuous hum of bees and twittering of birdsong echoes peacefully throughout the valley. There isn't a ripple on the surface as Shirley strips down to her bathers and dives in, spraying water that fans out over their feet. All afternoon, frogs croak in rhythm, drowned out only by the constancy of Shirley's squeals of delight. The twins laugh at how quickly her earlier protests are forgotten.

The holidays are over, but the sisters will be home again when the weather turns. By Easter, the boughs of the apple trees will be heavily laden and drooping with another crop ready to harvest. Jeanie loves the sweet aroma of freshly picked apples and the squelch of damp soil beneath her feet. It smells like home.

That night, Jeanie lays her head on her father's shoulder and plants a kiss on a cheek darkened with a five o'clock shadow.

'Don't you dare pick all the Grannies without me, Daddy!'

'Aww, Jeanie. This old place will be here waiting for you to come home. It always will.'

If only she had known that conversation marked the last day of her perfect childhood.

3

Beaulieu Ladies' College, 1951

The once glorious façade of Beaulieu Ladies' College is responsible for seducing many a prospective parent into writing a deposit cheque while seated with the headmistress and drinking tea. The Grecian-inspired mansion, built for a prosperous family in the late 1880s, offered lofty views over the wealthy pastoralist's land holdings that extended as far as the Yarra River. It is now owned by the church.

Rooms with eighteen-foot ceilings and festoon-draped windows frame a view to the gardens and hint at Beaulieu's past grandeur. But the grand old lady is distinctly out of place amongst the street's suburban pre-and-post-war homes: the sameness of sturdy redbrick bungalows nestled on half-acre blocks with immaculately manicured, newly sown front lawns.

The current headmistress, Miss McIntyre, is determined to keep the minds of her young ladies well-oiled and extended in every subject. Since two women were newly elected to the Australian Parliament, she insists that anything is possible for *her girls*. The vice-president of the Australian Federation of Medical Women is a

Beaulieu girl and one of Melbourne's leading doctors of women's medicine.

Jeanie is a favourite of the college with a bright future ahead of her. Earmarked as a fine madrigal singer, she tops her class in history and shows promise in the arts. Remarkably, she also holds the school record for the hundred-yard dash. But she's leaving her future study options open.

Her twin has no plans for university and has set her sights solely on Fred. Jeanie doesn't want him thinking Evie is too eager, especially after she said that when they returned home for the holidays, she might let him get to second base. So, on correspondence evening, she persuaded Evie to leave the hearts and kisses off her letter. Unfortunately, Fred was slow to reply—and Evie didn't appreciate Jeanie's candour when she suggested his romantic aspirations might be flagging.

With their previous discord now forgotten, the twins are seated in class while a visiting tutor paces the aisles, immaculately dressed in a smart double-breasted suit of navy serge. Mr Golding is running a workshop to assist students with their entries for the Victorian Schools' Drawing Competition. A delicious scent of mandarin with hints of spice and pine trails behind him, reminding Jeanie of Christmas. The tutor wears his sandy hair slightly longer than is fashionable which perfectly fits his artistic image. Instead of appearing dishevelled, he resembles the boyish portrait of the poet Percy Shelley in her literature textbook.

He moves past Jeanie and lightly sweeps her bare forearm with his fingertips. She startles and looks up, but aside from Evie scowling beside her, nobody is paying attention. The girls are unusually silent this lesson with heads lowered, focussing on their work. It appears no one wants to disappoint him.

'Great work, Jeanie.'

Her cheeks flare with heat as she meets his intense gaze. Teachers always call her Jean. His stare lingers, moving from the page to her lips. *Golly it's hot in here.*

The previous evening, boarders were in fits of giggles after noticing Miss McIntyre flush a furious shade of beetroot and clench her hands to her chest whenever Mr Golding addressed her. They made a show of kissing their elbows and running hands up and down their backs in an imitation of the spinster lost in the throes of passion.

Jeanie focuses on the lines of her sketch, resisting the temptation to look up again. She can feel him watching. But why? Is something stuck on her face? Heat burns a hole on the top of her head like the sun in January.

When the bell rings at the end of the lesson she breathes out a sigh. *Almost finished.*

'Jeanie,' Mr Golding smiles and calls her to his desk. 'You show great promise—you know that don't you?' His eyes sparkle like a cloudless sky lit in sunshine. 'It appears you have your mother's talent.'

'Thank you, sir,' she sways from one foot to the other. 'I love drawing and painting.'

'Then it's important to study the masters if you're serious about your art. Have you visited many galleries?'

'No, I haven't.' Jeanie blinks. His gaze is so strong it unnerves her. She looks away and rubs a charcoal mark off the back of her hand with her thumb.

'I should suggest an outing to Miss McIntyre as an incentive; a prize awarded by me to the highest placed artist in the college. What do you think?' He smiles again and his fingers inch closer; a minuscule flicker of movement bringing his fingers so close they almost touch the underside of her wrist.

'I think the winner would be extremely fortunate, sir.' Jeanie swallows to dislodge the imaginary piece of apple peel stuck in her throat.

'Perhaps, it will be you I escort to the gallery, if you win....'

The drama class bound in through the door accompanied by giggles and high-pitched chatter. Jeanie scurries away to the next classroom; her heartbeat pounds in her chest and the rush of blood echoes in her ears. She just has to win that competition.

The bell's decisive gong silences muffled groans as the rows of boarders open their eyes to the dawn. Jeanie's day begins with a perfect score on her spelling test. Then, she auditions in the music room and is successfully chosen as the soloist to represent her house in the college's annual Choral Competition. She's floating on a cloud of excitement and success.

'You're having a day out today!' says Evie, flicking a dark plait over her shoulder. 'Do you have a guardian angel watching over you or something?'

'Don't be ridiculous.' Jeanie swats at her, good-naturedly.

They take their seats in the two-storey building known as the monkey house—so named by an eccentric previous owner who had housed his pet monkeys there. Given the height of the ceiling and enormous floor-to-ceiling windows, the light-filled space is the place of daydreams; it's like a tree house perched in the clouds.

For weeks Jeanie has dissected every word Mr Golding has spoken, every comment, praise, or conversation replaying in lengthy scenes inside her head. She's been careful to keep this from Evie, as well as the dreams she's been having that wake her with a flush of heat flooding her body and send tingling to the innermost centre of her private parts. It's too embarrassing to discuss, even with her twin.

Lost in thought, Jeanie stares out the window towards the military drill hall, seconded to Beaulieu for use after the war.

'Silence, ladies. Before we begin our lesson today, I have an important announcement.' Miss McIntyre's glasses fall from the bridge of her nose, held by a twisted silver chain attached to the arms.

Could this be the moment she's been waiting for? Jeanie chews her nails.

'The winner of the Victorian Schools' Drawing Competition is—

'Jean Champion! Congratulations on being awarded first place in the state. Your prize is a book detailing the illustrative techniques of Australia's top artists.'

'Thank you, Miss.' Evie pats her on the back.

'In addition, on behalf of Beaulieu College, I'd like to reward you with a gift for winning the inaugural competition. A complete set of Derwent and Cumberland pencils.'

'Oh, my goodness!' Evie exaggerates.

Jeanie rolls her eyes at her sister's Shirley Temple impersonation and returns to her seat. 'Well, *I* appreciate them even if you don't!' She opens the packet and reverently breathes in the scent of grainy graphite. Her pocket money merely extends as far as purchasing the glorious cedar wood pencils one by one.

'Everyone knows how great you are, Jeanie. It's really no surprise that you won,' Evie sniffs. 'I guess you deserve it.'

But when Miss McIntyre turns back to the chalkboard and scratches an endless stream of sums on the black surface, Jeanie pushes down the swell of disappointment. There is no mention of a gallery visit after all.

Weeks later, Jeanie is called to the office to take a telephone call and worries there's been an accident on the farm. But the pain leaves her chest when she hears the excitement in her father's lilting drawl.

'She's gone and done it, love. Your mother has won the Archibald. I'm that proud of her I could burst!' Jack's voice is thick on the end of the line. Outside the window, Shirley and the other junior school girls are spinning cartwheels on the front lawn. Jeanie feels like joining them. How exciting!

'Give her our love, Daddy. What happens now?'

'First, she'll meet with her patron in Melbourne. But there'll be a party to celebrate soon—for all of us.'

When Jeanie shares the news with her sisters, Shirley's squeal brings Miss McIntyre running.

That evening, Miss McIntyre addresses the boarders. 'Mrs Champion is the first woman to win the prestigious portraiture award. It is indeed a triumph.'

Jeanie thanks her graciously. She's immensely proud of her talented mother.

'Once again here is proof, ladies, that if you strive, you will indeed, succeed. A lesson to us all,' she proclaims and dabs at her eyes. 'Now, to celebrate Mrs Champion's success, I have taken the liberty of instructing Cook; we shall have a treat tonight.'

'Bread and butter pudding?' Shirley asks hopefully.

'Peach Melba,' Miss McIntyre replies. 'Named after another of

Melbourne's famous and talented women. Now hurry along, ladies—your homework will not finish itself.'

Aurora is an overnight success. A star. The Champion sisters are given special permission to leave the boarding house to attend a party in her honour at the ritzy Menzies Hotel in the city.

The girls have been treated to new frocks that arrive in a George's of Collins Street delivery truck to a fanfare of enthusiasm. Jeanie's full moiré taffeta skirt is cinched at the waist and falls like turquoise petals over a frothy white petticoat edged in scalloped lace. Evie's dress is a similar style in a flattering shade of rose pink while Shirley's frock in snowy *broderie anglaise* with a Peter Pan collar and sash with oversized bow, far more suitable for her age. She looks almost angelic.

Jeanie's godmother, Hazel, collects the sisters in her new pillar box red Packard convertible, complete with two-tone upholstery. The top is down as they leave the boarding house, and Hazel hands chiffon scarves to the twins to tie over their lacquered hairstyles. Jeanie feels like an actress on the cover of *Screen News*.

'My, my young ladies, how splendid you three look!' Hazel's bright-lipped smile reveals slightly protruding front teeth. She turns back to the steering wheel. 'But far too grown up for my liking—you make me feel positively ancient!'

They set off and as the car reaches the end of the long driveway, a group of men jump out of the shadows and force them to a stop. Photographers thrust cameras in their faces and the flashes blind them.

'Mrs Champion, how does it feel to be the first woman to win the Archibald?' a man shouts close by.

'Mrs Champion, Aurora! This way if you please!'

'Gentlemen, you are quite mistaken. I'm not Mrs Champion,' Hazel laughs.

'But aren't these her daughters?' A man pokes his pad under Jeanie's nose, and she recoils into the upholstery. 'It says three daughters, Jean, Evelyn and Shirley—' He refers to his notes. 'I'm certain that's correct.'

'Yes, we're her daughters,' cheeky Shirley pipes up from the back seat. Jeanie turns and glares at her.

'Miss Champion!' The reporter leans against the passenger door. 'Tell us your mother's favourite recipe? Does she cook lamb or beef for the Sunday roast?'

Jeanie screws up her nose. *What ridiculous questions.* Aurora is not your typical mother, so why aren't they asking serious questions about her skill and endeavour as an artist?

Immersed in a world of imagery and slathering paint on canvas, Aurora often loses track of time in her studio, her thoughts miles away. If not for the lady she occasionally employs to help, they'd be lucky to eat anything more than what grows in the orchard. Jeanie learnt from an early age how to boil an egg or make toast and jam or Vegemite sandwiches so they didn't starve.

The men refuse to budge, and Jeanie's stomach turns uncomfortably. She never imagined Aurora's win would attract such vigorous attention.

One man is louder than the rest. 'Having a famous artist in our midst is exciting for Melbournians—especially an attractive woman. Our readers deserve to know more about her; can you tell us which department store she frequents?'

Jeanie clenches her fists. The fact that Aurora is a woman is irrelevant.

Hazel grips the steering wheel and shifts the gearstick into first. 'Gotta fly, gents,' she waves.

'Where are you heading, girls?'

The Packard lurches forward and rolls onto the road, leaving the men and their questions in its wake. 'Now I see why they call them vultures!'

'Golly, I had no idea Mummy was so popular.' Evie voices precisely what Jeanie is thinking.

'Let's hope she doesn't draw *too* much attention.' Hazel frowns.

Darkness closes in and the streetlights flash by as the Packard's headlights shine on the main road towards the city. Jeanie is pensive and smooths her new dress over her knees. Aurora rarely encourages talk about herself—a double-edged sword for an artist who strives for recognition. But perhaps the press exposure will be good for her and help bring in more commissions.

Hazel parks the car in Bourke Street, a short distance from the Menzies Hotel, and the group alight amid a buzz of excitement. Jeanie's eyes widen at the sight of a ruby carpet, a riot of pattern that sweeps them from the entrance foyer into a private dining room. The overall grandeur of the hotel interior is heightened by lofty ceilings and decorative cornices, each room a showcase of bulky colonnades and arches, and walls moulded with impressive art deco wainscoting.

Aurora looks divine standing in the centre of the room in a strapless mauve frock and bolero ensemble, illuminated under a glittering chandelier that covers the floor in fragments like speckled stars. Jack hovers beside her, strapped into a suit that strains across his stomach when he reaches to shake a hand. Hazel hurries towards him and loops her arm through his. When she whispers in his ear, colour drains from his face.

He recovers in time to envelop his girls in a hug and crouches to Shirley's height to let her crawl into his lap.

'What have we here?' he chuckles. 'My very own bevy of beauties. How wondrous you are.'

A fracas erupts in the doorway; three reporters, trying to gain access to the function. Jack rushes to assist the man remonstrating with them. Only the man's arm is visible; the crisp white cuff and gold cufflink are in sharp contrast to his dinner suit sleeve; a signet ring flashes on his index finger. Jeanie's stomach somersaults. *What is he doing here?*

Jack returns and nods towards him. 'It's a good job Michael Golding is here—Aurora's patron. He's helping promote her work and has invited art collectors and society people to meet her.'

'Is that how Mummy knows him?' Jeanie can barely tear her eyes away. He moves from group to group with his hand on the small of Aurora's back, urging her forward like Shirley's walking doll.

'He's an old friend—' Jack's face is blotchy after his exertions. 'They've only recently become reacquainted.'

'We met him at school,' Evie says, and sits with her legs crossed on the sofa. Shirley is already wriggling.

'At Beaulieu?' Jack frowns. '*Hrmm...*'

All night Mr Golding hovers by Aurora and tops up her drink or leads her by the elbow to be introduced to well-dressed people from art circles. Jeanie lets out a sigh, but he completely ignores her.

Soon the girls find it difficult to stifle their yawns. The evening is less of a family celebration, and entirely more about Aurora's introduction to the art world inner sanctum. It's a shame the winning portrait of Miss Sorokin is still on display at the gallery of New South Wales. Jeanie was hoping to view the finished work.

She excuses herself and makes her way to the powder room. A sweep of air rushes into the hallway when a door opens behind her.

'Jeanie.' Mr Golding reaches her in a few steps and smiles down at her. A glow of heat lights her cheeks, as she notices the tilt of his head indicating his appreciation. 'You look simply ravishing tonight. Like a duckling who transforms into a magnificent swan.' He bows his head over her hand like Prince Charming.

'Thank you,' she whispers.

He kisses her fingertips in an old-fashioned gesture, and a shiver runs down her spine as his lips trail over her knuckles. 'Enjoy your evening, little one. *Au revoir*, for now.'

Jeanie lets out the breath she's been holding.

Like most of the hotel, the powder room is opulent. For the first time Jeanie examines her full-length appearance in a gilt-edged mirror, the largest she has ever seen. Her figure is entirely feminine; the sweetheart neckline of her dress flatters her décolletage and hints at the gentle swell of developing breasts. Sculpting her body with her hands from her chin to her chest, Jeanie follows the curve of her breasts and down the bodice to her waist. *What does he see when he looks at me?*

Her pulse is beating faster when she returns to the party. She takes a few minutes more to recover and watches him from a distance.

Evie appears by her side. 'He's far too stuck up if you ask me.' She points her nose towards Mr Golding as the waitress approaches with a tray of canapés. 'Mind you, he's easy on the eye. Just look at all the old girls clucking about him like chooks with a rooster in the henhouse. That one with the French roll and the diamonds is clinging like a vine. Poison Ivy!'

'You can be coarse sometimes, Evie.' Jeanie turns away and steps closer to the silver punch bowl that Daddy has banned them from touching.

'Time to call it a night, my loves. Better get you back to the boarding house before Miss McIntyre skins me alive.' Jack takes a deep breath and reaches into an inside pocket for his pipe, then stares at it longingly.

Jeanie has noticed how quiet he's been all night, clearly uncomfortable out of his overalls. His tie is askew, and he's wrestled with a suit jacket that has seen better days. Meanwhile, Hazel has completely forgotten them; she left the hotel blowing kisses and raced off with a group in high heels and furs to a party elsewhere.

Jeanie stands. As though invisible fingers span the room to connect them, Mr Golding turns, and his gaze meets hers. She feels giddy when he nods and raises his glass with a grin. How peculiar to have someone stare as though they see right into the very heart of you.

She gives an awkward wave and returns his smile.

'Come now, my beauties,' Jack calls, breaking the spell. 'Don't worry about finding your mum to say goodbye. She's a busy lady. Let her enjoy her moment in the spotlight. She deserves to shine tonight.'

But Jeanie is shining too, warmed by the memory of the admiration and promise in Mr Golding's smile.

4

Melbourne 1951

A week after the night at the Menzies, Jeanie receives an invitation that makes her heart sing. With a squeal of excitement, she presses it to her lips.

I promised you a gallery visit and will take you to tea. Do say you will join me?

The note goes on to explain that both Aurora and Miss McIntyre have wholeheartedly approved the day out.

Afternoon tea at the Windsor Hotel is certainly a treat. *Evie will be green with envy.* Jeanie decides to keep that part of the outing from her sister who had been glum since Fred broke it off with her (though it shouldn't have been a surprise).

'I'd rather poke sticks in my eyes than spend hours looking at boring old paintings!' Evie rolls her eyes emphatically. 'No *siree*, you can have that on your own! Besides, I swapped a romance novel with one of the day girls—a saucy one too. I'm keen as mustard to finish it.'

The extent of artwork at the gallery is mind boggling. Jeanie's floats through the rooms in a delicious dream; her creativity on high alert and senses alive at the interplay of colours and texture. Mr Golding imparts a melodious stream of superior knowledge about the artists and their subjects. The epitome of elegance, he is dressed in charcoal trousers paired with a silver sports coat in a subtle check. He insists Jeanie call him Michael.

When the tour is complete, the gallery blurs in Jeanie's thoughts as she anticipates the most exciting part of the day—tea with her handsome escort. He flatters her across the table, praising her knowledge of the artists she admires with a cigar tip glowing between his manicured fingers. Although somewhat older than she first thought, he appears blessed with the spirit and liveliness of a much younger man. His athletic build and yearlong tan combine to exude a certain magnetism that Jeanie finds strangely attractive.

Michael's attention remains focussed on Jeanie as though there's no one else in the room. When the dining room lighting dims, his eyes darken, but it's his lazy grin that makes Jeanie's insides melt.

She tries not to giggle but is flattered by his attentions. The girls at school moon over handsome film and magazine idols, or their favourite crooners, but Jeanie knows very few boys and certainly no men who show an interest in her. Michael is a commanding presence; his smile shines so brightly it stings her eyes to look at him. He listens intently and shows interest in everyone he speaks to. Even the hotel staff gravitate to him; his charm undeniable given the way the waitresses blush and hover by the table. Michael is generous and thoughtful. Jeanie is fortunate to be his guest.

When she confides that she wants to be an artist, painting from an easel on the streets of Paris, he promises to help with her career.

'You are a rare talent, Jeanie—you know that, don't you? I feel the essence of Aurora's creativity in you. It's true—and already, you are as beautiful. I'm certain you will become a famous *artiste*.'

Then he claps his hands. 'And you must be painted one day! Yes! Perhaps dressed as a woodland sprite... or a goddess in a diaphanous robe of gossamer.' He throws back his head and the sound of his husky laughter hums through her.

He goes on to describe the Gothic architecture of the cathedrals of

Paris and the Norman churches of Britain. He speaks of the azure waters of the Mediterranean and beaches shadowed by treacherous rocky outcrops of granite and limestone; of first sighting white-washed cliffs quite unlike those of the Mornington Peninsula. He encourages her to embrace nature and consider painting the countryside she loves so much.

Jeanie is curious about the European countries he mentions but far too well-mannered to ask about his experiences during the war. *No one likes to talk of it.* His stories are about joy and life, fun and fabulous things—artists, writers and the famous people of his acquaintance.

He speaks about classical music; his love of the opera (which Jeanie isn't sure about) and the ballet (which she adores). Then he laughs when Jeanie mimics his pronunciation of exotic-sounding places—not in an unkind way, because his eyes darken and glow as though he finds her attempts charming. Michael is glamorous and interesting, quite unlike any person she has ever met.

His hand closes over hers, and he suggests driving her back to school. Jeanie sighs. It's their last moments alone. First, they take the short walk to his apartment in Collins Street to collect his car keys.

'A little bird told me it was your sixteenth birthday recently.' He sweeps a strawberry lock of hair from her forehead. 'You are the image of your mother, my sweet. You have her eyes—the luminous quality of amethysts, but with more vivacity. More verve.'

She giggles, overwhelmed by his flattery.

'We should celebrate. I like to drink champagne in the afternoon.' Michael grins, 'and one should always drink champagne in the company of a beautiful woman.'

Jeanie is happy to prolong the outing.

In his apartment, she jumps when the cork pops from a bottle of French champagne like a firecracker on bonfire night. But she's eager to taste it.

He pours the liquid into a crystal glass shaped like a saucer. Tiny golden bubbles rise to the surface.

She, Jeanie Champion, feels worldly. How glamorous to be here with this handsome man surrounded by art and music and drinking champagne like a lady of sophistication. Like a woman.

She savours the champagne and holds the cool taste in her mouth, afraid to screw up her nose for fear Michael might think her childish. The champagne burns as it coats her tongue and slides down her throat; the bubbles burst like popping candy and make her giggle. It's a similar sensation to the tingling of a Wizz Fizz in a Melbourne Show showbag. Delicious. She feels light and carefree, decadent. Her body lightens and releases like a ripple of waves rushing the shoreline.

'Just one more, thank you, Michael,' she says....

TATIANA

5

The Winter Palace, St Petersburg, 1898

It started as a mere flirtation, whispered in the silent language of fluttering eyelashes and wavering fans across a ballroom; in the seared heat of lingering fingertips on the barest hint of naked skin.

I trail away from the end of the official procession and steal into the portrait gallery before my absence is noticed. A reluctant page ushers me inside, his startled ovoid eyes like a pheasant dressed for supper. I oft wander the capacious rooms that have housed the many Romanovs before me and pause in the private apartments that were formerly the domain of my mother. If only the walls could speak.

Tsar Nicholas II permitted Mama's return to court once the dust had settled on what came to be the last of her scandalous affairs. It is said she died of a broken heart when the scoundrel she was in love with replaced her with another—one of an age closer to mine. Although she had passed some months before, I still sense her presence and imagine her bell-like laughter echoing through the hallowed halls.

Surrounded by a splendid collection of works by the great masters, my attention alights on the portrait of my handsome great uncle. Alexei Alexandrovich's virile strength shines in the crystal clarity of his stare.

'I see you share my appreciation for one of our empire's heroes.' A voice disturbs my study. 'But how ever did you manage to escape the tedium so swiftly?'

'My apologies, Your Imperial Highness,' I hastily genuflect and my heart lurches as the pleasant scent of wooded pine and musk surrounds me. 'I was not expecting—'

'Tatiana Vladimirovna? I scarcely recognise you! How can this be? You have grown so—'

The Tsarevich, Georgiy Alexandrovich, takes my hands and raises me, then swivels me from side to side as if I am still in short skirts.

'—spectacular. I confess, I'd forgotten how spectacular this collection was.'

I was a child when the Tsar's brother left Russia to pursue a life of freedom and hedonistic pleasures—the much-envied role of a younger son. I had not encountered him since.

'I was admiring the fine brushstrokes, Imperial Highness,' I recover. 'The way the clouds are perfectly appointed and appear to glide across the canvas. See how they settle into the background, behind the subject? It's quite remarkable.'

'Remarkable,' he replies, with the slightest quiver of lips. He takes in my appearance as if he might swallow me whole. 'An extraordinary transformation.' The words hang in the air between us; all that moves is the blush of heat that inflames my cheeks.

It occurs to me that my feminine armament is indeed lacking; a bolder approach might be required to deal with a man such as this.

Lifting my chin, I hold his gaze. 'The artist deftly perfects the popular style—realism, I believe it is called. I am told he witnessed the assassination of our grandfather, Tsar Alexander II....'

His eyes linger on my lips; the heat of his stare weighs heavily upon me. He appears as unnerved as I am.

'Indeed...,' he straightens and clears his throat. 'I've always believed this a fine example of Korzukhin's work.' He considers the painting with a hand cupped to his chin. 'Of course, it is said that while Alexei Alexandrovich had many lovers, your mother was his favourite.'

My mouth is as dry as the sacramental *prosforka* at Holy Communion. My relatively sheltered upbringing was, in fact, quite the antithesis of what one might presume for the daughter of the infamous Grand Duchess Katya Romanova.

'I expect he would have married her had it been permitted.' The hint of sympathy in the Tsarevich's gentle tone creates a tightness in my chest. Mama is more commonly spoken of with opinionated and ill-concealed contempt.

He extends a hand as though to touch my hair, but instead adjusts the gold *aiguillettes* at his shoulder. 'I believe you favour her—although, your fairer-colouring is entirely more becoming. Perhaps, the shape of your mouth?' He shrugs. 'The grand duke was well known for his impeccable taste when it came to both art and the female form.'

I hold my tongue, doubtful of a clever enough response, and focus on the sound of running water outside the window, picturing the fountain in a feeble attempt to still the flow of my thoughts.

'It has been a pleasure to make your acquaintance again, little cousin. Good day to you.' He inclines his head over my hand.

Then my heart beats in time with the swift march of his boots across the marble floor, and I'm barely able to ease a breath from beneath my stays.

As the leaves of the great linden trees in the Summer Gardens turn from gold to amber, a celebration to welcome our foreign dignitaries is planned, to be held at the sumptuous Yusupov Palace. The great and the good of St Petersburg will be in attendance. It coincides with the evening of my eighteenth birthday.

In the company of my dear friend, Miss Rosalind Brassington, the British Ambassador's daughter, I had chosen a magnificent length of imported silk for a new gown. The seamstress hastily finished the last stitches of embroidery only minutes before dressing.

The full skirt of rich sapphire feels decidedly buoyant as I twirl, and excitement spikes in the pit of my stomach. I examine my reflection in the mirror; confident my appearance is at its best. The Tsarevich is certain to be there. I picture his face. It has been less than a month since our encounter. Dare I hope he might speak to me tonight?

When he saunters through the doors of the White Column Hall and greets our hosts, his clear grey Romanov eyes gleam like Karelian granite. His magnetic smile sends butterflies tumbling through my stomach. The metallic sheen of gold braid glows on the collar and cuffs of his scarlet and midnight blue regimental dress coat, the cut and style a perfect foil for features that reveal the fine Danish heritage of his mother, and the height and noble stature of his father.

I'm not alone in thinking Grand Duke Georgiy Alexandrovich the most compelling man in the room. Ladies slip fans into their left hands and open them in a flash. His importance in the line of succession is undeniable; we have long-awaited a direct male heir to the imperial throne. Regretfully, the Tsar and the Empress have recently been delivered of a third daughter. Indeed, she is healthy, thanks be to God.

Before the proceedings commence, Georgiy makes his approach. The blatancy of the act shocks me. If only dear Rosalind was by my side to help steady my quivering.

'Tatiana Vladimirovna. How delightful it is to see you again. You will allow me to accompany you to supper. I insist.'

It's most unseemly to require my company so early in the evening. But I well understand the Tsarevich may choose the company of any unmarried lady of the court—or even a married one if he so desires.

From the perimeter of the reception hall the ladies-in-waiting watch on in flowing gowns of ruby velvet crossed with ceremonial sashes or St Andrew blue ribbons pinned to the left. I glance towards the elderly dowagers, resplendent in gold-embroidered robes of olive green and bejewelled from head to toe. Ever ready to preside over the younger ones and keep our conduct in check, they peruse the scene with frowns set deep in their foreheads.

'*Insist*, Imperial Highness?' I set my resolve with an unwavering stare—a difficult task given my heart is racing. 'I regret, I am already engaged for supper.'

From the tilt of his eyebrow, I see he realises I will not pander to his imperial fancies, yet his eyes glitter in good humour. 'That is indeed my great misfortune.'

He deflects my insolence with a shrug, then proceeds to regale me with an amusing and somewhat fanciful tale of his encounter with a performing dog in a railway carriage en route to Paris.

Our repartee is a game I know well enough. Flirtations are as common a pastime at court as cards or gambling, or the occasional visit to a spiritualist to commune with the dead; mere tournaments played between a man and woman for entertainment and bonhomie. Yielding your heart unreservedly is another thing entirely; an act committed but once in a lifetime.

My breathing steadies, my pulse recovers and our conversation flows with ease. I find him both amusing and interesting. Is he flattered by my questions? I cannot be certain, but he addresses me with the utmost respect—or perhaps in the manner of a kindly tutor, answering one whose curiosity seeks to be quenched. His manners are impeccable.

'You simply *must* visit Paris in the spring, Tatiana. The city has the charm and beauty of an intelligent woman—and the Eiffel Tower—such masterful engineering! The exquisite symmetry! Perhaps one day we will promenade the *Avenue des Champs-Élysées* together...'

My fan unfurls to cool my rising blush. 'Is Paris a favourite of yours, Imperial Highness?' His attention, though somewhat intense, is charming, alluring. I find myself eager to spend more time in his company.

'If I am to share my deepest secrets with you, I insist you call me Georgiy, like you used to.' His eyes brighten. 'Indeed, the city of Paris is enchanting, but England—*ahh*, the modernity I discovered in terms of engineering and production. Now that *is* impressive.'

The Tsarevich's voice elevates as he exudes the merits of the English way of life, and particularly the rise of new manufacturers of automobiles. He pronounces Great Britain remarkably progressive and almost as powerful as our Russian empire.

'Your Imperial Highness,' our hostess, Princess Zinaide Yusupova, appears with a smile of apology, 'the proceedings are about to begin.'

Georgiy bows his head over my hand, and his breath warms the opening of my glove. 'I will return to claim a dance, Tatiana.'

And then he whispers, 'I believe you intend me to play the hound to your fox. I assure you I will enjoy the challenge.'

My heart skips a step and loses its rhythm. I feel certain it will stop beating altogether.

Trumpets sound to mark the beginning of the evening's formalities. Tsar Nicholas II, Emperor of All the Russias, makes his entrance with his darling Alix, the Empress Alexandra Feodorovna on his arm. The Empress is pale and wan after the birth of the newest grand duchess but bravely carries out her duty. I well know how she detests such fanfare.

Georgiy follows solemnly behind them, escorting his mother, the Dowager Empress Maria Feodorovna. His resigned expression is as cool as the vacant space he has left beside me.

Finally, the orchestra take up their instruments, and the dancing begins. I hold back a squeal of delight when my favourite cousin, Oleg Igorevich, appears at my elbow. 'Come, Tatya. Let us away,' he seizes my hand and winks to remind me of the eyes upon us.

My jewelled slippers fly as I follow him across the floor. He whisks us into the centre of the merrymakers, then bows and draws me into the crook of his arm for the waltz. My head feels light and airy as we whirl across the dance floor in looping circles, keeping perfect time with the melodious notes of the music. It's no falsehood that I dance well; the one thing my mother did not fail to teach me. My cousin, too, is accomplished, and we soon draw the attention of one man transfixed in the corner with a smile lighting his grey eyes. Satiated by the mood and emboldened by our performance, I raise my chin and ignore him.

Once Oleg returns me to the younger ladies, we follow Princess Zinaide into the drawing room. But moments later a nonchalant Georgiy joins us with her son, Prince Felix. The Tsarevich stands within an arm's breadth of my chair yet does not seek to engage me in conversation. Is it deliberate? The heat of his body is like hot coals on my bare shoulders. I hold my countenance but feel awkwardly rigid; I must resemble one of the Yusupov's Roman statues in the courtyard.

The ardour of the Tsarevich's attention perseveres, and his regard follows me to every corner of the grand palace. It is apparent that I am, indeed, the one hunted—although, perhaps more startled deer than wily fox. I am immensely flattered, but surely he isn't to be taken seriously? I cannot deny the thrill of the prospect thrums through my body and trills like the notes of a nightingale in springtime.

Cousin Oleg is another none too subtle in the manner of his pursuit, although his desired quarry is my friend, Rosalind. As the evening ensues, our companionship circle grows. While he keeps a respectful distance, the Tsarevich's mien is expressionless, listening to the thundering politics of three, snowy-haired diplomats. I am aware of his gaze upon me as though I am the planet Saturn and he the fixed ring surrounding me.

The music slowly lures the more youthful members of the party to the dance floor; two by two the numbers fall away. Left without the expanse of a more captive audience, the diplomats return to attend their wives. Suddenly, we are a quartet, alone.

'Miss Brassington?' Oleg's dark eyes are eager and expectant in admiration. Rosalind's fair skin blushes; she nods and accepts his hand with charm and grace. The pair looks handsome together as they take to the floor.

With Georgiy so near, I can barely breathe. A pocket of air shifts around me, and I shiver.

'Your *joie de vivre* is enchanting. One with such life and spirit should be encouraged to embrace every moment.' His eyes glitter with challenge. 'Will you do me the honour of this dance, Tatiana?' Then he demands my hand from an arm's length away—an ostentatious gesture, and one not easily refuted in a crowded room.

Heat burns through my gloves; his touch sustaining like a life force holding me upright. From the moment we take our places in the line of the dance, I feel at ease. Georgiy spins me masterfully across the room and my feet skim the floor, lighter than a feather in the breeze. I dismiss my previous apprehension—instead I am lost in the spirit of the music and the magic of the dance, the company and admiration of my companion. Never before have I celebrated a more glorious birthday.

On our return, Georgiy sweeps glasses of champagne from a tray to quench our thirst. My skin is alive and tingling. While he engages with Oleg, Rosalind raises her eyebrows and draws me aside.

'The Empress appears in remarkable ill humour this evening,' she whispers, *sotto voce*. 'She's been glaring at our group with displeasure…'

I exaggerate an effort to appear aloof, but it's impossible to ignore the scowl tainting our Empress's beauty, the cool incline of her head making clear her dissatisfaction. *Of me.*

'Dear Alix has forgotten what it is to have youthful enthusiasm,'

Georgiy replies, raising an eyebrow. I hold back a smile. 'Since their marriage, Nicky too has become positively dreary. He used to be such fun! Now he hovers over his family like a lovesick bear with her cubs.'

The evening comes to an end in the light of the early dawn. Alix summons me with a toss of her head.

'You are young, Tatiana Vladimirovna. Foolish.' Her sibilant whisper makes it appear a curse. 'Do not make the mistake of ruining yourself, like your mother before you, with a man you can never have. Nicky would never permit it.' Her cool eyes hold a threat.

I clench my jaw, and my face tightens during her scolding. Would my cousin the Tsar agree? With practised reverence I apologise for my supposed misdemeanour of singling Georgiy out above any other beau. But is it fair to be sentenced with a lifetime of unhappiness in penance for the poor choices of my mother?

6

Marthe curtsies before me. 'Good morning, Your Imperial Highness.'

'Don't fuss with such nonsense in private,' I chide good-heartedly, for she is my favourite maid and the nearest in age. 'And not whilst carrying my tray.'

'You have received a message...'

The breakfast tray is extended over the counterpane. There is no sign of a note on it.

My heart beats swiftly. 'From whom?'

She shrugs. 'It came from Hercules, the Abyssinian. I did not enquire about its origins.' Dark eyes flash at me mischievously, and her scar wrinkles over the corner of one eye.

Hercules is one half of the sentinel guarding the doors of the Blackamoor Hall. While many of the servants have little to do with him, he fascinates Marthe who constantly peppers him with questions about his homeland in the American South that she repeats to me with relish. She insists he is trustworthy.

'Marthe?' Her playful nature is a tonic, but there is a hint of menace in her tone too. I hold my hand out.

'He slipped it into my pocket as I passed.' She props the ivory-coloured parchment beside my teacup.

Last night, Marthe was as excited as I was when I shared news of my evening in the Tsarevich's company. Our lives are entwined as one—any small conquest in terms of the admirer stakes is as much my maid's victory as mine.

Of course, not all the nobility is as congenial or amenable with their servants. Alix is known to keep her maids and her ladies at bay. Marthe heard it said that none are permitted to attend her until she is completely dressed. What use that must be, I cannot comprehend.

'And Oleg Igorevich asks that you meet with him to walk in the gardens this afternoon on the condition you convince Miss Brassington to accompany you.'

'I see.' And I do with a smile, immediately recognising the ruse beneath the wax seal bearing the Tsarevich's crest. 'Fetch me my notepaper. And send for a boy to deliver this to Miss Brassington at the British legation at once.'

And thus my first assignation with Grand Duke Georgiy Alexandrovich is secured.

Following our initial promenade in the Summer Gardens, the Tsarevich and I meet on several occasions (strategically) designed by chance. Georgiy absconds from the dowager's palace and cites various excuses by way of explanation, ranging from business meetings to the inspection of fledgling automobile factories.

We wander the paths, accompanied by Oleg Igorevich and Rosalind, ostensibly to view the geometry of garden beds of rainbow-coloured tulips in bloom or to debate literature observed under the taciturn stare of allegorical statues. I quickly discover Georgiy knows the best places to sample the famed apple *pastila* confectionary, the restaurants with the most secluded private rooms, and the merchants who profess to procure the finest blend of tea. With Georgiy as companion, I learn more about St Petersburg than I imagined possible.

Our reckless game of cat and mouse fast becomes genuine: I fear my heart is lost to him. How long will it be until those closest to us ascertain the depth of our relationship?

Two months after our first meeting, a message is relayed via the Abyssinian once again. I am collected in a hired turnout, a carriage so unobtrusive that a passer-by might presume me to be a mere merchant's wife going about her business. This morning, Nevsky Prospekt yawns its approach to the day. The white nights of summer are upon us; the time of year when the midnight sun holds darkness at bay and parties revel long into the evening, lit by sunsets that dust a rainbow glow across the Neva.

With very few out on the streets, St Petersburg appears to still be recovering from events of the previous evening.

Georgiy rises to greet me at the Restaurant Leiner, a well-known haunt of artists, poets, and ballet dancers, and where a portrait of the musical maestro, Tchaikovsky, stares down on patrons from the wall. Never before had I dared frequent a bohemian place such as this. It is here the literary master Pushkin is said to have taken his last drink before succumbing to injuries from his fateful duel.

'You are truly ravishing, *chérie*.' Georgiy rises to greet me, as though I am the Empress above him. He kisses me three times in the Russian manner and then takes my hands, holding them longer than necessary.

'Do I detect Madame Chechenka? Delightful. The ensemble perfectly reflects those brilliant eyes of yours.'

The ladies of St Petersburg have adopted the slender new Parisian silhouette, aided by a certain gifted seamstress whose salon by the embankment is fast becoming a favourite haunt of the nobility. My fashionable dove-grey silk gown is inlaid with creamy lace; a soft frill sways from the knees and flounces as I promenade while matching flared cuffs float from my wrists.

His adoring gaze lifts my spirits immediately.

'I require at least two hours of your precious time, Tatiana—then with much regret, I must leave you and return to the Caucasus.'

My heart thumps in my chest. Foolishly, I hadn't considered his return. Has he been toying with me all along? I push the thought aside and lower my eyes to the strong *lapsang souchong* cooling in front of me.

'Of course. Indeed, what a shame—'

'I am a man of service, as you know. Required personnel.' He winks.

'Military service? Will you be in danger?'

'No, *ma chérie,*' he chuckles, 'the Tsarevich is only employed in an official capacity—even during times of war. However, the Russian Empire is quite secure from the threat of usurpers and invaders at present. I assure you, my head remains completely safe!'

I humour him with a smile.

'It is unfortunate, but I have business matters; enough to plough through until winter if it takes that long. Let us say there are certain strategies to enforce for the future. But please, do not fret.'

Of course, I worry. The thought of him leaving—or that he might forget me—tears at my heartstrings. How in so short a time have I allowed myself to be won over by this man; one whom I can never expect a future with?

I daren't simper like a fool and beg him to stay. Instead, I lift my chin. Perhaps it is best we part now, like this, before I am further invested…

'*Chérie,* I have something to show you. A surprise.' He playfully affects a pout. 'Will you come with me?'

I follow him without question. How can I resist? We exit through the rear of the café, and I'm so relieved that I laugh. On reaching the obscured entrance to a building, Georgiy winks at me and taps three times on the door, then twice, then three times again. He waggles his eyebrows as we wait. Inside the bolt to the heavy door lifts with a groan.

The man before us is dressed in a white coat; like those worn by the doctors at the hospital opening I attended recently with Georgiy's sister, Grand Duchess Olga Alexandrovna.

'Your Imperial Highness, Your Highness,' the man bows, respectfully. 'Allow me to escort you to our showroom.' We pass through the open door and past a workshop where I gauge from the industry inside that we are in the bowels of the beautiful Fabergé store.

From the Romanov crest of the double-headed eagle affixed to the wall to a sign stating 'Suppliers to the Court of His Imperial Majesty', the patronage of the imperial family is evident. A metallic smell hovers in the air; the industrial and gritty masculine scent mingles with sawdust and oil—a stark contrast to the beauty and femininity of the objects the renowned makers create.

Glass cabinets line the walls of the showroom. The shelves display a cornucopia of exquisite jewellery and ornaments, from decorative ormolu clocks to ornately inscribed golden cigarette cases, and collars and lockets bejewelled with precious stones. The front door is locked, and windows cloaked by shutters that block us from the street. Our visit appears an entirely orchestrated and covert mission.

'What is this?' I whisper as Georgiy holds my elbow.

'Monsieur Perchin. Please show us your selections.'

You cannot live in St Petersburg without hearing of this craftsman's talents. Some would say he is a visionary artiste. As master of the artisan workshop, Michel Perchin's fine enamel pieces adorn many a palace.

He bows his head and retrieves a silver tray from a cabinet. Arranged on a cushion of crimson velvet is a glorious collection of diminutive and unique enamelled pieces encrusted with diamonds, rubies and sapphires.

Georgiy's hand hovers and he makes a great show of selecting an exquisite little pin. A closer inspection reveals the life-like representation of a ladybird, with scarlet *guilloché* enamelled wings that shine with distinctive black spots. Two rows of tiny square cut diamonds separate the head from the body while the golden minutiae of perfectly curled legs line the undercarriage.

'And what has Monsieur Perchin engraved here?' Georgiy hands me a jewellery loupe with a smile.

Engraved in entwined letters so tiny they are impossible to discern with the naked eye are our initials. It truly has been commissioned for me.

Startled by his generosity I begin to babble. 'Ladybirds bring good fortune. They are a sign of protection and prosperity and were once named, Our Lady's beetles. Serfs on our estate pray to Our Lady Mary to bless the crops...'

Georgiy's raucous laugher ripples through my body. 'Dear girl. You are a veritable fountain of knowledge. Indeed, perhaps this charm will bring us both good luck.'

'What luck do we need?' I ask with a coquettish pout. I do not add that every woman knows that encountering a ladybird commonly signals your true love will soon appear. Is this his more subtle intention?

'We *will indeed* need it,' he leans in and his breath tickles my ear, 'because when I return, I will demand Nicky permit us to wed...'

What bliss it is to be in love. Although I long to squeal my delight, I press my lips tightly closed. Of course, I want to marry him. I am flattered and overjoyed.

I pray we receive the Emperor's blessing, for without it, we cannot.

Over the following weeks, Georgiy's letters advise the progress of his pleas and petitions to the Tsar to sanction our marriage. The volley of exchanges accelerates, and our private correspondence increases in tone and ardour as though he is frantic in his thoughts of me. It's a powerful thing to be so desired by a man. I dream of my beloved constantly. The longer we are apart, the harder it is to face the thought of losing him. I admit, I am besotted.

My lineage and bloodline are more than adequately pure enough to appoint me into an equal marriage in any of the royal Houses of Europe. Yet it appears, I am lacking in worthiness as a wife for the Tsarevich. None of our station may be married without the Tsar's approval, and we dare not oppose him. To do so would risk dishonour and banishment. And I have no wish to leave my homeland.

With each refusal, Georgiy becomes more insistent. He reaffirms his love for me in poems and prose, stating his avowed intent to wed. *I cannot wait*, he writes. At other times, more perplexingly, I receive ramblings that make little sense, cursing the reasons why we are refused and scribbled in haste on scraps of notepaper.

I am in no position to displease the Tsar. I cannot risk having my imperial allowance reduced, or worse, losing my entitlement entirely. No doubt the Tsarina is well informed of Georgiy's petitions. I imagine her displeasure. It's common knowledge the Tsar shares all matters of rule with her; in truth, he daren't choose which fork to use at luncheon without Alix's expressed permission.

While Georgiy and I remain parted, I refuse so many invitations to the theatre and parties that Rosalind begins to think me gravely unwell. But then I attend a dinner party at Vladimir Palace, in honour of the Grand Duchess Vladimir's name day. Her parties are the finest social events of the season. To my delight, Lord Brassington and his daughter are invited too.

Guests are ushered through the brilliant white and gold halls to a large reception hall where *zakhouski* are laid out on an elegant table for our pleasure. I spoon a piece of cold smoked *sigué* onto my plate with a portion of caviar, conscious of the need to have food in my stomach before partaking of our customary vodka toasts.

'Your Highness,' Rosalind smiles, 'how well you look this evening.'

I nod in thanks, noting Rosalind's fair colouring suits the soft lavender hue that is entirely fashionable. The circlet of lilac in her hair is a delightful addition. 'The finesse of our favourite seamstress, no doubt?'

'An extravagance, indeed. When Papa permitted me a new gown, I could not resist.'

'It is enchanting, Rosalind. Now tell me, what news do you have from the summer? I have missed you...'

She leans in to whisper the tale of the Swedish ambassador's daughter embroiled in an intimate liaison with a member of the Gardes de Cheval.

'It is quite the scandal. Apparently, she had been sneaking out of their *dacha* all summer while her mother believed she was attending a sick friend nearby. The pair were discovered in the woods together, more than once. She was riding with him *alone*.' Rosalind leans closer.

'No doubt they will swiftly marry her off—'

'Sadly, it appears the poor girl will not marry her *amour*. Papa believes the man is already married.'

I let out a sigh. Are we women to be picked over for men to savour like an assortment of brightly coloured jellies in a box?

'The scoundrel sorely tricked her. *And* has done this before. She is a sweet girl, but young and foolish. Now she is ruined.' Rosalind sips her thimble of vodka, and my lips twitch. Though my friend tries hard, she is yet to take to all our traditions—the sooner she tosses it down, the easier it will be.

She swallows and coughs; then her eyes dart the hall. 'And have you heard about the Tsarina?'

'Do tell,' I encourage, for the impish look on her face cannot be denied.

'As you know, Olga Alexandrovna has left for the dowager's country estate in Yalta.'

Indeed, Georgiy's sister is currently enduring self-imposed social isolation with their mother, the Dowager Empress.

'Before she left, she told me the Tsarina has engaged a new spiritualist, one who promises to assist her in begetting a son.'

'Is that so?' My stomach flutters in anticipation.

The pronouncement conjures up images of Alix and Nicky in a cloud of heady incense, with an ethereal boy-child rising from the smoke.

'Their imperial majesties remain confident. And as we know, the empire is desperate to continue the line.' Indeed, all of Russia is eager for a son to be born.

I affect a laugh and encourage her to do the same. 'Hush, dear. This is not the place. It will start everyone off...'

Many here tonight have a brood of sons, the various direct lines descending from the Tsar's grandfather, as am I. In centuries past, that alone was excuse enough to wage war between them to gain rule.

As guests carry on with gaiety and *bonhomie*, my hopes rise. I pray Alix is with child soon. Optimism for both my and Russia's future is intrinsically linked to her success in producing a new heir.

Just when it appears there is little hope of deliverance, our wish is granted. The Empress is with child once again. The Tsar is overjoyed and pronounces their new mystic, Monsieur Philippe, *Our Friend*, a prophet of the highest order.

Georgiy's letters change from dogged persistence to missives filled with a modicum of hope: He writes:

My love, we will marry once the new Tsarevich is born, and travel the globe with the freedom to go as far and wide as we choose.

And Georgiy will be released from his imperial obligation. There is but one provision.

Nicky insists news of our marriage remains private for the time.
being. There is a diplomatic entanglement to be resolved. We need not delay a moment longer. Once the little Tsarevich is born (and following his churching), we will announce our union publicly and mark our marriage with a wedding celebration. Thank the Lord my dear brother has seen sense!

Dearest, let us elope immediately. Arrangements are in place with a priest who swears on his life to keep our secret and will be well rewarded.

We will take a short honeymoon in the Caucasus. I regret, there are matters there for my concern that I must attend to following our marriage and while you return to St Petersburg.

I make a note in my journal of what is needed for my trousseau. How will I arrange the ensembles in time? If the court dressmaker places my order ahead of the other ladies, it will be questioned. I tap my pen on the marble topped écritoire.

'Marthe, I require a discreet appointment with Madame Chechenka, immediately.'

I cannot bear the excitement. When Marthe advises of an appointment the following afternoon, I look up from my hurried penmanship and smile.

'Lay out the contents of my wardrobe. Everything. And cast aside anything the Tsarevich has already seen. I want the most current fashions, the *très chic*.'

'Yes, Your Highness.'

'I shall have a new gown for my wedding day. And a fine hat trimmed with ostrich feathers. You might make an appointment with the glovemaker too. I will need summer weight for my journey to the Caucasus.'

'Yes, of course.'

'I insist on your complete discretion, Marthe.'

Her eyes lower and shoulders drop. I regret offending her.

'What is it?' I wait for her to meet my gaze.

'Forgive me, Highness, if I have disappointed you in the past. I do not intend to do so now.'

'Of course not.' How foolish I have been. Marthe is loyal and would never do anything to jeopardise my plans. 'Marthe—do make sure to pack lightweight clothing for yourself, won't you? You will need them.'

'Yes, of course!'

'Indeed,' I wink, 'and not a word outside this room, do you hear?'

My absence is explained by way of an invitation. I'm to stay with an imaginary acquaintance named Dorothea, in a village south of Moscow, known for its vast apple orchards, and one unlikely to warrant further attention. The location proposed for our assignation, however, is farther afield, and we've entrusted Oleg to accompany me. It pleases me that Georgiy has taken him into his confidence. Oleg Igorevich is truly the brother I never had.

My cousin plays his part one afternoon, loudly declaring to all our circle that he cannot in good conscience allow his dear cousin to travel alone. His theatre is a well-rehearsed pretence, one perfected over years of idle summers at our *dachas* by the lake where we performed the plays of Chekhov for entertainment under the shade of long verandahs. If not for his appointment to the Chevalier Guards, he might have been afforded a role on the stage. He insists to all that he is tasked with overseeing the workings of an armaments factory close to our fictitious destination.

Oleg's bravado finishes with a jest. 'I will deliver Tatya safely to her friend on the way. I assure you dear cousin, I dare not insist you accompany me to investigate the weapons. I know how you shy from the sight of a loaded gun!'

The party laugh raucously, and then, with a wink directed at me, our ruse is perfectly executed.

Beyda, Voronezh Province

The ancient wooden church where we are to marry is perched on a hill in the village of Beyda, its sloped roof emerging above a grove of cypress trees. Once inside, the sweet fragrance of my bridal bouquet of wild bluebells is immediately overpowered by the scent of incense and frankincense absorbed deep into the timbers of the sacred house.

My hands shake and I turn to Georgiy, but his gentle countenance is set and determined. I'm overcome with excitement and yet momentarily waver—in the turning of one season he has progressed from convivial confidante to ardent admirer. *And now, husband.*

Is it too soon?

Then his face transforms with a smile so tender that my foolish reservations disappear. I am at peace once more in his company.

I solemnly lower my head, my face covered in a veil of fine lace, and step forward to join Georgiy on the rose-coloured fabric before the *iconostasis*. The priest invites us to light candles to mark our journey together, symbolic of the illumination of a new path and the transformation of our relationship. Then with stirring resonance, he sings out the same litany of holy vows to commend our marriage that have joined man and woman for centuries.

His joyful chanting grows louder when he removes his stole to bind our hands together, and continues while Oleg assists with the crowning ceremony and hovers the two gilded crowns over our heads. Tears prick my eyes as we circle the analogion three times, taking our first steps as man and wife, joined as one by the length of ribbon attached to each crown. I brave a shy smile, grateful for the profound honour this wonderful man bestows upon me.

We drink from the common cup, and when the time comes to bow our heads to our saviour and offer up our prayers, I praise God most heartily for my good fortune; for the gift of a husband who truly loves me as I love him. A shiver of delight thrills through my body.

While I blink away tears of elation, I confess my euphoria is bittersweet—there is regret for the temporary absence of friends to witness the good blessings offered for our future. Then all is swiftly forgotten as we emerge from the church into sunshine and Georgiy turns to me. In a fit of laughter, he makes a grand display of bending his knee and vows with a flourish of hand to shower me with everything my heart desires.

'May your joys be doubled, and your sorrows halved,' Marthe smiles with honesty in her eyes. Already the joy I feel is far greater than double.

She takes my bouquet, and we walk to a charming wooden *dacha* on the outskirts of the village. She and Oleg have arranged a feast and assure us the owners have been paid handsomely to vacate their home. No one will recognise us secreted behind these cheerful vermillion curtains.

When Marthe insists we must respect our Russian traditions, Georgiy laughs at the old ways but nods in agreement. She opens a cloth and the aroma of a loaf of freshly baked bread makes my mouth water. We break portions from the round loaf to dip into salt, and feed pieces to each other with a smile before offering it to our two guests.

For a time, we drink champagne and eat and sing, but Marthe is reluctant to join in and is at pains to make herself scarce. Examining the meagre possessions in the cottage, my husband and I laugh and toast the incongruous surroundings we find ourselves in, far from the glittering halls of our own world.

Finally, we farewell our guests and are alone. Georgiy takes me into his arms and hums the tune of '*Valzer dei Fiori*'; we dance until the candles burn low.

He nestles into my neck. 'My beloved. I am the most fortunate of men. We will have such fun together.' His eyes are bright with love. 'I wish this escape could last forever.'

I bite my lip. I love him so much I can barely breathe. 'As do I. You are dear to me, Georgiy...'

Our hands are clasped between us as he kisses my brow. He raises my fingers to his lips, and my skin burns at the touch. I glance towards the bed and back to him. Reading my intent, he sweeps up my feet as though I am little more than a beech sapling. Then he lays me down with reverence on the brightly embroidered coverlet and unpins my hair until the waves uncoil across the lace pillowslip.

I stare unblinkingly into his eyes. Sensing my nervousness, he smiles and tenderly reassures me. 'We needn't...'

But I whisper agreement, embarrassed by my eagerness.

His lips trail from my eyelids to my throat, and he presses kisses on my exposed skin as deft fingers slowly remove my garments. When my body is fully revealed he gasps; I immediately cover my breasts and between my legs, and then close my eyes.

'You are beautiful, Tatiana,' he whispers.

His praise is a tonic. I take his face in my hands and draw his lips to mine. Then I kiss him with a hunger so fierce the intensity frightens me.

'I love you, husband.' My eyes fill with tears.

'My love, I do not intend to hurt you—'

Anticipation stirs inside me, and I hold my breath as he divests himself of his trousers. My eyes moisten with tears of happiness at the touch of his warm skin on mine. Our limbs entwine and I draw him closer, willingly accepting his manhood, his love, as our bodies awaken in a slow dance of rhythm and our hearts beat in time.

I press my lips to his shoulder and rest my head into the soft hollow of his neck. Moments later, Georgiy shudders in release and spills his seed, and then stills beside me. 'I'm sorry if I hurt you...that it has to be this way...'

Moved by his sensitivity and care for my loss of innocence, I kiss tears away from his wet cheeks. In that moment, the fact that our marriage must remain secret is far less important than my joy in the act of love that has cemented it.

JEAN

7

Potts Point, 1982

For the past few months, Milton, Wilkinson and McMillan have been busy picking over the middle management staff and head-hunting employees for the new DJ's store in Melbourne. There's been a total overhaul of every department. Together with the implementation of a new personnel appraisal system, the restructuring has everyone on tenterhooks, with employees vying for positions.

Jean anticipates that with all the movement south it leaves the door wide open in Sydney—for Head of Department.

Then she is called in for an interview.

Before facing her nemeses, she paces the floor in the corner of the storeroom where her makeshift desk is stacked high with the new season's look books. The thought of facing the trio across a table is a necessary evil; she's determined to stay positive. It's what she's been waiting for since the fashion parade's success. She's the best person for this role, and after twenty-odd years it's time she is recognised.

For years, Jean has watched men with less experience promoted above her. This time, like the words of the song that repeats in her head, she's *gonna head in the right direction*.

She takes the seat offered in the unfamiliar territory of the board room and rests her hands in her lap. Jean is confident of her ability —*and* that her pillar box red suit (paired with an ivory blouse and flouncy bow tied at the neck) is the perfect balance of business-savvy sharp and feminine charm. Not that she cares one iota for charming this lot. They wouldn't hesitate to sell their mothers if there was something in it for them.

McMillan taps a biro on his notepad and his gaze drifts past her to the clock on the wall. 'You did okay with the parade...your sales figures are up and reflect decent growth—'

Ross Milton lights a cigarette while Wilkinson adjusts his coffee-stained tie. But it's the fleeting glances that cause Jean to hold her breath. She expected this to be tough; they must see she deserves this promotion. *What are they not saying?*

'Based on your performance, and long association here, we'd like to offer you the role as Head of Department for the Australian Designer Floor—'

Jean's shoulders relax as she eases out a breath.

'—at the new Bourke Street store in Melbourne.'

'Pardon?' *Melbourne?*

'It's a great opportunity.' Wilkinson's face flushes.

He should be embarrassed. How can they offer her the golden ticket —the role she's worked towards—but in Melbourne? A move interstate was not on her radar.

'Yes, thank you,' the words stick in her throat, 'although it's not what I expected.' She attempts a smile. 'I imagined I'd continue on here with the staff I've trained and the contacts I've established—'

'Come on Jean. You can source salesgirls anywhere. They're expendable commodities in retail, as you well know. The business model can be replicated in Melbourne—the suppliers, fashion agents, training methods etcetera. The components for any new team are transferable.' Milton leans back and bends his fingers into a bridge on his stomach.

'Yes, I imagine that's true.' Jean purses her lips. 'It's...quite a big step.'

'Of course, the salary is commensurate with your age and experience. This promotion is quite a coup for a woman of—' he checks his notes '— almost fifty.'

'And do my years of experience carry the equivalent salary of a male in the same position?' She eyeballs them. This promotion is well overdue.

Noel Wilkinson, the accountant, has the good grace to look abashed. 'Err...no. But it's a substantial increase in salary, Jean, with all the relevant superannuation benefits and packages afforded a role at this level. It's an *exceptional* promotion.'

'Look, Jean,' Milton leans forward and rests an elbow on the desk.

Jean waits for the put down. She's known him long enough to predict his *modus operandi*. The man can't help himself.

'To be honest—the company have thrown a lot of dough at the refurb of the old Buckley and Nunn's. We can't pay top dollar for all the new staff straight up. That's why you're such an appealing candidate. But there'll be an appraisal in six months, and we'll see how your figures stack up. Check how you're tracking then...' He winks.

Jean seethes, noticing his smirk. She takes a deep breath. 'Thank you for the *generous* offer, gentlemen. It's a great opportunity—and a huge commitment. I'll need a few days to consider it.'

'Naturally, the initial relocation costs will be taken care of. A month should be sufficient an allowance for accommodation, right, McMillan?'

McMillan looks up and then checks his paperwork with a frown. 'So, no partner—no kids or schools to consider in the relocation?'

'No,' she feels her flush rise, 'just me.'

'Well, that's a win-win for management. No plans of running to the altar, hey Jean?' Milton chuckles deep into his second chin. 'And I guess we don't have to worry about you getting knocked up.' His pink-blotched cheeks puff out like a baboon's backside.

Jean stares at the smoke curls from the burning cigarette on the ashtray in front of him. She's tempted to pick it up and tip the contents on his head. *I'm tired of all the bullshit.* All the sucking up and smiling and *playing the game* according to the boys' club rules. All the ways she has to concede. She has the highest figures on the sales floor— her years of experience surpass half the managers of other departments too. *Of course, she damn well deserves a promotion!*

At least in Melbourne she'd be removed from the constant scrutiny of these Neanderthals.

'Take a week to consider the offer,' McMillan stands as she pushes open the door. 'It's a great opportunity. Might be your last chance at this stage of life.'

Holding back tears, Jean returns to the designer floor and slams the door of the stockroom behind her. She needs a few minutes to recover.

While the offer is humiliating, there's more to consider than the potential promotion. Is she ready to return to Melbourne permanently? Her thoughts fill with scenarios. She pictures taking the job, addressing her past, and soldering the links she severed all those years ago, to Rick... to Aurora...to her family. In the Alcoholics Anonymous twelve steps program, making amends to those you have wronged is a major step towards rehabilitation.

With her parents both gone, and Shirley too, there's only Rick and Evie left. Is she ready for a family reunion, or the memories a return to Melbourne would stir? How will she ever make them understand?

Evie and Fred are divorced. Fred's the director of an international harvesting company and Jean spotted his wedding photo in the social pages—he married the chairman's daughter. He's come a long way since Champion's. They all have.

Like Jean, they are very different people now.

This promotion would be great for her career. A fresh start. But is it too late to start afresh with her family?

8

A sequence of sharp, high-pitched rings disturbs Jean's silence then is cut off by the heavy click of the answering machine that screens her calls. After one long beep the recording begins, and she stares at the blinking light. She'd read somewhere that anticipation was a form of masochism. As a child, she let her Easter eggs remain on her dresser for months, and to this day, she painstakingly unpeels tape from the wrapping paper on her gifts to drag out the surprise.

At the sound of a man's voice her hand hovers over the receiver. 'It's Rick, I guess you're not there.' He sounds...cautious.

She strides the four steps to the kitchen and slides a cigarette from the Glomesh purse on the island bench. The anguish of guilt and ache of regret that Rick stirs in her surfaces. With a defiant strike of a match on the Redheads box, she holds the flame to her cigarette and then blows a steady stream of smoke between her teeth.

'I have a couple of Mum's portraits. One looks like you—at least, I assume the kid on her knee is you—pretty sure you're the only redhead in the family.' His laugh is forced. 'But hey, I'm coming up to Sydney soon and thought we could—'

A click cuts him off.

She swallows the dryness in her throat and draws in the calming effect of nicotine masked in menthol. He's talking about the painting on the wall of her bedroom. The one she'd awoken to every morning before he was born. Her niggling curiosity surprises her.

A second call quickly follows the first.

'Sorry, the bloody thing ran out. The other is the self-portrait. I guess you've heard by now that Mum left it to you. But, hey, if you don't want it, it'd be great at the winery—I ditched Dad's apples and planted vines a while back. Aurora Estate, the old place is called now. Anyway, thought we might catch up when I'm there? Give me a call, Jeanie, when you can? Tell me what you're up to....'

When Jean left home, she severed her connection to the family orchard—or anything apple-related. To this day, memories of the cider-rich scent and tang of Grannies on her tongue hurt too much.

She frowns. *But a winery, of all things.*

Out on the balcony, she blows out a circle of smoke that drifts towards Sydney Harbour and dissipates in the cool breeze. She has no idea why Aurora's self-portrait was left to her and has resisted contacting her solicitor. Then she turns, staring through the glass doors to the rich timber panelling of her Art Deco apartment.

Jean collects pieces like a bowerbird, and her home is filled with an eclectic mix of styles—a spray of feathers in an opaque blue vase, a pearlescent abalone shell from Bondi beside it. But her home is transient, merely a place where her possessions rest. Once upon a time the orchard was her home. Now Rick has put his stamp on it and made it his.

A half-finished painting waits on the easel for her attention. While painting was suggested as a creative outlet to improve her mental health, the unfinished canvas also reminds Jean of what she hasn't accomplished. But facing the past is painful—twenty years of therapy has taught her that.

Taking an atomiser from her pocket she sprays the minty freshener into her mouth. It hits her like a sign from the universe—first, the offer of promotion in Melbourne, and now Rick is reaching out. Perhaps it is time to address her mistakes.

Things came to a head with her drinking when she'd woken up in a sleazy motel room to the sound of a man's husky voice on the phone, bragging how he'd 'pulled a live one'. She had no idea how she got there. Feeling dirty and ashamed, she had fled the room, with a thirst for the bottle so bad that it physically hurt.

That was the day she stopped drinking and took action. She swore she would never be placed in such a vulnerable position again.

Jean calls her psychotherapist for an appointment before she changes her mind. She can't afford to let anything derail her and tempt her back to the bottle. And every alcoholic needs a support team behind them to pick them up when they make mistakes or to lean on if they start to slide.

Jean's psychotherapist is grounded and conservative, but he's also in touch with New Age methods. One of his mantras is that Jean makes a list of her thoughts before making a major decision. 'Write it down. Set your intentions.' He says the perfect time for setting intentions is on a new moon. It makes your goals clear to the universe.

Jean isn't sure about all that, but she's never had cause to doubt him before. Not even when he demanded she prostate herself on the smelly shag pile carpet at his feet and writhe like a snake. She'd snivelled on the floor while the clocked ticked away until she was finally brave enough to follow his calm instructions. 'Hold your head up and repeat the affirmation, I am worthy. I deserve love.' At the time his method seemed out of line. It was a traumatic experience. But it *had* helped initiate a significant breakthrough.

Appointment made, she presses the rewind button on the machine and stabs a finger at the 'play messages' arrow to hear Rick's voice again.

Calm rises like a wave before breaking inside her; her body swells with confidence like it had in the days when she was young and sanguine. The opportunity is in Melbourne. What is she waiting for? Meeting with Rick in Sydney is the first step to face.

Her fingers stretch for her cigarettes. *If it is to be, it's up to me. Write it down.* Writing makes it real. She picks up a pen.

9

He's hard to miss. Rick is awkwardly balanced on a dainty Louis XVI repo chair when Jean enters the dining room of the popular *nouveau cuisine* restaurant. Thick blond hair is surfer-boy unruly and a lock of heavy fringe falls across his tanned face.

'Wow Jeanie, you look amazing!' Rick beams, rising from the table to greet her. 'Love the power suit.'

She braves a smile and nervously brushes fingers down her sleeve, her diminutive frame imposing in the new triangular style where padded shoulders taper to a narrow tube skirt and kitten heels. Jean's cobalt jacket perfectly complements her rosy gold hair that has lightened over the years. But the quintessential modern woman appears out of place in an old-world dining room bursting with ornate mirrors and prism-glass chandeliers.

'How wonderful to see you at last!' Rick envelops her in a hug.

She squirms out of it gracefully, embarrassed by his physical display. 'It's lovely to see you.'

A tuxedo-wearing waiter pulls out her chair and offers Rick the wine list with a flourish. Crystal glasses sparkle in the light as linen napkins are ostentatiously twirled across their laps. Why do they only offer men the wine list? The fact that she won't partake is not the point.

Rick grins and rolls his eyes at the charade. 'It's been a few years since I've been anywhere this fancy. In my corporate days, I was wined and dined in places like this all the time. We'd chug back Bollinger like lemonade and smoke enormous Cuban cigars!' He holds up his hands to demonstrate. 'Geez, I can still remember coughing up the vile taste of spice and tobacco the next morning. What an absolute wanker I was!'

Jean laughs and immediately feels more at ease. 'I imagine there are still a few of *those* around.' She directs a raised eyebrow towards a table of raucous businessmen. The dessert cart is parked to one side and the sherry trolley on the other; the sommelier stands to attention wearing a mask of servility while patiently awaiting their instructions.

'Takes all kinds,' Rick smiles. 'Now, I thought we might try a red. What do you think?' He licks his lips and concentrates on his selection.

'Just a lime and soda for me,' Jean answers with a curt nod. The waiter has reappeared with the stealth of a panther.

A small frown wrinkles Rick's forehead. 'Tough workday, huh? I'll grab a glass of the Heathcote Shiraz from central Victoria. I'm keen to see what that vineyard is doing.' He hands the wine list back with a slow smile. 'It's all research while I'm here. But Jeanie, tell me all about you?'

Butterflies circle her stomach as she offers the Glomesh cigarette case across the table. Rick shakes his head.

Where to begin? 'Before we start, there's something I need to explain —' She slips a cigarette between her lips and lights the tip before meeting his gaze. *Rip the band-aid off, Jean.*

'I'm an alcoholic.' She lowers her voice. 'I joined AA and I'm twelve months sober. It's the best thing I've ever done for myself.'

'Wow—Jeanie, that's great. Must be tough though. But I'm proud of you...' The magnitude of her effort is reflected in the concern knotted between his brows.

'Yes. I feel like a new person. I live for my job and I'm in a good place.'

'I'm happy for you. It takes guts to turn things around like that.'

Jean affects a carefree smile and then draws deeply on her cigarette. Talking about herself threatens her composure. She changes the subject.

'On the phone you mentioned changes to the orchard. Why don't you tell me about it?'

'Given your news, it feels a little difficult.' He takes a deep breath. 'When I lived in Europe, I became interested in winemaking. And Red Hill has the perfect growing conditions for shiraz.'

Rick explains that the idea of opening a winery and art gallery was a concept he had considered for years. It was the perfect blend of his past —bringing together the two people who had been the prime influences in his childhood.

'I spent months in France working with a winemaker there. His family's methods of biodynamic farming appealed to me, and I'd been looking to buy land to replicate the process here. When Dad suggested the orchard was getting too much for him, I ran my idea past him—the apple industry just didn't do it for me.'

'Biodynamic—that sounds like hard work.' He'd certainly taken some intense steps towards change. And Jack had encouraged him. 'Does that mean no pesticides?'

'That's right, and yes, it has been hard. But the vines I've planted are well established now,' he continues. 'The thing is, I'm planning to have the gallery open soon, and I'm hoping you can help. I have several of Mum's paintings, but—'

Jean never refers to Aurora as 'Mum' and his use of the word startles her. She makes a fuss of squaring up her knife and fork on the tablecloth.

'—I thought you might be able to offer some background info on them? I understand you're the most artistic of us, and you probably know more about her earlier pieces than I do. Wait till you see the self-portrait. The photos don't do it justice.'

Jean draws deeply on her cigarette as their drinks arrive, and Rick takes a cautious sip.

'I'm not sure how much I can help.' She stares through a window behind him that overlooks the path to the building next door—an illegal abortion clinic. One that is such an open secret, it's common knowledge throughout Sydney. The irony is not lost on her.

'Jeanie?'

Jean stubs her cigarette in the ashtray and folds her arms. Bright vermillion nails splay like drops of blood against her sleeve. 'If it's background, you're after, I'm really not sure I'll remember anything helpful.'

'Look, I know our upbringing was a little unorthodox compared to other families, but with Shirley gone and Evie overseas...' His voice is strained. 'I was kind of hoping for some understanding. For your support.'

The word hangs in the air.

'I'm sorry.' Jean's tone is clipped, and she looks away. She knows what it's like to be without support. 'You might have been told that Aurora and I didn't get on. When I was a teenager, things—changed—and I went my own way. I can tell you that the painting of me as a child was done in the mid-1940s, but I've no idea about her other work...'

'Did you notice anything of interest in the photo of her self-portrait? I'm not sure of the significance of the symbolism. Unfortunately, there's no information or reference notes for that one, and nothing in her preliminary sketches.'

'I really don't know.' Jean sips her drink.

'I guess when you see it.... I mean, once you receive the painting, then it might jog your memory.'

The solicitor's letter suggested she would understand it too. Jean isn't sure.

Their entrees appear beneath domed silver covers lifted with exaggeration. A supercilious voice interrupts their discussion with a long and elaborate description of the nouveau dishes. The tension is palpable as they sit silently, waiting for him to leave.

Rick tries another tack. 'So, tell me about your work. DJ's, isn't it? They're a great company—'

Work is safer to discuss. Jean explains her role as a buyer offers her the freedom to express the creativity denied in sales. She praises the virtues of her latest success, Lisa Ho, fresh out of art school. Her beautiful designs are sexy and stylish, but with spunk and attitude too. Rick leans forward and nods at intervals as he listens. He's a handsome man with his father's eyes.

'You obviously have a knack for fashion. And I guess there are opportunities for further advancement within the company?'

'Yes, there can be,' she hesitates, taking a delicate mouthful of seafood mousseline terrine. The heady scent of oregano and thyme has the clarity of a morning walk. 'The company recently took over the old Buckley & Nunn building in Bourke Street.'

'Wasn't that Mum's favourite haunt?'

'In my day George's was her preference.'

When Rick laughs, Jean joins in.

'With the stock market up, business must be booming for DJ's...'

'Actually, they've offered me a promotion to head up designer fashion at the new store.' She surprises herself by volunteering the news.

'In Melbourne? Well, that's wonderful, Jeanie. The company must be impressed with your work.' He holds his glass up in salute.

'I'm still considering the offer.' She sips from her glass. 'It's quite a big change—my life is here.'

Rick's fork stops in mid-air. 'Surely, they've offered you a substantial incentive to move interstate? It must be a step up, career wise?'

'Yes. But it means starting over again, finding a new apartment and everything. Sometimes I feel I'm past it.'

'Good god, Jeanie, you're in your forties, not your nineties!'

Rick's smirk and comical expression offer support, not ridicule. She has the good grace to laugh. He's lovely.

'You're welcome to stay with me, you know. Obviously, I'm a way out of Melbourne, but it might help until you get set up. To be honest, it'd be great getting to know you better. I always felt a bit like an only child growing up—'

'I imagine you did.'

'The olds were more like grandparents by the time I came along. I used to think my birth was a mistake—except blind Freddy could tell Mum and Dad had a pretty special relationship.' He takes another sip of wine and smiles. 'I know how fortunate I was to have the love and support of such great parents.'

Jean can't help the twinge of envy. Aurora was far from a saint. But Rick has her on a pedestal. It's clear a great deal has been kept from him.

She places her napkin on the table and stands. 'Please excuse me.'

The waiter rushes to pull out her chair and pre-empts her needs by pointing in the direction of the powder room.

Inside, Jean examines her makeup and reapplies her lipstick, relieved she has the powder room to herself. Of course, she loves him. He can't possibly understand what the separation has cost her. She needs to explain.

But when she returns to the table, they chatter about general topics, safe and impersonal, as their main courses arrive. Jean is mesmerised by Rick dissecting the guinea fowl on his plate with precision, and how he pushes the strawberries to the side of his plate. She dabs at her lips with the napkin. *He saves the best for last too.*

The wine continues to loosen his tongue. He speaks with confidence of his plans for Aurora Estate. His idea for a gallery to help foster the careers and profiles of local artists is not too far removed from Jean's own vision in fashion. Then he mentions establishing an Aurora Champion Prize, one that will provide a scholarship for a young artist. What a wonderful opportunity for a burgeoning creative.

'It was one of Mum's last requests. She was always so considerate of those less fortunate.'

Jean's plate still bears traces of the dish she has barely touched when the waiter appears. She sips her soda to quash the uncomfortable squirm in her stomach. She can't tell him now. 'I must get back to work, Rick.'

'Already?' He leans back in his chair and runs both hands through his hair. 'Let me know if you need help with the move. I'd be happy to put out some feelers about your role at DJs too—in fact, I might still have a connection on the board. I could put in a good word for you, if you like?'

Jean presses her lips together. 'Thanks, but I'm fine.' Fine? *Fucked up. Insecure. Neurotic. Emotional.* Far from fine!

'Let's stay in touch.' He kisses her cheek.

Jean steels her voice before her guard shatters completely. 'Thank you, Rick. It's been lovely to see you.'

Collins Street, Melbourne, 1952

It was raining when she arrived that day. It was easier—kinder—to forget the shock on Michael's ashen face; the blank stare as he pursed his lips and the realisation took hold. His brilliant blue eyes had filled with tears and glassed over so swiftly that Jean might have questioned her arrival on his doorstep unannounced if only she had read the situation correctly.

'Jeanie? What a surprise. What are you doing here?'

'I heard you were back in Melbourne...'

She had sobbed with relief when Aurora mentioned her patron had returned from his business trip. He'd been gone for months. At least that explained why Jeanie hadn't heard from him. But now, at last they were here, together.

It had been hard to keep their relationship secret, especially from Evie. Many times, she had wavered and been tempted to share it; even again today, when she asked Evie to cover for her, pretending she was meeting a fictitious schoolboy. Her sister had no idea what Jeanie had been up to.

It was a tad embarrassing—and private. Although Evie had once boasted of intimacy in her relationship with Fred, Jeanie tried to imagine telling her twin that she had actually *done it*—and with an older man no one knew she was seeing?

Now that Michael had returned from overseas, she would share their news.

'Please forgive my appalling manners. Do come in.' Michael directs her through to the kitchen. Jeanie screws up her nose. The strong fragrance of whisky wafts from the glass filled with amber fluid on the table.

'Can I offer you a coffee, or tea, perhaps?' He folds his arms.

'Michael,' her voice trembles. 'It's wonderful to see you. I have news I've been waiting to tell you...' She reaches out and places her hand on his arm.

He steps back so sharply that her hand falls away. 'Jeanie... You really shouldn't have come here. Your mother would be furious.'

He's about to say more, but Jeanie frowns, noticing his lips clamped into a tight line as he turns away. The thread that attaches them inside of her draws tighter.

'Well, I...I can't stay away any longer. Mummy doesn't know what we mean to each other.'

'Oh Jeanie,' Michael takes her hands, 'please forgive me. What happened between us was inexcusable. I don't know what came over me. I assure you it won't happen again. I sincerely regret what fell between us that day, and any harm I caused you. I would never hurt you intentionally...'

'But you didn't. I know that you care for me.' Perhaps he doesn't realise how she feels about him. She *must* make him understand. 'I...I love you, Michael.'

Her face flushes with the heat of laying her feelings bare: her heart is spread wide open. She's dangerously exposed, as though lying naked before him once more.

'*No Jeanie!* No! I'm sorry! That....' He runs a hand through his hair.' No, that was not love, sweet girl. I should never...I took advantage. It was wrong. A terrible mistake. How will you ever forgive me?'

A mistake? Jeanie and her sisters had been brought up to believe the act of making love was the coming together of two people in love. To respect and save themselves for marriage. Her hand rests on her stomach, and she sinks into a chair.

'But Michael, I'm going to have a baby... your baby.'

'*Shit!* Are you sure?' He paces the floor.

Jean nods and her tears spill onto the linen tablecloth. *Of course, she is sure.* She let out the side seams of her school tunic until the pleats stretched out of shape. Her shirts strain across her breasts and the bottom buttons remained undone. All winter she hid under her dressing gown and squirrelled her clothes away in a bathroom cubicle to get dressed away from prying eyes in the dormitory.

'We—you—must tell your mother. She will know what to do. *J'emmerde*, she will never forgive me!'

My mother? Jeanie has no intention of asking Aurora for help when there's a simple solution. 'I thought we would be together. We could... get married...'

But when she looks at Michael, all she sees is his anguish. And inaction.

He slumps against the wall in the corner of the room with hands covering his face as though he wants to be as far away from her as possible. 'I can't. It's not possible. I'm sorry...'

Didn't he care for her? She hangs her head and closes her eyes. How could she not have seen it? She gave herself to him. She allowed him the most intimate of acts possible between two people and all that time—was he just pretending?

But then she remembers his tears when he sobered from the fog of heavy drinking, and the disbelief in his eyes to find Jeanie in his bed. The way he skulked from the room…

Shame churns inside her. Jeanie takes a deep breath. It's her fault. She should have stopped him before things went too far. She could have said no. He had seemed so interested in her, praising her talent and beauty. He made her feel special…

'I can't marry you. Forgive me.'

His pleas fall on deaf ears. Jeanie must be strong now. If she is to be a mother—an adult—it's time to act like one.

She looks him in the eye. 'Can't or won't?'

In the hallway, the clock on the chiffoniere chimes the hour and breaks the silence. Its echo hollows through the apartment.

'What do you suggest I do?' She holds back her tears.

'There are places to go. I will make enquiries. A clinic where they—can end it.' He shrugs.

Her eyes widen. Of course, she had heard the stories of backyard abortionists. But that is not for her.

'You expect me to…? No, no I could never!'

His gaze meets hers briefly, and then he stares past her to the doorway that offers exit from both her and the situation.

'Then it is best if you go away to a home for unmarried mothers. I'm sorry but that's your only choice. You're too young, Jeanie. Have the baby and then give it up for adoption—'

'No!'

'You'll need money. Of course, I'll pay—'

'I don't want your bloody money!' Jeanie swears, the first curse she's ever allowed herself. 'I'm keeping our baby. How dare you disrespect me by trying to pay me off like a common….' She can't bring herself to say the word she hears in her head, no matter how much she feels like one.

'I apologise. That was not my intention.' He places a hand upon her shoulder, but she shrugs him away.

Thoughts rush through her head as she plans how she will care for a child. She'll go back to the orchard and explain it to her parents. They'll be upset at first, furious, but eventually they will come around. Michael might too.

'I'll do whatever is necessary and provide whatever you need.'

How disappointing, that his immediate reaction is how to best wash his hands of her.

Michael leaves the room. Jeanie's knuckles are white as her fingers grip the arms of the chair. It's all that keeps her from sliding to the floor and curling into a ball. She thought he'd be happy. Supportive. Loving. *What a silly little fool she was.* Why would a man like Michael, an intelligent man of the world, be interested in a love-struck schoolgirl like her?

'I understand you don't want to take my money, but I insist.' He hands her a cheque, the sum greater than a full year's tuition at Beaulieu. He opens his hand to reveal a silk purse. 'This belonged to my mother. It's only a small token, but I'd like you to have it. It's all I have of my family.' His eyes are glassy.

The thrum of her heartbeat echoes in her ears as she considers his words. Perhaps deep down he does care.

Jeanie stuffs the purse into her coat pocket. 'I have to go.'

Taking one last look at him—the man who she believed loved her the way she loved him—she holds her head up, realising she must face the consequences alone.

Her first life lesson is a hard one.

But she will never forget Michael's expression, the one that aged him immediately. And his look of remorse remained indelibly imprinted in Jean's memory for the rest of her life.

TATIANA

10

Abbas-Tuman, 1899

My husband vows the small town of Abbas-Tuman, secluded in the forests of the Caucasus, the most restful place on earth.

'I value my privacy,' Georgiy confesses on the final part of our journey. 'And the Cossacks are far more liberal in their views. I don't feel the need for great halls full of people wasting hours in idle conversation. I simply cannot wait for Alix to deliver a son to relieve me of my imperial duties.'

I laugh, somewhat nervously, conflicted by both the thrill of freedom and the question of solitude it affords. He suggests Abbas-Tuman will become our main residence after our marriage is announced in St Petersburg.

'There's much to entertain us there!' he continues. 'Bathing in the thermal springs, riding, walking—the landscape is perfect for drawing or painting. The air is clean and the climate temperate, if not a little hot in summer. It is a great improvement on the city.'

Although he is not enamoured of St Petersburg society, I'm sure we will still entertain. I imagine intimate parties and picnics, playing hostess to my friends and welcoming them to our country estate.

The scenery grows more spectacular as we edge nearer. A rich and lush canopy of pine trees leads from the forest to Georgiy's summer residence. The first of two mansions appears in the verdant valley, cleaved into the side of heavily forested mountains. The tranquil setting is as picturesque as Georgiy had promised.

A sudden wave of nervousness overcomes me. I'll be the mistress here. But I know little of the customs of the local people, or of running a household, to be frank. Nor do I fully understand the expectations of a wife. I barely know Georgiy in many ways. I draw a deep breath and brave a smile as the automobile comes to a halt. An elderly footman appears as Georgiy and I prepare to alight and shades me from the bright sunshine with a parasol.

The edifice of Georgiy's summer mansion is predominantly wooden with stone-trimmed turrets and corbels. Oriental-inspired windows are framed with pretty, decorative arches and painted wooden latticework.

'It is enchanting, Georgiy.' I smile and grip the crook of his arm tightly. 'Truly delightful.'

Servants line either side of the entrance hall, wearing livery embroidered with the Tsarevich's crest. They respectfully study their feet. However, I try to engage them, repeating their names, wishing them to find me an amenable mistress. I frown when Georgiy introduces me as his cousin, rather than his wife, then in a hushed voice, advises it best.

'If you take a walk and cross the bridge over the Otshke, you'll reach the winter mansion. Or rest if you like, after those infernal dusty roads. Do make yourself at home—'

'Oh Georgiy! Can you not escort me?'

'I have work to do, *ma chérie;* matters to attend to. But have a good poke around. There is a fine tempered roan mare in the stables, Saperavi. She would be perfectly suitable for you to ride.'

'Saperavi? As in the grape?' I laugh as he nods.

'The wine! Nevertheless, make yourself comfortable and wander at your leisure. We will meet later once you are settled.'

He instructs the housekeeper to show me to my apartments and waves me off with a chaste kiss to my forehead. Perhaps he is right; it is not yet prudent to expose our relationship.

With Marthe at my heels carrying a compact personal valise, we take the stairs to find guest rooms opening off the wide hallway and bathrooms conveniently located on the same floor. I hesitate at the door to the library and take a few steps inside. The walls are lined with mahogany shelves bursting with leather-bound books while a large desk and chair rest under the window, providing views over the grounds below. It's the largest library I've seen in a private residence, and I am delighted. It reminds me of our first meeting. I can't help but smile. 'Has His Imperial Highness read all of these?'

'*Nyet*, Your Highness,' the housekeeper answers, her accented dialect accompanied with a look of disdain. 'What His Imperial Highness does is not my business.'

The housekeeper has an officious manner, but I offer my brightest smile, hoping to express the sincerity of my intentions. She walks on with scarcely a backwards glance.

We turn into the north-facing wing and to my quarters, on the opposite wing to the Tsarevich's. Marthe is immediately shooed down a narrow hall to a servant's room.

My boudoir is delightful and will be perfect until Georgiy and I share a suite, as I am eager to do. The view from my sitting room reveals an undulating expanse of vibrant green foliage, unfolding into a quilt of forested wilderness.

It is beautiful here, and I am excited to begin my life as Georgiy's wife. A pang of guilt has me wishing I could share the joy of our marriage with dear Rosalind. And Olga.

I've lived in solitude in the past, but quite prefer company—particularly female companionship. Is there sufficient to amuse me here? I may well do without the conviviality of the theatre for a time, but will I miss the vibrant city I love?

I n private, several days later, I kiss Georgiy's cheeks appropriately, then brush my lips across his to reacquaint him with my ardour.

Lingering for his response, I stifle my disappointment when he backs away at the sound of shuffling footsteps in the hall.

A man in the uniform of the Cossack Hussars strides confidently into the room. My first thought is we have been caught out, and the man's thunderous expression is a reminder that people will be surprised by our marriage.

It's been days since we have been intimate, first hindered by the restrictions of our travel lodgings, and then by Georgiy's insistence on us resting after our journey. I long for the unbridled passion I felt rise in me at every touch of his hand on our wedding night and can't wait until we are united once again.

'Imperial Highness, I apologise for the interruption.' The hussar looks from Georgiy to me and back again. 'I was not aware you had company.'

The ruggedly handsome man appears a little older than Georgiy with curling jet-black hair that shows the finest whisper of turning to grey. His expression is serious, but his eyes are hard and cool. Judging by his dust-covered *sapogi* boots, he has arrived in much haste.

Georgiy's face glows pink. 'Indeed. Grand Duchess Tatiana Romanova, may I present my adjutant, Lieutenant Ivan Borsky.'

I tender a generous smile of welcome. A man so close to my husband is one important to befriend.

'It is…a pleasure, Your Highness.' His manner fails to affirm his greeting as he turns to Georgiy. 'Sir, we have matters to discuss. If you will excuse me—' Then, clicking his heels, he leaves as swiftly as he appeared.

Georgiy peers through the window towards the mountains.

'Darling? Is there a problem?'

He turns to me with one of his treasured smiles. 'No, *ma belle*. Nothing to concern you. However, I regret we will have to postpone our outing today. I must discuss affairs with Borsky. Might you make your own plans? Perhaps you can take the brougham into the village this afternoon? Marthe can accompany you.'

'Do not concern yourself,' I kiss his cheek. 'I'm quite able to entertain myself. I have no intentions of interfering with matters of state.'

Little did I know it was merely the beginning of my husband's many burdensome affairs.

11

Matters of covert military importance have kept Georgiy busy for days and nights on end. Borsky provides him with an endless stream of imperial communiqués. It seems there is much for the pair to attend to in the villages too. Georgiy and I have barely managed an hour alone.

Since I was a girl in Veliky Novgorod, my private journal has been my constant companion and provides welcome respite. I smile, reading over problems that once seemed insurmountable. There were times when I chose not to write at all, instead using the blank pages to make sketches of people and the places I had visited, or scenes that amused me. Conversely, my deepest thoughts are confessed here, moments when all hope of a bright future appeared lost. A habit I'm not willing to forgo.

I ponder the marital relations between man and wife. Had my mother possessed the same fervent desires I feel for my husband? With my father? Her lovers? My skin flushes with heat, recalling the gentle touch of Georgiy's hands on my body. Does he love me as I love him? Is it indecent to long for him so passionately? I lay down my pen and close my eyes, imagining my hands on his chest and fingers trailing lower, brazenly taking hold of his firmness....

When at all Georgiy attends my bed, I confess to disappointment. I must content myself with little more than a brotherly kiss or holding his hand as he falls to sleep in exhaustion. Most evenings I am abed with only a novel for company and the decisive sound of silence.

The Tsarevich holds a pivotal role in Russian rule, and Georgiy is diligent in all his undertakings. I'm fascinated to witness his efficient and conscientious approach. I had no idea of the extent of politics that require his express attention, but he is a man of the people, devoted to a life of service. He promises not to bore me with political matters and avoids discussing them in my presence, despite any interest I might harbour in Russia's affairs. 'Do not concern yourself, my darling. Borsky and I have best knowledge of these matters,' he says with a dismissive wave.

One morning he adds, 'It's a tedious business, and one must do as one is told but...,' a wracking cough breaks his flow. 'My apologies.' He recovers and sips the glass of tea beside him. 'As I was saying, the documents will remain in my study today, so I may devote my attention solely to you. I refuse to allow affairs to impose any longer on your restful stay.'

I am indeed a visitor. I long to show him that as his wife I'm willing to shoulder his burdens. We shared intimacy during our courting, laughing together, speaking of travel and art and all the freedoms we hoped to experience in the future. Marriage to Georgiy is proving not at all as I expected. I resent the matters of state that shut my husband away from me, and ponder the question: once our marriage is made public, what further matters might I be excluded from?

But instead of informing Georgiy of my bitter disappointment when he once again cancels our planned picnic, I express the concerns in my pages.

I endeavour to find new and interesting ways to make a satisfying life here. I will host charity events and bazaars, visit those convalescing and offer alms. Yet will this be enough to fill my days? The niggling doubts keep me awake, oft until dawn.

The day before I'm due to return to St Petersburg, having woken far too early, I throw a shawl about my shoulders and take a walk. The seasons are turning, and dew is heavy underfoot. Although I have enjoyed the forest and its seclusion for the past month, I'm eager for the company and gaiety of my friends in the city.

On my return I approach the courtyard to hear muffled voices coming from an open window. Dearest Georgiy is already hard at work in his study. The boughs of a large chestnut tree make it impossible to see inside; a canopy of evergreen leaves obscures my view. When I hear my name, I stop.

'How can I believe you? You married in haste without my knowledge. It's too late now—'

'What would you have me do, Vanya?' Georgiy's tone holds irritation. 'I have a responsibility to my family—'

'And what of me?' Borsky's voice rises. 'What of your responsibility *to me*? The thought of you...'

I lean against the building, and then chastise myself. I must have imagined hearing the words: *touching her.*

'Nothing needs change. It will allay rumours. It's a precaution. Besides, Tatya returns to St Petersburg tomorrow.'

With a hand on my aching chest, I swiftly scale the staircase to my rooms and brush past Marthe in the hallway, my thoughts racing like a whirlwind. *Indeed, they must be discussing another matter entirely....*

'Your Highness? What is it?'

'Leave me be,' I wave her away, a bitter taste on my tongue. 'I'm merely fatigued. Inform His Imperial Highness I will join him for breakfast in due course.'

Half an hour later, I'm composed well enough to face him. But Borsky follows on my heels and bursts into the room, fluttering behind my husband as is his habit. The man has the uncanny ability of appearing whenever we're alone, finding the precise moment to adjust a tray or produce a letter requiring Georgiy's signature. While not unusual to have servants in constant attendance, the adjutant's constant presence verges on intrusive.

A maid serves my tea from the samovar and places a plate of fruit before me. I'm silent as Georgiy reads the document. I want to question him about what I'd overheard. Is our marriage truly what he wanted? Or was it a foolish whim offered in jest to irritate his brother? A pain lodges in my chest. The scent of pine is strong, and I swallow down a salty taste in mouth. I suddenly feel too warm, too uncomfortable inside the room. Claustrophobic. Even the aroma of freshly baked croissants makes me nauseous and offers little appeal.

'My dear, you look quite unwell,' Georgiy pats my hand. 'What can I get for you? I'll have something brought in, something sweet perhaps?'

I shake my head and dab at my mouth with a napkin.

'My physician is due to visit today. I shall insist he examines you.'

'No, Georgiy,' I wave away his hand. 'I'm afraid I did not sleep well.' I direct my gaze at Borsky. 'Lieutenant, if you don't mind, I'd like a *private* word with my...cousin.'

Borsky's cool response borders on insolence. Cow-dung eyes appraise me as though I'm refuse beneath his nails. With a scowl on his handsome face, he sets his jaw square. Georgiy grimaces when the door slams behind him.

His cheeks are decidedly grey. He could use a tonic. I've heard Alix takes a protein drink for her health each morning. 'I hope your physician is bringing something for your cough.'

'Yes, he suggests an elixir. I expect I spent too long in the thermal waters last week. Nothing to worry about, my dear. He is due around noon.'

'It's no surprise you are run down, working all the hours you do. However, I was hoping we could spend my last day together...'

'An excellent idea. Although, I'm afraid we must wait until after *he* calls.' Georgiy smiles at me, as you would to indulge a child.

What I really desire is for Georgiy to hold me—to love me again completely. After this morning's events, I'm even more confused by his lack of intimacy.

The parlour door opens, and Borsky materialises once more. I glare over Georgiy's shoulder.

'Imperial Highness. The telephone call from the Tsar you were expecting. Will you take it in the study?'

Georgiy rises and kisses my brow. 'Excuse me, my dear.'

I clench my fists. Once again, I am excluded.

12

St Petersburg

Despite missing Georgiy, I slip back into my life in St Petersburg as seamlessly as fingers into a silken glove. Mindful of telephone exchange operators, our calls are brief, and discussions guarded. I pen dates in my journal for parties and theatre performances to fill the emptiness, all the time hoping Georgiy might surprise me with his arrival.

After weeks of light tea gowns and simple daywear of lace and muslin, tonight I'm restricted by etiquette to return to the armour of court dress for a state ceremony at the Winter Palace.

The afternoon before I left for Beyda, my new court gown arrived while I was out riding. When I dressed that evening, Marthe was left to pin me into it; the neckline had slid from my shoulders and the ivory bodice sagged; the full satin underskirt hung loose at the waist. I could barely sit down for fear of pins scratching me.

I was furious, having assumed there was no need to doubt the quality of needlework from the salon that singularly supplied dresses to the court as required by the *Edict on Dress*. However, I suspected

Madame Brissac's young seamstress had not given me her full attention. I recalled her sour expression when I ordered the embroidered panels and velvet for my *sarafan*, in the sky-blue reserved exclusively for Mama's, and in turn my, use as was our due with the rank of grand duchess.

'Has my gown been adjusted?'

Marthe's cheeks redden; she smooths a hand over the folds of fabric billowing from her arms. 'I apologise, Your Highness. There was little time before we left for the Caucasus.'

'Oh, Marthe,' I sigh, 'You'll have to pin me into it again.'

When she eases me into my gown a short time later, remarkably, the gold acanthus leaves embroidered on the bodice flatten out and the velvet sits smoothly across my bust.

'It appears the clean air at Abbas-Tuman stimulated my appetite,' I frown. With little to occupy my days, I had availed myself of every opportunity to exercise in the lush surrounds with walks into the nearby forest where I'd sit and sketch.

Marthe bobs a curtsy and returns with the fillet *kokoshnik* headdress worn by unmarried ladies of the court. She affixes the satin ribbon at the back of my head and arranges the veil over my shoulders.

The procession's montage of colour begins at the rose-coloured Corinthian columns and trails along a line of pristine scagliola walls. We glitter and shine under sparkling Bohemian crystal chandeliers. The men, impeccable in full parade uniforms, wear jackets adorned with more gold medals, regalia and braided *aiguillettes* than are fixed on the gilded walls.

I suffer under the weight of my gown, despite the slits in my velvet jacket that allow my arms freedom of movement. It requires all my energy to make the slow progression from the Malachite Hall dragging the heavily embroidered six-foot train.

I'm exhausted by the time Oleg joins me, having escaped a party of elderly dowagers seeking news of his parents.

'Are you well, dear Tatya?' He is resplendent in the white parade uniform of the Chevalier Guards.

Before I can answer, the Empress approaches. She's a little pale, but her cheeks are plump and her hand drifts protectively to her stomach.

Oleg bows and then tactfully disappears.

'Your Imperial Majesty,' I curtsy. 'You look well this evening.'

Her greeting kisses surround me with the scent of violets, the hint of spring in an English garden. Her bloom cannot be denied. I notice the fullness of her neckline exposes more flesh than usual. While many ladies rejoice in the lower décolletage of court dress, our Empress professes to loathe the style.

A wave of excitement trills through me. *Can it mean that Georgiy and I will be seen together soon?* There's no joy in hiding our love when all I want is to sing our marriage to all around us.

'Indeed, God willing. I am remarkably well this time.' Her blush is comical for someone who has been with child several times. 'Walk with me, Tatiana Vladimirovna...'

We do not move far; the train of the Empress is more than double the length of mine. 'I am pleased you have come to your senses and restrained your behaviour with the Tsarevich. He remains in Abbas-Tuman. It is for the best. It would never do.'

'Your Majesty?' I frown as her cool stare meets mine.

'It's high time you found a suitable husband. As is your duty.'

Later that night, I lay in my bed, the ache in my shoulders eased by Marthe's thoughtful use of a warmer on my linens. The conversation replays in my head but puzzles me. I thought Nicky told her everything? I roll to my side with my hands beneath my cheeks and close my eyes with a smile. She doesn't know about us. I can't wait to see her face when she finds out. And once she gives Russia an heir, all will be well.

Georgiy's letter arrives a couple of days later.

'*My dear girl,*' he writes. His hand carries a grand flourish on all the capital letters and takes an effort to decipher. '*The weather has been ghastly since you left, but last night we took supper outside and felt the breeze cool a shade or two. Borsky was saying how quiet the house is without the continual hum of your voice.*'

I press my lips together.

'*Nicky reports they intend making a new home at Tsarskoye Selo.*

More comfortable for you too, I imagine.... There was a names day celebration in the village on the banks of the Alazani last weekend. The Cossacks were out in their splendid traditional costumes, and much vodka was consumed, as well as the fine Saperavi you so enjoyed while you were here.

'I long to see you but won't return to the city until after winter. I do so miss the kind welcome in your beautiful smile.'

I skim the lines for words of passion and endearment but find none. I can't help a tug of disappointment.

That afternoon, I call for my carriage to join Rosalind at the British Legation for tea.

'My dear Tatiana! I've missed you so...' Rosalind draws me to her. 'You cannot imagine all that has happened since you've been away. But your friend, Dorothea? Did you find her well?'

Tears spring into my eyes at her heartfelt welcome and cheery smile. I avert my face, ashamed of my mistruth. 'Yes, indeed. It was restful, fresh air and the like; endless afternoon teas and soirees, as you well understand.' I shrug and remove my gloves, then smooth my gown over my knees. 'Enough of that. I see the Empress is in fine health...'

'In almost every discussion, talk leads back to Their Imperial Majesties announcing the arrival of an heir before summer. I pray they aren't proven wrong.' She inclines her head.

'It is unwise to speak of it.' I frown. *Voicing it aloud might bring on bad luck.* I can't imagine how devastated they would be to have another daughter. And I have more reason than most to wish the child a tsarevich.

'Oh Tatiana, how incredibly superstitious you are!' Rosalind laughs. 'I meant no harm. I am sympathetic to the Tsarina and her situation. It is clear their imperial majesties are still very much in love. I sincerely hope they are blessed with the son they wish for.'

'Indeed.' The subject is far too sensitive. I struggle to maintain my façade. 'Tell me, who have you called upon? Or whom, shall I ask, has called upon you while I was away?'

'Oh Tatiana. Your cousin Oleg Igorevich is a delightful man.' Rosalind's porcelain skin flushes with colour. 'However, some time ago he disappeared on a mysterious mission and was quite evasive when explaining it.' Rosalind lowers her eyes. 'Do you think…I mean, should I presume he is seeking the affections of another?'

I press my lips together, wishing I could explain the details of his absence. He is fond of Rosalind, far fonder than is wise, and I have genuine concerns regarding her ardent admiration for my cousin. Oleg is an intelligent man, but like many in our position he is prone to exaggeration and flattery. Flirtations are one thing, but in the Russian court, marriage—as I well know—is quite another.

Rosalind is the daughter of a British Lord, and eminently suitable as a wife within the noble classes of Britain. However, whether her birth is considered equal to the bloodlines of dear Oleg Igorevich, is another thing entirely. Tsar Nicholas II is yet to sanction a request from anyone of imperial rank in a morganatic marriage. While it's an antiquated law; it is one that threatens us with banishment if opposed.

I seek to allay her concerns. 'We are fortunate to be surrounded by numerous eligible *beaux*. If Oleg saw your interest in another, perhaps it might further inflame his feelings?' I stare at her with raised brows to make sure she understands.

'There are few I admire, certainly none like Oleg.'

'Surely one or two have tempted you…'

A frown wrinkles her fair brow. 'There is one who is terribly dashing, but far too aloof for my liking. Lieutenant Vorontov.'

'Vorontov? Have I met him?'

'You must have. He's one of the dowager's Life Guards. The lieutenant is a giant of a man! Rather dark and brooding, the way I imagine Heathcliff from *Wuthering Heights*—'

'Heathcliff?' I laugh. 'Oh Rosalind, you are amusing.'

'My goodness, Tatya, is that a new brooch?' Rosalind's swift change of subject surprises me. 'One of your mother's? Although not her typical style—' She points to the ladybird pinned in the folds of my blouse.

My mother's baubles are easily spotted from the length and breadth of a reception hall. The settings of her rings hold jewels so enormous I can barely raise my hand whilst wearing one.

'—I don't recall seeing it.'

'A gift, I suspect.' I hold the lie between my teeth and curse the necessity. 'Let us take a stroll along the embankment. I feel the need for fresh air.'

Though longing to share my news of my good fortune, I pray the secret will not be my undoing.

13

A week later, leaves swirl past my window and twigs ravage the street. I feel quite ill at ease. When Rosalind calls unannounced, I'm partaking of a strong brew of Assam with a large serving of sugar to restore my flagging energy. In recent days, my social calendar has been decidedly hectic.

'Rosalind dear, it's madness to venture out today!'

'Your Highness.' Her gloves are chilled as she squeezes my hands tightly and lowers her head. 'I take it you haven't heard the terrible news...?'

'Has the ambassador been reposted?' I would dearly miss the Brassingtons if they were to return to Britain. I hold my breath.

'Tatya...I know how close the two of you were; it is indeed a tragedy. It's Grand Duke Georgiy. He is...dead.'

'*Dead?* No!' I grip the mantelpiece, willing the words from existence. 'That cannot be—'

'I'm afraid it's true, dear. Papa was notified this morning by official communiqué from the palace before the newspapers were alerted. A motoring accident, I believe. I came as soon as I heard.'

I want to drop to the floor, to sob and scream like an infant for the man I love and have lost. But I keep my back to her, schooled not to show any sign of the pain that twists in my chest. *My darling Georgiy.* Whatever will I do without him?

'I know this must come as a terrible shock. I wanted to offer my condolences.'

With effort I lift my head and pull my shoulders back. 'Thank you. Tell me...how...?'

'It appears his new automobile lost control and careered into tree. The wreckage was found some hours later.'

Borsky's face appears in my thoughts. 'Was he alone?'

She nods and inclines her head as I take my seat. 'For a time, I suspected there was more between you. But then you went to stay with your friend, Dorothea, and have not mentioned him since. The Tsarevich was delightful company. Such fun. It's a terrible shame. I'm deeply sorry for your loss.'

It is incomprehensible. How can Georgiy be dead? I'd read his last letter, mere days ago. It was written with such liveliness.

Our marriage is wiped away as swiftly as chalk from a slate.

'Olga Alexandrovna and the Dowager Empress were planning to visit him in the Caucasus. Now I expect now they'll be arranging his funeral. It is simply too awful!' Rosalind holds my hands in hers. I avert my gaze from hers.

My mouth opens but the words still on my tongue. I must grieve in silence, with no more fuss than I would for a distant relation. My vision distorts as though peering through a foggy haze. I make my apologies, but when Marthe shows Rosalind out, I take to my bed, caressing the ladybird at the neck of my blouse, with my body convulsing.

My darling Georgiy. I will never forget his love. Our marriage offered the promise of far more independence than a woman of my position is entitled to. He opened my eyes to the possibility of a richer and freer future. But now he is gone.

Without him, my days will remain as closed and claustrophobic as the coffin he will rest in for eternity.

And I must bear my sorrow in silence.

Less than a week after Georgiy's death, servants report the discovery of the body of Lieutenant Borsky. It appears (in details passed from the dowager's valet to his sister who works in the Winter Palace kitchens) that Borsky had taken his own life. A note was found, stating his regret at not keeping the Tsarevich safe.

While indeed a tragedy, I choose not to contemplate the sin he has committed against God. I had never warmed to the man, and his avowed dislike of me was clear. However, I deeply regret he felt such an extreme measure necessary; the accident was not his fault.

Georgiy's final journey to St Petersburg takes weeks, with details of the extensive route of the funeral cortege reported daily. I have neither the will nor the energy to leave my bed. I hover in limbo, trapped between reconciling the shock of his death with the dread of attending his final interment. *Alas—I have no choice.*

The fateful day of the funeral is bright and full of warmth, but my heart is frozen. I'm determined to maintain decorum, despite the high cost to me.

'Your Highness, it is time.' Marthe stands at the foot of my bed. Her kind smile of sympathy brings tears to my eyes. I slide from the bed and then sink to my knees, sobbing.

'Please, Tatya.' She rushes to me, comforting me in her arms. 'You must be brave today—remember, you are mourning a relative, not a husband...not yet.'

My head hangs low, and I try to find the courage to stand. How can I face life without him? *How will I live?*

When Marthe fastens me into the mourning gown I last wore for the funeral of my mother, her mouth downturns.

'What is it?' I ask, irritated by the tedium of the task. I want it over, want the day done with.

'Your stays need to be pulled tighter to secure these lower hooks.' She spans her hands around my waist and a flush a colour floods her cheeks.

'Try again,' I instruct, holding my breath. But as she draws the laces, I sway, lightheaded. 'Stop!' I push her away and double over. 'I can't breathe.'

'Your Highness,' Marthe takes my hands. 'You have not had your courses since we left St Petersburg.'

'*What? No!*' I absorb the implication of her words.

She guides me into an armchair, and I lose all resolve, as the severity of Georgiy's loss sinks in. The tears I've been fighting drip in rivulets down my cheeks. How will I hide the extent of my loss? And bear his child without him?

I feel somewhat stronger by the time I hear Oleg's voice in the parlour. Marthe has loosened my laces and my gown is hidden under a full-length coat. With my face covered by a sheer funereal veil, I am ready.

The mourning procession leaves Nevsky Prospekt with Georgiy's coffin draped in flags and transported by a team of twelve horses as befits his station. Grateful my face is concealed, I avert my gaze from the hearse as we pass the Summer Gardens, blinking away memories of our secret liaisons and joy of newfound love. *Was our time together just a dream?* It's been barely a year yet feels like a decade has passed. My fingers rest briefly on the base of my bodice: I push one foot in front of the other.

Mourners with tear-lined faces gather at every point of the journey to the Peter and Paul Cathedral. The streets too, are cloaked in black funerary crepe; banners and bunting cover the balconies and windows of every block. Without Oleg at my elbow, I daren't imagine how I might have survived the interminably slow procession. When we finally reach the fortress, my limbs are weary and my lips dry. I draw in a deep breath to prepare for our final farewell.

The church bells are struck, and the solitary notes peal hauntingly above the priests' chanting. Incense swung high in an arc leaves a foggy trail of smoke that stings my eyes. I cannot believe Georgiy is gone.

When I emit an audible gasp during the Divine Liturgy, Oleg squeezes my elbow. The true cost of Georgiy's death is evident too, in the pain on the faces of the dowager and her daughters. The Tsar too. While I'm obliged to bear my agony in silence, the women's muffled sobs mock my exclusion and echo in my ears. My chest tightens as we stand before the priest and pray for the repose of Georgiy's soul.

He is to be interred inside the open crypt alongside his father, Tsar

Alexander III, and infant brother Alexander, who died in the first year of life. The lowering of the coffin almost brings me undone.

Supported by her daughters, the dowager covers her eyes. 'No! It is too much, too much to bear! Why? Why take my Georgiy too?' Her face is wracked with the precise grief and agony I endure. I press my lips tightly to stifle my sob.

I do not recall the return journey, or how I managed to contain my desolation from scrutiny. But the significance of my situation is clear. The sooner our marriage is acknowledged publicly, the better. Perhaps the family will find a grain of hope and optimism, knowing part of Georgiy lives inside me? Then our child may assume its rightful place as a Romanov.

Like the chill of a moonless night, a sense of doom washes over me. Whatever happens, a child born into this family will inevitably become a pawn of the court. While likely a daughter might be offered in marriage to secure a foreign or political alliance, there is a greater threat—one that presses deep into my chest and draws pain that slices through my heart like a blade.

If I have a son—Georgiy's son—he would remain the heir presumptive until a tsarevich is born.

I pray the Empress carries a son, not only for the sake of the Russian Empire.

JEAN

14

Melbourne, 1983

Jean wrestles the butterflies in her stomach on the morning she is to begin at the Bourke Street store. It's been decades since she visited the city.

Aurora insisted the Champion girls have one magical day *in town* each holiday break. Dressed in our best frocks, hats, coats and gloves, we caught the train from Red Hill station—the same weekly train the orchardists used to freight their produce. Shirley would swing her little pink dillybag by the drawstrings, right up until she spent her sixpence on a Darrell Lea Bo-Peep jar. Then she'd tuck it carefully inside, next to a handkerchief ironed into a perfect triangle.

Jean is surprised to find a section of Bourke Street has been closed off outside the store creating a shopping mall between Swanston and Elizabeth Streets. Traffic is reduced to a constant stream of people hurrying about their business while the clang of bells warns of trams approaching in both directions. Jean dodges between Melbourne's distinctive modes of transportation and deftly crosses the tracks with her heart racing.

The redesign of the old Buckley and Nunn store is based on Le Bon

Marché in Paris. The modern open spaces are welcoming with light entering the store through a multitude of artificial lights and full-length mirrors. Jean steps into the elevator, noting the ornate black metal cages are now enclosed. She recalls the jump and surge in her stomach during those holiday visits as the elevator operator perched on a stool and manoeuvred between floors, calling out the goods for sale on each level. The staff's official-looking uniforms of pencil skirts, blouses and blazers which once impressed her seem terribly impractical now.

Jean can't afford to let the past take hold of her. She's determined to show how much she wants this role and what a damned hard worker she is. She doesn't need anyone reminding her it's a big step—her own insecurities are enough. She's ready for the challenge.

Outside the personnel office on the top floor, she wipes her hands down her houndstooth skirt. The only low point of her promotion is that Ross Milton is heading the Melbourne store.

When her paperwork is complete, she makes her way to his office for her appointment. He's on the phone and she hesitates, but he nods at a chair and carries on speaking.

'I told you—' he hisses between his teeth '--I told you already! I'm busy all week. Just leave it will you? Stop bloody breaking my balls!'

Jean wriggles in her seat; she'd prefer not to eavesdrop on his private conversations. Leafy ferns trail from a hanging basket in the corner of the office. Aren't plants meant to ease stress?

The level of anger in Milton's voice increases. Jean realises he's addressing his wife. A knot clenches in her stomach—if that's how he speaks to her, how will he interact with his staff?

A moment later he slams down the receiver and yells at his secretary from the doorway. 'If she calls again, tell her I'm in a Board meeting—all bloody day! See if *that* stops her nagging!'

He slumps back into the leather armchair, muttering to himself as he makes another brief call. Finally, he turns to her. 'So, here you are. Now, tell me, Jean, how exactly does this new styling caper work?'

When Jean presented her expansion plans for the designer floor to the executive management in Sydney, her proposal was accepted. Now it's up to her to bring the Style Salon to life. She's convinced it will be successful, but Milton's ongoing support is essential.

'Stylists are fashion consultants. They provide a personalised service to clients and advise them on their wardrobe requirements and how to put outfits together. We show them what suits them best and how to wear it. And of course, our sales staff will cross sell, suggesting accessories to complement the outfits and arrange alterations if necessary...'

'Explain this in terms of financial growth. I need to see substantial profit in at least the first quarter of trade.'

'Yes of course.' She sits ups straighter. She's confident of her vision and expects an increase in sales figures. 'The Style Salon is the perfect way to introduce fashion to the average woman and open them up to a world of possibility. It's about exclusivity and one-on-one appointments; the opportunity for customers to benefit beyond a solitary shopping experience. If you like, think of it as an additional service that increases purchasing power in the same way access to the new store cards and credit accounts do. It's all about repeat custom. My staff will be encouraged to offer outstanding personal service and build relationships, so the customer keeps coming back.'

'It sounds a bit pie in the sky to me although "up-selling" certainly has worked for us in the past. I guess consumers *are* spending big now the economy's flying. If anyone can manage it....'

That's about as close as he gets to a compliment.

Milton lights up a cigarette, and Jean licks her lips. She's given up smoking since she arrived in Melbourne.

'So how long before this salon makes a profit? With all the extras you insisted on, it's cost us a bomb. We can't have every other department demanding expense accounts for grog and finger food if sales only equate to a couple of dozen hankies!'

'That's certainly not my intention, Ross.'

'You're damn right,' he answers with a smirk. 'Now let's meet the team.'

By nine thirty, Jean is questioning how she will cope with the many ways Milton irritates her. He gushes at the sales staff when she introduces him, and his eyes hunt every woman on the floor. While the girls smile and politely laugh off his tasteless jokes, Jean takes care to keep her distance—and notices a few quickly follow her lead.

An hour after the end of a busy first day, Jean's head is swirling with names and procedures to remember, items to restock and tills to balance. When she finally boards a crowded train, she gratefully takes the seat offered to her.

The serviced apartment arranged by the relocation company is in Richmond, only a few kilometres from the city. She received a welcome pack from the company and was appreciative of the peppermint teabags included along with some grocery staples. And she gave the removalists the bottle of champagne and six-pack of coolers (although they didn't appear to be champers drinkers any more than she was).

As the red rattler moves past the MCG, she can't wait for a nice hot cuppa and to submerge into bubbles in the bathroom's trendy corner spa.

Cloying sweetness greets her as she opens the door to the stuffy apartment. *I must call Rick and thank him for the flowers.* She slips off her work clothes and into a fluffy pink bathrobe, then makes the call while water fills the bath.

'I just wanted to say welcome home and good luck—it was nothing much. Did the florist write that on the card?' She can hear the shyness in his tone as Rick laughs and searches for conversation.

Jean briefly describes her team and the lovely modern surroundings she'll be working in. But each word is carefully chosen and spoken with caution. This is new to them both—as with all relationships it will take time. It's a matter of taking things slowly.

Once she feels comfortable Jean will reveal her news, but while listening to him chatting about pruning the vines and the gallery renovations, she bites her lip. *What if he can't forgive me?*

'What do you think about coming down one weekend?' She hears his intake of breath and her stomach flips. She doesn't want him to feel awkward. 'Can we lock in a date?'

'You mean, to stay?' Her heart is thumping.

'I'd love to show you what I've done with the old place. I've got a bit on now, but how about the first weekend of next month?'

Jean counts to five, not wanting to scare him away with her eagerness. 'That would be absolutely lovely, Rick.'

Jean taps her fingers on the desk. Sales figures are ahead for the end of the month. Bookings for the Style Salon have risen to several consultations a day. She's ready to look Ross Milton in the eye with conviction at the department heads meeting—even he can't ignore the facts in black and white. That'll wipe the smarmy look off his face.

When she returns to her office an hour later in a swell of euphoria, a yellow 'Post-it' note is stuck on her desk.

'Did Summer Harrington leave a message?' Jean asks.

'She just said to call her back if it wasn't too much bother. She was very polite. What do you think she wants?' Debbie, her senior sales assistant, replies.

'I'm not sure.'

At the fashion parade after party, Summer indicated she was keen to source additional work. Jean had taken to Summer immediately and identified a depth of kindness in her. She feels mildly protective. It might not be what Summer had imagined, but seeds of an idea come to mind. It's ambitious, but worth a try.

'Summer!' Jean smiles into the phone as if she can see her. 'How lovely to hear from you.'

'Hello Jean. Thanks so much for returning my call.' She sounds a little breathless. Perhaps she's been doing those aerobics—the staff talk constantly about the new fitness craze. High cut leotards and leg warmers have been selling in crazy numbers.

'What can I do for you?'

'Unfortunately, I'm still considered *persona non grata* in the industry. Until they decide to use mature age models—'

How ridiculous; she's barely thirty. But Jean can certainly relate and senses where the call is heading.

'Summer, I have something I'd like to run past you. It's a little left of centre given your level of professional expertise, but the Style Salon has been rolling along beautifully, and I need another fashion stylist. There's commission, of course, on top of your base salary, although I'm afraid it's nowhere near what you're used to.'

'A fashion stylist? Oh, Jean, that's terrific! I was actually going to ask about... but you beat me to it. I appreciate the opportunity.' Summer's sigh of relief comes through loud and clear. 'It will be a great help with Mum in the nursing home now.'

'Would you like to come in and have a look around? As I said,' Jean taps a pencil on her desk calendar, 'you have a great eye for detail and the customers will adore you. It's a far cry from shoots in the Caribbean or the ski slopes of Aspen, I'm afraid. But it's steady work. What do you think?'

'At least there'll be no more stripping off to my knickers in front of sleazy photographer's assistants while they adjust the lighting!' Summer stifles a giggle.

Jean laughs. 'How true!'

'Jean, I'll be honest with you. I'm extremely grateful, but I'm studying interior design at night school. It won't interfere with a day job, and it'll take ages to build up a client base. I hope that won't be a problem?'

'No, not at all. It sounds fabulous!' She's a little envious if anything. It's a career move Jean might have considered herself: the perfect way to combine her love of colour, texture and style. 'I'll have to clear everything with personnel first. Not that I think they won't jump at the opportunity to have you on our books!'

'That's wonderful, Jean.'

'But just a suggestion—perhaps don't mention the course? They need to hear you're committed to DJs, so ham it up a little if you can.'

'Yes of course. And thank you, Jean.'

'I'll pass on your details, and personnel will be in touch for an interview. A formality, I assure you. I look forward to seeing you soon.'

Resting her elbows on the desk, Jean cups her chin in her hands. There's time to arrange a promo shot and introduction piece welcoming Summer to the team before the forthcoming customer catalogue mailout. *What a coup.* Even without experience Summer will be a huge asset. The salon is sure to be inundated with appointments.

15

Castlemaine

P art of the journey through the Alcoholics Anonymous steps program is to make amends with the people affected by the actions of an alcoholic. They call it *making a searching and fearless moral inventory*. Jean is slowly ticking off her list. While it's too late to mend her relationship with Aurora, a weekend in Castlemaine is the perfect place to begin facing the past. A great way to blow off the week's cobwebs too.

With each kilometre up the highway towards the goldfields, a cache of memories surface. When Aurora won the Archibald Prize, Castlemaine—Harriet Sorokin's hometown—shared in her triumph. But what happened there is the ultimate source of Jean's pain.

She's rented a cottage not far from the one they stayed in back in 1952. A new home has since been built on the site, but the memories of the old cottage swiftly return: the scent of the country; the silence; the plans she had imagined for her future once she returned to Melbourne.

It's so long ago it's hard to believe it wasn't a dream.

It started with Aurora informing the family of an artist's residency placement. She then notified the headmistress at Beaulieu that she was taking Jean with her for life experience. Aurora insisted Jean would have plenty of opportunities to return to study if she wished; her whole life was ahead of her.

Following her success, Aurora was offered several commissions, but decided to work from photographs instead of live models. The two painted together in a makeshift studio in the back room of the cottage, and Jean's excitement grew as she and her mother prepared for the new baby. They stayed away from the town. Aurora had somehow arranged for a weekly grocery delivery that arrived on the doorstep. Jean can't recall the details. While her mother worked, Jean prepared meals and kept house. She was grateful to spend the time alone with Aurora, and it was the closest she ever felt to her, but she missed her sisters, her father, and school.

The name never mentioned was Michael's—until it came between them, the day Rick was born.

Jean stops outside the church where people are filing out after mass. She stares through the doors from the gate, recalling the time she had gone inside and prayed (something her family were not accustomed to), *actually prayed* for everything to work out.

It takes a few moments before Jean realises her cheeks are wet with tears. She shelters from the squalling wind under the eaves of the Theatre Royal and pulls her coat closer, wrestling her fingers deeper into new leather gloves, a luxury purchased with last month's bonus. Grateful now for the extravagance, she considers her options for refuge. Left is the Criterion Hotel, and to the right, a bottle shop. Instead, she marches around the corner and into a café.

Jean takes a seat at a laminated table by the window. Dappled grey shadows shine the last traces of daylight across a handwritten menu clipped on Masonite. She flicks through the pages distractedly as fragments of a time she thought forgotten flash through her mind.

'Hello, love. What can I get you?'

Jean presses deeper into her chair as a woman stares down at her with one hand resting on her hip. 'Looks like you need a good cuppa to warm you up. English Breakfast or Earl Grey?'

The face that studies her appears kind. *Genuine.* Deep wavy lines express the story of her life. An interesting subject to draw. 'I'd love a coffee if you have it?'

She nods with a smile. 'Anything else, love? My cakes are freshly baked…'

'No but thank you.' Coffee might settle her stomach—and her thoughts.

Taking out her notebook, Jean flicks through the first few pages listing details from her recent AA meetings. She begins a fresh one. Her pen scratches furiously as recollections flood the page.

'Here y'go.' The woman stands in front of her expectantly. The strong sharp aroma of coffee beans gives Jean reason to smile.

'It smells fabulous.'

'I've brought you a slice of my famous Lumberjack cake too—on the house. Looks to me like you need a bit of a lift, love, if you don't mind me saying. Give old Merle here a yell if you need a friendly ear. There's nothing I haven't heard before.'

Jean smiles and shakes her head. While appreciating that Merle means well, she's reluctant to share details of her life with anyone, let alone a stranger.

She sips the bitter coffee, and the caffeine hits the spot. Cradling her cup in both hands, she squeezes her eyes tight. Snippets of her life appear beneath her eyelids like pages of a family album. *The girl most likely to succeed.* What a joke that turned out to be. On the magical day she won the art prize, Jean had felt invincible. But her life had peaked, and in the following months, dived into the abyss.

She grapples for a handkerchief. Earlier, Jean had picked a few stalks of lavender and popped them in her pocket. The sweet and earthy notes are a comfort. Enormous old-fashioned camellia bushes are what Jean remembers most about the cottage she stayed in with her mother. But lavender reminds her of home, the orchard in Red Hill. She can't wait to see Rick and what he has done. It won't be the way she remembered. Her childhood had been almost perfect.

Keen to escape further scrutiny from the well-meaning café owner, she returns to her accommodation.

After breakfast she wriggles her feet into boots and checks through the window for signs of rain. A bouquet of damp soil and chook poo wafts from the chicken coop nearby. Fog spreads a ghostly blanket over the garden, but despite the brisk temperature, the sun shines across the garden and patches of aqua sky emerge between fluffy cumulus clouds. Although a city girl for many years, Jean is sensible enough not to trust them. She loves her new easy-care perm and the spring and volume it gives her thinning hair. No doubt it will frizz at the first hint of moisture; she doesn't fancy being caught in a downpour.

She grabs her coat. Too hot she can handle, but the thought of being cold might tempt her to refreshments stronger than tea to warm her. She's been sober for eighteen months, ten days and four hours, and feels healthier for it. But the threat of falling off the wagon is always there.

People are up and about in the main street with the market open for trade, perusing stalls selling home-grown produce, various knickknacks and old wares. A trio of young boys with sports bags slung over their shoulders come hurtling towards her; stones scrunch underfoot as they handball and kick a footy, seemingly unaware of her presence. Like seasoned professionals they zigzag around invisible opponents in an imagined match. Quick as a flash, they leg it over a fence and disappear across the railway tracks, taking a short cut to the footy ground.

She smiles and the strong scent of jasmine increases as she turns the corner; the warble of a birdsong symphony plays in the trees. It's as if Jean has woken from hibernation; the sights, scents and sounds of the countryside seem more vivid now. Her senses are slowly returning since she curbed her drinking.

Continuing east, Jean raises a hand to shade her eyes. Harriet Sorokin's homestead is on the crest of the hill. She remembers seeing the name engraved on a brass plate on a gate of Brunswick green: Magpies Rest. Aurora told her that the house overflowed with Harriet's needlework and the assorted crafts and handiwork of her equally talented sisters. It's now open to the public as a museum.

She begins her climb. There is an ice-cream cake beauty in the houses with curling white iron lacework—the filament adornment a well-recognised feature of the Victorian and Federation periods. Some of the more modest cottages are of weatherboard while those made of brick are set back on larger blocks of land, possibly the homes of successful gold miners and landowners of the period.

Jean feels the peaceful serenity of the town. Her busy life is filled with noise—the constant chatter of customers and staff, the mindless gossip and small talk and pretentiousness she has no interest in but must endure. Cities are filled with the clamour of transport, car horns and sirens, the consequences of existing in a burgeoning population. Her short-term accommodation in Melbourne is just that; perhaps she could call a place like this home? Castlemaine. Imagine it. Somewhere with an ease of life, yet not too far from Melbourne.

With each step the idea of a permanent relocation grows. Her focus is so intent on thoughts of country life she barely notices the grind of an ancient truck ascending the steep hill. With a cough and a shudder, the truck's wheel hits a ditch, and a heavy stream of muddy water sprays her from head to foot.

'Hey! Watch out!' She raises her fist as the driver crunches gears and jams it into second without a second glance. The truck lurches forward and continues its climb.

Jean dabs at spots on her camel-coloured coat that resemble coffee stains. Her feet have copped most of the puddle; the insides of her boots are soaked through. Why on earth did he take the corner so close to the kerb? It's bad enough she's drenched, but he could have killed her. She turns around. Now she'll have to change her clothes. Her visit to the Sorokin home will have to wait.

At boarding school, they used to stuff the insides of their wet shoes with newspaper. With that in mind, Jean heads to the news agency. On the window of the real estate agent's office next door is a picture of an old worker's cottage. She hesitates. The front garden is overgrown, and the lavender hedge could use a good prune, but the leaves of the magnificent mulberry tree in the centre sweep all the way to the ground.

'Morning, pet. Buying or renting?'

Jean opens her mouth in surprise. Merle balances two cartons of milk in her arms and squints at the photo. 'That one there's a nice street. When are you moving in?'

Jean holds back a retort and blinks. *What's stopping me?* The train line runs direct to Spencer Street Station—she has nothing else to consider.

From the smug look on her face, Merle seems to know what Jean is about to say.

'I'll think about it.' She shrugs, and the weight rolls off her shoulders like droplets of water.

'Won't we be the lucky ones to have her here, hey Pete?' Merle speaks over Jean's shoulder to someone behind her. 'Mark my words, I reckon she'll be here soon.'

Jean turns and faces him with heat rising on her face. He's a silver fox in the calibre of Terence Stamp, but his lips and cleft chin are all Timothy Dalton.

Merle really has taken the bull by the proverbial. The thought has barely entered Jean's head and now it's a done deal and broadcast to strangers. She smiles and shrugs but the man staring down at her frowns.

'I expect I owe you an apology. That *was* you I saw walking...?'

'Ah, you're the one I send my dry-cleaning bill to?'

'I'm so sorry, and yes, of course you can. It's lovely to meet you—?'

'Jean—' she extends her hand

'I'm afraid I couldn't stop. My poor truck's on is its last legs and struggles to make it up that hill with a full load of timber.'

Merle coughs to remind them of her presence. 'I was going to tell her about your work! You'll have to pop in and have a squiz, pet. Pete makes tables and chairs. *Beautiful* woodwork. I do like to look after my best customer.'

He gives Merle a wink. 'I'll be in for a cuppa and a piece of my favourite cheesecake as soon as I've finished my errands. Nice to meet you, Jean. I hope to see you around once you settle in. And I owe you a drink for spoiling your clothes. I apologise once again.'

Jean stares at the advertisement and glances at the agent's door as he flicks the sign to *open*. She takes a breath. And as easy as that her decision is made.

16

Melbourne

On Monday, all goes well at the department heads meeting until Milton informs Jean that he's cut the Style Salon's budget for the next quarter. She's furious that she's forced to reduce her winter coat order. He'll see how that ends, when the women of Melbourne choose to shop the wider selection at Myer next door.

Taking a break from her paperwork, she checks in with the stylists. A luxurious floral arrangement cascades from an enormous vase on the bureau in the waiting area while plush velvet sofas and armchairs of salmon-pink are endowed with feather-filled scatter cushions. Soothing music pipes through invisible speakers in the background.

Informed that a new client has walked in expecting an immediate appointment, Jean prioritises her duties to accommodate her.

'Welcome to the Style Salon. My name is Jean. May I call you Odiel?'

The older woman barely glances from her glossy magazine. 'I am *Mrs* Di Maggio.' She rolls her eyes.

Ignoring the affectation, Jean accompanies her into the salon, chatting about the new stock they have received. She introduces Mrs Di

Maggio to Debbie, with the assurance that she is in the hands of her best stylist.

'Please let us know if we can assist you with anything at all,' Jean smiles. 'I hope you enjoy the experience.'

The client shrugs with vague disinterest as Debbie points her towards the large dressing room assigned for her exclusive use and instructs her to slip out of her clothes and make herself comfortable in the thick white robe.

Jean's mind is racing. Stock sheets and payroll forms need to be processed, and she's misplaced her notebook with details and the new address for the AA meeting tonight. It was in the Salon yesterday—she's sure it was. Perhaps, it's still in her desk. Menopause brain again.

As Jean searches beneath the counter, she hears Debbie explaining to Mrs Di Maggio about her seasonal colour consultation, designed to specifically establish the range of colours most complimentary to the client's skin tone.

'These colours should be considered to form the basis of your entire wardrobe. You'll receive a personalised record of the most flattering shades, for future reference.'

A short time later, Debbie reappears. 'I'm sorry Jean, but I'd like a second opinion if you don't mind.'

Jean follows her to the dressing room where Mrs Di Maggio is draped in a swathe of apricot fabric.

'I want to be sure, Mrs Di Maggio,' Debbie blurts with uncharacteristic dismay. 'I've asked Jean to confirm my analysis.'

'Well, do not expect to charge me double.'

Jean assures her that isn't the case and steps back with a finger poised to her lips.

As they replace the fabric with a darker shade, Mrs Di Maggio looks from one to another with her arms outstretched like a store mannequin. 'I look like a model,' she chortles and twirls in a full circle. Jean nods politely but a tiny smile teases her lips.

'You're quite right, Debbie—Mrs Di Maggio is an *autumn-metallic*. It's an unusual combination.'

Mrs Di Maggio appears to take the description to heart and lifts her head high.

Debbie immediately marks down the details. 'Now we can make the selections for your wardrobe. Are you shopping for a special occasion, today?'

'My *husband* and I,' she exhales, and stares pointedly at Jean's left hand, 'are invited to the Veneto Club Gala Charity Ball. We are the president's *special guests*. I *must* have a new gown. Something *sophisticated*.'

'How lovely,' smiles Jean, trying to place her accent. She's definitely not Italian, as her name suggests. Her accent is thicker—perhaps German or Dutch.

'I'm certain we'll find you the perfect gown. And Debbie will be happy to assist with accessories to complement your outfit. Now if you will excuse me, I have another appointment.'

'A hot lunch date?' Mrs Di Maggio smirks.

Jean's eyes widen in surprise. She opts for humour in response. 'Ah, Mrs Di Maggio,' Jean exaggerates a grin, 'it seems you have caught me out. A date with my paperwork. Business rather than pleasure, I'm afraid. Let me help select some garments first, and then I'll leave you in Debbie's capable hands.'

She leaves Mrs Di Maggio in front of the mirror with a glass of champagne and returns a short time later wheeling a liquorice-all sorts rack of high-end labels. Mrs Di Maggio laps up the attention. Debbie pops in and out of the dressing room like a cuckoo through a clock door as the client demands alternative colours and smaller sizes and then refuses point blank to consider a pair of perfectly tailored pinstripe trousers.

She ignores Debbie completely and will only address Jean. Jean winks to convince Debbie she is doing her best with a difficult taskmaster. But she can't find a way to extricate herself without looking neglectful or rude. She checks her watch discreetly.

Finally, after another two glasses of bubbles and a round of dainty club sandwiches, Mrs Di Maggio finds something to smile about. An hour and a half past the allotted time slot, she decides on a stunning full-length silk gown in a shade of russet brown with strappy gold shoes and a handbag to match. Then she adds a floral blouse in shades of a tropical sunset, paired with a hip-hugging chocolate sun-ray pleated skirt that fans out at the ankles when she walks. The ensemble is fabulous.

'I look so young,' she croons. Jean and Debbie nod politely. 'My *husband* says I still have the figure of the hourglass.'

'How... lovely,' Debbie stammers.

Mrs Di Maggio stares at Jean. 'He likes curves on a woman—straight up and down like the bean's pole is not attractive to a man.'

A few minutes later, she re-emerges from the fitting room and appraises her new crimson lipstick in the large mirror. Jean wraps her garments in tissue paper, a smile barely clinging to her lips as she conducts the final transaction.

Finally, Mrs Di Maggio turns on her heels and waltzes out of the Style Salon. Jean and Debbie sag against the counter.

'I'm sorry, Jean,' Debbie raises her brows. 'I tried everything. She didn't take to me at all.'

'You're not alone.' There's no doubt the woman was rude, but customers often lorded it over the sales staff. 'Don't worry, Debs, some days are harder than others. Sometimes it's not anything we're doing; it's about what's going on in the client's life. Our job is to make women feel better about themselves and what they wear—we can't fix their personal problems—we're only dealing with the surface. Now go on and take an extra break. You deserve it after that.'

'Thanks Jean. You're the best,' Debbie gushes.

Jean receives an impromptu call from Rick. He's in the city for a meeting and asks to catch up. She happily makes time for him.

She rushes into the little Italian bistro at the Paris end of Bourke Street and takes a seat beside him at the bar. He's sipping a glass of red and the scent of blackcurrants wafts around her. *Delicious.* She sips the sparkling water Rick has ordered for her.

'Are you eating today?' He kisses her cheek. Jean's heart beats a little faster.

'I'm starving. I can't seem to last these long days without a big lunch.'

'Shall we eat outside?'

The sun filters through the trees as they take their seats at a roadside table. Rick waits for the clatter of trams passing on the road beside them to subside before speaking again. But instead of his typically sanguine expression, his attention flicks from Jean to the passers-by. A twist of concern catches in her stomach. His problems are beginning to matter to her, very much.

'I've been so busy, and things got away from me. Don't get me wrong. I love working the land, but I have more important issues at the moment.'

'Oh? I thought everything was on schedule? Last time we spoke, you said the harvest was coming along nicely...'

'There's a disease that can affect the vines: *phylloxera*. It ran rampant in the early days of wine making, so I made damn sure I had all the protective measures in place after everything I'd learned in France. But it was bloody expensive to invest in. The thing is, now I'm low on cash flow to set up the gallery, and I'm only halfway through.

'I've just come from an appointment with the bank. I guess I should have taken it as an omen when I left all my figures behind this morning. I had to improvise and give calculations off the top of my head...'

Jean's stomach growls as two bowls of steaming *linguine alla norma* arrive. She can feel Rick's tension rising.

'The bank is unwilling to extend my loan for a hobby venture, as they called it. You'd think after the years I spent working the financial markets, they'd understand I'm not a risk taker when it comes to investment. I've seriously considered this, Jeanie. I've done the figures. I've researched. I've bloody well given everything to get this vineyard up and going!' When he runs his hand through his fringe, Rick looks strangely childish. 'I'm shattered. Just shattered.'

Jean is surprised by his outburst. She'd considered him to have a rather nonchalant disposition. But the passion and faith he has for the venture astounds her. She's impressed with his focus. He is determined for this to work.

'I'm sorry, Rick, you're obviously disappointed. Perhaps you could delay plans for opening the gallery. I'm not sure what else I can suggest...'

'Look, it's my problem, and I'll find a way to sort it. But thank you.' Rick runs his hands through his hair again and looks up. 'Please make sure you come down next weekend. I'd really appreciate your help—especially going through Mum and Dad's stuff. There are things you might like to keep. But so much crap. They kept everything! And you'll want to see your painting, of course.'

Jean quickly slips on her sunglasses to hide her watery eyes. Rick doesn't seem to notice. She swallows a large mouthful of water.

'Thanks for spending your lunch break listening to me moan.' He looks up at her with a cheeky smile, one that catches Jean so unawares she feels a sharp jab in her stomach. 'We've barely had time to catch-up since you arrived. I started to think you were avoiding me.' He laughs.

Of course, he's uncertain of her. Jean has done nothing to make it easier. She brushes her hands down her skirt and smiles at him. 'Well, we can rectify that next weekend.'

17

Red Hill

The long, winding driveway is achingly familiar, but the landscape is distinctly altered. As Jean reaches the last rise of the gravel road, her eyes widen at the breathtaking sight of Rick's vineyard. Where a heavy brow of apple trees once flourished, row upon row of vines now fill the orchard in a sea of forest-green. It's impressive. She slows to a stop on the crest of the hill for her first glimpse of the old homestead and blinks back tears.

Heartened by the sight and resilience of the century-old weeping elm she climbed as a child, Jean pulls into the circular driveway. The wide verandah still hugs the homestead, as much an extension of her childhood as the orchard itself.

It was where she played games of chasey or hopscotch with Shirley and Evie. She can still conjure up the thwack of footfall on timber as they hopped from one white-chalked box to the next, and their lithe bodies in seersucker frocks spread star-shaped across the boards, waiting for the whisper of a breeze to cool them from the summer heat.

Sometimes the sisters reclined on long wicker chairs and read until the afternoon sun lowered into a lilac haze. Or marvelled at how the leaves of the apple trees changed to three shades of green with the seasons. And always there was Jack, in his faded overalls, beside them, the curls of smoke from his pipe fading into the evening as mist settled into the valley.

'Jeanie! It's great to see you.' Rick emerges from the homestead and leaps off the deck, flipping open the boot of her car. He grabs her overnight bag and slings it over his shoulder. 'A bit different, hey?'

His exuberance triggers a catch in her throat. 'Too right,' her words are muffled by his bear hug, 'but it looks fabulous!'

They walk to the rear of the homestead. The old lean-to sunroom is gone, and Rick explains that the extension will soon incorporate the cellar-door area. While different, the homestead feels disconcertingly familiar. Unnerved by the jumble of past and present, Jean feels the well of tears.

'Oh Rick, it's just...wonderful. You've done so much. Marvellous.' She pretends to focus on the landscape and fights the urge to flee. Rick's boundless enthusiasm is bringing her undone. She very much wants to be part of his life. But what if she's not good enough? 'I'd forgotten how quiet it is here.'

Jean has been strong for so long, but the vulnerability of standing in surroundings that were once her sanctuary is claustrophobic. Generations of Champions passed the estate down through the male line, following somewhat archaic male primogeniture laws. While a ridiculously old-fashioned rule, Jean was grateful; she'd wanted nothing to do with the orchard and all it represented. Nor did she expect it. No, she was happy for Rick to have that responsibility.

But here on family land and faced with Rick and his charm, she sees what she has missed by leaving them all behind. When did she last think of what this property had meant to her?

'What would you like to see first?'

'Show me the vines. I need to stretch my legs after that long drive. And you can tell me about this vinification process of yours.'

'Are you sure? I mean...'

'*Rick,*' Jean touches his arm, reassuringly, 'I can't promise I'll ever taste it, no matter how good you believe your wine to be, but I'm keen to hear about the growing methods and the ins and outs of the process.

Please don't ever think that because I'm an alcoholic, it means you can't talk to me about your passion.'

Rick explains that his plans for a vineyard grew wings during his time at Lichtenstein Pharmaceuticals. His role sent him around the globe visiting various manufacturing plants and operations. He found the culture and lifestyle of Europe appealing.

'So that's when your interest in the French vineyards began.'

'Yeah. I was punching numbers and managing investment portfolios to secure funds for a team of scientists to develop an organic range of healthcare products. It was increasingly corporate, and the next career move was a permanent role in Geneva. But I missed home,' he tells Jean with honesty. 'The idea of country living—and an escape from the corporate world--was pretty appealing.'

As they wander down the valley towards a wide path of leafy vines, Jean looks back to the homestead. It will be beautiful here in summer. She imagines people wandering the property and picnicking on the grass, laughing, smiling, enjoying the fruits of Rick's labour. *He's passionate about this.* She sure he'll succeed.

'Do you remember the big red rattler? I loved that old tractor—it seemed so much a part of Dad it could have been another limb.' Rick folds his arms across his chest. 'He'd sit me on his knee, and I'd navigate through the apple trees, or we'd lay out fertiliser. Then there'd be the grafting, and when the time came, the harvest. I guess I loved everything about growing up here.'

Jean's smile is forced. His memories are painful for her to hear. 'Your love of the land shows through, Rick.'

'Yeah, I hope so. Dad was really supportive when I told him I was keen to plant grapes. The orchard was getting too much for him. He helped out in the last few years until the end. It was probably a good thing he went first...before Mum.'

Tightness spreads in her chest. *Dad.* She'd let him down too. She sincerely regrets it, but once she left there was no looking back. It had been a huge price to pay to never see him again.

'Evie said she had no interest in the orchard, and I assumed it was the same for you, but I never really understood what happened...'

His gaze searches hers, but she is quick to divert the question. 'And so, you decided to work the land?'

'The wine economy started to pick up after the sixties and has been steadily building ever since. It felt the right time to get my hands dirty.'

'It sounds like you've laid the perfect groundwork...'

'Yeah, and I'm lucky a whole new generation of Aussies are opting to drink wine instead of beer.'

'You've done really well. It looks like the vineyard has been here for years.'

'Thanks.' He stretches his neck, rolling his head from one side to another. 'My dream is to produce a fine, full-bodied syrah like they make in Montpellier. Here we call it shiraz. The orchard's position and past success prove that the conditions and climate are right for growing vines; I've studied enough scientific reports to have thought this through.' He scratches his head and sighs. 'But sometimes I ask what on earth made me think I could pull it off?'

Jean smiles. 'I admire the way you're getting on with it, Rick.' She fights the urge to hug him.

They head to the cellar where both stainless steel and oak barrels are laid out in rows. The combination of a strong earthy and metallic scent instead of alcohol is sobering. Rick taps ruby liquid from a marked oak barrel into a waiting glass.

'By fermenting in a tank, and then pressing before it goes into a barrel, the integration of the wood stays with the wine for a long time. I prefer brand-new oak. It's almost counterintuitive. It's the oak that brings through the oxygen and stabilisation processes and draws out the spice and berry flavour I love. I use facilities nearby to press, and then we transfer it into the barrels and store it back here.' He shakes his head and inhales deeply, taking a sip of the first batch made from his own vines. 'That's a great nose.' He smiles. 'Sorry...'

'No, go on. I understand how special this is for you. Is it ready?'

'A little heavy on the tannin, but the oak is blending through nicely. It has notes of rich soil spiced with pepper. Getting there...'

Jean smiles again.

'I get carried away here.' Rick sets the tap right again. 'Sorry, you must be starving. Come on. Let's get back to the house. I've made us soup. And not out of a can, I promise!' Rick's raised eyebrows hover, and he has a cheeky gleam in his eyes.

The changes inside are less pronounced. Beyond the extension, the rooms in the front part of the house are much the same. He's kept the old Aga but repositioned it in the new Baltic timber kitchen. The joinery is beautifully crafted with a central bench and a high return that features decorative capped moulding and turned posts.

All he's missing is someone to share this with. Jean hasn't pressed him for details about his personal life. Or shared hers.

'Are you okay in your old bedroom? Heaps of your stuff is still there. I didn't like to go through your things. I've no idea what to do other than pack it up and store it in the loft or the barn. Or you can have the spare room if you'd prefer. I can make it up for you?'

'No, no—my old room's fine,' she shoos him away. 'Don't fuss. I'll pop my things in and wash my hands.'

Apart from the missing painting, her room is as she left it. Lowering onto the bed, she remembers the last arguments with Aurora when she packed her bags to leave. All she wanted was for her mother to draw her into her arms and tell her she loved her; that it wasn't her fault....

'Jeanie, it's ready!'

'Coming.' She wipes her tears and checks her appearance in the mirror of the Queen Anne dressing table in the corner. *This might be harder than I thought.*

After lunch Rick asks Jean to help pack away their parents' belongings.

'Some of the stuff I've found!' He laughs. 'Here, check this out. He reaches into a box and holds up one of his footy trophies.

Then he pulls out a package folded in tissue paper and begins to unwrap it. 'What's this? Geez, she really did keep everything!'

A baby jacket with matching bootees and a bonnet. He laughs and places it beside the box with a shrug.

It's the set I knitted. Jean lowers her head, remembering how proud she was of her work.

Rick doesn't notice as he continues to chat about his plans to redo the master bedroom.

Nothing has changed. The antique walnut chest of drawers stands in pride of place against the main wall—a wedding present from Jack's parents. Jean empties the drawers of Aurora's clothing and places them in garbage bags. She tries not to feel regret for the collection of diaphanous Lucas lingerie, unworn and still in boxes, and removes several unopened honeysuckle soaps inserted between colourful layers of fabric to prevent silverfish—a remedy Jean employs to this day.

At the back of the third drawer, safely tucked beneath hand-knitted woollen jumpers exuding the scent of camphor wood and cedar, is Aurora's jewellery box. Jean sits on the bed as she did as a child and takes out the pearl earrings and matching creamy necklace she wore on special occasions. Next, a watch with a tiny clock face and intricate marcasite detailing that's quite out of fashion. The feeling of loss catches her by surprise.

Aurora's diamond engagement ring is in its box. Jean passes the beautiful Catanach's jewellery store on her way to DJ's every day. It's been a prominent fixture at the corner of Little Collins Street and the Royal Arcade since last century. The ring had been handed down through the family, and as the eldest, was intended for her.

Jean notices a false base in the jewellery box and opens it with interest. Inside is a letter bearing the Beaulieu letterhead, the paper almost transparent. The loops and exaggerated 'J' in the sign off suggest Jean was the author.

'How's it going?' Rick smiles at the childish hand. 'From you? Oh, there's no date.'

Jean holds it at arm's length to read, but Rick peers over her shoulder, reciting in a childish high-pitched voice:

To Dear Mummy

I am very glad you have already won first prize. I met Hazel on Sunday morning and she invited us to tea. I do not expect you to write back. Daddy told me he had plenty to do.

With heaps of kisses
xxxxxxxxx

With love from
J

'Who's Hazel?' he asks. 'Is she a relative?'

'No, Hazel was Aurora's best friend—and my godmother. Wasn't she at the funeral?'

'I didn't see her. I don't remember her at all.' Sadness clouds his face at the sight of Aurora's jewellery.

Jean feels loss too—for what should have been. What could have been. With the weight of so much left unsaid, Jean feels the sudden need to explain the past to him.

'Rick, things happened between Aurora and I that I felt were unforgivable. Everything went pear-shaped. But my behaviour was out of line. I've made a lot of mistakes and have many regrets—but how I treated my family is the one I need to address first.' *I'm opening a can of worms now.*

'We all have stuff we regret, Jeanie.' His eyes are soft and kind when he smiles. 'Stuff we're not proud of. Let's make a deal to move on and put it behind us.'

A reply chokes in her throat, but she nods as he pulls her into a hug, and she buries her face in his shoulder. With his arms around her she feels safe, safe from the hurt the past had caused her. But she owes him the truth. She pulls back.

'You know,' Rick looks down to her. 'Mum and Dad were such great parents, I can't imagine anything being too much of a problem with them, to be honest. I'm sorry if they were harder on you. Dad used to talk about you all the time. Mum kept herself busy with her art, of course, but I'm sure she would have loved you to come home, no matter what disagreements you might have had. We all pushed the boundaries. But Mum was pretty open. I think she would have understood if you had have given her the chance.'

Jean takes a deep breath. *He thinks it's my fault.*

'They didn't know where you were for years. Mum told me you just disappeared. I miss them both. They were great role models. Mum was a real powerhouse. She was the best! My mates were all envious.' Rick smiles fondly. 'The olds were a perfect match too; it was clear how devoted they were to each other.'

Jean clenches her fists. *But the lies...so many lies....*

'You know, Jeanie, I want a love like they had. There was a time when I thought I'd found someone special, a love like theirs. Sadly, it didn't work out—'

'I'm sure you'll find it, Rick. Now, how about I put the kettle on?' Jean forces a cheer into her voice that she doesn't feel.

Then she stands and turns away. *How will I ever explain it to him now?*

18

The next morning Jean packs away her gumboots and follows Rick to Aurora's studio. One paint-splattered wall has been replaced with angled plate-glass windows offering breathtaking views over the undulating vines. Jean is lost for words.

'What do you think the mystery is, in the portrait she left you?' Rick asks.

Jean has no idea. Nor has she considered what she'll do with it. But she's strangely eager to view it up close.

She imagines Aurora working on her portraits as they move through the studio, surrounded by a sunlit treasure of oil palettes and linseed and turpentine, scents she always associated with her. It's now replaced by the whiff of timber shavings and traces of plasterers' glue.

'Are you ready?' Rick looks set to pull a rabbit out of a hat.

At the door to the room that was Aurora's office, he punches a code into the security pad before they enter. Inside it's clean and neat, with shelves lining the wall. A large packing crate stands in the darkest corner.

'Once the tradies have finished, I can bring in the rest of the artworks for the installation.'

The family didn't own enough of Aurora's works to fill the gallery for the opening, so he's gained permission to borrow some. He also plans to exhibit works of local artists.

'It will help establish them in the community *and* showcase the winery. Ideally, I hope to build a loyal customer base from there.'

He carefully lowers the portrait onto an easel. It's larger than Jean had realised.

'Oh, Rick...it's exquisite.'

'Yes. And much brighter than some of her earlier works. I'm not sure when it was painted. She hasn't dated it.'

Jean moves closer, examining the tiny details painted into the background in a treatment that looks like wallpapering. The painting is layered with texture and movement in both theme and composition. It seems out of place amongst the replastered walls and bare floorboards but is uniquely Aurora. Jean is speechless.

'I had no idea until Mum's solicitor notified me of her wishes for the funeral. He insisted I find the painting. I hadn't been into the studio for years; it was always out of bounds.' Rick laughs and runs a hand through his fringe. 'I found it hidden behind her boxes of sketchbooks in the storeroom under a blank piece of canvas. It was wrapped in paper and covered with an old hand-knitted rug. I have no idea when she painted it.'

Surrealist artists often paint self-portraits introspectively, with their faces as muse. An illogical juxtaposition. But Aurora's is unique. Jean can't deny the expression of satisfaction on her face. She looks proud. But there's a sadness in her eyes too. Instead of exposing dreams and illusions, her portrait appears to be telling a story.

'I thought it might have been meant as a surprise for Dad? Either way, it's a fine piece of art,' he hesitates, 'and what you do with it is up to you. But given it's her only self-portrait....'

Aurora Estate. It belongs here. 'Rick. It wouldn't seem right if she wasn't watching it all unfold here. I'm happy for you to display it. It's gorgeous.'

'There's some writing that I can't read. Is it backwards?' Rick's nose is almost touching the canvas. 'Nope. No idea.'

Abstract motifs are scattered in the background like scraps of bread for Hansel and Gretel to follow. Aurora's lips are slightly parted and her eyes glow like amethysts—the depth and emotion in the painting exudes pure happiness. While the foreground conveys lightness and an expression of hope, the objects connected in the background reveal a mystery. A shadowy figure inside a darkened window; gold spires atop a Byzantine building; a stretch of sea in a mirror image. Curious, indecipherable words smeared beneath a translucent film of oil paint. And the ladybird brooch.

'I've got a magnifying glass here somewhere,' Rick says. 'But I didn't notice *that* before.'

Jean had avoided commenting on the ladybird. *What happened to it?*

'So, what do you think it means? See a ladybird and make a wish? Fly away home? I don't get it.' Rick frowns. 'Unless the ladybird relates to preventing phylloxera and disease in the vines?'

'What do you mean?' Jean tilts her head.

'I told Mum how ladybirds and certain other insects keep pests off the crops,' memory clouds his expression, 'and Dad insisted that when they were around it meant there'd be a good harvest. In some cultures, they prayed to Mary to bless the crops believing she was the 'lady' referenced in its name. It developed from Mother Mary, or Lady Mary, to ladybugs or ladybirds.'

'Really?' Jean's smile tightens. *It's nothing to do with the vines.*

'When I was in France, they believed that an infestation of ladybirds could sour the wine because when under threat, their bodies release a secretion as a means of defence. That's why it's essential to get the balance right in biodynamic farming.'

'Which ties in with your research for the different types of vegetation to plant amongst the vines?'

'Yeah, partly. I've cultivated an insectarium and planted specific grasses and vegetation that encourage good insects around the crop. But it's a pretty amazing coincidence that a ladybird is in the composition.'

Rick moves closer to the painting. 'Hey, see these spires? They're like the ones I saw on a church in Leningrad, I think it was.'

She follows his line of vision to the tip of tile-like shapes of Tiffany-blue. There's something in the painting's composition that reminds Jean of another artist, aside from Frida Kahlo.

Jean claps her hands together. '*Red Square*—that's the name of the painting I was thinking of. Kandinsky*'s Red Square. Moscow.*' Jean stands in front of the portrait, nodding.

Snapshots of childhood memories filter through her thoughts. Jean once chose Kandinsky for a school project because Aurora had admired his work.

Rick shrugs. 'Well, whatever it means, it's great that you'll let us exhibit it, Jeanie. It'll be like having Mum watching over us. She'd have loved having you here too. It's like it was meant to be.'

A cool mist signals an end to the day and lowers over the vines. Jean promises to visit again soon.

Rick smiles good-naturedly, and his farewell is warm and genuine. 'I can't wait for the building to be finished.'

'You've done a great job—of everything.' Jean waves in the direction of the vineyard.

'It's been terrific to have you here. Come back soon, Jeanie.'

When Jean leaves Red Hill and the winding trail of peaceful country roads, a tangerine sunset paints the sky in the west. A wave of sadness creeps into her thoughts. Being in Rick's presence has forced her to contemplate more of the past than she has for years.

She stops at a set of traffic lights in Mornington and grips the wheel with both hands, waiting for the lights to turn green. It's not Rick causing her agitation. The scenes replay over and over: packing her bags and catching the bus to Sydney; her mother's change of behaviour; the look of horror on her face when Jean revealed his name...

A car horn toots behind her and she startles, holding her hand up in the rear-view mirror to apologise as she eases the car forward. Then, it dawns on her. Is it possible there was more to Aurora and Michael's relationship? If that were the case, the only one left who might be able to explain it would be Hazel.

The idea of tracking Hazel down draws deeper memories. The Hazel Jean recalls was impressively organised and active—a competent and independent woman. She was one of Beaulieu's first students back in the 1920s. But at some point, over the years, it appears Aurora and Hazel had lost touch. Or had fallen out.

Hazel was a qualified accountant—it was unusual at the time for a woman to hold such a senior position in a predominantly male field. She was always furiously busy and carried herself with an air of importance. She imagines Hazel tallying figures with a fountain pen resting between her scarlet lips.

But why wasn't she at Aurora's funeral?

It's dark by the time she reaches Castlemaine, and her to-do list is growing. She finds Hazel's address in the telephone book and copies it into her notebook. She'll call her soon.

Taking kindling from the wicker basket beside the hearth, Jean lights the fire, and the air fills with the smoky scent of gum and eucalyptus. As the flames take hold, the feeling that Hazel was involved during the time in her life she's coming to terms with makes her stomach flip uncomfortably. She can't remember the details. Pictures flitter in the flames, faces that had been decisively pushed away in the ensuing years.

Hazel and Aurora were complete opposites. Hazel would never have baked a loaf of bread until it disintegrated into dust or forgotten altogether about cooking a meal for her family. When Aurora returned paint-stained and blurry-eyed from her studio, Jack would laugh good-naturedly and shake his head.

Perhaps Hazel might feel better able to speak of it now Aurora was gone. And as Hazel's goddaughter, surely Jean was able to inquire about any long-held grievances?

Settled with her mug of tea and the warmth of the fire, Jean's memories are muddled. The stories contrived in her head are further clouded by the fond memories Rick has shared with her. She'd spent years believing Aurora a witch of a mother and her father a saint to put up with her. What if the truth was more complicated?

TATIANA

19

Alexander Palace, Tsarskoye Selo, 1899

A week after Georgiy's funeral, I seek counsel with the Tsar. I pray I remain composed to face the challenge it presents.

I'm ushered into Nicky's commodious study at Tsarskoye Selo and approach his great desk, clasping my reticule tightly in one hand and my skirts in the other.

'We apologise for our poor state today, Tatiana. It is perhaps, not the best time to hear your petition.' He indicates he would like to smoke. I acknowledge his request with a deferential nod and take my place in the Louis XIV chair opposite.

'Georgiy and I were more dear friends than brothers. It is a terrible circumstance to lose a sibling.' The trace of a catch in his voice makes me look up.

'Or a husband, Your Imperial Majesty,' I murmur and turn from the clear grey eyes that shock me as always in their likeness to Georgiy.

'No one expected his death so soon. He was far too kind, too young....' He taps fingers on his writing set while drawing back on his cigarette. 'We were surprised to receive your note. Georgiy made no mention of you.' His voice is wary, and he glances past me, rather than meeting my stare. 'Whatever the state of your relationship, indeed, whatever you may have believed of him, it is best put behind you. The less said, the better. Your reputation remains intact and you are free to—'

'Imperial Majesty,' with a tremor in my voice, I interrupt, 'I'm afraid that is impossible. There is more pressing news that, while unexpected, I hope will be of some small comfort to you now.' I take a deep breath and smile. 'I am carrying Georgiy's child.'

'*His child*? No—' He frowns and runs a finger between his brows as if to press the thought aside. 'But that's impossible! Scurrilous talk—'

'I understand it comes as a surprise—'

'This is a sin—a *grave* sin in the eyes of the Church. You are unmarried, Tatiana, and the granddaughter of a tsar. We did not expect this from you. And Georgiy would not—'

'Indeed, Georgiy and I *were* married. It was sanctified in the Holy Russian Orthodox Church. He insisted we elope as you suggested—'

'*Elope!* We suggested no such thing. Why on earth would we agree to a secret marriage for the Tsarevich of all the Russias? It appears we have underestimated your influence, Tatiana Vladimirovna.'

He stands and grips the desk, resting his weight on his hands. 'As you are no doubt aware, the Statute on the Imperial Family insists upon the Tsar's sanction *before* any marriage of the court. We have never failed to decree banishment for those who oppose our rule—as our father did before us. We expected you to have more sense. What did you hope to gain by deceiving the Tsarevich and luring him into your bed? It is, indeed, a grave seriousness.'

'Your Imperial Majesty,' I clench my fists to stop them from shaking. 'I would never lay with a man before marriage. My cousin, Oleg Igorevich, was our witness....' I lift my head. Why doesn't he believe me? My eyes prickle with the threat of tears.

'You say the child is Georgiy's? But it cannot be...' He shakes his head, and the empty words hang between us. 'We will not hear of it.'

'I love—I loved him.' Nausea swirls inside me, and I grip the arms of the chair for support. 'May I have a glass of water?'

He breathes out a sigh and pours from a lead crystal decanter then places a glass in front of me. 'We need not inform you that this places you in a preposterous position. However, we refuse to allow our Romanov name to be dishonoured by your behaviour. No one will believe in such a marriage, any more than we do. A suitable husband must be found for you—immediately.'

'A husband?' I loathe the wavering of my voice. I've barely survived seeing the love of my life buried, and here is the Tsar thrusting another man upon me.

The clock on the mantelpiece chimes the hour as he expels a furious stream of smoke in my direction. I cover my mouth.

'Given your family's past, you, Tatiana, can ill afford such a scandal. We will not permit our cousin to give birth to an illegitimate child.'

The scent of roses in my handkerchief does little to settle my thoughts. 'Our marriage *was* legal,' I press my lips together. The truth in my words does nothing to release the pain in my heart.

'This business with Georgiy—this mistruth you attest to: quite frankly, we find it appalling so soon after his death. You will marry immediately. We will arrange it.'

'I beg of you—'

'We will not speak of this again, Tatiana Vladimirovna. Not. One. Word. We bid you good day!' He dismisses me with a flick of his wrist.

In light of the Tsar's refusal to accept or recognise my marriage, I have no alternative. To be married in secret is one thing, but for a Romanov—the granddaughter of one of our Empire's most powerful tsars, to be unmarried and with child; that is another matter entirely. Yet what will a new marriage mean, in terms of my and my baby's security?

Around the world, women are making progress towards independence. There are female doctors, architects, and engineers. Here in St Petersburg, I am confined by the edicts of an autocratic monarch ruling Russia as though we are in the middle of the dark ages and not the centre of a modern and industrial transformation.

Alas, I have no choice but to obey him.

Following a military ceremony on the day before our wedding, I am briefly introduced to Captain Nikolai Zolotov. While his face is familiar, it is not impressive, nor is his indolent manner and irreverence towards me. The Tsar and Tsarina are present while my estates are discussed and assigned to my future husband: a man whose station is eminently unacceptable under ordinary circumstances. I'm in no position to argue.

Zolotov's dark hooded eyes light up when he realises the prominent position of my townhouse and value of an asset (on one of the best *prospekte* in St Petersburg) with views across the Neva. He is rewarded my entire inheritance. My greatest disappointment is that it includes my family's country estate in the old town of Veliky Novgorod.

I toss in my bed, uncomfortable at the thought of the day to follow. I am raw with grief. The burden of Georgiy's loss is enormous, but I cannot afford to let my mask slip in public. It is some relief that our relationship is kept from my husband.

My husband. What will Zolotov expect from me as his wife? I am carrying Georgiy's child. The thought of making love with another man is abhorrent. Nothing must risk our child's safety.

My wedding day is experienced as though viewed through a veil—I would prefer it a figment of my imagination. We are married in the private chapel at Alexander Palace in mourning dress (as required and out of respect for Georgiy) with no members of the imperial family in attendance. It is clear this is no celebration. Only a small group of courtiers bear witness, selected I imagine, for their loyalty to the Tsar, along with two naval men Captain Zolotov insisted accompany him. No doubt they will commend his sudden vicissitudes in station and good fortune.

Nausea overcomes me as incense rises in the chapel. The urgent chanting of a requiem performed for Georgiy's funeral merely weeks ago feels decidedly offensive. I hold back tears with every note of the priest's guttural tone, with every prayer muttered under his breath.

At last, it is over. The Tsar grants me one small concession—I am to keep an honorific. Furthermore, I am to be known as, Her Highness, the Princess Zolotova.

We leave the chapel, and the priest ushers us to the internal courtyard to greet the Tsar and Tsarina. When the Tsar kisses my cheeks in congratulations, I feel nothing in his touch or manner to offer generosity in his blessing, or the kindness I once thought him capable of. As my husband marches past and follows the Tsar without so much as a glance back at me, a hand catches my arm.

'Tatiana Vladimirovna. You would do well to make the best of this.' The Tsarina hisses, reverting to English as she does when tired or under duress.

How foolish to assume she might feel sympathy for my position. We have much in common—we carry the children of two brothers, created from love. It would give me greater pleasure to be a friend, not an adversary.

'Nicky has been far too lenient. Make no mistake—he will not be as tolerant if you embarrass him further.' Her hand lingers on her stomach. Her figure is filling out the folds of fabric caught in a rosette at her hips.

'I understand, Your Imperial Majesty.'

When we arrive at my townhouse, Zolotov is given a tour by my valet. He spends the next few hours investigating (taking inventory of) my personal possessions. Afterwards he leaves, and for a few hours the household lies in peace.

It is dark when I wake from a nap, ravenous. Marthe brings me a small plate of *zakuski*, some sweet cakes, and a pot of tea. Later she removes my tray, with eyes lowered and unwilling to engage, and discreetly shuts the door to my bedchamber. My stomach fills with butterflies; she will have laid out a nightgown and matching lace peignoir for my wedding night. I will not allow her to witness my nervousness.

Without notice, the captain swaggers into the room with his hands caressing a bottle of my finest brandy. Turning his back to me, he approaches the mantelpiece and picks up a violet Sèvres porcelain vase to study. He catches my reflection in the mirror and glances to the bed and back.

I clear my throat. 'I was not sure when you would return ...'

'You need not concern yourself on my account, *wife*.' His tone is flat, but his lascivious smirk sends a shiver through me. 'I have no interest in bedding you—I'm well aware someone has ploughed that ground before me.'

I look away, feeling shame when there should be none.

'Nor do I intend to remain in this gilded birdcage.' He swigs from the neck of the bottle like a savage. 'I intend to resume celebrations of my good fortune at my sailing club. I return to the naval base, tomorrow.'

'Indeed—'

'What you choose to do is your business,' he interrupts. He steps closer; brandy and the stale scent of cigars linger on his breath. I recoil, unwilling to bridge the space between us.

'However, I demand you rein in your excessive spending and have your accounts ready for my steward to examine when I return. From now on, it is I who pay for you—and your bastard.'

'Yes, Captain.' The deference in my tone sounds hollow. I close my eyes, imagining the life ahead—for me, for my child, under this man's control. I clench my fists.

'And I suggest you leave for the country house immediately and remain there until you have the brat. Once I return this will be *my* residence—then I will decide what to do with you, *Princess*.'

He closes the door and I sink into an armchair with my face in my hands. From the outer rooms I hear laughter and boisterous male voices increasing in volume. Zolotov and his fellow naval men seek the type of clubs and bars that would never entertain any decent woman. What makes him a suitable prospect as a husband I have no idea.

A few minutes later Marthe reappears.

'The men have gone, Your Highness. The Captain will not return tonight.' Her colour is high. I regret to think what has been said in her presence.

'Oh, Marthe! What a terrible mistake this is.'

She draws me to her, and I sob like an infant for all I must endure. But I am greatly relieved too. For the time being, I have no husband in the true sense of the word. I have no wish to share my life with him, even less, my bed.

While he is far away at the naval base in Vladivostok with elevated status and increased wealth, I will leave St Petersburg for the serenity and sanctity of Veliky Novgorod. And there I will await my confinement, with my reputation preserved.

My life from hereon in will never be the same.

20

Veliky Novgorod, 1900

One afternoon, heavy with child, I walk the banks of the Volkhov River overlooking the ancient fortifications of the medieval Kremlin village. The last vestiges of daylight linger, and the air is crisp; patches of ice are beginning to cover the ground.

Suddenly, three robust black crows block my path, and my raised walking staff does little to frighten them. I circle my arm wildly to shoo them away, but the trio stare back with mocking disinterest.

I'm reminded of an old folktale my nursemaid recounted when I was a child.

The tale was of a tsar who had offered a reward for anyone who could rid his palace of three noisy and unruly crows that were disturbing his peace. Many had tried, but none were successful. Then came a young man who had travelled the world as a boy, and by the time he was grown, was able to speak and translate the language of every species of bird. He arrived at the palace and when he listened to the crows, he learned that one was the father and one, the mother, while the third was their son.

The reason for the constant caw was that they sought the Tsar's answer to a question: when it is time to leave the nest, which parent should the son follow? 'A son must always follow the father,' proclaimed the Tsar. And with that decided, the crow son took to the skies and flew after his father.

So close to my child's impending birth, the notion of a poor mother being abandoned by her family and left all alone is one I dare not imagine. How could I bear being parted from Georgiy's child?

Finally, I force the crows from my path. The largest caws in protest and sweeps high into the snow-dusted branches of a pine, continuing to observe me. Reason prevails over my dread of such omens. Yet the forewarning leaves me unnerved. I pull my fur cloak to my chin and tread carefully as I make my way home.

The following afternoon a telegram arrives from the naval base, informing me of an accident. It reports that the captain fell victim to a misfired cannon aboard his torpedo ship and was fatally wounded. He died instantly.

The news is a great shock; any death is regrettable, and this is a tragic waste of a young life. But I confess, I feel nothing beyond that. How can I grieve a man I hardly knew? The captain and I were forced into positions beyond our control like two pawns on a chessboard. Not yet twenty and twice widowed, I'm more alone than I have ever been.

Now the river has frozen over, life outside my window appears eerily dormant. Trees bow under the weight of branches sifted with powdery white snow and icy fingers that droop to snow-cloaked ground.

Fatigue overcomes me. I expect I have overexerted myself. My limbs ache and I recline on my chaise longue in the parlour, dozing before the fire burning in the grate. An hour later, the light has faded and softened outside when a sharp dig beneath my ribs causes me to shift position and close my eyes.

My last thoughts are of returning to St Petersburg once my baby is born. With a sigh, I draw the bearskin rug over my body, giving up a prayer of thanks for my peremptory release; as a widow, it may be possible to resume life as before. Then I whisper a prayer for the healthy birth of my child—and for the repose of Nikolai Zolotov's soul.

Within hours of retiring for the evening, I'm awoken by a tight pain that restricts my movement. I writhe on the bed as discomfort grips my body and dissipates, just as quickly. Marthe sends for the village midwife and a reputable physician.

'It's a little soon, but all will be well.' She smiles and wipes my forehead. 'You are strong, Tatya.'

I heave out a sigh.

But as the cockerel's crow signals the dawn, I am tired, exhausted, and have made little progress. Marthe stands by me, bathing my face and holding me in her arms. Images flicker beneath my eyelids: terrible visions of Georgiy with an unlikely frown on his face; of Alix screaming, her fists raised and silver eyes glaring across a darkened room. Next, I am dancing, twirling across the floor with my cheek pressed to Georgiy's.

'Princess Zolotova! You must bear down and push!'

I open my eyes to the doctor's command, shocked by the rawness of hearing the title. 'Push now, the baby is coming.'

And through burning pain and stinging relief, tears of sorrow and joy, my son—our darling Misha—is born.

My precious son is small but perfect. His tiny rosebud lips puff out a sigh as I lay him in his cradle, ignoring the nursemaid who insists it is not my place to do so. I simply cannot stop staring at him. His skin is velvety soft and rosy pink. His eyes are the blue of lapis lazuli. And the delicious smell of him—I struggle to accurately describe the milk-sweet tender scent in my journal. He is heavenly. My heart bursts full of a love so fierce I can barely comprehend the emotion nor sate the desire to watch him, to watch over him. To never allow him from my sight. I'm a vixen with a cub, my love protective and unwavering. We share an immediate and intense attachment.

Yet I must continue. There are matters to attend to.

'Excuse me, Your Highness. Miss Brassington is on the telephone.' Marthe smiles and ushers me to the valet's room where a telephone has recently been connected. I take the heavy handle to my ear and lean in as close as I can to speak into the mouthpiece.

'Rosalind? How lovely to hear from you....'

'Dear Tatya, are you well? And the baby?'

We're caught in a muddle of straining to hear and waiting to speak but work out a system through the long silences and soon find our rhythm to converse more freely.

'Have you heard from Oleg Igorevich?'

'Oleg?' I frown. 'No? Not for some time.' I wonder what has happened.

'I thought he might have told you. Now that the Empress has given birth, simply everyone is walking on eggshells--'

Eggshells? Sometimes Rosalind's English idioms are beyond me. So, Alix has given birth at last. I hold a hand to my stomach.

'—fortunately, the Empress and the little grand duchess are both quite healthy.'

'A grand duchess, did you say?' A pain twists and pulls once more, low in my abdomen. 'Are you certain?

'Yes, of course. The announcement was held off for some weeks, but Papa received an official notification now that they have named her. Anastasia. How is Novgorod—still as lovely as ever? We do miss you here.'

'I apologise, Rosalind, but I must bid you goodbye.'

I have little energy to process this news. All I can focus on is the fact that Alix has given birth to her fourth daughter, while I have the son that Russia dearly desires.

F ollowing Zolotov's death, two notaries arrive to make an inventory of the household.

'Who has authorised this?' I say, while my steward stands firm beside me with fierce concern on his face.

'It's written in the terms of your marriage contract. The Tsar's signature is on the documents,' the more corpulent of the two replies. 'In the event of his death, Captain Zolotov's brother is beneficiary.'

I glance over the legal jargon until my eyes glaze with tears. I had paid so little attention to the details, never once imagining such an outcome.

'The entire estate is to be inherited by his brother with various possessions left to his relatives,' the other man holds out his hands in a show of apology. 'But please, Your Highness, take your personal belongings and anything of the child's.'

'What provision is made for our son...?'

'None, Your Highness,' he looks away. 'Our client made no provision....'

The other coughs until he is red in the face.

I read over the documents once more, and see the paragraph quite clearly stating that in the event of his death, neither Zolotov's wife nor child would inherit the estates brought to the marriage. Veliky Novgorod has been in my father's family for centuries. Now that heritage is completely lost.

I admit Georgiy and I made a mistake in not waiting for Alix to give birth before we married. But this is harsh retribution indeed.

After negotiating for two weeks grace, I take stock of my personal belongings. The period is long enough to dismiss and settle the wages of my staff and to pack our trunks. Thankfully I've been granted consent to retain the paintings from my suite; I would despair of having them left to one with no appreciation of art; one who might ignorantly toss them aside or sell them off.

'Where will we go?' Marthe asks that night as she turns back my covers.

'I have no choice. I will request the use of Mama's apartments in the Winter Palace.'

The sleighs are packed, and we bundle under furs and warm coats as the horses make haste to the railway station for our return to St Petersburg. The merry tinkling of sleigh bells is at odds with my goodbye. I sense, deep in my heart, that I will never see Novgorod again.

I farewell the ancient walled city and whisper stories of the past victories of our ancestors to my son. As we go, I carefully describe the scenery, naming the various monuments while praying that one day Misha might return.

Marthe's widened eyes declare our fears; for what we know about my son; for the state we are faced with, and for our unknown future. I retain an allowance and Mama's personal effects and am far from destitute. However, as a Romanov, Misha is as entitled as I am to an imperial allowance from the treasury. And so, I'm forced to return to St Petersburg to petition the Tsar for his mercy and beg his forgiveness.

However, the strain of having a son while Nicky and Alix do not gnaws away at me.

With surprisingly little argument, I'm permitted counsel with the Tsar at the Alexander Palace, where the family now reside for most of the year. Alix is not in attendance: having severely suffered the disappointment of another daughter, she barely leaves her rooms. It's of no surprise that Monsieur Philippe, the fraudulent spiritualist who promised them a son, has been banished from Russia and warned never to return.

Experiencing a moment of *déjà vu*, I face the Tsar across the walnut desk with my head held high.

'Our condolences, cousin,' he smiles, somewhat cautiously. Does he imagine I will rant and scream and cry? Does he want me to throw myself prostrate at his feet? I will not grovel. This is our right. Mine and Misha's.

'Let us not dwell on my widowhood,' I nod in acknowledgment, satisfied to see colour blot his cheeks.

He lights a cigarette and turns to the window. 'What is it you are asking?'

'I ask only for what I am entitled to as Georgiy's widow.'

Hard eyes stare back at me. 'You will never repeat that.'

I raise my chin and wait; the air shifts in temperature as though a shadow lingers.

'Misha is entitled to an allowance. Under the terms of the *Statute on the Imperial Family,* you and I both know he must be taken care of, given his position.'

'The matter is not for discussion, Princess Zolotova.' A slight tremor in his hand gives away the anger he withholds. 'There will be no talk or acknowledgement of a marriage—there is no proof.'

'Our marriage was sanctified and witnessed by Oleg Igorevich.'

He turns away. 'We will give you access to private apartments in the Winter Palace. However, regarding a greater purse...you and Prince Zolotovsky will be required in the imperial household from time to time, and on occasion, to accompany us to our various estates. Guests, if you like. Is that understood?'

'Why is this?'

'It is best we take an interest in your son, and his future.' He curls his hands into fists and rests them on the desk. 'You will want for nothing. We will review the matter as is necessary....'

I catch my breath and feel the walls closing in on me.

'We have faith. There is still time...,' his voice lowers as he lights another cigarette and rises, 'once Alix gives birth to a son, we anticipate a change in circumstance. But until then....'

He waves a hand dismissively. 'You are a loyal Russian subject and my widowed cousin, Tatya. We will endeavour to support you.'

'Imperial Majesty.' I curtsy. *Support or control?* 'Please pass on my felicitations to the Empress on the birth of Grand Duchess Anastasia. She is blessed with a beautiful name.' I hope my smile is warmer than I feel.

The Tsar's face briefly crumbles in a mixture of emotions, and the weight of it drags me down and pools at my feet. For inadvertently, we have both confirmed Misha as Russia's rightful heir. And neither one of us chooses for it to be known outside the walls of this room.

JEAN

21

Castlemaine

Jean dials Rick's number. *How are his vines coping with the cold?* It's been days since she's spoken to him, and she's keen to hear the latest on the renovation. With a sigh of resignation, she leaves a message. No doubt he has his hands full.

The visit to the orchard has inspired her. Nudged on by Elton John singing about an empty garden, she hums along to the old transistor radio and sets to work. Dormant during the winter months, pockets of greenery now sprout in the garden revealing vegetables like zucchini and broccoli she's never considered before. Boarding school put her off Brussels sprouts for life—she can't stomach the lingering stench of them cooking. Perhaps any surplus veggies can be offered to Merle or the local farmers' market?

When the afternoon breeze turns damp and heavy, satisfied with her endeavour, Jean gathers her gardening tools and packs them in the shed.

Once inside and alone, it's inevitable that her thoughts drift. She's spent her life trying to mask her mistakes behind a brave face, but Rick's warmth and good humour is slowly chipping away her reservation. There's no denying that by uncovering the past, she risks vulnerability.

She can't bear the possibility of their fledgling bond breaking. The thought is too terrifying.

When the brass knocker raps on her front door she's startled to the present. Jean certainly isn't expecting visitors and approaches with a frown. She peers through the peephole, surprised to see Peter from the workshop holding a large bunch of silver beet with curly leaves that gleam like jade in the grey light of the afternoon.

'Hi Jean. I hope you don't mind. I have more of this than I can use. It'd be a shame for it to go to waste. I thought you might like it?'

Her mouth remains open until she makes the conscious decision to close it. 'Thank you. How kind.' The pair stand at cross-purposes, on either side of the doorway. When Jean reaches for the produce he turns slightly, using his body as a shield. But his eyes are soft and kind.

'My mother insisted it was bad luck to receive gifts across a threshold. Do you mind if I come in—or perhaps you might step out?' He shrugs apologetically. 'An old wives' tale, but I daren't put it to the test.'

'Oh,' she eases out a breath, 'I've never heard that one before. Would you like to come in?' Jean pats her hair self-consciously and steps aside, grateful to have showered and changed out of her gardening attire.

'No problem,' his deep voice fills the hallway. 'I like to remember some of her traditions.'

He follows her into the kitchen, and she removes her knitting bag from the table. A fisherman's rib cowl of deep purple mohair is her latest creation, large enough to cover her head on the frosty morning walks to the station. She click-clacks away on her commute each day while peaceful scenes unfold outside the window. The gentle rock of the train offers a welcome release after a day dealing with fashion agents, designers with creative temperaments or competitive staff driven by sales targets.

'How are you settling in?' Pete sets the silver beet on the sink beneath the window. 'Make sure you wash it well—there might be a few slugs. The soil here sticks like glue.'

'I'm sure I can manage.' He might think her a city slicker, but Jean knows quite enough about soil and gardens. 'I grew up on an orchard.'

'I almost brought you tomatoes, but I see you have them. Don't they grow well here?'

'Yes, extremely well.' His eyes are lovely. Like Caramello centres. She pushes the thought away. It might be his surprise appearance, but something about him unsettles her. Her hands dangle by her sides. 'Would you like a coffee?'

'I'd prefer tea if you have it.'

Jean flicks on the electric kettle and takes two cups from the overhead cupboard. 'I prefer tea of an afternoon, too,' she offers, compelled to fill the silence.

He shuffles from one foot to the other. 'I haven't seen you around the town for a few weeks. Merle told me you'd been to visit your brother. I hope you won't feel this an imposition, but I know what it's like to be new in town and thought you might use some company. I assure you I'm no axe-murderer.' He grins and his face softens.

She smiles at his turn of phrase. 'Well, if you are, I'm in big trouble!' They laugh.

The kettle takes an age to boil. The ticking of the station clock on the wall sounds like the opening bars of the *Sixty Minutes* promo. It's been a long time since Jean made small talk with a man.

'Do you see that tree?' Peter points to the green gage plum outside. 'You probably know about the disease that affects plum trees. This one's rife with it. I'll bring you some spray.'

'Thank you. I'm afraid dealing with pests is more my brother's domain. He runs the property now.' Jean motions for Pete to sit down at the circular table near the bay window.

'So, he's the farmer, following in the family's footsteps?' He appears quite at home in her kitchen, reclining in the seat with a smile. The usual anxiety she feels in male company falls away with his casual ease.

'Actually, several years ago he replanted the orchard with vines and they're already producing. He'll be opening the cellar door soon, with his first vintage. I mentioned your furniture to him too. He'd like to see your work, at some stage.'

'I appreciate the recommendation. I'd be happy to show him.' Peter bows his head. 'No doubt it's a huge effort to get things up and running.'

'I expect he'll manage. He has a good head for business.' She smiles proudly and spoons leaves into the teapot, breathing in the soothing blend as it steeps.

'Were you pleased to see the orchard transformed?' Peter accepts his dainty teacup, pinching the narrow handle awkwardly between two large fingers.

'It's nothing to do with me.' The tone of her voice rises a notch as the words dart from her mouth. 'It's Rick's venture, and I wish him luck with it.'

He mirrors the frown on Jean's face. 'It's okay, Jean. I understand. Family can be difficult.'

'We've lived apart for years. We're getting to know one another again now, I suppose.'

He reaches out to pat her arm but his hand stills. 'Of course.'

'Perhaps I can send him photos of your pieces. He's just so busy—'

'You're welcome to drop by anytime. You don't need to wait for the open weekends,' he laughs. Crow's feet fan like stars from the corners of his eyes.

Pete glances to the back verandah where Jean's easel is set up and the second of her botanical paintings almost finished. A Delft blue and white vase on a weathered pine table holds a bouquet of burnished amber marigolds, bluebells and various shades of pink dahlias. A spool of sapphire ribbon uncurls at the base.

'This is your work? You're a painter?'

'It's just a hobby.' She looks away.

'It's beautiful. You have captured the light well. The petals look soft, like velvet. I like it, very much.'

'Thank you,' Jean's face grows warm. It's difficult to accept such an energetic compliment.

'Your secret passion might turn out like mine. My woodwork began as a hobby. I didn't want to share it with anyone for quite some time.'

'My mother was an artist,' Jean offers. *Why did she tell him that?*

Pete smiles and nods. 'Then you never know where this might lead. What do they say about the apple not falling far from the tree?'

He waggles his eyebrows, and Jean bursts into laughter.

One afternoon, Jean arrives in the lunchroom to find Summer on her tea break at the pristine Formica bench, reading through a large pile of paperwork.

'That looks serious. Are you memorising the new work-relations manual?'

'Very funny,' Summer giggles. 'Sorry to disappoint you, but I'm studying for an exam. Design Specifications.'

'That sounds ominous. How's the course going?'

'I'm really enjoying all the creative exercises, the storyboards and fabric concepts, but I'm lost when it comes to art history and architecture. Trying to remember the various styles and periods is overwhelming, to be honest.' She waves Jean towards a seat at the table. 'Now Mum has passed, I've got plenty of free time to study up on it.'

'I'm sure she appreciated you being there at the end, Summer.'

'Thanks.' She braves a smile. Summer had been throwing herself into extra shifts since the funeral. 'Isn't the salon going well? I think the gorgeous fabrics help me with inspiration for the design exercises. But tell me, what else have you been up to, outside of work? It's been ages since we've had time to chat.'

Jean is not about to discuss her personal life in the lunchroom. 'A bit of gardening—not much else.' She takes a breath, thinking of how often she and Pete have caught up in the café in the past weeks. 'I've mainly been focusing on buying for the new season. That's about all.' She takes a bite of her sandwich.

It takes one loner to recognise another. And Summer is quite the loner. Jean rarely sees her join groups during her breaks, and although she's popular on the floor and the customers love her, she staunchly avoids gossip. The thought of this gorgeous woman lonely and alone seems absurd.

'You know, I've always been interested in art history,' Jean offers impulsively. 'Maybe I can help you with it—'

'If you're sure you don't mind, Jean? I'd really appreciate your help.' Summer chews the end of the pencil, then places it in front of her. 'I'm out of my comfort zone defining these architectural periods. Some of the field trips make it clearer. We visit properties to study the various design elements, like the Federation style of the Royal Exhibition buildings.'

'I'd love to help. In fact, I live near a beautiful homestead with an Italianate façade that might also be useful in terms of its unique arts and crafts period furnishings. It's well regarded in artistic circles. Maybe you'd like to see it? You'll have to find a weekend to come and stay.'

Summer beams her supermodel smile. 'That would be wonderful! I've spent so little time in the countryside since I came back. You live near Bendigo, don't you?'

'Yes, Castlemaine. Why don't you come up the weekend after next?' The invitation is unforced and genuine. It will be lovely to have company.

'Fabulous. It's a date.'

22

Melbourne

Jean has a pile of stock orders to check and has skipped lunch yet again. Rick's unexpected arrival is a welcome reprieve.

'I've just come from the bank,' he offers as soon as they sit down in the store's cafeteria. 'They've agreed to extend the loan. What a bloody relief! It'll be much easier now.'

'That's terrific,' Jean is genuinely relieved. 'Now you can finish setting up the gallery and brand your wine exactly the way you planned. It's going to be amazing, Rick!'

'The scholarship's coming together too. It's to be presented the week after the gallery opening.' The proposal to provide a girl from a disadvantaged background with a scholarship had been presented to Beaulieu's school board and heartily accepted. Aurora had stipulated the inaugural scholarship be based purely on artistic merit.

Rick hands Jean a wallet of glossy photos in a larger format than she's seen before. 'These are the portraits on loan for the exhibition.'

One by one she works through them, overwhelmed by the intensity of emotion in Aurora's paintings and her familiar artistic technique and style. But the scope of her talent is unfamiliar. She has missed so much.

'Aren't they amazing?' Rick flicks aside a fringe that's longer than usual. Overseeing his building work and production at the vineyard has given him time for little else including haircuts.

'I can't believe her work. It's—'

'Unreal, huh? She was an absolute master.'

Jean checks her nails. *He praises her in every conversation.*

'And hey, would you present Aurora's scholarship at Beaulieu. Is that okay?'

'It depends on my roster.'

She sees he's puzzled by her response, but now is not the time to explain. She checks her watch. 'I must get back, Rick. I spoke to my friend Pete about what you're looking for in terms of furniture. You'll need to find time to check out his work—'

'As much as I'd like to, now I've got the green light with the funds, why don't you go ahead and order the pieces I need? I trust your judgement.'

'Are you sure...?'

'Yeah—and didn't you say one of the girls here was helping you? The interior designer?' He collects the wallet of photos. 'Seriously, I'm happy if you just fax me the quote. You know the look I'm going for.'

'Sure.' She kisses his cheek and picks up her purse. 'I'm positive Summer will be pleased to offer a second opinion—'

'Summer?' His colour fades beneath his tan.

'The interior designer.' Jean tilts her head to the side. 'Are you okay?'

'Yeah, must be something I ate. I'll let you get back.' He squeezes Jean in his trademark bear hug, and she savours his arms around her.

Most nights, by the time Jean's train reaches the station, Pete has collected the evening papers and is waiting to walk her home. He enquires about her day and says that since he's been bent over a woodwork lathe all day, the walk helps stretch his legs. *It's no trouble at all*, he insists. Both know it's an excuse but neither draws attention to the fact.

Even Merle has made light of the shift in their friendship, none too subtly offering Jean tips on Pete's favourite cakes and slices, while suggesting that 'Jean works too hard and deserves a night off from cooking.'

The pair has fallen into an easy rhythm, an unspoken habit of similitude. Jean finds Pete respectful and a great listener; she's grateful he encourages her to unwind as she shares the challenges of her daily routine on the walk home.

When Pete suggests that once Rick's tables are finished, they can deliver them together, Jean is delighted.

'I'm looking forward to meeting him. And of course, I'd love to see where you grew up.'

She nods into the shadows of the evening. 'Would you like to stay for dinner? I picked up a lovely lasagne today. It won't take long to reheat.' The Food Hall at DJs is a godsend with its ready-made meals.

'That would be lovely. Invitation accepted.' Pete coughs to clear his throat.

'It's so peaceful here tonight,' Jean muses as she unlocks the door.

'You know, many who live in smaller country towns are lost souls, but there are happy, uncomplicated people here too, choosing to make the most of life.'

Castlemaine has given Jean greater sanctuary than she could have imagined. The space to face what she's running from. For the first time she admits that a deeper friendship with Pete would be safe too. Enjoyable. Possible. Maybe this really is a second chance.

'I must say I have not missed the city at all. And I agree, Castlemaine has much to commend it.'

After dinner, he lights the fire, and the careful and considerate manner of their conversation does little to dampen the energy between them. But it's getting late. Pete stands to go, and Jean follows him to the hallway. She rests one hand on the doorknob.

'Stay?'

Pete takes her hand. Warm eyes, liquid with kindness and care stare down at her. 'Are you sure?' The slow flicker of a smile makes her legs feel unsteady.

'Never more certain,' she says, and tilts her lips to his.

23

Jean studies the photo of Aurora's self-portrait. Questions hang over the symbolism, stirring up ghosts of the past and the minutiae of memories that are no clearer. She has put off speaking to Hazel for long enough. It's time for some answers.

On her rostered day off, Jean lifts a bouquet of blousy pink peonies from the seat of her car and then juggles them to press the nursing home buzzer.

The door opens from the inside. 'There you go, love.' The cheeky young staff member winks, his hair is cut in the latest style—business in the front, party at the back. A recognisable scent of pine assaults her nasal passages—it's popular with the younger ones and generously sprayed from acorn-shaped bottles at the fragrance counter.

Jean finds Hazel seated with ankles lightly crossed in a sunroom of beige and bland, looking anything but ordinary. Fuchsia-lipped and studying the form guide, she's immaculately dressed in the height of fashion in a psychedelic quilted silk bomber jacket, and an Edwardian-style blouse with a frilled collar that curls to her chin. Instead of the sensible flat heels worn by women of advancing years, she's sporting a shiny pair of cherry-red court shoes.

Hazel springs from her seat and claps her hands as though the decades have melted away. 'Jeanie, my dear girl. How wonderful you look! The spitting image of your dear mother, God bless her.'

Jean gasps startled by Hazel's positive reference.

'Come and sit. Tell me all about yourself. I've plenty of time, dear, so don't leave anything out!' Hazel's nut-brown eyes widen and wrinkled fingers grasp Jean's hand, stroking the back like ruffling fur on a cat's spine. 'Married? Children?'

Jean doesn't want to talk about herself. That's not what she's here for.

'No, I'm a working girl, Hazel, a career woman like you,' she rephrases. 'I'm head of Australian designer fashion at David Jones.'

'Well done, my girl!' She pats Jean's hand again. 'You know, my career as you put it, wasn't solely my choice. I lost my fiancé, bless him, in Hitler's damn war though in the end it was the Japanese who did him in. Afterwards, well, I was afforded strong sensibility and a stubborn streak that set me apart from women of my time. "Too headstrong," dear Mother used to say. Not an admirable trait in a woman of marriageable age. I expect that's why I got on so well with Aurora. I really was better off alone.'

Jean suspects Aurora might have preferred a solitary life too; the struggle between her artistic self and her role as a wife and mother must have been difficult. Jack walked in her shadow, allowing her the freedom to create and paint, to do what she liked.

'I'm sorry I didn't write to you the way I did as a child. You were always good to me...'

'Oh *phfft*! I was busy too. I regret that between work and my travels —well, I was ever the poor correspondent. Unlike Mother who was a dab hand with a pen.

'But, when I heard Aurora had died—' She sighs and reaches for a handkerchief, balling it into her hand and then uncurling the wrinkled mess once more. 'I must say, it broke my heart. I should have tried harder to mend our relationship. But I had lost her trust, I suppose. She did mean a great deal to me once, you know.'

Jean frowns, not knowing at all. 'How did you meet, the two of you? I never asked.'

Hazel explains how her friendship with Aurora grew in England before the war. 'It was through Mother of course—and Michael was like a son to her. As a child I adored him.'

Jean runs her tongue over her teeth. After ignoring him for decades, his name intrudes on their sunny afternoon conversation like a rising phoenix.

'*Everyone* loved Michael. Of course, when he and Aurora were in London, there was no doubting their connection. Then, to our surprise, she became engaged to Jack quite out of the blue.'

Hazel picks up the glass beside her and takes a sip. Jean feels the walls closing in on her and loosens the scarf around her neck. 'I thought she and Michael were work colleagues.'

'*Work colleagues?* Oh, goodness no,' Hazel laughs and waves her hands. 'Michael worked as a translator at the Home Office. That must have been *before* he became an art dealer. Anyhow, your mother was studying at the academy. He was totally wrong for her, of course, but he had such an immensely magnetic personality. She wasn't the first artist to fall under his spell.'

'But why didn't she tell me?' Jean's voice wavers.

'Why? Why do you think, dear?' Her brows arch as if to say, *if you know what I mean.*

Jean moistens her lips.

'Dear child, you must have suspected....'

Jean isn't sure of her meaning. Perhaps Hazel has the wrong end of the stick, as her father would have said.

'Of course, when your brother was born, there was no hiding it. Your parents were barely together by that stage. Aurora took off and fled to the country when she was pregnant. But to her credit, after Rick was born, she became the faithful wife and she and Jack turned their relationship around. She committed to Jack, to the farm—I expect she had to, after everything she'd put him through.'

'I'm sorry,' Jean purses her mouth and tilts her head to the side. 'What do you mean?'

'The war, dear. The Great War, we call it now, since we suffered Hitler after that. It left a mark on him, as it did for all who fought in it. It was a catastrophe for families who lost loved ones, *and* for those who returned. But women—well! They were left to jolly well get on with things.'

Jean frowns. Jack never spoke about his service years. All she knew was that he had fudged his age and run away from the orchard to join up.

'I think Aurora tried her best to resist him,' Hazel smiles and pats Jean's hand again, 'but I never understood it. I thought things were well and truly over between her and Michael. Mind you, beautiful women were always his undoing.'

Michael? Jean thinks back to when her pregnancy was discovered—and then the night Aurora decided her fate. She was in love with Michael. Aurora was jealous. She kept Rick to punish her.

And now, Hazel is professing affection for the wonderful Michael, and telling her that women fell at his feet as though she is proud of it.

Hazel didn't know him the way Jean did, or what he was capable of. What he had done to her.

'He was too handsome for his own good—,' Hazel carries on, unaware of Jean's internal struggle, '—he was always one to crave attention.'

How foolish she had been. It had taken years to escape the shame of his betrayal. Michael was a self-indulged narcissist, only concerned with his own pleasure.

'Still, when Aurora had another child to him—'

Another child? Jean wants to unhear the words, but Hazel's lips keep moving and forming, opening and shutting like a trapdoor.

Her stomach convulses.

'—Naturally, Jack agreed to marry Aurora without question. But then when it happened again, I considered it a gross injustice.'

If Jack isn't my father...

Jean sucks in a breath and an iron-hot flush rushes through her. By voicing it aloud, she would be forced to admit the truth. It's horrific to even think it.

'Of course, Jack loved her—for better or worse,' Hazel's diatribe continues.

Bile sours Jean's mouth. 'Excuse me—'

She rushes from the room and into a toilet cubicle, retching. *It can't be true!* No wonder Aurora was so furious when she learned of her pregnancy.

Dear God, what have I done?

Castlemaine, 1952

Jeanie promises she won't stray far, but she needs fresh air; the continual smell of linseed oil, paint, smoke and heat is giving her a headache. Wrapped in Aurora's fashionable swing coat, her expanded girth is well hidden from sight of the neighbours.

A burst of sunshine lights her path. Golden budded wildflowers dot the wayside, while the sweet scent of dewy roses in shades of pink, cherry-red and apricot swirl in the breeze.

When she reaches the home of the Sorokin sisters, a young man runs out in front of her with a parcel under his arm. He doffs his cap. 'Sorry, if I gave you a fright, just off to do my deliveries, quick sticks!' He leaps onto a red bicycle and clatters away. Jeanie giggles at the awkward formality of his mannerisms.

When she returns, Aurora is pacing back in front of the cottage with her face pinched in disapproval. 'Come inside, young lady.'

'What is it?' Jeanie asks, a little out of breath. The last block had been far harder than when she set off. She rests against the gatepost, and then breathes out slowly as pain tugs in her lower back. She might have overdone it.

'Inside, now!'

Both mother and daughter had needed time apart. Jeanie doesn't want a repeat performance of the argument from the night before. She has no intention of giving her baby up for adoption, despite her mother's entreaties that it gives Jeanie the best chance for the future. She can't imagine being parted from the child she already loves. Aurora has no right to insist. Once the baby arrives, she'll see what a good mother Jeanie will be.

Michael might think he doesn't want her or their baby, but in time he will see sense too. She'll bring up their child. Adoption is not an option.

Aurora insisted on knowing the name of the father, but Jeanie refuses to give him up, conscious of compromising her mother's business relationship.

Releasing a stream of breath, she follows Aurora inside; each step is an effort.

'Where did you get this?' Aurora opens her hand to reveal a trinket fashioned like a ladybird. 'Where? Tell me, NOW!'

Jeanie steps back in surprise. 'I've never seen it before.'

It's a brooch, with shiny patterns in the black and scarlet enamel that are remarkably realistic. Three lines of white stones cover the surface, while underneath are six tiny gold legs like those of the slater beetles Shirley collects in the garden. Then she notices the silk purse in Aurora's other hand.

'Don't lie to me, Jean Elizabeth Champion! Not after—,' she points to Jeanie's stomach as another pain digs deeper, '—I found this in your room.'

Jeanie had never bothered to open Michael's gift; it reminded her of an ending to what she had hoped was their beginning. The purse had been bundled in with a matinee jacket she knitted for the baby in the drawers of her room.

'You went through my private things?'

'I went to wash the baby clothes. We need to prepare. Instead, I find this. I know it's Michael's. But why, how do you come to have it?'

Jeanie has never seen her mother so incensed; her lilac eyes are lit with an almost frightening fury. How does she know? Jeanie hadn't lied but didn't want to anger her further. 'He gave it to me.'

'*GAVE it to you!* When? Why would he?' She folds her arms. 'Jeanie Champion, I swear you tell me the truth right now! He would *never* give this away.' Aurora paces the floor and runs her hands through her hair. 'Did you steal it?'

'No.'

'Then tell me, or I'll ask him myself.'

A sharp pain twinges harder, and Jeanie lets out a cry. Amidst the shock, her mind plays tricks on her. *Where is she? What's going on?*

Seconds later, a gush of liquid pools between her legs, and Jeanie drops to her knees.

'Oh god, Jeanie, not now!'

She looks up at her mother and tears blur her vision. 'It hurts, Mummy, it hurts so much. Please, I don't want to do this. Make it stop. Make it go away.' She sucks in a breath. 'I want to go home—'

Aurora helps her into her room and onto the bed. She squeezes Jeanie's hand. 'Don't move, darling. I'll take care of you. Stay calm, and I'll be back in a jiffy!'

Jeanie labours through waves of contractions but progresses far too quickly. Her senses dull as she focuses inward. Soon enough, pain breaks through her self-control. Around her the light is dim. Between intervals of twisting discomfort that wrack her body, she hears the blur of voices, soft and incoherent. Someone else must be here, but Jeanie doesn't care, she just wants the pain—the sharp, knife-edged tugging and stretching, the burning—to stop.

Aurora's arms wrap around her body, supporting her, urging Jeanie to push. With the next contraction she bears down on the rising tide, and as her body opens, she gives in to the force of nature. Jeanie lets out a primal scream, screaming out the name of the man she loves—the man she is trying to protect—as one long, violent curse. Seconds later, an exhausted Jeanie delivers her son into the world.

In the days that follow, Aurora forbids mention of Michael's name. Then she tells Jeanie that he has no interest in seeing her again. To forget him. It's best for them all. And when Jeanie raises the question of his gift, she's hit with a blunt reply. 'It no longer concerns you.'

They've been away from the orchard for months, and Jeanie longs to return. The night before they leave Castlemaine, Aurora informs Jeanie of the plan she has made for the future.

'There's no need for an adoption, darling.' Her tone is gentle... cautious.

Jeanie smiles down at her son in her arms. She knew Mummy would understand.

'It's all arranged. His birth is registered in my name, with Jack as the father—a *change of life* baby. They happen all the time.'

'No! No, you can't!' Jeanie removes the bottle from her child's sleeping lips and cradles him closer.

'From now on, all decisions regarding him will be made by your father and me. I won't have it any other way.' Aurora's eyes are steely. Jeanie sees pain behind them too.

She never saw the brooch again—the only connection she had to Michael. Aurora stole everything. Everything and everyone she loved.

Before returning to Hazel, Jean splashes cold water onto her face and pinches her cheeks like Scarlett O'Hara. She has questions only Hazel can answer.

Back in the sunroom, the elderly woman is staring out the window. 'My dear, I don't have time on my side, and I need to ease my conscience.'

'The reason you lost touch?'

'Yes. I sincerely regret it. I thought Jack deserved to know the truth. I was angry. Furious. Perhaps a little jealous of Aurora too, I'm not too proud to admit. Jack was older, and the last thing he needed was a fourth child to rear.'

Hazel takes a perfectly ironed handkerchief from her pocket. 'I told him the baby was Michael's.'

She sniffs, flicking the handkerchief open. 'Aurora never forgave me. It destroyed our friendship, of course, and I'll never forgive myself for that. I tried to mend it—I drove to Castlemaine to have it out with her, but she barricaded herself inside the house and wouldn't come out. She demanded I leave.'

'I returned to Melbourne and told Jack what I knew. Aurora was furious, and rightly so. I should *never* have interfered.' Hazel sniffs again.

Hazel has part of it wrong. Rick is her son. 'I don't know what to say...,' Jean's feeble attempt to speak masks her inner turmoil; even *thinking* it makes her feel filthy. Tainted. Disgusting.

'I should have let sleeping dogs lie. But I couldn't bear the thought of standing by and watching Aurora fussing over Rick when he wasn't Jack's son. Yes, I was envious. Of everything she had.'

Jean can't catch her breath. The air is thick around her, and the pain that clamps her chest is so tight she feels ill. She moves to the doorway, dazed and confused. She can't hear another word.

'It was a tragedy what happened to Michael in the end—'

'I have an appointment, Hazel, I must get back.' Jean ignores the powdered cheek offered for her to kiss.

She stumbles to the car, her mind full of slow-motion images of her with Aurora and the hiss of hushed voices and vile accusations.

Until now, she had no idea about Aurora's long-standing infidelity —or the devastating consequences of her affair on the whole family.

TATIANA

24

Winter Palace, St Petersburg, 1903

The palace is overrun with servants and activity in preparation for tomorrow evening's Grand Costume Ball. The four grand duchesses begged to attend, but Nanny promised them a celebration in the children's wing instead. At three years of age, Misha is too young to dress as a *boyarin* however often Nanny suggests it.

I'm very much looking forward to joining the four hundred guests gathering in honour of the two-hundred-and-ninety-year anniversary of Romanov rule. Even Olga Alexandrovna is eager to join the festivities—more so, I suspect, because her husband is in Paris, and once again in the company of friends. (Sadly, a regular occurrence since their marriage two years ago.)

I've spent an age surrounded by costumes and feathers and excuse myself from gowns and seamstresses. I'm eager to escape the unrelenting stream of gossip too, rife from the first of the anniversary celebrations the previous evening.

The chill of the courtyard takes me by surprise; a fresh dusting of snow is yet to be cleared and sludge lies underfoot. The clatter of hooves approach and voices pepper back and forth through the courtyard like shots of rapid gunfire. The two horsemen are *cuirassiers*; their uniforms are trimmed with the signature blue that marks them as officers of Her Imperial Majesty's Life Guards. Men of the regiment are required to be tall and dark haired and mounted on reds such as chestnuts or sorrels.

Deep in discussion, the pair steer the horses overly close to the palace walls. I hurriedly step back and press against the cold stone. Although the more dashing of the two inclines his head as he rides by, the wilful curl of his mouth suggests he is entirely non-apologetic and displays a distinct lack of regard for their reckless behaviour.

A short time later, to my chagrin, the crunch of *sapogi* jackboots signals the approach of the very same *cuirassier*. I turn to retreat, but my boots slip on the cobblestones and a sharp twinge in my ankle restricts my movements. Fortunately, my skirts cover the injury, which smarts terribly. But he reaches me in moments, sweeping his *Fokin* cap from his head and under his arm.

'Might I offer assistance, Your Highness?' He has the temerity to smirk, and brazenly meets my gaze when he rises from his low bow. 'It appears the mere sight of me has set you off balance…'

Heat burns my cheeks; and for some peculiar reason, the thought of my ungraceful steps and my mother comes to mind. She would never have been wrong-footed by a handsome man.

'You are insolent, lieutenant. I do not recall our introduction.'

'In that case, allow me to rectify the error. Lieutenant Ilya Petrovich Vorontov at your service.' He raises his eyebrows. 'It is, indeed, my pleasure to make your acquaintance at last.'

From the beginning Lieutenant Vorontov stands apart from the rest. While most of his regiment sport neatly manicured moustaches, his face is clean-shaven. His conceit is immediately apparent—as clearly defined as his cheekbones or the line of his angular jaw sculptured with the mastery of a Grecian statue.

I am lost for a reply when he seals his introduction with an irritating tilt of his chin, the cleft of which infers a rakish charm. More disconcerting is the breathlessness constricting my chest. The lieutenant has most unusual toffee-coloured eyes that flash with gold dust like a tiger's when he smiles. The man is altogether too attractive.

The voice inside my heads tells me to ignore him. This man means trouble. And I have already had more trouble in my short lifetime than any one woman deserves. I dismiss him with a curt nod and gather my skirts. Pain shoots through my ankle, and I wince again, before righting my composure.

'Your Highness? Ah...your foot. You would not be the first young lady attempting to avoid me. Allow me to assist.' He holds out his elbow.

I glare at him. His lack of deference is most curious. Here is a man who will not be cowed by the rules. I note the smooth and rich tone of his voice, steady and confident. I imagine he is a man used to getting his own way. But to court the solitary attentions of any one man is a lesson best learned early; I have no interest in him, no matter how handsome his jawline or brilliant the fit of his white uniform jacket.

'I can manage *perfectly well*, thank you, Lieutenant. Good day.'

His boots echo in retreat, and I stagger the first steps along the path. Then shuffling to the wide doorjambs, I lean on my parasol and wait for a footman to aid me inside.

The next evening, I don my costume and embroidered slippers, ready to step into the seventeenth century like Cinderella at the fairy tale ball. The ivory lace and gold-threaded brocade of my traditional *Boyarishnya* costume, is exquisite. I'm delighted with my headwear too—the traditional diadem *kokoshnik* is decorated with creamy white pearls and set in the centre with a luminous topaz the precise shade of my eyes. With my ladybird brooch pinned close to my heart, Georgiy is with me too at this important Romanov celebration.

From the hallways to the reception rooms, the Winter Palace is awash with courtiers and guests in shimmering garments embroidered in threads of silver and gold. The men are resplendent in an array of bright costumes; robes of turquoise or rich crimson velvet are worn over the voluminous bloused breeches from various times before Peter the Great. They mingle with ladies wearing elaborately decorated *sarafans* and bejewelled *kokoshniki* in countless degrees of height and width. It's as though we have stepped straight from the canvas of a master's painting; a vision as rich and vivid as the portraits of my Romanov ancestors who line the gallery walls.

Accompanied by the sound of trumpets, the Tsar and the Empress make their entrance. A truly spectacular sight! Dressed as Tsar Alexei Mikhailovich and his first wife, Tsarina Miloslavskaya Maria Ilyinichna, they lead the procession to the Nicolas Hall. There, they are seated on the imperial thrones and two by two we approach the dais while the Grand Marshal announces our character titles with a deep and throaty bark and the tapping of his staff. Olga and her mother, the dowager, progress together, while I am further down the line, accompanied by a recently bereaved general of advancing years.

Preeminent foreign ambassadors have been invited to the evening's celebration; no doubt the marking of two hundred and ninety years of Romanov reign is enough to make other countries envious. The symphony orchestra take up their instruments on the platform above, and their Imperial Majesties make their way to the floor for a polonaise. Olga and I join the line with the younger ladies.

A short time later, Rosalind weaves through the crowd. Hazel eyes twinkle beneath a demure but becoming veil of almond-white silk, edged in intricate handmade lace that she explains is crafted in the north of England. 'I'm pleased to see you without a limp tonight, Tatya. The bedrest worked, I see?'

'Indeed, it did ease the swelling,' I smile. 'I spent the evening on the chaise with a cold compress while Olga read chapters from the novel you recommended. I am fully recovered.'

'I'm pleased to hear it.'

Suddenly a deep voice behind me sends a tingle down my spine. 'Good evening, Your Highness. Miss Brassington.'

While bowing over Rosalind's hand, he still manages a glance in my direction.

'How delightful to see you again, Lieutenant Vorontov.' Rosalind's voice tinkles like a bell. My friend never fails to swoon over a man in uniform. 'I imagine you know Princess Zolotova?'

'I've briefly had the pleasure.' He reveals a sardonic smile.

The exaggerated puffed sleeves of his medieval falconer's costume emphasise the breadth of his muscular physique. Proudly emblazoned across the chest of his black tunic is the Romanov crest—the double-headed eagles embroidered in gold survey the vast expanse of the empire from the east of the globe to the west. It does not escape my notice that his costume tapers firmly over his buttocks. I confess the brevity of ignoble thoughts about what lies concealed beneath.

I flick open my fan in courtly language he should understand. The mother-of-pearl and gold *rocaille* scrolls on the guard-sticks sparkle in the light as I wave it slowly, conveying my disinterest.

His head lowers over my glove in greeting, but he holds my hand for longer than is polite. To retract it from his grasp without making a scene, I relax my fingers to fall limp.

'You are fully recovered, I see.' Though spoken with mirth, it appears the man cannot resist a taunt.

'You did not mention you knew the lieutenant?' Rosalind whispers.

'Would you do me the honour of allowing me to accompany you for the next dance?'

After my encounter yesterday I would prefer any partner, any guard or tiresome statesman, over Lieutenant Vorontov. I silently count to five before acknowledging him, but when I look up, his attention is firmly fixed on Rosalind. A rosy blush covers her cheeks in her pretty English way as she effects a curtsy. 'I am honoured, Lieutenant.'

I affix an indolent smile on my face despite the affront. But as he leads Rosalind to the dance floor, he glances over her shoulder, and his eyes meet mine. To my humiliation the insufferable man has the audacity to wink.

Though I am not without company, I lose count of the number of ladies Vorontov partners during the cotillions and quadrilles. I dance with several officers and one dear man with a luxuriant horseshoe moustache whose wife scowls at me from behind a pilaster each time we circle past.

Yet as the evening progresses, I feel more aggrieved. He is the size of a bear and hard to miss, rising head and shoulders above those around him. The glow of crystal chandeliers reflects the sheen of his chestnut hair like a beacon. Why am I so intent on avoiding him? I cannot shake the feeling he is covertly watching me although with so many guests it's likely my imagination.

Soon the announcement is made for guests to take their partners for the *mazurka*. I hold my breath to still the tightness in my chest. It is the dance of promise, of passion, and is at the very heart of every Russian celebration. The dance of love and life.

A wave of sadness washes over me, and I turn from the dance floor. My path is swiftly intercepted.

'Your Highness. May I?' He raises an eyebrow. Despite his cordial manner, it feels suspiciously as though Vorontov is offering me a dare.

Our gaze connects. I'm surprised that instead of arrogance, his tiger's eyes are lit with levity and merriment.

I incline my head. 'Lieutenant, if you will excuse me...'

But then I notice Lord Brassington beside me; he smiles at our exchange. Though my refusal catches at the base of my throat, it would be the height of bad manners to make a scene in front of the British ambassador.

I set my jaw and extend my hand. 'Thank you, Lieutenant.'

His grip is firm and unwavering as he leads us to take our place.

At the opening bars of the most famous of all the Chopin *mazurkas*, my nervousness disappears. Expectation thrums through my body and a tremor of excitement extends from my chest to my toes.

'I saw you dance this once,' Vorontov whispers as he rises from his bow, 'it was intoxicating.'

We part to take our positions and my stomach lurches. From the first step, the guests smile and throw themselves into the heady spirit of the dance. The *mazurka* is the dance of defiance too.

Conversation shifts between us like quicksilver as we weave and change partners. Each step is liberating; I feel confident, triumphant. With my head held high and shoulders back, my steps are light and care-free. I almost believe *I am* a woman from another time.

'Did you know Chopin was a Pole?' Vorontov rejoins the gentlemen's line. 'This was composed while Poland was valiantly opposing Russian rule. Amusing, don't you agree, that the oppressor appropriates the finest attributes of the country it dominates in victory?'

'I wasn't aware you were so well-versed in matters of musical composition,' I quip, when next we partner. 'I understood military men only ever thought of victory.'

We clasp hands and he raises an arm high over my head to clear the height of my *kokoshnik*. When he slides his arm down and extends it across my back in the hold, I feel the warmth and sense of protection that first inspired the dance.

'I can think of far more delightful pursuits,' he winks and my stomach flutters as he lowers his mouth in line with my ear, 'but that is not for your pretty ears, Princess.'

Heat shoots through my body, and my steps falter. His eyes do not leave mine as I skip to catch up.

All too soon the music concludes. We applaud the orchestra and thank each other in the formal bow that social niceties require. Then, with an exaggerated click of his heels, Vorontov drops my hand and retreats, his dismissal as swift a slight as the sting of a blister from a new pair of slippers.

I barely catch my breath before he has crossed the room and is laughing with a group of fellow officers, their faces flushed with the excesses that celebrations such as this encourage.

Indeed, the man is incorrigible, just as I had first predicted.

The next day, as is our habit, Olga joins me in the parlour adjoining my apartments. After a break in conversation, I argue with a voice in my head that refuses to listen, and broach the subject, interested to learn what she knows of the man.

'Lieutenant Vorontov?' Her head rolls back as she laughs. 'Oh darling, Tatya, now, he is one to avoid! Trouble from all accounts. And hardly a model of duty and service. *Why* Mama insists he remain in her precious guards' regiment is beyond me.'

I avoid her eyes. *What is it about him that arouses my curiosity?* I expect that I am unaccustomed to the ways of ill-mannered men. 'He is indeed insolent.'

'I assure you, he is somewhat cast with the reputation of a louche.' Olga's eyes widen with her intonation.

I focus intently on my embroidery and slip a fine stitch through the frame.

'Will you continue to read for us, Olga dear? I am quite enjoying *The Wings of the Dove*.'

Olga takes up her book while I blink the memory of Vorontov's eyes from my thoughts. I have my son's future to consider. I do not need any such distraction in my life.

25

Livadia, Crimea, Spring 1904

While reluctant to accept the invitation to accompany the family to Livadia, our presence is demanded. Olga Alexandrovna too. The Crimean coast is the perfect refuge for members of the aristocracy, far removed from St Petersburg. After an interminably long winter, a sojourn to the country may well agree with us, and we will attempt to make the best of it.

Just as bees and beetles are dependent on rose buds for sustenance, Misha and I are never far from the reach of the imperial family. The fact that my son's position is never referred to is both a blessing and a curse. He remains entirely unaware of the obligation.

For the most part our life is none too difficult. I'm a dutiful subject, one who curtsies with respect and follows orders obediently; a role I play to perfection. My reliance on the imperial purse serves the purpose of keeping us close. But it pains me to admit my silence was bought for thirty pieces of silver.

However, thoughts such as these are best expressed solely in the privacy of my journal.

Livadia Palace has a façade of gleaming white marble and limestone, and when viewed from the sea, rises high above a verdant woodland. Olga and I take breakfast on the terrace this morning. Snow-white clouds float above us and then sweep the azure sky to the coastline. I sip my tea and contemplate the soft breeze on my face, the first kiss of promise in a new day. The imperial family intend to spend the day on their yacht, *The Standart*, and we are to accompany them.

'We shall refuse,' Olga decides, her pretty mouth drawn in determination.

It is futile to oppose her once she sets her mind on a mission. While generally quite accomplished at getting her own way, sadly attempts to have the Tsar annul her marriage have so far eluded her. She speaks of little else; unhappiness in her marriage has tempted her to look elsewhere for attention. Until now, I had not realised her connection to the quietly spoken Captain Kulikovsky of the Life Guards was so strong.

The Tsar and the Empress join us. With the briefest of greetings, they take up their papers. We might well not exist. Their devotion to each other is obvious in a conversation punctuated by the pout of a lip, the murmured whisper of endearments. The way the Tsar curls and stretches his hand beside the pages reminds me of Georgiy. And Georgiy is never far from my thoughts, his expressions so clearly mirrored in our son's mien.

'Nicky darling,' Olga leans into his line of vision, 'would you be terribly disappointed if Tatya and I remain behind? We certainly would prefer it. We are quite content here, reading in the shade of the palace gardens.'

A glance passes between the Tsar and the Empress. Neither looks to me for a response.

'If you *insist* upon staying behind....' The Tsar shrugs while the Empress exudes an audible sigh and returns to her page.

'Thank you, Nicky,' Satisfaction shines in Olga's eyes. 'Please extend our apologies to the admiral for our absence.'

Reading indeed. Olga has surreptitiously proposed we seek the skills of a mystic, one of the Old Believers living on the outskirts of a neighbouring village. When she suggested the ruse, I admit, curiosity had the better of me. 'I want to be with Nikolai more than anything!' she confessed. 'No matter the cost. I love him, Tatya. The old woman will tell me if it will come to be.'

As soon as the sails of the imperial yacht billow in the distance, cast white against the indigo sea, a prickle of anticipation touches the back of my neck. I follow Olga to the stables, my fists clenched tight at the prospect of the Tsar uncovering our subterfuge.

'There you are, Vorontov. Are the horses ready? Saddle them please.'

My breath catches as I register his name. The grooms have been released from duty: with his shirt undone to the waist and coat hanging on a fencepost nearby, it appears he is tasked with brushing down our horses.

My face floods with heat as I glimpse the broad span of his naked chest and close my eyes to a healthy covering of dark hair trailing lower. I am confused by my reaction to such virile masculinity. He quickly slips arms into his shirt sleeves and rearranges his livery.

'Where is he?' Olga asks eagerly, and I see that I, too, have been caught out, oblivious to her scheme. Of course. The two are in the same regiment; a *rendezvous* has been arranged.

'He will be here shortly, Imperial Highness. But I must warn you, I think it unwise...'

'Enough, Vorontov!' Olga lifts her head.

A few moments later, Captain Kulikovsky appears from the opposite direction.

'This is not wise, Olga,' I warn.

Kulikovsky barely acknowledges me. He dismounts and rushes to take Olga's hands.

I hover by the stable doors. The thought crosses my mind that having anyone bear witness to the pair's meeting is not ideal, although I expect my presence gives it some validity. My apprehension is mirrored in Vorontov's look of disdain, or perhaps disappointment, at the bright face of the grand duchess.

'Shall we leave the grand duchess to her privacy, Princess Zolotova?' He looks to me with a modicum of sensitivity. My immediate reaction is to refuse, but at Olga's eager nod, I cannot.

We stroll through the stalls and he begins a commentary on the breeds and names of the horses. One name is so amusing that I laugh aloud. I smile as he reaches for the thoroughbreds and strokes their ears, brushing long fingers through their manes like a mother untangling knots in a child's hair. When he feeds a mare oats from his hand, his voice is soothing and gentle as she nuzzles his palm. I almost forget all I've heard about him.

'I'm pleased to see you smile, Your Highness. It offers me a challenge.' I blink at the intensity of his eyes as the gold flecks flare. 'Perhaps you might delight in my company, after all.'

Soon we reach the darkest end of the stables. How foolish I am to be lured here. I'm no plaything for a man who spends his time in mockery and tomfoolery, nor am I a conquest to boast about. Yet as a widow, I expect I am regarded as fair game for any ambitious man who seeks to rise in the ranks. As I have learned, position and estates have long been the reward of men seeking to align with those in imperial rule.

'You are forward, Lieutenant. I will remind you of whom you address.'

His laughter is like the crack of a whip. 'So, this is to be the way of our relationship, is it?' He smirks with an arrogance that riles me and leans on one elbow. 'Is this how you speak to a man who will risk his life in the coming days?'

'Risk your life?'

'While you recline here in your high tower without a care, our troops are in the city, preparing to face the Japanese. The day after tomorrow we embark for Vladivostok.'

'The Japanese? I was unaware…'

'Nor would I expect someone like you to see beyond your gilded walls.'

His criticism stings. He has no idea what sort of person I am, or what I think and feel. 'Lieutenant Vorontov. I assure you, I did not realise the gravity of the situation. Had I known, I would never have drawn you away to accompany us.'

There have been reports of the Japanese and a treaty with terms they have refused to agree to. But war? I was unaware it was imminent…

His demeanour changes once more and an impish grin settles on his full lips. 'Yours might be the last charming face I ever see. I could be dead by Sunday, carved on the battlefield like a stag after the hunt...'

'Stop this at once!' I raise my voice and hold up my hand to silence him. 'How dare you speak of death with such carelessness! Do you have any idea what it is like, to lose the one you love? No, because when it comes to war, men like you see only excitement and adventure—the thrill of the conquest! Every man's death is a woman's source of pain.'

My vehemence shocks me. But with the threat of war on our doorstep, I'm reminded of the great cost of life.

Vorontov's expression is condescending as he reaches for my hands. 'Your Highness, I was not aware the loss of your husband pained you so greatly.' His tone is mocking.

I realise, of course, that he speaks of Nikolai Zolotov. Not Georgiy. I step back, and a chill sweeps me from head to toe.

'I was acquainted with your late husband, in ways in which I expect you are unaware. I did in fact envy him his good fortune. Quite the prize for a man such as he. A beautiful bride and a fine healthy son—'

'How dare you.' I walk away, only to find I am boxed in at the end of the stables. 'To speak ill of the dead is in poor taste.'

'Your Highness, I apologise for my indiscretion and any offence caused. Perhaps I was ill informed.'

'Indeed Lieutenant, yet I doubt your apology is sincere. You are forward and insolent. Speak plainly. What exactly do you imply?'

'It is of no importance. Shall we join the others?' He raises his elbow to escort me and I ignore it.

'I demand to know.'

He turns with a grin and arms folded across his chest. '*Demand*, do you?' His eyebrows raise and he leans against the wall, still blocking the narrow pathway. I feel the heat from his body in the confines. 'And what if I refuse your demands?'

A ripple of uncertainty pulses through my body as we hold each other in a defiant stare. The scent of horseflesh and cigar exudes from his clothing and mingles in the cool air.

Before I have a chance to read the change in his eyes, he steps towards me and gently touches my cheek. I'm caught like a child staring at a firefly, drawn into the light in his eyes. I hold my breath as his lips quiver. I'm sharpened with desire—a flicker of heat bursts from my feminine centre to spike higher in a delightful sensation I haven't felt for some time. This man gets under my skin, and while my head tells me to stop, my body refuses to obey.

The warmth of his breath touches my lips but I pull back in a flash of clarity. Does Voronov assume that as a widow I am powerless to deter his pursuit? My chest tightens. I panic as the fear of losing my liberty again passes before my eyes. I lash out and beat his chest with a fist. 'Leave me alone!'

He steps back with surprise painted across his face. 'Your Highness, I assure you, I would never hurt you!' He rakes a hand through his hair and bows before retreating.

I turn away from him.

'Tatya!' Olga sings from the doorway. 'We are ready to leave.'

I straighten my skirt and march towards her without a backward glance.

'You're as pale as a ghost, Tatya. Are you feeling well?' Olga asks as Kulikovsky helps her into her saddle.

'It is nothing,' I dare Vorontov to speak. His face is ashen beneath his tan. I do my best impression of a cheerful smile.

Kulikovsky shakes Vorontov's hand. 'I'll see you back at the garrison tomorrow.'

Olga braves a smile as the captain gallops away.

Vorontov is silent as he assists me into the saddle, but I ignore both the man and the question in his eyes.

'Let us be off.' Olga turns her mount to the gates and trots ahead.

I feel Vorontov's eyes on my back as we leave the stables. When he reins his horse next to mine the heat of his body stifles me. I'm not sure I have the patience for him or his cryptic remarks. But I make an effort for Olga's sake.

My mood lightens as we ride into the breeze, taking the route along the Tsar's Path, a horizontal pathway linking palaces of the nobility beneath the shade of vase-shaped hornbeam trees. We pass the Gothic-style *Schwalbennest* that hovers on the edge of a clifftop overlooking the ocean, like a fairy tale castle in a Grimm brothers' tale. In the distance lie the ruins of a Grecian-style temple on the crest of the mountain.

When we reach the sundial, we dismount to investigate crudely carved artefacts within sight of the pathway. I kneel beside a broken tile the colour of an autumnal leaf.

'Will anyone remember us one hundred years from now?'

'What morbid humour you have brought with you today!' Olga growls.

Rough-hewn household tools and burial holes remain beside the walls of an ancient fortress. I sigh and replace the tile on the grass. 'How could people leave their lives behind like this?' The feeling of loss and destruction are evident.

'They moved away or died. Who knows the reason?'

'Perhaps they were driven from their land by usurpers.' Vorontov takes hold of the horses. 'Or were left with no choice.'

Olga's eyes dance with mischief. 'Do you ever remember your place, Vorontov?' Her pout makes me smile. Olga's constant good humour is a tonic.

'My apologies, Your Highness.' Despite the brief bow of his head, Vorontov's deference is insincere.

We return to the path and he trots beside me, leaving distance between us.

'Your Highness—'

'Not a word, Lieutenant.' I refuse to speak of what has occurred between us—I suspect the man is someone I cannot trust. There is mystery to him, and together with the knowledge that he is a rogue and a womaniser, I would be sensible to avoid him.

Suddenly he looks up. He holds my gaze with the same hungry stare that penetrated my resolve when I first met him at the Winter Palace. Tiny hollows draw in the corners of his mouth. I grasp my reins tightly, discomfited by the sense that I am the fawn of a musk deer stalked by a wolf—all the reasons to avoid him come flooding back to me.

Olga takes up her chattering, unaware of our silent exchange. We ride to the edge of the village and skirt around it until we reach the seclusion of a protected clearing. A fine trail of smoke signals life beyond a dense copse of spruce; a narrow path leads towards a scattering of huts. We hand our horses into Vorontov's care, and Olga instructs him to find them water.

'I insist you reconsider, Imperial Highness.'

Olga holds up her hand.

A scowl of dissatisfaction appears on his face. How apt his family name is. Vorona, the crow, and like the predator, he is lurking over our shoulders.

'We are merely peasants from a neighbouring village, Ilya Petrovich, nothing more. Wait here for our return.' She lifts her head, daring him to refute her instructions. 'And not another word.'

With a grunt he leaves us.

Our disguises are hidden beneath our riding attire and we squirm out of our layers. The freedom of movement in my simple peasant dress worn without petticoats or stays feels strangely playful. I run a hand down the calico, much cooled by the lighter fabric. But my excitement is tinged with caution at the illicit nature of our quest.

'You do realise we'll be sent back to St Petersburg if discovered?' I warn.

The look on Olga's face is comical. 'Darling Nicky will pretend to be cross but then he will forgive me, Tatya. We played games such as this as children, you know.' Her eyes widen as her voice elevates. 'One day, Mama caught us hiding in the corner of a storeroom. Dear Georgiy was wearing one of Nanny's aprons, pretending to be the wise woman, while Nicky and I waited patiently for our fortunes to be told.'

'I can imagine your games.' I smile at the excuse to speak of him. 'Georgiy Alexandrovich had a fine sense of humour.'

'Indeed. But do you know what happened next? Instead of scolding us, Mama laughed and sat down to join us!'

'I expect Georgiy found it intriguing too. He was a great one for secrets.' I swallow a lump in my throat.

'Yes, he was.' Olga frowns. 'Even after all these years, you can't imagine how much I miss him, Tatya.'

She allows me to draw her into a hug, and I'm grateful she cannot see my face. Nothing can erase his loss or replace the plans that we had for the future.

'Now, let us make ourselves ready.'

We hide our identities behind brightly embroidered traditional headscarves and make our way down the grassy path towards the shepherd's huts. As we approach, a group of children look up. Their clothing, flashes of scarlet, russet and daffodil yellow, is vivid against the thriving greenery of the forest, like players on a stage. The tallest girl stops and shades a hand over her eyes. A moment later they turn away and return to their games.

Olga beckons a grubby faced boy and places a few kopeks into his hand. When she whispers her request, his smile reveals several missing teeth, and he skips off without hesitation. We wait, surrounded by the scent of pine from the forest, while the floral sweetness of wildflowers and juniper abounds from meadow grasses. I begin to feel drowsy in the heat of the day.

Just as we think the boy has forgotten us, he appears between the trees and signals for us to follow. He leads us to a dilapidated cottage set apart from the village. Outside, an old woman is seated on a fallen log, drawing a stick through the charcoal remains of a fire. Hard life has ravaged her face. Her skin is lined and weathered, brown and roughened from toiling the land and its harsh elements.

Olga's hand grips mine as we await her invitation. The woman squints into the sunshine and tenders a toothless smile, reaching for the payment with trembling fingers. She sniffs it greedily and runs the currency between thumb and forefinger, as if doubting the authenticity. Then in a flash, she pushes it into the apron she wears over her *sarafan* and signals for us to sit.

We crouch as she shouts instructions in a guttural Russian dialect I barely comprehend. A black-flecked mirror is positioned to reflect a portion of the ground between us. Nearby are two plates. One holds a few grains of seed while water is ladled from the pot alongside her into the other.

The boy reappears holding a squawking rooster firmly under his arm while a second boy dangles a white hen by its legs a short distance away. I hold my breath.

The woman takes the rooster and pins him in her strong arms until he settles. Slowly she releases him and signals for the hen to be freed in the same way. She holds up a hand to warn us to be silent. Olga's fists are clenched to her chest, nervously awaiting the outcome of the test. I pray she receives the answer she seeks.

The birds scramble and flap their wings, screeching and startling as they shy away from their reflections in the mirror. We watch anxiously to see which direction the rooster will take. He lets out a cry and leaps towards the hen, but quickly changes course and scurries instead towards the plate of water.

The old woman looks up. 'Your man likes the drink,' she says to Olga. 'I suspect he likes women too. But he loves you. He is not as bad as some.' She closes her eyes. 'Life will be difficult, the travel, the distance... but you will end a long life together. The weaker man will step away without a fight.' She finishes with a short nod and folds her arms.

The woman's eyes are glassy, and the whites are bloodshot. Despite the warmth of the sun, the hairs rise on my arms as she fixes her stern glare on me. It chills me to the bone.

Mirror in hand she shoos away the chickens and beckons us to follow her into a hut that reeks of fetid cabbage and the stale stench of sweat. I try not to show my distaste, covering my nose discreetly with the ends of my scarf. She seats herself before the mirror in the darkest corner of the room and lights a candle.

The woman stares at her reflection, and a swirling sensation builds inside me. The effect is mesmerizing. I'm frozen in place while she seeks answers within the mirror. Olga reaches for my hand and squeezes it tightly.

Suddenly the woman gasps, her gnarled hands fly to her chest and then grip the fabric over her heart. The candle hisses and extinguishes. Her stare captures mine in the mirror's reflection.

'Death surrounds you,' she hisses, 'and blood... much bloodshed.'

Olga gulps and covers her mouth. The heat in the room is oppressive, yet I still shiver.

'You, with the golden hair,' she points a crooked finger at me, poking the air three times. 'I see love and death, and a man who will never be free from the past.' She glances sideways. 'Help set him free.'

I shake my head. I've already lost the man I loved. I have no wish for another.

'Death rides on his shoulder. Your token of good luck is needed to protect those you hold dear. One is your past and one is your future—you must protect them.'

We leave the clearing wordlessly, the woman's voice ringing in my head. My chest feels tight as we return to our horses, tethered beneath a sprawling oak. Is Misha's life in danger?

I ignore Vorontov and ride ahead, leading the group in silence with my eyes fixed firmly on the path. Olga avoids engaging me in conversation, the excitement of her future happiness somewhat overshadowed by the sense of impending doom in mine. By the time we return to the palace, we are subdued and pensive.

That night, I dream of running barefoot in a meadow of wildflowers, with my hair loose and free and Georgiy by my side. The sun sets over the fortress of St Petersburg, and light touches the Cathedral of Saint Peter and Saint Paul, the final resting place of all the Russian emperors since Peter the Great.

Across the Neva, a gilded spire glimmers above the domes as twilight bathes buildings of cerulean and ivory in amber rays and paints the city in a band of colour.

The scene changes. The plangent strains of a requiem sing out from the Church of the Saviour of the Spilled Blood, the traditional influence of both east and west evident in the architecture's Russian design. A dark cloud hovers overhead.

I shudder. The church was built on the site where my grandfather, Tsar Alexander II, was assassinated.

Next, I'm standing alone watching the moon rise over the river. The earth tremors as a hussar arrives on horseback; I hold out my hand for his message. I fear the loss before I see it. Slung across the horse like a sack of rye grain is a body with evidence of an enemy sabre slashed across his back. To be struck down from behind in battle is an act both unchivalrous and despicable.

I dare to glance at my beloved once more, but he disappears, and instead all I see is the face of my precious son.

26

St Petersburg

One joyous evening, bells peal in celebration across the city. After ten long years, the wait is over. Alexei Nikolaevich Romanov, the Tsarevich of Russia is born. Our prayers for the continuation of the direct imperial line of Romanov rule have been answered.

I do not complain when we are called on less by the imperial family. No one is more grateful for his birth than I. Now Misha is freed from the burden of position in the line of succession, we may retreat into a more peaceful life.

Several months later, Olga Alexandrovna calls on me, her distress and lack of composure apparent. Once behind closed doors her demeanour crumbles and sends a stab of fear into the pit of my stomach.

'Whatever is the matter?' I take her hands and ease her into a chair. My thoughts run immediately to the numbers of men lost to the Japanese and talk of sending forces to Persia. 'Is it your captain?'

'No, thank the saints, he is well.' Olga shakes her head. 'I have come from Mama. Oh, Tatya, it is terrible news! It concerns little Alexei...'

I see it written on her face. Rumours of doctors that come and go from the palace have been whispered everywhere from salons to servants. My stomach somersaults as Olga presses a handkerchief to her mouth.

'I cannot tell you the number of physicians the Tsarevich has seen. I took to the gardens with my nieces, just to avoid the dear child's pitiful cries. The screams of pain. *Oh, Tatya!*'

I take a deep breath; little in St Petersburg is kept secret. *The Tsarevich will not live a long life.*

'Only the family's inner sanctum is permitted to know the truth,' Her eyes fill with tears, and I reach for her hands. 'His agony is cast over us like a dark shadow of fate looming in the distance.'

'Hush, dear. I'm sure they will find physicians who will heal him—'

'But you see, Alix is ignoring serious discussions or diagnoses regarding the cause of his illness. It's the same blood disease that took the lives of her brother and uncle. It appears to run through her family. And Tatya, there is no cure.'

I press my hand to my chest to hold down the rising fear. 'Indeed, it is a tragedy.' I avert my gaze.

'There will be squabbles amongst us. With no heir, there are those in the family who will jostle and demand power. It's too late for Alix, for another child. She did not cope well this last pregnancy. Whatever will become of us?'

It is true. Alix suffered significantly. Several physicians have attended her since, with her back giving her great discomfort.

But Alix is not my concern.

'Olga dear. I will see to some tea.' A wave of nausea swells inside me. I struggle to my feet and make my escape.

Leaning against the cold metal door does nothing to resolve the trepidation that courses through my body. If the Tsarevich is suffering from haemophilia—what does it mean for my son? I thought we had escaped the bonds of rule. But the Imperial grip squeezes Misha tighter still—.in fact, nothing will change if Alexei fails to live.

I reflect on the conflicting mood on the day of Alexei's birth; perhaps I should have taken more notice, the signs were there. Russia's collective joy was somewhat subdued, following poignant reports from the North China Sea that the Japanese had destroyed a considerable number of ships from the Russian fleet, and the commander of the Imperial Navy was killed on the flagship, regrettably named, *The Tsarevich*.

That night, I snuggle Misha to my breast, breathing the sweetness of honeysuckle on his soapy clean skin, the fresh scent of the darling boy whom I love more dearly than I imagined possible.

Whatever the future holds, I will face it with him. I will find a way. The safety and health of my son—Georgiy's son—is all that matters.

October 1906

Their Imperial Majesties increasingly demand seclusion. While Alix's disdain for our numerous pageants and ceremonies is well versed, it is rare, indeed, for the Tsar to neglect his duty. He has not been seen in public for months; people begin to wonder if the empire rules itself and question why he ignores his responsibilities and disregards the court.

Gossip throughout St Petersburg continues as speculation about the health of the Tsarevich grows. The fact that Alexei is desperately ill is the worst kept secret of all. Alix commands physicians from every part of the globe to heal her son. *I would do the same for mine.* She is more devout than ever in her prayers and appeal to God, and when God does not heed her prayers she returns to the old practises, seeking help from mystics and spiritualists who profess to know all the higher truths.

'Have you heard?' Olga is decidedly bright as we walk the gardens one morning.

'About what exactly?'

'The Black Peril have discovered a new spiritualist,' her eyes widen mischievously, 'and *we* are invited to attend their salon to meet him.'

Known as the Black Peril, the two daughters of the King of Montenegro who married grand duke brothers, hold the most outlandish soirees of all the nobility. They are known for gathering an oddity of people from all walks of life to entertain the ladies of the court.

'His name is Father Grigori and he's a monk from the farthest province of the land. They also say he's a brute who smells like a mule and curses like a peasant. He *is* one, after all. But it appears he has fascinated and bewitched the ladies.'

Olga looks over her shoulder. 'You will come to meet the mysterious mystic, won't you? Simply *everyone* is going to be there. Do say you will?'

'Is it absolutely necessary?' I turn to her, shading us under my parasol. 'What are this man's special powers?'

I wonder if he's accompanied by a performing troupe of monkeys from the Orient or recites poetry in the language of the Zulu warriors. There's no doubt he is another charlatan here to fleece the bored ladies of St Petersburg of their time and coin.

'It is said he communed with God and helped a man to walk again. It appears he can heal all kind of ills. They say his powers are magical.'

'I was hoping to spend time with Misha after his lessons. His English is progressing nicely, and I promised we would read together.'

'We will be back in plenty of time, Tatya. I promise.'

Olga and I arrive at the stylish Palace of Znamenka, home of Grand Duchess Militza. The mood is electric as we enter the parlour where the women giggle and jostle for position and crowd around a man in the centre of the room as though he is the flower and they the thorns.

'This is him? Judging by the sisters you'd think him a saint.'

'Militza insists he is particularly charmed when it comes to improving the health of women, those with...the more feminine ailments. Nervous conditions and intimacy complaints.' Olga widens her eyes in exaggeration.

'Do you believe what they say?'

Tall and dark haired, he wears the full thick beard of men of religion that resembles a hawthorn bush, and his gaze is a piercing ice-blue. While I'm surprised by the slovenly appearance of a man of God, I'm more dismayed by the behaviour of the ladies prancing about him like prize thoroughbreds at a military parade.

'With luck he will invoke his magic on my husband and encourage him to leave me for good.' She grasps my hand.

Despite Olga's years of petitioning, the Tsar still refuses to permit her divorce. I would love for her to find happiness and have a child of her own. Perhaps that is why she is so interested to meet this mystic.

Princess Militza drags us closer to the group, and he regards us from one to the other, until his eyes settle back on me.

'Come closer, my exquisite bird,' Father Grigori pats a seat close to him, almost eager in his attempts to shoo away a young baroness who glares at me as though I have won a prize. 'What is it that ails you?'

He strokes my arm and I shudder as fingers scratch like talons through the fabric of my sleeve. There is a distinct stench about him; that of a festering wound and overwatered soil. His skin is leathered and dirty, although it surprises me later to overhear that he is a frequent visitor to the bathhouses of St Petersburg.

I lift my head and meet his stare. Again, I shiver. I can't wait to leave but feign a carefree tone. 'Nothing at all, Father Grigori. I am merely here to enjoy the company of my friends. But I thank you for your concern.'

He rises when I stand; I am tall, but he towers above me. I am grateful for my gloves when his rough hands rub mine between them. 'Bless you, my little bird, for indeed the Lord watches over you and sees your challenges. You have a charm in your possession. I feel its presence now. In time, one who holds it will reveal the truth.'

'Is that so?' I smile, coolly. 'I'm afraid I do not recall one,' I answer with little conviction.

He draws me closer and his sour breath washes over me. I hold my breath, afraid of what I read in his eyes. 'When your soul needs cleansing, as all souls do, be certain to call for my assistance, Princess. I will cast out the pain inside and release you.' He frees me with a raucous laugh and turns to the next woman.

That night I scrub my body so hard that I almost break the skin. The man has shaken me with his mocking eyes—as though he is all seeing, all knowing. Not only does he commune with God, but I sense the power of another, more evil spirit. I will certainly avoid him in future.

I remove my brooch and hide it in a tiny box behind my book of poetry. If Father Grigori Rasputin does have magical powers, I cannot risk him knowing more than he presumes. Any link to Georgiy exposes us to danger and is a far greater risk to Misha than me.

JEAN

27

Melbourne, 1983

Jean's thoughts are foggy; she's barely able to focus on orders for the summer range. All this time she's been waiting for the right moment to tell Rick—about her—about Michael—but how does she explain *this*? Her situation is repulsive.

It was a mistake to have skipped the last few AA meetings. She could use the support of people who understand the difficulties of facing life's roadblocks and speedhumps. But Hazel's sinister revelation spins in her head like the revolving doors of the State Bank building. This is far more complex. And she'd been doing so well.

Fight it, Jean. Fight the feeling. The temptation to drink and wash away the shame is creeping in. She can't afford to let the beast take hold of her.

With a second coffee on her desk, she rifles through the drawers one more time. Her notebook is missing and it's the second time she's misplaced it in as many months. It must be here. Apparently, (according to lunchroom consensus) forgetfulness is one of the side effects of menopause. It's out of character for her to be so careless; now more than ever, it's essential she focus on method and routine.

Jean closes her eyes but all she sees is a bottle of vodka. She imagines the cool burn in her throat and relief as it hits the spot; the veil of calm over her consciousness and the feeling of weightlessness. The temptation to step out of her world and forget. *No!* It won't help. No amount of booze will wash away the stain of her birth.

While checking the filing cabinet for the third time, a commotion sounds from the Style Salon. Jean hurries to the reception area to discover the problem. An irate customer has baled up one of the younger members of Jean's team and is pointing holes in the air with her finger.

'I said,' the set of her jaw demands attention, 'I demand to speak to the management at *once*!'

Two women seated in the waiting area look up from their magazines and frown. With a grateful glance at Jean, the stylist hurries them away to their consultations.

'How may I help, madam?' Jean addresses the customer politely, working through the letters of the alphabet as she tries to recall her name.

She lifts her chin and scowls, thrusting a bag branded with the store's logo at Jean. '*Mrs* Di Maggio!'

'Of course, Mrs Di Maggio. What have we here?'

'I came to you for assistance and you forced me to purchase these dreadful things. They are unsuitable! You call this high-class service? It is not good enough.'

It's times like this Jean wishes she were in her twenties again—in the days of the House of Merivale with its cutting-edge sixties style. It was far more pleasant dealing with free-spirited bohemians and hippies than pandering to self-obsessed women with airs of entitlement.

'I apologise, Mrs Di Maggio. Please, let me take a look.'

The customer picks a piece of fabric between two fingernails and drops it as though it's poison. Her heavily ringed fingers ball into fists on the counter. 'This is hideous—it looks like I'm wearing a sack. Credit them back to my account. All of them.'

'May I offer you a seat, and perhaps a tea or coffee? Let me see what we can arrange.'

This is the last thing she needs today. Jean sends Summer to fetch a coffee and keep Mrs Di Maggio calm while she sorts through the bag. There's no doubt the evening dress has been worn; the scent of perfume lingers. And the purchases were made outside of the standard exchange period. Jean's expert touch notes the texture of matted fibres indicating the other pieces have been washed. Even if returned to stock they can't be re-sold.

'I insist upon a complimentary appointment—with you—the one in charge.' Mrs Di Maggio refuses to let Jean out of her sight. The counter is all that separates Jean from the invasion of her personal space.

Every customer is important, but this woman believes her needs surpass everyone else's to prove her importance. Jean curses under her breath. From experience, she knows it will make things difficult unless the store bows to her demands.

'The evening dress was a complete disaster! You will refund it *at once*.'

Jean ushers Mrs Di Maggio into the lounge as Summer returns with a coffee and a selection of petit fours, served with her winning supermodel smile.

'Mrs Di Maggio, this is Summer Harrington. I hope you won't mind if she assists me today. As she was previously an international model, Summer has intimate experience with European fashion trends as well as our local designer brands.'

Mrs Di Maggio appears suitably appeased to have a woman of note fawning over her.

'Why don't you discuss your preferences with her while I find something special for you.' Jean mouths a 'thank you' as Summer ushers her into the changing room. 'Shall we begin with evening gowns?'

For the next hour, they bend to Mrs Di Maggio's demands, and smile politely as she insists on trying on gowns from the bridal couture collections of Marianna Hardwick and Linda Britten. When she gravitates to a boxy jacket by international giant Yves Saint Laurent in a shade of puce that makes her skin look sallow, Jean reminds herself that the customer is always right.

Finally, convinced to try an elegant Carla Zampatti pantsuit featuring flowing pleated culottes, Mrs Di Maggio lifts her head, visibly delighted. The silky copper-coloured outfit is embellished with sequinned motifs on the wide padded shoulders. It's perfect for her.

'I feel like a supermodel too,' she gushes and struts in front of the full-length mirror, oblivious to the two customers whose view she has blocked. 'Yes, I'll take it. Wrap it up.'

'We'll meet you at the desk when you're ready,' Summer smiles. Jean rolls her eyes in relief as the dressing room door closes.

A few minutes later Mrs Di Maggio walks over the expensive pile of silk and satin pooled on the floor and exits the dressing room after dropping one last dress on top. The flick of a hand at Summer says, *pick it up; that's what you're paid for.*

Jean grimaces as the refuse is scooped up and empty hangers retrieved. Battling her inner turmoil is hard enough; she swallows the lump in her throat. This woman has fast outstayed her welcome.

'Mrs Di Maggio. I'm delighted we've found you something suitable.' She takes a breath, 'Unfortunately, we're unable to offer a full refund on the returns. Several of the items you've returned have been worn and—'

'I BEG your PARDON! I have returned them. What are you accusing me of? I *demand* a full refund.'

Jean offers a sympathetic smile. 'I can offer a thirty per cent discount on your purchases today.'

'What is this?' Mrs Di Maggio's accent is more pronounced as her voice rises. Customers in the vicinity stop and stare. 'No, no, no. This is NOT what I expected from an establishment such as this. It would *never* happen in Europe, would it?' She looks to Summer pointedly.

'It's a difficult position, I agree,' begins Summer, with characteristic tact and diplomacy, 'but if an item is not returned with the tags in place and in original condition—'

'I will speak to the management! The *man* in charge.' Mrs Di Maggio stands with one hand fixed on her hip.

Jean presses her lips together as heat courses her body. Not today. Not now… She would prefer to settle this without Ross Milton.

'I'm sure that won't be necessary,' she evens her tone—the first rule of dealing with disgruntled customers. 'How can we assist you in a way that will be satisfactory? What do you suggest?'

Mrs Di Maggio lets out an effusive sigh. 'A full credit and thirty per cent off the price of my pantsuit. This is what you offered!' Her glare is unwavering.

'I'm afraid that's impossible.' Jean hands her the original purchases with a tempered smile. 'But you may keep these.'

Her pout would out-do a two-year-old. Jean stands firm. She has already worked the figures as far in the customer's favour as possible. When Jean politely suggests that she has already been extended a discount beyond the usual bounds of DJ's returns policy, Mrs Di Maggio finally shrugs and leaves.

But as she walks through the glass doors, her parting glance at Jean is worthy of a vigilante set on retaliation.

28

The next day, lethargy drags at Jean's body, and she can't stop the ache. She'd like nothing more than to stay in bed with the fluffy doona pulled over her head and music playing softly on the clock radio in the background. But with Hazel's bombshell, and yesterday's customer's diva performance, it's best she keeps busy. It's too quiet at home, and isolation and sleep-deprivation are recognised triggers for recovering alcoholics. In her current frame of mind, she's vulnerable. She fought and won the fight the day before, and she'll do it again.

After her tea break, Jean throws her handbag into the cupboard in her office and sighs when she sees the message directing her to go straight to Ross Milton's office.

Debbie pops her head around the door. 'Jean.' She points to the Post-it note on the desk and raises her eyes to the ceiling. 'It's about the trouble yesterday. Mr Milton insisted on knowing which of our staff were present with that customer—Mrs Di Maggio? I'm so sorry,' she shrugs, 'I wasn't sure what to say.'

'It's all right, Debs. I'll handle it. You've done the right thing.' Jean pats her arm and turns to collect a folder from the small filing cabinet. Summer's not in to corroborate her account, but Jean had taken the precaution of making notes of the details in the same way she would report on a workplace accident. While her actions weren't strictly by the book, Jean did what was best under the circumstances. Milton will understand the dilemma when she explains it. Part of her role as manager is to use her initiative.

'Jean. Come in.' He points to the chair opposite with a typically smug look on his face. He swivels the wand on the slimline Venetians and secures their meeting from view.

Jean perches on the edge of the chair like a schoolgirl on her first visit to the principal's office. She takes a deep breath.

'I've had a customer complaint about your behaviour. I just need your version of events. Odiel Di Maggio is a delightful woman but you've really ruffled her feathers. It's not how we do things here—not at all. Now, tell me from the beginning.'

He leans back in his chair and rests his fingers into a bridge on his rotund stomach. Under the fluorescent lighting, his dyed hair appears a washed-out orange. Jean notices tiny scabs on his scalp; a series of flaking crochet-hook holes, reaching from his side-part and receding hairline to the mottled dry skin across his forehead.

She takes a breath and explains.

'What happened to the stock she originally bought?'

'The garments couldn't be sold. They had been worn and washed. I gave them back to her.' Jean frowns.

'Pretty difficult to prove our position if you don't have the goods. Who authorised the substantial discount on the purchase? It was new season stock.'

'I did. It was the fairest margin I could offer. As you would understand, she's not entitled to a refund or a replacement for worn goods. There are no exact measures for a situation like this—'

'So, you went rogue, making it up as you went along? You gave her the garments *and* a discount. Far more than you are authorised to offer.'

Jean presses her lips together. What could she have done differently? Perhaps she *had* been too hasty to be rid of the woman.

'And now we've been forced to refund the original purchases too.' He sits forward.

'But that's ridiculous!'

'Well, she's got some pretty big names in her circle. I'm not willing to mess with her. I don't know what you were thinking, Jean. This is what we pay you the big bucks for.'

Jean swallows down a retort. Women managers are still only paid half of what the men earn.

'I tried to make the customer happy, but she was making quite a scene and the salon was full of new clients at the time. Under the circumstances it was the best I could do. It was damage control, Ross.' Jean breathes deeply to settle her anger. What did he expect? 'I did my best. We all did.'

'Listen. Just apologise to the old bird. I don't want you to fuck it up for me. She knows all the right people and has promised me a ticket to Flemington. Even gave me a tip about the horse she's got running in the Cup. We had quite the lengthy chat—'

'You know what it's like when a customer decides they're not happy with a purchase.' Jean forces a smile. 'I honestly don't believe she would have accepted anything we suggested in the end.'

'Well, something's got her goat that's for sure. She did say you were a bit too big for your boots,' he leans back again, 'and that you made certain judgment calls about her character. Sounds to me there was a little prejudice involved, given her background. She suggested as much—'

'Not at all!' Jean is affronted. 'I can assure you I made no reference to her nationality. Nor would I.' She pulls back the strength of her voice, lowering her tone. 'You wouldn't have stood for her behaviour—'

'You're wrong there. First rule of retail, Jean. The customer is always right. But more of a concern,' he looks at her pointedly, 'is the alcohol she detected on your breath. That, Jean, is unacceptable. In fact, it comes damn close to an immediate termination of employment.'

What? 'I assure you I *had not* been drinking.' Jean's hands are clammy as she grips her folder tighter.

'Well, that's harder to prove. But we both know you have form, Jean. I've heard all about your past exploits. You're no saint are you, love? Stories from the old days make their way down here too, you know. Staff talk. Especially when the subject is juicy enough—' He lifts his eyebrows and leans in, addressing her breasts. A leer spreads his lips thin.

The ghost of a memory walks down her spine.

'You're not a bad sort… for your age. I daresay there've been any number of beneficiaries of your talents over the years. But having someone like that as head of any department here at David Jones doesn't make for a good bedfellow—pardon the pun. Our objective is to make money, not lose it by pissing off influential customers.'

The sound of blood rushes through Jean's ears. 'What exactly did Mrs Di Maggio say?'

'Forget the details. But your little *problem*—well, if anyone knew it, wouldn't be a good look for us, would it?' He leans forward. 'We don't need shit like *that* getting out.'

Jean closes her eyes.

'Must be a bloody nightmare, eh? With your brother and the winery? For an alcoholic?' He slides her missing notebook across the desk.

'Where did you get this?' Heat flames her face.

'You've got some serious shit going on. *Alcoholics Anonymous?* I know you used to sink a few with the boys, but this is the real deal.'

Shame and disgust billow in Jean's stomach. She'd tried so hard.

'It's highly unprofessional to leave personal information like this laying around for customers to see. Mrs Di Maggio found it in her changing room and questioned the kind of people we employ. It's not a good look at all.'

Nothing Jean can reply will take away the hurt of his accusations. She *is* an alcoholic. Not just sometimes. *For life*. She bites her lip to hold back the tears.

'Listen. If you fuck up like this again, you're out. As it is, the loss on the merchandise will be taken out of your wages.' The contempt in his expression freezes her in her seat.

'Yes, Ross. I understand—' Jean is seething.

'Of course, there is another way. I *could* inform the GM of the increase in your sales figures for last month. It might save your skin for a bit longer.'

Jean holds her tongue and clenches her fists in her lap.

'You owe me, Jean. All this shit is stressing me out.' Milton's voice has an edge of warning. She looks up. 'How about you be a good girl and make it go away.'

It's as though the next few seconds appear in freeze frames. It isn't until she hears the sound of a zipper being opened that recognition dawns.

'Or I can make the complaint go away for good. No one has to know. Just cop a mouthful of this—' His expression is ruddy and eager and his cheeks sag like the jowls of a bulldog, but his eyes are hard and cold. 'Come on love, our secret—'

'You're DISGUSTING!' Jean staggers to her feet. She has to get out. 'How dare you!' She grits her teeth. 'How DARE you treat me, or *any* woman like that! I'll report you to the GM.'

'Sure, you can, but then I'll explain that you're an alcoholic. I'll show him the choice pages I photocopied from your book that talk all about your sordid little secret,' he smirks. 'Your social life must be pretty shot if all you have to look forward to is your Wednesday AA meetings.' He chuckles. 'Might be a great place to pick up a root with a no-hoper or two though?'

Ross leans back in his seat. 'If you don't want to play the game, I'll tell him how you insisted I cover up your fuck-up. How you've been leading me on since we came down from Sydney. How you *made a scene* and threw yourself at me. I'm pretty sure he'll have my back, so you're fucked, Jean, either way. Now get on with it!' He indicates his crotch.

Jean's heart is racing, and the walls are closing in. First Hazel's bombshell and now this. The room begins to spin. *I have to get out of here.*

'You repulse me!' She grasps the door handle and swings it open wide. 'No woman deserves to be spoken to like this—your wife, your secretary and *definitely* not your colleagues! Working for you is the last thing any woman with a shred of decency should do! You can stick your job where the sun doesn't shine.'

'Good riddance to you too, you stuck up old bitch. You're dried up. Go get a drink, you bloody pisshead!'

Jean staggers back to her office, barely registering the echo of her feet on the pristine tiles. She grabs her bag and slams the door behind her, holding her shame close and ignoring the wide-eyed stares of her girls. She shouldn't have lost control. She let him get under her skin.

'Jean! Whatever is wrong?' Debbie calls. 'Please, what can I do to help?'

'I'm done, Debs. Finishing up.' Jean holds up her hands.

'What?'

'It's okay. I have to leave. Have to get home....'

The walk to the station seems to take forever. Tension knots her from her head to her shoulders; her mouth is so dry, she can hardly move her lips. She has to make it home before she does something she's bound to regret.

Lowering her eyes, Jean marches past the bottle shop, the same one she has been so proud of ignoring every single day. *No. I won't.*

A man crosses her path, and she stops and closes her eyes. It only takes a few seconds to change her mind. She doubles back and darts inside, holding back a sob. Jean grabs two bottles from the shelf, hating herself for what she is doing but unable to stop the loathing she feels. She slaps a twenty-dollar note on the counter and thrusts the vodka into her knitting bag.

During the journey home, temptation rests on her lap, taunting her with its weight. Her hand cradles her bag like a mother protecting her child. Jean's resolve wavers. She fights the urges for the duration of the journey, debating the voices in her head.

She denies her body's craving, holding off until she's at her front door. Then it swings open and hits the doorstop and she leans back against the cold timber. The twist and crack of the bottle top sets her heart beating faster, and as the clear liquid pours down her throat, relief washes through her veins and drowns her thoughts away.

TATIANA

29

Livadia Palace, 1913

An arid breeze warmed with the scent of gardenia carries the echo of children's laughter throughout the palace gardens. They frolic at play on the lawns, dancing the steps of an imaginary tennis match, and the mood is delightful. Soon they move on to a game of tiggy, dodging the thick trunks of centuries-old fir trees. I smile indulgently and peer into the sunlight with a hand held to my eyes.

My son adores playing tricks. Once he set a live frog on a plate beneath a silver cloche before it was served at tea while another time, Anastasia's face pursed into a grimace as she sipped a glass of fresh juice, flavoured with salt and honey. His father would have been highly amused by his antics.

Grand Duchess Anastasia squeals, and I look up, smiling as a flash of white chases Misha across the grass. How nimble he is, easily staying a step ahead of his favourite cousin. Like the newly birthed Mongolian deer on view in the Alexander Palace animal enclosure, both the fawn and Misha have legs too long for their bodies.

Nearby, the little Tsarevich laughs at their antics, the wheels of his special chair locked into position to avoid movement. His skin has the translucence of a porcelain doll, but his waxy complexion belies his spirit. *Alexei looks frail today*, I think, as the Empress appears in a lavender coloured tea dress. Indeed, I dare not repeat my thoughts aloud.

I rise to greet the Empress and bow my head. She nods and takes up her book, Olga's highly recommended English novel, *A Room with a View*, and reclines on a chaise nearby. I'm content to watch the children. Their games have reached the perimeter of the manicured lawn. I let out a sigh; wouldn't it be wonderful to freeze this moment in time; for Misha's life to remain this tranquil?

'I fear Anastasia admires your son a little too greatly.' The Empress breaks the silence. I notice the line of her lips, the thinly veiled indication of dislike. 'She will learn soon enough what is expected of her. There is no future there. Nicky will never agree to a morganatic match for any of our girls.'

I adjust the lace shawl across my shoulders to shield the sudden chill. Why *would* he agree to it? A first cousin marriage opposes the degrees of consanguinity stated in the Pauline Laws. Yet the added slur debasing Misha's dynastic state is an insult intended to remind me of my place. The Tsar is fully aware Misha is the son of Grand Duke Georgiy Alexandrovich—*and* the great-grandson of an emperor through both his bloodlines. His lineage is pure.

It is safer to ignore rising to her bait. If Misha is afforded more freedom in his life than his parents were granted, I will have done my best for him. He receives an excellent education and has unquestionable connections within the court by vestige of my lineage alone. He is a bright and amiable boy. He will go far, of that I am confident.

'Prince Zolotovsky shows signs of his father's exuberance,' Alix says. 'However, I expect it may do him more harm than good if not curbed.'

He is Romanov, not Zolotov. Once again instead of responding, I smile politely and then carefully choose my reply.

'Indeed. Misha is spirited, as all young boys are inclined to be.' I nod towards the Tsarevich with a smile. Alexei has insisted his faithful sailor guardian, Nagorny, carry him closer to the children. They are hidden behind a fountain and protected by a thick cloak of fir trees. 'I pray the Tsarevich enjoys his continued good health.'

Alexei is armed with a bow and rubber arrow—a weapon he routinely inflicts on the unsuspecting, waiting in stealth for them to come into range. He might be sickly, but has the heart of a lion, combined with the cunning of a snake. Nagorny is his constant companion, guarding Alexei to ensure his safety at all costs—any knock or injury has the potential to cause him grievous harm.

Two years ago, when he almost died from injuries sustained in a fall, the people were finally informed of the gravity of his illness. Ever since, the Empress has become frantic to the point of zealousness in her defence and pursuit of methods to sustain his health.

'The air here is good for us—for Alexei, most of all. Regretfully, we must return to St Petersburg soon. *Our dear friend* believes that given the recent unrest, Cousin Willy will soon make war on us.

'There is news of a disruption with the railways through Serbia. It seems he is his ever-evasive self when it comes to halting Russia's progress.' Alix's attempt at humour does not reach her eyes.

'I expect, if war is the outcome, we must consider further recruitment of suitable young men to follow the call to arms and undertake military training.' She nods towards Misha.

I do not care for this line of discussion. My jaw clenches. A cloud passes the sun and the sky dims for a moment. I stare towards the sea.

'The Kaiser is known to be foolish, reckless at times. Nicky is at his wits end dealing with him.' She lets out a sigh and lies back on the cushions, returning to her book.

A minute later she stops to address me once again. 'Perhaps your son should enter military service immediately. It is necessary for Russia's defences to be prepared. We refuse to be caught off-guard as we were with the Japanese. Don't you agree?'

'Yes, Imperial Majesty.' My body tenses at the mention of war in the same breath as my son. I pray my expression conveys poker-faced resolution. The thought of Misha bearing arms is not something I have anticipated. However, it is foolish to believe military training will be avoided. All Russian noblemen undertake military service; it is their right and obligation. I cannot expect Misha to be excluded.

'It appears he has an affinity with the water. He asked a great many questions of the commander on board the imperial yacht. I mentioned his curiosity to *our dear friend* when he enquired about him.' Her silver eyes are filled with derision as she meets my gaze.

Why is Rasputin asking about my son?

'You must allow me to arrange his entry into the naval academy at Kronstadt to serve as a cadet in his father's regiment. I insist, my dear.'

His father was not a naval officer. My reply tangles in my throat. 'Thank you, Imperial Majesty. You are most thoughtful.'

The children run towards us, and I focus on their shining faces, full of innocence and vitality. Alexei and Nagorny trail behind them.

Misha slows as he approaches the Empress. He stops respectfully and effects a perfect formal bow, as he has been taught.

'Mama, darling,' Anastasia pushes past him and grins. Her hands are cupped around the treasure hidden inside. 'I have a precious gift for you. In truth, Misha found it but—'

'Anastasia Nikolaevna! Where *are* your manners?' The Empress recoils as Anastasia hovers her hands under her mother's nose. 'Take it away and free it beyond the garden. I do not care for your foolishness.' Alix waves her daughter aside with a scowl.

I stare pointedly as Misha looks to me, willing him to read my thoughts. Stay silent. Be respectful.

Anastasia sighs, and turns back to the pathway with her head hung low. There is no doubt she is a mischievous young lady. But the sense of humour she shares with other members of the family is lost on her staid and serious Mama.

'Tell me, young man. You are growing like a reed in the marshland. What age are you now?' The Empress's voice is pure sweetness, but her eyes remain cool.

'Almost thirteen, your Imperial Majesty.' My son smiles so brightly his teeth catch the sunlight, white against his tanned skin.

'Thirteen years old!'

She well knows Misha's age. A stab of fear nudges me. I cannot help that Misha is healthy any more than the Empress can prevent the illness in her son. I well understand why she envies his good fortune. My son is everything hers is not.

'The perfect age to begin your military studies. I will speak to the Emperor and arrange for you to begin as soon as possible. There's no time for chasing butterflies and beetles when Russia has need of accomplished young men to protect us.'

'Yes, Imperial Majesty. I am eager for the opportunity to do my best for the Russian Empire.' Misha's eyes gleam like brilliant sapphires before he drops his gaze. A glow of golden light shines on his face.

Like all young boys he longs for the company of men and talks endlessly of battles and war. But it makes me shudder to see him play at tin soldiers with the Tsarevich, as though war were a nursery game. Men are killed in battle, and I want him kept safe. How can I bear to have him leave me and sent away to the naval academy? The prick of tears rises with my anger.

'There we have it, Tatiana Vladimirovna.' The Empress's voice crackles like ice breaking the Neva in springtime. 'It is settled. When we return to the city I shall speak with the commander in charge and arrange for Misha to commence his studies.'

Misha is so excited that after spilling his drink at tea, he is banished to his room to calm down. But I cannot stay cross with him for long.

'Mama,' he grasps my hands as I bend over him to say goodnight. 'I have always wanted to travel beyond the Russian Empire. Imagine the far-away places I will see in the Imperial Navy! I'll stand on the bridge and command the Tsar's entire fleet one day. Anastasia says she can imagine me with a pipe and a beard and a row of young men in white, swabbing the decks and obeying my every command.'

His cherubic face is changing from child to man before my eyes. His high cheekbones are covered in fine down; his brilliant blue eyes implore me to smile.

'Have you forgotten, darling? I thought you wanted to pursue the arts? You insisted you would paint your own symbolist series?'

After we had viewed the audacious, Jack of Diamonds exhibition earlier in the year, Misha talked for weeks about the artist's talents. The works were astounding with abstract colours and shapes in bright hues that were a far cry from the staid portraiture of the past. The mythology associated with the subject of Kandinsky's works—Saint George and the Dragon—had awakened a passion in my son that surprised me.

Before that, he vowed to own the biggest *pastila* factory in Russia; the fluffy sweet is his favourite, just like his father. Then, he was determined to be an anthropologist on a dig in Egypt, and after helping wash the elephant in the Alexander Palace lake, he suggested he might open his own zoo park.

'It's true, I had intended it, but Anastasia insists she will only marry a man in uniform.' His brow furrows. 'She'll never consider an artist.'

It appears he has taken her at her word.

I cough into my handkerchief. 'You are both a little young to concern yourselves with marriage. Now, enough chatter, *mon chér*. You can read for a time, and I'll see you in the morning.'

His long arms wrap around my neck and I nuzzle into his shoulder, holding back tears with a gulp. He will soon be grown. How long will we have as mother and son before our world moves speedily to the next stage of his life? If I can prevent him from facing life's harsher challenges, then I will have done my part.

With a tender kiss I leave him and pen a note to Nicky. I must speak to him about this nonsense of the naval academy. I refuse to allow Alix to dictate terms to me. I was born a Romanov—and so was my son.

Olga has left us to paint when the Tsar makes his way towards me in the garden the next day. I curtsy, and in reply he kisses my cheeks.

'Your Imperial Majesty,' I lower my eyes, waiting for him to acknowledge my request to meet with him.

'Tatya.' He surprises me with my diminutive, the one used by those closest to me. 'We have no need for formalities today. What is it you wish to discuss? Your allowance, I presume?'

A hot flush rises from my neck to my face. I detest the way I have to ask for assistance and approval in everything I do. 'It is about Misha. The Empress suggested he might study at the naval academy, but it is not what I prefer.'

'Hmmm.' He draws a hand across his jaw, in thought. 'Though it would be an admirable solution for him.'

'Yes, but,' I daren't say anything that provokes antagonism. I want to ask outright for permission for him to be in the same corps as Georgiy was, but bravado leaves me. 'I'm not sure the naval corps is right for his military education. After all, it's common for members of *my* family—that is, our family—' I take a breath. 'Might Misha enter the service of one of the more prestigious regiments? Perhaps the Preobrazensky or Semyonovsky?'

'Indeed, you do have a point.'

He blinks and promptly looks away before lighting his cigarette. 'What about the academy of the Corps des Pages? Then, once he has graduated, he may choose his own regiment.'

Students from the Corps des Pages can easily move into a diplomatic corps, or civil service. Both are considerably safer options and far more suitable for Misha.

I sigh in relief. 'Thank you, Nicky. I am deeply appreciative.'

'No doubt, you will direct him to follow the right path.' He nods with a smile and raises an eyebrow as though he can read my mind.

I see Alix from the corner of my eye and sigh. She is using her parasol as a walking stick, poking holes into the lawn as she marches towards us.

'Tatiana Vladimirovna.' She pivots to direct the Tsar's eyes to her and smiles. 'Come, Nicky. *Our dear friend* has asked us to pray together, all of us.'

This morning Alix was close to tears as Alexei's cries were heard throughout the palace. Father Grigori was immediately sent for. Olga and I had shooed Misha and the girls away and entertained them with games.

'We were just discussing young Prince Zolotovsky. He will join the Corps des Pages once we return to St Petersburg.'

'Nonsense! Not the naval academy? Tatiana? We agreed...'

I lift my head and speak clearly, 'I did not realise the matter was settled, Imperial Majesty. I presumed it was merely one of your many kind suggestions.'

Her face flushes as she reaches for Nicky's arm.

'A far better option for the boy, my dearest.'

I hold back a smile and whisper a prayer of thanks to the saints. It does no good to irritate the empress more than I already do, but inside my heart is joyous.

30

St Petersburg

The St Petersburg season appears busier this year, with more parties and social activities than ever. Tonight, in celebration of Rosalind Brassington's birthday, guests are invited to a banquet in one of the private rooms at the Café de Paris. On this fine June evening, an interesting mixture of personalities gather including a French poet and a famous baritone about to embark on a concert tour of Europe. Several premier musicians have been engaged to provide entertainment and serenade our hostess.

I catch my breath when Ilya Petrovich Vorontov enters the room. Over the years, idle talk spoke of his insubordination during the Russo-Japanese war and being caught *in flagrante* with an unsuitable woman. Some of it, I imagine, is pure fabrication, no more than salacious innuendo, gossiped by wide-eyed ladies of the aristocracy over tea.

The intervening years have done him no harm. In his crimson uniform coat and tight elk-skin breeches, it is difficult to look away. I regret that I was unreasonable and impolite the last time I encountered him. I make a silent promise to behave with civility tonight.

'Your Highness, Miss Brassington.' He appears beside us with a formal bow. Then he kisses our hands in greeting, holding Rosalind's a touch longer. 'What a vision of beauty you are.'

Rosalind flutters her eyelashes coquettishly and after a short discourse, excuses herself from our company to greet the last few guests.

'How delightful to see you again, Princess Zolotova,' Vorontov grins. 'Your beauty remains unchanged, and yet, you seem strangely aloof—'

He stares at me with such naked approval I gasp in surprise. How could I have forgotten the mesmerising quality of his golden eyes?

'Merely an observation, of course.'

I am wrong-footed once again and retort with attack. 'I have no interest in your observations, nor have I need of them.'

His throaty chuckle sends a shiver through my body. 'I hoped by now that you had found a way to break through the restrictions of the imperial circle although as a woman in your position I understand the need for subjugation—'

'Much like your opinions, my position is none of your business. As you are aware, I am a Romanov, and obliged to do my duty.'

'Perhaps…although, I fear it unwise to blindly accept what you are instructed to do when what is happening in front of you is clear enough.'

'Enough, Vorontov.' I am ashamed of my terse tone. Why does this man rile me so? I was to keep my temper in check tonight and instead, have failed miserably. 'Enjoy your evening.'

We are ushered to the table and to my chagrin he is placed to my left. I opt for levity to lighten the mood. 'What can it be that you fear tonight? Merriment? Entertainment? What more do *you* see here?'

He pulls out my chair and bends close to my ear. 'You do not fool me with your grand opinions, Tatiana,' my name growls from his lips, 'you and I are more alike than you choose to admit. We both receive scraps from the table of the imperial family. But I will not always be a servant. And one day—if the rumblings in the rest of Europe are any indication—they will be the same as you and me.'

'The people of Russia hold the imperial family in high regard—'

'Not all are as believing as you. What I have seen, where I have been…I am concerned for our future, and you should be too. Your fine education would have shown you that history can be repeated. In countries across Europe, it has been so. Why should Russia be different?

'Russia *is* different.'

'I disagree. There have been strikes amongst the factory workers for days now, have you not heard? Change *will* come. It is time Russia placed her own best interests ahead of the rest of the world.'

We are the subjects of a powerful empire; the Tsar remains in the hearts of the faithful people of Russia. Where has this come from?

'Cease this talk at once!' I hiss and fold my hands in my lap. 'I do not care for rumours of change or unrest.'

He shrugs. 'Greedy extravagances keep the ruling *boyars* wealthy while peasants in the fields and the factory workers continue to slave for a master with no reward—just as serfs have for centuries.'

I turn away from him and speak to the gentle and earnest young man seated to my right. I find him mildly amusing. As a devotee of the ancient Greek, Plato, he insists he does not believe in the pursuit of pleasure merely for the sake of it. I hold my tongue, looking at the excesses around us.

As the student continues to praise the philosopher's theories, I'm surrounded by the hum of carefree voices. Our behaviour *is* indulgent and some part of me imagines that peace might well be attained by living a life of moderation. I have noticed people on the streets, beggars, people disfigured in factory accidents, but what have I done to assist them? *For shame.* If we should go to war what happens to the weak and the sick? Who will support them?

Once the celebrations are over, the guests decide to continue on and revel into the evening.

'Are you joining us at the theatre?' My new philosopher friend looks to me eagerly; his swift move from Plato's teachings is precisely the reason I resist.

'Do say you will come, Tatya?' Rosalind's sweet voice rings out.

'Not tonight, dear,' I kiss her cheeks and promise to visit soon. 'It's a beautiful evening, and I shall enjoy the walk.'

I signal to the waiter for my cloak, and Ilya Vorontov appears in front of me. 'Perhaps you will permit me to escort you home?'

'Thank you, Ilya, an escort is a sensible idea,' Rosalind smiles. 'Good evening to you both.'

Vorontov stands silent before me, eyes darkening until I break their hold. Heat fills my body as if his very presence warms the room.

Outside the moon is high and bright lights sparkle over the Moyka River as we walk along the embankment. My mood has softened over the course of the evening, and I pull my fur-lined mantle over my gown.

'I love the city when it is like this,' I muse as we stop on the bridge. 'I believe, the people of Russia *do* love the Tsar. He is our ruler. It is God's holy will that he rules our beloved country.'

'Let us agree not to argue,' Vorontov's breath brushes the tips of my ear, 'but if one day the people protest, you would do well to listen. It is in your best interests for you and your son to be ready. I assure you, I have no cause to ever wish you harm.' Golden light flickers and the moonlight is reflected in his eyes. 'You are a woman, and alone—'

'Your arrogance will be the death of you, Ilya Petrovich. You would do well to follow the instructions of your betters, as I do.'

'You think those Romanovs are *better* than you?'

Like a hunted animal I step back. His distinctly male scent and the hint of the forest overpower me. 'Our respect is demanded by our rulers.'

'You are wrong. Respect must be *earned*, Tatushka.'

My stomach clenches at the audacity and intimacy of the derivative.

'The Tsar and Tsarina are man and woman; flesh, the same as you, or me. The monarchy is destined for reform, and it's time the Tsar listened to his people. He is more intent on looking to fight a battle in Europe than facing the unrest raging inside our borders.'

I do not care for the pomp and veneer of palace politics, but I know their imperial majesties take little counsel from the ministers who attempt to attend to cabinet affairs. Have they been so intent on the health of the little Tsarevich that they aren't aware of the plight of the common people? And if we are in danger, how will that affect my son?

'Have you not heard of Napoleon? His country's oppression of the *bourgeoisie* rose like a tide for centuries before his fate was met. The French people rallied behind him and turned against the crowned heads of France. No man, anointed by God or not, should inherit and rule by either divine right or autocracy of power and fail to listen to the voice of his people.'

'That was a hundred years ago! Next, you'll predict a repeat of the 1905 uprising.' I toss my head.

'Do not be foolish in assuming that a repeat is not possible. When flagrant extravagances persist inside the palace with such carelessness that those in power fail to see it, and those outside its walls lose hope, history shows that the people *will* rise up.'

'No! What happened in France will never happen here.' My voice is shaky. I look towards the Winter Palace, and gauge how long it will take me to reach the doors. I walk briskly with hands over my ears, but he strides alongside me.

'One day I will show you how wrong you are. And if they and their kind are cursed—tell me—where does that leave you, Tatiana Vladimirovna? It is time you had as much care for your safety as others do.'

I do not stop until I reach the front steps and leave him at the foot.

Later that night, I replay the conversations from the evening in my head. Vorontov's suggestion that the people of Russia will rebel against the Tsar verges on treason. He is wrong. The people love the Tsar, the Grand Duchesses and the Tsarevich most of all. When I last travelled to Livadia, people lined the roads smiling and waving and showering the imperial train with flowers as it passed the countryside and through each village. Surely, only the radical few agree with him?

Is it dangerous to be cast in the imperial family's close circle? I dare not risk the ire of the mob by mere association. The question is, how do I disentangle myself and my son from their grasp?

31

It's been six months since Misha last had leave from the Court des Pages academy. I had hoped to catch a glimpse of him at the annual troop review where I peered through opera glasses as the hundreds marched on Palace Square. Alas, to no avail.

But tonight, he has been given leave to accompany me to the theatre. Clothed in black from head to toe, my son has grown tall. The gold trim of his cuffs and collar and the spotless white gloves of his dress uniform add to his handsome visage.

In something of a miracle, the grand duchesses are also permitted to attend and ride in the automobile ahead of ours, chaperoned by Olga. She is the perfect aunt and eager to spoil the four sisters who range from thirteen to nineteen. Sadly, the Tsarevich is not included. It is rare for Alexei Nikolaevich to be seen in public these days.

By the banks of the Neva, the avenue of Nevsky Prospect is a frantic display of life and merriment as crowds spill out of the palatial buildings of shell pink and sunny lemon. My beloved St Petersburg is lit by the glow of a white night—the rare weeks encompassing evenings when the sun barely sets and the city appears to forgo sleep. Trams and trolley cars rattle over rough cobblestones as merchants raise their awnings to ready for the nightly trade, and lovers and families enjoy a leisurely promenade before supper, savouring the cool evening breeze. St Petersburg is alive and vibrant; filled with enchanting spirit.

But tonight, there is uncertainty too.

'Why are the troops out this evening, Mama?' Misha exclaims.

'It appears they're on parade, *mon chér*.' I shrug and move closer to him.

Facing the river and standing to attention beneath the opulent stucco pediment that spans the breadth of the Winter Palace, the formations are regaled in spectacular dress uniforms that contrast the pastel exterior.

'It's customary for the troops to parade before the Tsar, but he is at Tsarskoye Selo. Our Emperor should be here. His people expect it.'

'Hush, Misha.' I purse my lips at my son's impertinence, grateful for the hum of the automobile engine. Like all Russians, we must guard our comments to ensure they are never misconstrued.

To change the subject, I point out the equestrian statue that rises above us in Senate Square. The Bronze Horseman rests on a piece of granite so enormous that the magnitude of its message cannot be ignored. As our automobile slows, Misha sits up taller for a closer examination.

'Our tutor said the snake under the hooves is symbolic of Russia's power over her enemies. I asked to know more, but Alexei was in one of his moods; he dismissed the tutor and made his sailor take him outside to play.'

'Legend attests that while the magnificent statue of Peter the Great stands, the city of St Petersburg will never fall to an enemy force,' I smile and adjust my cloak.

'So, Russia relies on such superstitions to win our battles, Mama?' he states. His handsome face displays a wry smile. 'You've always been a devotee of the mystical, and, of course, the silver age of symbolism.' He chastises me as though he is the parent and I, the child.

'If by that you mean I embrace and appreciate beauty in art, theatre and literature, then yes, I am indeed a devotee.'

'Using symbols as a way to discover the higher ideals of eternal truth?' he chuckles.

'Indeed, I believe such art influences your destiny—it transcends reality and speaks to us through the soul.' I snuggle into my sable-trimmed opera cloak and lean against him. 'And what do you believe?'

'I believe there is more to experience from the world outside this city.' He presses into the corner of the seat with his stare fixed firmly on the view.

He is almost my height now; soon, he will be a young man. I conjure the image of Georgiy as though he is here with me. I hope I am doing what he would have expected for our son.

A *troika* pulls alongside us, and the rapid gait of the three fine horses drawing the carriage sends a tremor through my body. Misha smiles as hooves clatter over the stones and bells tinkle merrily, his eyes bright with excitement. For too long he has been locked away at his studies.

Our chauffeur follows the path of the imperial automobile, and the people cheer and wave when they recognise the grand duchesses inside. I notice small groups of men amassed on street corners. Some are dressed in the simple clothing of Cossacks, with *astrakhan* hats and long coats, while others carry the grime of factory work on their clothes and turn their backs on the imperial vehicles. A few call out roughly, their angry faces gnarled and frowning as they hurl insults that are lost in the swell of wind. I recall Vorontov's caution of people who have no love for our Emperor and his wife.

'The people flock to observe the imperial family like exhibits in a zoo,' Misha scowls just as confused. 'But what are they saying? What have the grand duchesses done to anger them?'

'These people do not know them as we do.' The four grand duchesses are blessed with sweet temperaments, and, despite their naiveté, there is a gentle wisdom about them.

'The sisters are kind…except for Anastasia,' Misha chuckles. 'She can be quite wicked, but she's also the most fun.'

His alarm is forgotten as we pass the Yusupov Palace and approach our destination.

Outside the magnificent imperial Mariinsky Theatre, we wait for the grand duchesses to alight. Apart the elegant strands of pearls worn by the two older girls, their evening attire is simple and unadorned; the slight variations in their all but identical gowns give the impression of childlike innocence.

Like buds on the verge of bloom, the sisters smile and wave to their subjects, their shiny faces radiant with the signs of youth and good health and the promise of life ahead of them. The youngest pair are holding hands, until Anastasia breaks away to perform a *pas-de-deux* at the theatre entrance. Olga Alexandrovna gently ushers them inside.

There's no denying the lavish display of finery and extravagance of the Mariinsky's full house. In contrast to the ivory of the grand duchesses, ladies in fashionable evening gowns of Venetian red, emerald, and peacock blue strut and preen under golden lights, adorned in pearls, diamonds and rubies that glimmer against their bare skin. They are accompanied by dashing men ablaze in gold-trimmed uniforms. Others salute the traditions of customary Russian court dress and wear ornate *kokoshniki*. The rich, festival of colour spills throughout the theatre like silk threads from an embroiderer's *étui*.

I urge Misha forward and my heart beams with pride when he offers me his arm. He stands tall as we approach the staircase, surrounded by the great and the good of St Petersburg.

Rosalind greets us outside the door to our box. 'You look ravishing, as always, Tatya. Misha, my dear, I'm sure you will enjoy the performance.'

Once inside, Anastasia waves at us from the imperial box in the centre of the theatre. When she and Misha make faces at each other, I place a half-hearted hand on his leg to chide him. 'Do not needlessly draw attention to yourself, *mon chér*.'

Close in age, the pair is on the verge of adulthood, exuberant and fun loving. But the days of hide and seek are behind them. They will not remain carefree children forever. My hope for both is to find love and happiness in their futures.

No doubt the public are curious to see the imperial children after a long hiatus. Rumour and scandal are of endless intrigue to St Petersburg society.

Misha and I will be recognised too. His resemblance to the Tsar is more obvious as he grows—they share the same blue-grey eyes and wheat coloured hair that glints in the sunlight. In full view above the stalls, our Romanov resemblance is obvious. I angle my body, shielding him from prying eyes as best I can behind the drape of velvet curtains.

While my likeness has been ever my curse, I am grateful it offers a modicum of explanation for Misha.

Rosalind nods a greeting to the man in the box alongside as he takes his seat.

'That is Eugene—or I should say, Evgeny Throckmorton, the British steel industrialist. Quite the character,' she whispers. 'He appears somewhat taken with you, my dear.'

The brazenness of the man's stare continues during the opening bars of the first act. I avoid glancing in his direction.

I try to relax and enjoy the program, to ignore the curious gaze of people who should instead be mesmerised by the brilliance of Tamara Karsavina's performance. The ballerina is a pure delight—graceful and strong on her toes yet lithe and delicate in her steps. Watching her dance Swan Lake is like immersing into a deep dream and waking in a field of flowers.

The evening passes far too quickly, and the stage fills for the final scene. The ballet corps surround Karsavina, fawning over their star like swans; the ballerinas' naked arms and long necks are both provocative and elegant. A blush floods Misha's face. He tugs at the neckline of the formal jacket and embroidered collar he is unused to wearing.

His growing awareness of women is obvious. I find him increasingly shy with me and see the idea of launching into my arms with his head laid at my breast as he did as a small child would make him squirm. The realisation that he views me as a woman, rather than his mama, has me catching my breath.

Karsavina steps forward gracefully and addresses the rousing applause; she is presented with a large bouquet of flowers which overflows in her arms. Her face is still lit with a smile when the curtain falls.

'Wasn't it magnificent, Tatya?' Rosalind asks as we leave our box.

'Yes, indeed. A delightful performance.'

'And Misha. Did you enjoy the ballet?'

'I did, very much. Thank you, Miss Brassington.' His English is much improved, and his accent perfect. My heart swells with pride.

The man from the next box appears beside us in the foyer. He has the combination of fair skin and russet-hair common to the British. 'Miss Brassington.'

Rosalind smiles and bows her head. 'Princess Zolotova, may I introduce Mr Evgeny Throckmorton.'

He appraises me openly, like a specimen under glass. I feel my blush rising as I look to Misha to affix my cloak.

'*Enchanté*, Your Highness.' Throckmorton thrusts his chest out with self-importance. I notice a scar along the line of his cheek, shaped like a hook. 'Karsavina was quite the spectacle this evening. I don't know how that husband of hers stands for her behaviour. I'm interested in your opinion of the woman's moral ineptitude. Though I imagine you are familiar in terms of those who view infidelity and dishonour without shame.'

The hairs on the back of my neck stand in alarm. What a grand assumption! I refuse to condone language that denigrates women and certainly not when it conceals a veiled remark about my mother. I answer in a clear burst of French, and Misha looks up in surprise at the discourtesy. I make my excuses to Rosalind and sweep past Throckmorton towards the exit with Misha hurrying behind me.

The streets are full of people, and I quickly ascertain a mood that far exceeds revelry. The crowd is mainly men, angry men. The tone is hostile. My stomach churns, and I grasp Misha's arm, frantically seeking our vehicle. I search the faces of the theatre patrons, worried for Olga and the safety of her nieces. With relief I see the imperial flag flapping in the distance as the Tsar's automobile speeds ahead. They have safely cleared the mob approaching from the nearby square and must have exited through a rear door.

Rosalind reaches me. 'This trouble has been brewing for days. Possibly another strike. Come Tatya, follow me. It will be safer for you in the embassy vehicle. I will have my driver escort you home.'

In minutes, the crowd begins yelling abuse and chanting anti-authoritarian and anti-tsarist slogans. 'Power to the proletariat! Give voice to the people!'

Misha questions me with a glance, and then helps push us through the surge of people. We find the ambassador's chauffeur circling the fenders of the automobile like a hawk guarding a nest.

He inches the automobile away aided by the sound of the horn. We are aghast at the damage the mob has caused. Trolley cars and trams are overturned, and glass from broken windows is scattered across the cobblestones. Men brandishing revolvers and shouting curses band together like criminals, but others are bleeding, injured, forced back by Cossack troops on horseback and surrounded by the police.

I have never been this close to violence, and my heart races. The automobile slows and two belligerent-looking men sneer and point in our direction. I grip Misha's arm and cover my finery. If only my cloak had the power to render us invisible. In a shaking voice, Rosalind instructs the driver to continue.

Suddenly, gunshots ring out and men scatter. They push against our vehicle and it pitches like a boat bobbing on a lake. Two men jump onto the running boards and for a time ride alongside us as we move slowly. Misha's eyes widen at the unrest unfolding; understandably, he has lost his earlier bravado. Resuming the role of a child, he buries his head in my chest and wraps his arms around me.

The British Embassy is only a short distance away, but the way forward is obscured by the growing crowd. Streetlights are out, and the automobile comes to a complete stop. The cabin begins to rock and shake; men shout and barricade us inside, banging on the panels and beating the metal with sticks like a drum. The sound is deafening.

'Mama! What will we do?'

'Hush, Misha.' I kiss his head, but I am frightened too, terrified for our safety.

The driver's door is flung open, and two brutes stand over the chauffeur, shouting orders. The chauffeur yells in Russian: 'This is a British vehicle! See this flag! A British flag. Let us through—'

It takes the assailants a few moments to comprehend and move on.

The motor crawls a short distance and then stops again. My heart lurches when the door swings wide and rough arms reach for me, attempting to haul me from my seat. Rosalind shrieks and pounds on the roof, urging the chauffeur to drive. He shouts, repeating the vehicle's British status.

'Leave her alone!' Misha screams, but his hands fail to hold me back. The men claw at me and the fur slips from my shoulders. Their nails dig into my skin as they drag me free and my fingers slide from the leather upholstery. In the darkness, the street blurs behind my tears. Then three shots ring out, and I close my eyes, praying Misha is not hurt.

Firm arms enclose me so tight that I can hardly breathe. Am I hurt? Have I been shot? I'm afraid of what will happen, to me, to Rosalind, but my main fear is for Misha. *Please don't touch him!*

I'm hanging out of the vehicle when it lurches forward. I try to push against my abductor, but he forces me inside and lands on top of me on the floor of the cabin; the door swings open precariously.

'Move on!' he yells but his arms have me trapped. The automobile picks up speed, and the door slams shut.

I wriggle beneath him and try to push him away, pounding my hands into his chest. I am frightened and angry. Why are we the targets of such outrage? But then something triggers a memory...smothered beneath the musty scent of sweat and smoke is the familiar and spicy mix of cedar and bergamot.

'You're safe, *Tatushka*.' His tone is gentle and a soft kiss touches my brow. And then I hear Rosalind's sob of relief when she addresses him by name.

The automobile jerks through the streets, and I sob, curling my fingers into his jacket and clinging like a limpet on a rock. Never before have I felt more grateful for the menacing presence of Ilya Petrovich Vorontov.

32

Anichkov Palace, St Petersburg

The following afternoon, Olga and I join the Dowager Empress for tea in the sea-green and turquoise splendour of the conservatory at Anichkov Palace. The dowager is in a somewhat prickly mood; our discussion immediately sours when she admonishes her daughter for her campaign to have her marriage dissolved.

'I'm well aware of your dislike for public appearances my dear, but given the current sentiment, you must continue to show yourself. The people need to see you. Your husband, we pray, will see sense and stand beside you at some point. However, it is necessary we Romanovs do what we were born to do.'

Olga ignores her barb. 'It is not *me* they need to see. Who is at fault when the city is faced with unrest? Last night poor Tatya was caught in a terrible riot and dragged from Miss Brassington's vehicle. Show Mama the bruises, Tatya,' she encourages before I say a word.

The strike that turned to blood and disaster has greatly unsettled me —the vehement attack feels like a personal slight.

Now the city has ground to a halt, with factories closed and telephone, electricity and postal services no longer operating.

'I am quite well now, thank you.' *Though a little worse for wear.* My wrists and arms ache, and I'm covered in bruises.

The dowager offers a tight smile. 'And prior to that, did you and Prince Zolotovsky enjoy the ballet?'

Her question might almost convince me of an interest in our affairs. She and my mother had a long-held rivalry in their youth, but she appears to have warmed to me somewhat. As a widow herself, perhaps she feels sympathetic to my position.

'We did, Imperial Majesty.'

'I'm pleased to hear it. Indeed, I did hear of the incident. Count Vorontov alerted me to the matter this morning.'

Count Vorontov? My stomach turns a full circle.

'These infernal strikes are unhelpful—the threat of war urges men to behave with rash impetuousness.' The dowager faces her daughter, 'I have no doubt Nicky will stand tall against his foolish cousin. However, war and riotous men are not my only concern today.'

'Mama?'

'Although I would have preferred he remained in my Life Guards regiment, I have appointed Count Vorontov my aide-de-camp. He has been warned to leave trouble alone, but time and time again, he seems to find it! I pray he desists. I owe it to his mother.'

'His mother?' Olga and I exclaim in unison.

The dowager's expression indicates that whatever the reason, it pains her to speak of it.

'Maria was one of my ladies, a dear friend in my younger days. But when she died, her husband blamed his son for her death. The man was a fool. As we women know, there is always a danger in childbirth. However, an aunt raised Ilya and his older brother, and I assisted with their education. I regret that the eldest, Yuri Petrovich, fell in with the wrong calibre of people—revolutionaries and dissidents. More than once I had to rescue him from trouble.'

'Yes, I remember, Mama,' Olga says. 'He was convicted of plotting against Nicky. Was he placed in a gulag?'

'Indeed. He was one of a group who led a rebellion of dangerous students from the university where he was studying law. The same group who assassinated Grand Duke Sergei during the marching of the troops.'

I hadn't made the connection. It was a time of great concern within the family with the rebellion and our defeat in the Japanese war. *And Alexei's birth and subsequent ill health.*

'In any case, I did what I could to save Yuri from the hangman's noose, but I could not prevent his incarceration. Ilya Petrovich, however, is a good man, a more faithful follower of the Emperor than his brother. He has always shown gratitude for my charity.'

'You are extremely generous.' Olga touched her mother's hand.

'Indeed, Maria was dear to me,' the dowager says with genuine concern, 'but, unfortunately, it appears Ilya has offended his colonel with a personal insult and has fallen out with his fellow guards.'

Olga pales a little and moves uncomfortably in her chair. The man remains a curious anathema.

'The woman involved was unaware of the drama that unfolded as a result of her foolish behaviour.' Seconds pass and the dowager muffles a cough with her handkerchief. 'Russian men and their passions!'

Olga looks to me with raised eyebrows.

'Ilya's position has been further exacerbated by suspicion over the sudden death of his wife, the Bavarian countess...,' The dowager lifts her head at the sound of footsteps in the hallway.

My heart jumps a beat. *His wife?*

'He was of course questioned, and then acquitted of any wrongdoing. And at my insistence, Nicky agreed to release him into my care.'

'This is concerning, Mama. With such dubious links, is it wise to keep Count Vorontov so close to you?'

'Of course, it is! I merely wanted to make you aware of any gossip that may circulate. He is innocent, and I trust him implicitly, but many will question my decisions. Nicky would prefer Ilya join his brother and remain locked away. However, I took great satisfaction in reminding him that as Dowager Empress, I am entitled to appoint the staff within my own household.'

She inclines her head. 'There is one concession Nicky forced me to agree to. After his last transgression, any further accusations will result in Ilya Petrovich being stripped of his position and exiled from court.

'Nicky's concern is that given the estate he has inherited in Bavaria, Ilya might be tempted to side against us and take up his brother's cause. I can't imagine he would ever bow and scrape to the German Kaiser, nor prove disloyal to the Tsar, no matter what Nicky imagines. I have insisted Ilya offers no threat, but if he sides with his brother and his socialist factions, I doubt my reach will protect him.'

She leans into the cushion of the settee and takes up her fan. The discussion has taken a great deal of effort, and she appears unsettled. Always so regal and poised, this is unusual, to say the very least.

I sip my tea and reflect on our discussion. Count Vorontov is a man of considerable intrigue. And opinions. But it is not my business.

'Dear Maria was a gentle soul who would turn in her grave to see what has become of her sons and their compromised loyalties.'

'But Mama, the situation between our countries is fraught with danger. If war breaks out with Germany—'

The dowager ignores Olga and turns to me. 'It was fortunate the count was close by last night.'

'Misha and I are most grateful, Your Majesty.'

'Indeed,' she pats my hand. 'There is one sure way to assure Ilya's loyalty....' Her gaze meets mine. 'Tell me my dear, have you considered marrying again? I have a mind to suggest it to Nicky. Allow me to find a suitable husband for you.'

It is well known I have rejected the attentions of many a suitor over the years. But heat floods my face as I recall the tangle of our bodies on the floor of the automobile. His arms around me; his head nestled into my neck....

I am at a loss to answer. And try as I might to deny it, the thought of marriage is as frightening as it is exciting.

Within a week of the ballet night incident, I'm summoned to a meeting with Nicky at Alexander Palace. My heart is in my mouth.

When the Empress joins us, she kisses Nicky's head and stands beside him, resting her hands on his shoulders.

'A decision has been made regarding your future.' The Tsar smiles. 'Mama's suggestion in fact. However, we agree it is in your best interests,' he takes a breath, 'to marry again.'

It appears the dowager's extraordinary plan is well afoot.

'I have not considered a husband.' I picture Vorontov's full lips and unusual eyes. If I must marry, I could do worse.

'Nevertheless, the matter is settled, and we are obliged to make the arrangements.'

Alix curls her fingers into the Tsar's shoulders, reminding me of the eagle in the imperial crest. 'You were born into a noble lineage that any man would relish—and young enough to give him an heir. Your son has been fatherless for far too long. We have decided. Romanovs have long made marriage alliances such as this.' She offers a congenial smile.

'Might I be permitted to know why my marriage is necessary after all these years?' I do my best to know my place. But I will not give her the satisfaction of making this easy. I lift my head and affect a cool stare.

Her eyes narrow. 'The marriage will take place.'

'Do I have a choice, Your Imperial Majesty?' I soften my tone and direct my question to Nicky, hoping to negotiate civilly.

He shifts in his seat and strokes his jaw. His appearance is a shock, so like Georgiy in this moment that I need to pinch myself to believe it's not him.

'When he asked for your hand we admit, we were surprised. But his factories currently supply the steel for the construction of our railroad to Vladivostok. An alliance with Throckmorton is vital for Russia's future.'

Throckmorton? My stomach turns a somersault, and I slump in my chair. The mere twitch of the Empress's lips suggests her hand in this. I know little of the man. Why would he ask for my hand?

'I am content to live out my life as a widow. I have my own allowance.'

The Tsar clears his throat. 'Ever since the Japanese war, the *Duma* has demanded a reduction in costs. We are requested to reconsider the remuneration of all members of the family and, as you admit, you are one reliant on the imperial purse. We are reluctant to adhere to the *Duma*'s warmongering prophecies, but by taking a husband, your allowance will release strain on the imperial treasury. Indeed, if our troops *are* deployed, Russia's railroads must be further extended. Throckmorton's steel is an essential commodity.'

'So, I'm to be sold off to pay for cannons and railway sidings!' The words are out of my mouth without a thought. 'I cannot imagine what our grandfather would have said of this treatment!'

'He would have reminded you of your duty to the Russian Empire, Tatiana Vladimirovna.'

I hold my breath as seething anger courses through me. 'And what of Misha's allowance? He too, is entitled to a purse.'

Alix's glare shoots through me. 'As his legal guardian, Throckmorton will assume responsibility for your son. Prince Zolotovsky's future will become his decision until he reaches his majority.'

I dig my nails into my palms. 'And will a marriage be decided for him too when the time comes? Or, since he will no longer be reliant on the treasury, I assume he will be free to marry whomever he chooses?'

Nicky draws back on his cigarette and lowers his head.

'*Hmpf*,' Alix shrugs, 'it is of no concern, provided your son does not seek a marriage above his station.'

I am at a loss for words and shake my head in despair.

'Nicky darling. This is agreed, is it not?' Alix drops a kiss on his forehead.

The Emperor clears his throat. *Does he ever oppose her?*

'It's for the best, Tatya.' He rarely addresses me by my diminutive. But there is a flicker of warmth in his eyes. 'You offer a link to a distinguished branch of the aristocracy. As Throckmorton's wife, you and your imperial lineage will help sway influence and advance his position with those powerful in industry. It will be a comfortable life.'

'Indeed,' Alix's voice cuts the air, 'Throckmorton has factories to attend to, and with war on our doorstep, it is best you return with him to Britain. No doubt, you will acquaint yourself with the wives of his industrialist colleagues. I'm sure you will find numerous entertainments to amuse you in London. It is quite the place to be seen, and I know how you enjoy the theatre. I believe our dear Chaliapin performed

Borodin's *Prince Igo,* just recently at Drury Lane.' Her smile is intensely disingenuous.

'I know nothing of the man.' I look to my kid gloves and imagine another wedding ring on my finger. I'm to be passed on to a new master to be broken in like a horse bought at auction.

'However, Prince Zolotovsky will remain in St Petersburg and finish his studies. He will best serve the motherland here. As a Romanov, of course, you understand this.' The Tsar stands, and we are reminded who is in charge. 'And of course, we expect him to join us at Livadia in the autumn. The children have missed him.'

An unusual sound comes from Alix's throat.

I hold back a smile. The Tsar is holding his ground with more backbone than I've witnessed for some time. Perhaps he cares for Misha after all?

Nevertheless, his edict leaves a stale taste in my mouth, like when almond toffee grows thin and loses its sweetness.

How will I bear leaving Misha here without me?

33

Troops are marching in the streets when I visit Rosalind to prise out information about the man I am to wed. The uniforms remind me of Vorontov, but I push his image from my thoughts.

I'm shown through the doors of the British legation and to the Brassington's apartment on the first floor overlooking Nevsky Prospect. The balm to ease my reticence in marrying Throckmorton is the knowledge my friend and her lovely family will guide me in the ways of the British.

I consider life in a new country, recalling the paintings I've admired over the years. The Constables and Turners, the open fields and meadow flowers, the English landscape of mills and country streams and Norman style churches.

Yet nerves grip me relentlessly. How different will it be from my beloved homeland?

'My dear Tatya, how exquisite you look today.' Rosalind takes my hands and kisses my cheeks.

The gored inlays of my empire line skirt sway at my ankles in lapis lazuli and gold stripes, and a Basque coat in the same blue hue hugs my waist. But not even pairing my ensemble with new French-style millinery sporting a peacock plume has appeased my mood.

'Thank you, Rosalind. I hope you forgive my intrusion.'

'My dear, I'm delighted to see you. I've heard the most stupendous news. Is it true?'

'That is why I have arrived unannounced. The Tsar has arranged my marriage. I hope you might shed light on my future home.'

Rosalind's head tilts to the side with a frown. 'Indeed. Olga Alexandrovna informed me that the dowager had arranged for you to wed. And I am delighted, I must say. As you well know, I have long admired Count Vorontov...'

'Vorontov? No—,' Though at times, dear Olga is reckless with her gossip, it appears I am not the only one to have misunderstood the Dowager Empress. 'I'm to marry Evgeny Throckmorton.'

'*Throckmorton?* How extraordinary.' She recovers her surprise with a flutter of her handkerchief. 'I imagine he is hugely impressed with your links to the monarchy. He will assume it will further elevate his business interests.' Her nose turns ever so slightly as though overcome by a bad smell.

'Indeed, Throckmorton has powerful connections in trade.'

Rosalind's frown deepens. 'But Tatya, he is one not to be crossed. In fact, he has the feisty temper of the Scots. If you say you are to marry Throckmorton, but Olga says it is to be Vorontov...I do hope there is no cause for alarm.'

When I telephone the college to advise Misha of my forthcoming marriage, I am tersely reminded the pages are not to receive communications in this manner. *The telephone is not for Prince Zolotovsky's personal use.* However, I am eager for him to gain a pass. It is only when I mention my missive comes directly from the Tsar that Misha is permitted leave at all.

He arrives at my apartments that evening, his face eager and full of news. 'Mama, is it true? You are to be married?'

'Who told you?' His blush confirms Anastasia before he answers. 'Don't be angry with her. She is excited for you, Mama—'

I nod and take his hands in mine as Marthe brings in a tray of *pastila* with our tea, just the way Misha likes it.

'And, of course, I'm happy for you to be married and to have a father. But which man is it to be?'

A pain tugs in my chest. Which man? '*Mon chèr*, tell me exactly what you have heard.'

'Anastasia told me about the Briton, Throckmorton. But there is to be a duel fought tomorrow for your honour, Mama. With Count Vorontov.'

'That cannot be!'

'I've never been so popular! It's tremendously exciting. Everyone in the academy has been swarming around me for information.' His blue eyes glitter. 'The seniors are all seeking my opinion on who I think will win so they can lay their bets. Who shall I say? Which man do you expect will be victorious?'

Duelling is a tradition still upheld by the Guards. They are well known for it. Any intended or imagined slight or revelation of a dishonourable romantic liaison will cause one man to challenge another.

Count Vorontov is foolish indeed to engage in this dangerous quest.

The flutter in my chest is so rapid I can hardly breathe. 'Where and when is this duel to be held, Misha? Tell me the details.'

'Denilev's elder brother was present with the officers of the guards at their club. He said the Briton, Throckmorton, was at another table, and repeated something profoundly insulting.' He takes a deep breath. 'Count Vorontov took offence and asked Throckmorton to retract his comment. Instead, the Briton stood and slapped the count's face with a leather glove in front of *everyone*.

'The count is a loyal friend to us—to you especially. What else was he to do, Mama?'

He lowers his head. 'Denilev said the Briton made a certain comment about you...and my grandmother. He said she was...a...a woman of questionable morals.' Misha blushes a colour so bright against his fair hair that I see there is more to this slight than he is saying.

God knows what my son has heard. I take his hands in mine and draw him to sit beside me. 'Tell me exactly what was said. Perhaps I can explain…'

'He said he hoped the daughter was—as well-versed in the ways of women—as her mother. *That's* when the count punched him in the face and agreed to the challenge. He would never turn from such an insult!'

Misha tosses his head like a foal prancing his first steps. *So like his father.* 'Had I heard it with my own ears, I would have challenged the man myself. With your permission, I will offer Vorontov my support tomorrow and stand as his second. As your son, it is my duty. I will not have men speak of you this way.'

I place my hand along his cheek. '*Non, mon chér*, you will not. I refuse to allow you. I'm sure Count Vorontov has made his own arrangements. You will return to your studies, and I expect the college will most certainly forbid your attendance. I will not have you disciplined for absence.'

I hug him to my chest, filled with overwhelming sorrow. I shudder to think how my life will fare married to a man like Throckmorton. How dare he speak of me with such disrespect—and what does he hope to achieve by besmirching the reputation of his future wife?

Word of the impending duel spreads faster than ice across the Neva in the first grip of winter. As expected, the Corps des Pages are prohibited from attending. The act of duelling is a senseless one. But the code of conduct outlawed by previous rulers has crept back in recent times. Zinaide Yusupov's eldest son was killed in a duel just a few years ago over a dispute regarding his entanglement with an officer's pretty wife. The princess took an age to emerge from the despair of losing him. I cannot imagine her pain. Russian men are as impetuous as they are passionate.

I do not sleep all night with Ilya's gilt-lit eyes hindering my dreams. While unnerved by the discomfort the man provokes in me, I'm touched by his need to defend my honour.

But I refuse to silently await a fate I have unwittingly been the cause of.

In the hour before dawn, Marthe stealthily enters my room and aids me to dress. My carriage takes us to a stretch of protected land on the outskirts of the lake by the Chernaya River and to a field infamous for hosting this type of atrocious event. We hide behind a cluster of barberry and viburnum bushes, arriving just moments before the combatants arrive. I'm surprised to see my cousin Oleg Igorevich standing as Ilya's second; he must have travelled all night to be here.

After ten minutes there is no sign of Throckmorton's party. I clench my hands to my chest and pray he does not appear for then the matter will be voided and concluded by his absence. With no one injured, or worse, all that will be lost is bruised honour.

Just as the steward appears set to announce a termination, Throckmorton arrives, his face as pale as a shroud. The men begin a brusque discussion.

Marthe asks me to explain. 'This is the moment for them to make their reconciliation.'

Throckmorton is jumpy and fidgets with his coat. His second is almost Ilya Vorontov's height, but thin and reedy like a sapling that would blow over in a storm. Throckmorton paces while the seconds look over the weapons—pistols at dawn are the common choice of the duellists of St Petersburg.

Neither man takes a backwards step.

'Please withdraw while there's time,' I whisper, mouthing the words to the men in the growing light. I cover my face with my hands but peek between parted fingers.

The steward stands to the side with another man cloaked in a large overcoat, his mouth set in a grim line. A medical bag is gripped in his hands; the doctor is better-prepared than I to witness injury, or worse. Birdsong sails from the treetops and does little to allay my fears. The sweet dawn chorus feel distinctly out of place.

With the barriers set, the men ready themselves. My mouth is dry; I lower my head afraid to witness the event. Marthe wraps her arms around me and grips my elbows. She too, senses the danger; the possibility of witnessing a man lose his life.

I pray they come to their senses. Time seems to take a breath, and all is still and silent. Then, just as the steward shouts the last of his count, a crow caws from the branch above. Ever the opportunist, the predator is alert to the distinct possibility of blood and death. It hovers and then circles the field, eyeing the group for its quarry.

A white handkerchief drops, and I squeeze my eyes tightly shut, the prick of tears sharp beneath my eyelids. *What foolishness this is!*

Pistol shots crack through the silence, and voices shout immediately. My legs waver and give way. I sink to the ground, afraid to open my eyes.

Marthe reaches for me. 'It is done! It is done!'

I look up to see blood streaming from a wound on Ilya's arm; Throckmorton is on the ground. Oleg rushes to help his man lift him to a waiting carriage, and the doctor follows them.

I stagger forward and branches crack beneath my boots. Ilya turns and stares.

Oleg rushes to me. 'Tatya! You should not be here. You must leave. Quickly! We must not be discovered.'

'Is he—?' I dart a glance from Ilya to the departing carriage.

'Throckmorton will live,' Oleg says although a pained look suggests his concern, 'but you must go. Please Tatya.'

Ilya strides forward. 'I apologise, Your Highness. It appears I have disrupted your wedding plans—there is cause for delay.'

'You foolish man!' I find my voice now the outcome is known. Vorontov is merely grazed. Relief comes to me as anger.

Oleg silently retreats.

'It is unwise to be discovered here, Your Highness, but how kind of you to care.'

A blush heats my cool cheeks, at odds with my racing thoughts. 'You are hurt; you must attend to your wound—'

'You need not fear my death just yet, *Tatushka*,' he growls, his voice sending a shiver down my spine. He reaches with his good hand and strokes my cheek. 'Go, quickly, before we are all thrown into a prison cell.'

I turn away with a lump in my throat and a feeling I cannot explain. The weight of relief drains through me. Both men will live.

With gladness in my heart, I watch the sun rising ahead of me; a sign, perhaps, that I might hope for something more.

34

St Petersburg, 1914

Newspapers report that Evgeny Throckmorton has returned to Britain. Why a man should leave at such short notice, when Russia is under the threat of war and his factories provide work for thousands, is explained in terms both poignant and ambiguous.

'British industrialist, Mr Eugene Throckmorton, has been a great contributor to the Russian economy. Devastated in recent years by the death of his Russian wife, he has left St Petersburg, stating he cannot bear to spend a moment more in her country without her.'

Then, a week after the duel, I receive a formal missive from the Tsar:

By Imperial decree of We, Nicholas the Second, By The Grace of God, Emperor and Autocrat of All the Russias.

Proclamation to Our loyal subjects, Princess Tatiana Zolotova and Count Ilya Vorontov:

In the name of Our dearly beloved homeland, We ask Our loyal subjects above-mentioned to let domestic strife be forgotten at this hour of threatening danger and join self-sacrificingly and with one accord. We intercede in this marriage to safeguard the honour, dignity and integrity of Russia and pray the union be trusting humbly in Almighty Providence.

Compelled by the circumstances created, and in an effort to obtain a peaceable issue of negotiations, We call on Our faithful subjects to fulfil their sacred duty to Holy Russia and obey the Tsar in the moment of Our trials.

With a profound faith in the justice of OUR cause, We invoke prayerfully the Divine Blessing for this union and for Holy Russia, and furthermore, to help Him guide the Russian Empire on the road to victory, welfare and glory.

'Given at Saint Petersburg this day, twenty-eighth day of July, in the year of Our Lord one thousand nine hundred and fourteen, and the twentieth year of OUR reign.'

Our marriage is to take place immediately. Within days, the formal signing of the marriage documents is complete. There is no mention of gratitude to Ilya Vorontov for his service in defending my honour. Nor am I offered an apology for my swift transference from one man to another.

Misha, however, is overjoyed when he telephones from the Corps des Pages. 'Mama, I'm delighted. Count Vorontov has been extremely kind to me while I've been here. In fact, I'm seriously considering joining his regiment when my studies are finished, and I graduate.'

'Whatever do you mean, *been kind to you?*' I swallow down my apprehension.

'I've met with him many times, Mama. We have taken tea in the city and have discussed a range of interesting subjects. Count Vorontov has several extremely forward-thinking ideas on Russia's future—'

'Indeed.' *I can imagine.*

'Did you know his grandfather was a Finnish nobleman? Apparently, that is the reason for his great height. A family legend says the Vorontovs descended from Norse warriors.'

My son continues his praise for Vorontov and his deeds of greatness, and my stomach churns. Why has he sought to befriend my son? His motives are curious. Or, has he used Misha to pursue me? *No. It cannot be.*

Then I recall a conversation we had long ago about the death of my husband. Does Vorontov suspect the truth? Know more than he should? *About me? About my son?*

I cannot risk him unveiling the truth.

I burn my journals, sobbing as flames curl the pages. Thoughts I shared in private, revelations too intimate to reveal, lie in cinders in the grate. My memories of Georgiy and our love are in my heart and reborn in the face of our son.

His secret is one I vow never to expose.

The day before the wedding, the man I am to wed arrives on my doorstep. I would prefer not to be tied to him in marriage, nor in fact to any man. But as a Russian, he is a far better proposition than one who would take me from my son.

I intend to make clear *my* conditions. I am no brood mare, nor a possession to own and display. He has been awarded a healthy endowment upon our marriage, and I will make him understand the debt he owes me.

'Your Highness. A vision of loveliness as always,' his lips twitch.

I have chosen to greet him in a once sky-blue gown now faded from the strong light of Livadian spring times. Blotched patches give the overall effect of tumbled quartz. Marthe wears it in the laundry.

I indicate for him to take a seat and call for tea without seeking his preference on the blend or method to prepare it.

'Count Vorontov. I believe you have been spending time in the company of my son. However, in future, I would prefer that I am the one to counsel him.'

'My apologies, Princess. I enjoy the boy's company and seek only to answer his many questions. He tells me he has had little guidance in the way of men. But if that is your wish....'

He raises an eyebrow and reclines all too comfortably in the chair.

'Indeed, it is.' I nod to Marthe who deposits the tea tray and retreats.

Pouring tea into two cups, I hand him one and stretch my mouth into a tight smile. 'I believe it best we state our requirements before we begin, so there is no mistaking our intentions.'

'Then, perhaps we can cease with the formalities. We are to be married, after all—.' He peers at me over his cup as he sips.

'Of course, Ilya Petrovich.' Heat floods my face as I speak his name. 'As we are both aware, this is a marriage of convenience. Neither has a care for the other.'

'Is that so?' He leans forward and replaces his cup; his hand brushes mine as I reach for a plate.

I look up, startled by the shock of his touch. The heat in his eyes reminds me how his body cradled mine on the night of the workers' strike; the strength of the arms that shouldered me from danger. My eyes are drawn to his mouth, to his full lips. I take a breath and sip my tea.

'Tell me what *you* propose, Tatiana Vladimirovna.'

I take a deep breath. 'I presume you will reside here? It is convenient to Anichkov palace and large enough for you to keep separate quarters. That way we may continue with our lives as before.'

'Shall we indeed?' He meets my gaze. 'What are you afraid of?' he whispers.

What am I afraid of?

Rising heat forces me to look away. I ignore further innuendo and move on. 'I believe it best we maintain a platonic relationship. Naturally, when you seek the company of other women, I ask for your discretion—and far more than you have used in the past. I do not care for my son to witness any sordid liaisons.'

'I cannot change what you may have heard, Tatiana, but I am not who you imagine. I assure you I am no stallion who will force myself on you, nor will I ever make you do anything against your will.' His expression confirms the candour he is known for.

'But tell me, what if I require an heir? How might we resolve *that*? I hold land in Bavaria....'

My cup lands awkwardly in its saucer, and I mop the spillage with a napkin. 'I did not imagine you had need of an heir.'

As his wife, if he insists, I cannot deny him.

'Not immediately,' his eyebrow arches again, 'but the estate provides a small income and will need consideration. It is not prudent for the time being, but perhaps in time—'

I am not sure what to make of him.

We sit with the words between us, and I press my hands into my lap. Silence builds to a crescendo in my mind. I had not considered a move to Germany. How could I bear leaving Misha? And given the concerns of the dowager regarding his brother's traitorous allegiances, the need to protect the truth of Misha's birth from my husband appears a significant concern. My son will always be my first consideration.

'Of course, since I am so distasteful to my future wife, I will grant you time to get used to the idea before insisting upon my conjugal rights. It's the least I can do—given the great *wealth and favour* your position bestows upon me.'

I note the cynicism in his voice and meet his gaze. His eyes are lit with mischief, yet there is bitterness behind them.

I immediately feel uncharitable and admit that my body warms to his more freely than I care to declare. But I have more to lose in this transaction than he has to gain. I am ashamed of my duplicity.

'But if this is your wish then, yes, I agree to your terms.'

I breathe out a sigh of relief. 'I thank you for your understanding.' Inclining my head, I focus on my hands in my lap.

'Until tomorrow, Princess.'

His cool tone turns my stomach—but when I look up in a vain attempt to be more pleasant, he is already gone.

The ceremony is held in the cavernous grandeur of the magnificent St Isaac Cathedral. How curious that for our small wedding, Ilya has engaged the grand cathedral where my parents were married and where my baptism was celebrated.

All is aglow as we approach the iconostasis and stand before God, gathered at the base of grand columns of malachite and lapis lazuli, and topped by acanthus leaves painted in gold. Magnificent mosaics decorate this vast space and depict meticulously recreated holy scenes and saints.

But my admiration for the beauty is tinged with regret. Once again, I am marrying against my wishes, as my mother had before me. I wrestle to contain my emotions and am drawn to look up beyond the bright light of the crystal chandeliers and to the glorious, gilded dome overhead. A poignant reminder that we Romanov women are duty bound and obligated to follow the dictates of our tsar.

I suspect by the stern look of resignation on his face that Ilya, too, would prefer to attend to matters anywhere but here.

Then, just as our hands are bound together in silk ribbon, he stares down at me, and his amber eyes shine, catching the light of the glittering interior. I'd like to believe it is some semblance of admiration that I see in the set of his lips instead of resentment for his fate. *Our fate.* The heat of his body so close to mine overwhelms me and sparks of fire that have for so long remained dormant in my body flicker at his touch. I pray the heat burning my face does not betray my inner conflict.

When it is over, I breathe out a sigh. My husband politely offers his arm, and we lead a small group of guests on to a celebration. The reception is a gift from the dowager, although she is not in attendance.

I'm delighted Rosalind has joined us, along with Olga and, in a rare appearance, her Kulikovsky. My cousin Oleg's presence is sorely missed. I have failed in my attempts to contact him and assume he is busy in his role in production. I might have relied upon his good humour and support today. Our celebrations are brief, and as Ilya and I leave our guests and return to our apartments, I am left with no place to hide.

Time stretches endlessly until evening, punctuated by the ticking of the clock. I lie awake in my bed, wondering if my husband will break his promise and come to me after all. I strain at every sound, all the while imagining forms emerging from the shadows in each shift of the dappled light.

The next morning I arise alone, exhausted from lack of sleep and untold hours of anticipation, fatigued from the final heavy drug of slumber that seized me just as morning broke.

It appears I have succeeded in my wishes. I have control in my marriage in the manner I requested—and yet, perhaps, it is not what I want after all.

In the first days of our marriage, we barely speak. I pass him briefly in the hallways as though he were a guest on an official visit rather than my husband. While relieved, I struggle to maintain a cool deference in his presence.

His manner, in return, borders on hostility and his stare follows me as I move about a room or while giving directions within my household. And everywhere is the scent of him: cedar, bergamot and a hint of clove. I instruct Marthe to throw open the windows and walk in the gardens to escape it. Like his great size, Ilya appears to envelop every part of my life, from breakfast to the supper table and all the moments in between.

Then, as tension between us becomes so visceral that my resolve is weakened, and I feel disposed to be more sympathetic to keep the peace, news comes that Archduke Franz Ferdinand, heir of the Austro-Hungarian throne, and his wife Sophia, have been assassinated in Sarajevo.

The war we have ignored, yet been expecting, finally reaches our door. The Austro-Hungarian Empire, with the backing of Germany and Kaiser Wilhelm, declares war on Serbia. The Tsar has no option than to rush our forces to Serbia's defence. Then he patriotically distances himself from anything of German influence and changes the name of my beloved city to *Petrograd*.

At once, Ilya is called upon to serve. A man with his level of military expertise is in demand to undertake the training of soldiers.

'Do not trouble yourself to attend the station on my account.' His lip curls as he stands before me on the morning he is to depart for the front. 'I dare not consume more of your valuable time than necessary. I will burden my wife no longer, nor do I wish to add to your duties. I wish you well.'

'To be bound in this manner is by no means convenient for either of us, I assure you.' I reply.

My barb stings; I notice him flinch as he turns away.

I clench my fists in irritation. I did not mean to suggest I have no care for his health and safety. Indeed, all I feel is shame in the manner of our parting.

I regret our farewell is not an occasion I am proud of.

When the days turn to weeks, and then months, with no word, I attempt to convince myself that Ilya's welfare is not my concern. But this is entirely not the case. I find myself questioning those around me for word of his *corps*, for any clue as to his safety; but all is in vain.

Once again, I'm reminded of my visit with Olga to the mystic in Livadia. Was it Georgiy's death she foresaw—or the blood of Ilya Petrovich? Like a spring bursting from a box, my nerves are strung tight with worry. I will not survive another loss.

Ilya's face appears in my dreams more often than I care to confess. Too often I awake in the haze of morning light, filled with regret at the memory of his tiger's eyes glaring with distaste.

In the following months, men leave the city while women and children pour in from the provinces, starving and seeking refuge when their homes and fields are plundered in the course of battle. The rows of injured and dying men, and the state of their wounds, only serve to increase my concern for my husband.

The city's hospitals overflow with casualties, and the Tsar insists on making use of the state rooms of the Winter Palace. As soon as the Tsarevich Alexei Nikolaevich Hospital opens, I add my name to the roster and throw myself into my role as a volunteer under the direction of the matron, Lady Callaghan, a friend of Rosalind's. As the number of casualties rises, we take on daily shifts and share the workload.

And then one night I am asked to hold the hand of a handsome young man, returned from the front in a far poorer condition than he left. The sharp lines of youth jut from his face, accentuated by the shortage of food. The injuries he sustained in battle are life-changing. He is barely nineteen, just a few years older than Misha.

'Please don't leave me,' his voice breaks as he reaches for my hand, 'talk to me, for if you are speaking, then surely God will not dare to take me.'

His dark lashes are wet with tears and I try to allay the fear in his eyes. 'Hush now.' I pat his hand. He grips my fingers so tightly I am surprised at their strength. 'You are safe.'

'Safe?' Tears trail from the corners of his eyes. 'But what use am I? What use can I be? Like this?' A dressing wraps the shoulder of his left arm, but his elbow is nothing but a stump. 'How will I work the land again? How can I ask my Olenka to marry me now? I am not whole. I'm broken, less of a man.'

'Please do not speak this way. You must have hope. You will recover.'

I dampen a cool flannel and lay it over his face, pushing back matted hair from his forehead. I imagine how his mother would feel to see him here and tend him as I would a treasured son. I dare not bear the thought of ever witnessing mine so close to death.

He coughs, a horrible wracking cough that finishes with a violent burst of sputum, and blood purges from his mouth. I try to still him but hear the gurgle of blood as he struggles to draw air into his lungs—and fails dismally.

'Don't leave me, mother!' He pleads, and his hand grips my arm. Then he coughs and gasps once more, as a final burst of blood spills from his mouth.

As the light fades from his lovely brown eyes, my tears fall on to the starched white sheet below. I struggle to contain them and murmur the words of a prayer over his body. Then I close his eyes for the last time.

I beg the Lord to put an end to these battles and beseech Him to watch over my son and keep him safe; to spare him from the threat of war. *My husband too.*

That night, overwrought at having witnessed the first death of a patient I have nursed, I arrive home and swallow my pride. I cannot continue to ignore the turbulence of my emotions and take up my pen to write to my husband.

Then, like a foolish lovesick pup, I eagerly await his reply.

However, as weeks turn to months, no letter is forthcoming.

JEAN

35

Castlemaine, 1983

Jean grunts and stirs, startled by someone rapping at her door. *Who's there?* Attempting to lift her head from the floor is like hefting a bowling ball. She hears pacing back and forth across the verandah and turns to the sound of her name then gags as her stomach roils from the stench of a nearby pool of vomit. Time is immeasurable. *Is it minutes, or hours later?* She doesn't even know what day it is. Fast tapping cracks on the windowpane and she forces her eyes open. Who's there? The shady outline of a figure glows through the frosted glass. *Someone is coming to get me...*

Jean drags up her legs and tries to sit. A female voice hums in the background like a movie soundtrack. Next, there's a knock at the door, or the wall, or the window: harder, faster. How many people are here? Jean closes her eyes; *go away* she screams inside her head. *Leave me alone!* Her limbs are too heavy, and she sinks back to the lounge room floor.

'Jean! Jean, are you all right?'

The pounding in the back of her head is relentless. 'What do you want...' Jean thinks she's said the words aloud, but her tongue feels swollen and trapped inside her mouth. It tastes like she's licked an ashtray clean. She tries to swallow, but her throat is parched; the foul taste makes her gag again.

A doorknob twists and screeches until finally the back door is forced open.

'Jean!'

'Go away!' Jean moans and waves her arms, flinging them out aimlessly. 'Leave me alone.'

'Thank God,' she hears someone murmur close by. It sounds like Summer's voice.

Jean's view is lop-sided. From this angle, the sofa's chintz cushions lie sideways. Her eyes slowly adjust to the darkened room. She squeezes them tightly closed, and the patterned bouquets of lavender and roses blur.

'Let me help you,' Summer reaches for her with one hand, covering her nose with the other.

'No!' Jean slurs. 'Go away!'

Summer takes a deep breath and rubs her arm. 'It's okay, Jean. I understand.'

'I don't need you...'

She doesn't want Summer's questions or her sympathy and can't bear to be a victim. She's lost the fight. The shame is great, too great to bear. How can she explain her failings to Summer or Rick or Pete?

Tears fill her eyes. She's worked so hard to hide her alcoholism—keeping busy at work, staying strong.

While alcohol is always on hand for the customers in the salon, there's no time to drink if you're constantly gathering stock and attending to staff matters. It's almost a role requirement to have the odd glass of bubbles at management and sales meetings or when fraternising in social settings—it took an enormous effort for Jean to avoid it. And she had....

'I'm here to help. Come on. I'll get you into the shower.'

In the bathroom, Summer helps Jean strip off her clothes and leaves her to sit on the bottom of the bath with her head resting on her knees. The overhead shower rose sprays a continuous stream of tepid water over her head. By the time Summer returns with a steaming mug of peppermint tea, Jean is resting on the edge of the bath, wrapped in a fluffy towel.

'I'm so ashamed.' Mortified. 'What must you think?'

'I think you have a fantastic collection of teas, Jean, but coffee has always been my favourite,' Summer smiles brightly. 'I know this is hard for you. You've been so brave.'

'I'm far from brave. Stupid and pathetic, more likely.'

'Rubbish!' Summer rests her hands on her hips. 'I assume this was triggered by what happened at work with Milton. I get the way men like him operate. Tell me it's none of my business, but—'

'There's more,' Jean sniffs and closes her eyes. 'I've worked so hard all my life. But I'm an alcoholic. I've made such a mess of things.'

'Look, Jean. There's more to life than DJs. To give up drinking without support is extremely difficult. You're a talented woman with much to offer. Let's get you well again and then we'll worry about all the other stuff when you're up to it.'

'Oh God,' Jean covers her face with her hands. 'I invited you for the weekend, didn't I? I guess this isn't what you imagined.'

'No, but you're stuck with me now. Luckily, I swung by the food hall on my way out and have brought supplies. Looks like you could use a good meal.'

'It's too much—'

'Don't be ridiculous! It's the weekend and I'd love your company. But tell me, is there anyone I can call? Someone you might want to speak to?'

Jean frowns. 'I can't tell Rick. I was doing so well. What will he think?' She presses her lips together and looks away. 'I thought I didn't need AA. I guess that was stupid.'

'Not at all. I've seen people relapse before. It's all part and parcel of the process. The hardest part is working through the trigger points and finding the strength to trust your progress.'

'I really thought I was fine. It's been more than two years since I've had a drink. Now I'm back to scratch. I didn't see this coming. Losing my job was the final straw. The venom in the way he spoke! It was...I was....' Tears well in her eyes as she breaks off.

'I was really worried about you. All the girls were. As soon as my shift finished, I headed here.'

'You're very sweet, Summer. Thank you.' But Jean can see signs of the salacious gossip regarding her departure in the pity in Summer's eyes.

Later the pair settle in front of the fire. A freshly baked ginger cake sits on the coffee table along with a steaming pot of tea.

Jean takes a breath. 'I need to explain...'

'You don't have to, Jean. It's none of my business.'

'To be honest, it might be a relief.' Jean's voice is husky, and she's still pale. 'For as long as I can remember, I've turned to the bottle every time something happened to me. I lost myself in the drink...'

'I understand that when things are tough you find a crutch to sustain you. But it's no use beating yourself up about it.'

'With the swell of alcohol in me, I could forget—both the past and the present. It was the only way to stop my thoughts taking me to the dark places. The thing is, I just can't stop at one or two. The drink takes me over. My body reacts differently.'

'But how have you managed in your career?' Summer shakes her head. 'All the liquid lunches and staff functions?'

'I realised that once you've taken a glass at an event, most people don't notice what you're drinking. I try to make sure I'm busy or excuse myself if I see a waiter on his way with a bottle. I leave one group to chat to another and buzz around like a bee. Once people are slightly intoxicated, they lose track of what everyone else is doing.'

'It's not easy to accept and face your problems. I'm proud of you for being so courageous.' Summer takes a breath. 'But it must be tricky for you now, with your brother and his vineyard?'

'Yes, it will make life interesting.' Jean stares into the flames. 'I suppose you have to laugh, don't you? While he is attracted to every aspect of wine and winemaking, it's essential I have nothing to do with it.' Regret stings her voice.

'Oh, Jean,' Summer pats her hand, 'This is a trip up not a roadblock.'

Jean draws in a breath to hold back her tears. 'I met someone recently, and we've become quite close. He's a lovely, gentle man, but I'm sure he'd be shocked to see me in this sorry state. I had hoped you'd meet him this weekend. He's the one I mentioned, with the beautiful woodcraft.'

'That's wonderful. You *have* been keeping secrets!'

Jean looks up. *Should I tell her? No.* She doesn't know Summer well enough to expose the extent of the Champion family's skeletons. *That* is a far more serious problem to face. Thoughts of Rick are too difficult.

'What about you, Summer? Are you dating? Is there anyone special?'

'Actually, *there is* something I need to explain,' Summer's voice is low, 'about Rick.'

'Rick? My Rick?'

'Yes. I met him in Montpellier years ago. I hope you don't mind me not telling you. We...we had a bit of a thing.'

Jean sits back in her chair. 'I see.'

'I saw him visit you at work one afternoon. I didn't put two and two together at first,' Summer shrugs. 'Your surnames...'

'I changed mine to *Campain* after I left home.'

'Anyway, I faked a headache and took off when I saw you together. I hid in the storeroom like a rabbit in the headlights.'

'To avoid Rick?'

'Yeah—it was a touch dramatic—Cinderella on the stroke of midnight.' Summer smiles to make light of it. 'Anyway, he's probably forgotten me.'

'Somehow I think you'd be hard to forget,' Jean answers and draws the blanket across her knees. 'Maybe it's time you faced him and sorted it out?'

'Pot, kettle!' Summer laughs. 'Oh, Jean, you're one in a million. Let's just get you over this hurdle first, hey? Then we'll see where it leads.'

The next morning the two women clear away the debris of Jean's bender and open the house to fresh air and sunshine. The kettle is constantly on the boil, and Summer makes sure Jean keeps her fluids up. Into the afternoon they chat and sharing stories becomes easier with the blurry haze of Jean's intoxication lifting.

'Do you feel up to speaking to Rick?' Summer asks gently.

Jean notes the lurch in her gut. News of her relapse is bad enough. Telling Rick, she's his mother is even harder. How can she lump him with the sordid truth?

'No,' Jean presses her lips together, 'I'd rather not at the moment.'

Her shame is overwhelming as she recalls the conversation with Hazel. She doesn't have the energy.

Time to deflect.

'After what you've told me, maybe you're the one who needs to speak to him. He's a good man, Summer. I'd love you to be friends if nothing more.'

The wistful look on her friend's face is incongruent with her angular cheekbones. 'Not yet, Jean, but I'll consider it. Let's focus on you and your health, okay?'

Summer checks her watch. 'Do you feel up to a walk? How about you show me this town of yours?'

Jean points out places of interest as they follow the path in the fresh air. When they near Pete's workshop, she reluctantly agrees when Summer asks to see his work.

Jean stands back while he describes the timber he uses and shows Summer various pieces. But after a few minutes Pete turns to Jean. His thoughtfulness at including her in the discussion warms her heart.

'I sold that oak dining table to a couple of newlyweds,' he smiles. 'Do you think your Rick might like to take a look at the bar tables? You could come for lunch tomorrow.'

Both women freeze, open-mouthed. He frowns, glancing from one to the other. 'Sorry, did I say something wrong? I thought he was interested in them for the cellar door?'

'Oh Pete, it's not that, it's just—' Jean breaks off. Lethargy consumes her and perspiration is seeping from her pores. Her need for a drink is rising. She clenches her fists and works hard to push away the irritation that prickles her skin like a mosquito bite.

'I think Jean wanted this weekend to be a break for me,' Summer glances to Jean for endorsement, although from her expression, she too is reluctant to see Rick.

Jean's energy is flagging fast; the demon is rearing its head. She scratches at her hands. She has to get home. Fight it. Fight the feeling. Her friends might be willing to support her, but this is one journey she must make alone.

36

Verity House

Jean never imagined being the type of person to need 'rehab.' Undertaking drug and alcohol rehabilitation at the new Betty Ford Clinic in California is practically a rite of passage for rock stars, movie idols and celebrities. But affluence offers no escape from personal pain, and addiction is an ever-increasing societal problem. Jean needs help to wrestle her demons too. She makes the call to Verity House before Summer wakes.

As an ordinary person, Jean thinks it's a little over-the-top. She should have the fortitude to control herself; should never have lost it in the first place. She'd tried and failed to kick drinking, first on her own and then on the AA twelve-step program. Picking yourself up after you've been knocked down plays a huge part in recovery. Right now, accepting professional support is her best option.

At Verity House, Jean silently bears the physical pain; the chills, the sweats, the ache that ravages her body as toxins are expelled, day and night. It's part of what must be borne to face the mental anguish ahead. Only then will she be physically strong enough to confront those she loves; strong enough to withstand the shame of her actions and the possible rejection of those she has hurt when the sordid truth surfaces.

Patients contribute to the daily operations of the rehabilitation centre. Jean is delighted when assigned on gardening detail and finds the routine a balm. Not only does she relish the sight of sprouting shoots and blossoming blooms; the fresh air settles her thoughts and nourishes her body too.

One afternoon the sun glows through a parting in the curtains during a counselling session. Jean shades her eyes with a hand. Her progress has halted, and she's reluctant to press through to the root of her fears.

The psychologist stands and closes the drapes. 'There's one way to tackle this,' she resumes her seat. 'You've worked hard, Jean. It's time to face it. You *do* have the strength to get to the heart of what you're dealing with. Take your time.'

'But what if...?' Jean's words dissolve with her bravado. She doesn't want to sever the relationship she's built with Rick. But what has living a lie done for her?

'You have the tools to accept whatever you need to face, Jean. What's your next step?' The psychologist's dark eyes remind Jean of a doll she had as a child; the eyelids rolled open and closed as she moved but her face remained expressionless.

'Before I can tell Rick, I need to establish the truth about my father.'

'And how will that look for you? Tell me.'

Jean' stomach twists in knots. Evie. Dear Evie. This affects her twin too.

'I'll contact my sister and ask her what she knows. If she knows...'

The psychologist's sympathetic gaze rests on her. Jean breaks it to stare at her hands. 'I haven't spoken to her for years...'

'Once you have made contact, you will be better prepared to accept the knowledge, whatever it may be.' She offers Jean a smile. 'Significant events witnessed from your perspective may not necessarily reveal the truth. Take hold of your power, Jean, and you will find the way forward.'

Jean closes her eyes. She sees the past rising and bubbling to the surface, then flowing like lava from Vesuvius.

Essendon, Melbourne 1951

Jeanie and her sisters walked out of the school gates with glee. Stew was on the menu, and like Evie, she was relieved not to be eating it with the rest of the boarders. Evie complained that the dried-up mutton stuck in her throat and made her choke. With smiles that brimmed from ear to ear, they skipped across Buckley Street and headed in the direction of Hazel's house for tea.

Their father had phoned that morning, telling his daughters that Aurora was a finalist in the Archibald Prize.

'Fingers crossed that she wins!' Jeanie leaned into the mouthpiece.

'Well, even if she doesn't, it's been worth the effort to have entered.' Jack let out a cough. Jeanie imagined him taking out his big, checked handkerchief from the back pocket of his overalls. A muffled sound came down the line, and his sniffle faded. 'She's worked so hard for this.'

'Are you all right, Daddy? Do you have a cold?'

'A cold? Yes...yes, that's it.'

Poor Daddy, always out in the elements. No wonder he'd caught a cold. 'You must take better care of yourself,' Jeanie warned with a frown. Her father was a hard worker. She wished she were there to help him in the orchard.

'The Grannies are almost ready,' Jack's voice was full of pride as he changed the subject. 'I expect a first at the Royal Melbourne Show this year with these beauties. Best looking crop for a while.'

She immediately sensed the taste of her favourite green apples; the tart juice and fragrant perfume had the power to invoke a heady dream. 'Oh Daddy, you say that every year,' laughed Jeanie. 'When can we come home? Can you collect us soon? We miss you.'

'Sorry, love,' Jack sighed, 'I can't get up to Melbourne at the moment. We're snowed under with the harvest. It'll be a few more weeks. Perhaps mid-term break?'

'What about Mummy? When can we see her?'

Jack hesitated, as though choosing his words, 'I'm afraid Aurora's a little caught up in the art world. We Champions come a poor last for the time being.'

Jeanie read much into this statement in the ensuing years.

'I'm happy when she's happy. And if that's what she needs—'

'Do we make you happy too, Daddy?' Jeanie's voice held a smile.

'Ah, Jeanie, when you girls were born, it was the happiest day of my life. Except, of course, when your mother accepted my proposal.' He chuckled.

'When you gave her grandma's ring that belonged to your mother.'

'It will be yours one day, Jeanie. You're the eldest; only by a touch, but it's the family tradition. It only came to me because there were no daughters.'

'Golly. I don't expect I'll be getting married for a while!'

Jack chuckled. 'I hope not. You're far too precious for me to let go of just yet.'

The next day, Jean puts through a trunk call to Singapore from the orange pay phone in the reception area. She's grateful her fellow inhabitants have left her to speak in private. With group counselling and the power of an experienced rehab team, she feels stronger than she has in weeks. But she must address the issue of her birth. *Their birth.*

Once she has all the facts, then she will know precisely what—and how—to deal with her situation. Just what does Evie know?

It takes a few minutes for the operator to connect the person-to-person trunk call. Soon the static in the line changes, and Jean holds her breath as a woman answers. The operator puts her through.

'Hiya!'

'Hello, Evie, is it really you?'

'Yes, who's this?' Evie sounds cautious.

'It's Jeanie. Your sister.'

'Jeanie? Oh my god, Jeanie, as I live and breathe!'

After the initial shrieking (and crying) between the pair, the pain in Jean's chest starts to loosen its grip. The twins navigate the time delay and revert to their old habits of finishing each other's sentences while the ping-pong of cross-wired communication jumps back and forth. It's easy to begin with safe topics like the weather and Rick's work at the orchard. But when the pips sound, and Jean hasn't yet spoken of what she needs most, she feeds more coins into the slot and takes a deep breath.

'Evie. I'm sorry I let you down. But I have something I need to explain. I'm currently undergoing rehabilitation. Not for the first time, but I'm serious about making it the last. I'm an alcoholic.'

'You've had to cope with this on your own? Then, my god, we've all let you down, Jeanie. It must be a nightmare for you.'

'Yes, it's hard, but if I want it to work, I really must face my past. I've denied what I've tried to hide for too long. Firstly, I'm sorry I left without telling you—'

'You didn't seem to need us,' Evie sniffs. 'You pushed us out of your life, and no one was game to pursue you. I should have tried harder...but we all have our rubbish to deal with. I've missed you, Jeanie. It was never the same without you.'

'I never stopped thinking about you all.' That in itself was an admission Jean has only just faced. She might have locked memories of her family away, but once she began therapy, she found the love she once had for them still there, buried beneath years of doubt and self-loathing.

Suddenly, a second round of beeps sound, and the operator interrupts to ask for more coins if she is to continue. Jean drops every last cent into the slot.

'Did Rick tell you I'm coming home for the gallery opening?' Evie's voice wavers.

Jean is surprised he hadn't and tells her so. But then she breathes out a sigh. There's more to discuss, and it will be better with the three of them in person.

'Before we go, Evie, I need to ask you a rather odd...and awkward question.'

'Go on...'

Jean hears her sister's intake of breath and wishes she could spare them both the pain.

'Aurora's friend Hazel mentioned Michael Golding. He was her patron, but,' she closes her eyes, 'Hazel suggested he was always...*with*

Aurora. Perhaps, intimately. Do you think we really *are* Jack's daughters? Or might Michael be our father?'

Evie splutters on the end of the line, thousands of miles away. 'WHAT? No! No way! Of course, Dad is our father! But Jeanie, I thought Mum would have told you?'

'Told me what?'

'About Michael. He had a real thing for her. That's why they fell out in the first place. They grew up together in England. But apparently, he was distraught when she told him she was going to marry Dad and tried to stop her. He eventually followed her to Australia. Sounds like he was unhealthily obsessed with her.' Evie coughs again. 'Dad never trusted him. He said he was overly confident and cocky. That kind of thing never went down well with him. Dad was quite the opposite.'

Tears of relief prick Jean's eyelids, and she holds back a sob.

'Mum insisted she owed Michael's mother a great debt and had promised to watch out for him. I remember her saying, "He's my responsibility now." I didn't understand it of course. Not for years.'

'I thought they were close because Michael managed her career. He invested in her talent.'

'Surely, she told you about *that*, Jeanie? The carry-on when she won the Archibald—apparently, he flipped. As you know, she became an overnight sensation. Maybe he was jealous? He watched her like a hawk. But when she came home after having Rick, she was rarely seen in public. She gave up the interviews quick smart and refused to do any more.'

Jean sighs. 'I guess I didn't know her well at all.'

'Jeanie, I missed you more than you can ever imagine. I can't wait to see you again—and Rick. And the vineyard! I can't imagine it! Oh, by the way—'

Jean takes a breath, expecting the worst.

'I have to remind you—seriously—you're the only one of us with Dad's pointy nose!'

Tears well in Jean's eyes as she laughs. She need never give rise to the shameful words and thoughts again. Now, there's only one thing left to do.

'Thank you, Evie! I do have something important to tell you; something I've kept from everyone. But I'll explain it in person when you're here for the gallery exhibition. And once I'm through my recovery.'

Jean hangs up the phone and bursts into tears. But this time, they are tears of relief and happiness. Her heart is full.

On visiting day, Jean greets Rick in the sunroom. She'd waited until she was through the first torrid weeks before she allowed him to visit. Beams of light stretch the lawn; the variegated garden beds have the look of those in the Domain, the same Sydney gardens she'd walked through a million times, wondering what was happening in her son's life.

He bounds in like a puppy and squeezes her in an enthusiastic hug. 'I'm so proud of you, Jeanie. Look at you! You've done so well! The doc has kept me updated.' She hears the relief in his tone.

'I'm feeling really well. I'm certainly not proud of the weakness I have for drink, or for the way I allowed it to take over my life. But I'm putting it behind me.'

'Great stuff, Jeanie.'

'Now, tell me your news. I want to hear about the winery. How's it coming along? Have the painters finished?'

'Yeah, it looks amazing! Just a few things to touch up, and we'll be ready for the installation—' There's a flush of colour in his clean-shaven face. He brushes back his fringe. 'Actually, I've had some professional help with the decorating.'

'Good for you—'

'From Summer. I've been seeing her. She said she explained how we were together, years ago—'

And has conveniently left that morsel out of discussions when she calls to check in each night.

Jean is delighted that the two people she dearly cares about are working things out. She hadn't realised what she'd been missing all these years; the intimacy of a close friendship—the girl talk. But the inclusion Jean craves more than anything is for Rick to keep sharing every part of his life with her.

He shrugs. 'After she contacted me about your relapse, things just kind of clicked. It was full on back then, but I remembered how thoughtful and caring she was and realised what a chance it was to try again. I think she's the real deal, Jeanie.'

'I'm so glad for you.' Jean squeezes his hands. 'I think she's terrific.'

'It's great to have her back in my life. She's pretty special. I really mucked up last time and won't make that mistake again. I'm giving it a red-hot go,' he nods slowly, '*and* she's been a huge help with the renovations. She sure knows how to whip those tradies into line. They don't know what's hit them!'

'I'm pleased, Rick. I can't thank Summer enough for what she did for me.'

'Yeah, I couldn't agree more. We might have lost you, Jeanie.' He leans in and gives her a kiss. 'Just when you'd come back home too.'

The touch of his lips on her forehead almost brings her undone. Whatever happens now, at least she knows Summer will support him.

'Hey, I have those baby things you asked for,' he frowns. 'But what's this all about?' He lays out the white matinee jacket with its pretty scalloped pattern and rests the bonnet and bootees on top. 'Who are they for?'

It's time. She's put it off long enough.

Jean twirls the ribbon around her finger, noting the knobbly knot where her clumsy stitches had attached it to the bonnet, to secure under Rick's tiny chin.

'I'm not sure what I can say that will make this easier.'

'Are you okay?'

'I knitted this set for you—'

'You did? Wow, that's a bit cute,' He laughs his deep throaty laugh and holds his hand up. 'Thanks. But I'm pretty sure we have a way to go before I'll need them!'

Jean takes a deep breath and rests a hand on his leg.

'I made the set when I was *expecting* you, Rick. When I was pregnant with you. *I'm* your mother. Not Aurora—'

'Holy shit!' He stands and her hand drops away. 'No! No, you can't be.'

Jean's heart beats faster. 'I'm sorry, Rick, but it's true. An illegitimate child in the 1950s wasn't easily accepted. I was young and didn't have a choice. Aurora decided it was best to bring you up as her son.'

'But why didn't she tell me? Why didn't she ever talk about you?' Colour drains from his face as he paces.

'We argued. I left home. We never spoke again.'

'All this time she lied to me.'

Jean suddenly feels protective of Aurora, of her decisions and her reputation. 'I know this is a shock, Rick, but there's more to the story. I've been trying to piece it together myself...'

'Wait! You must have been at boarding school?' He turns, horrified.

This is harder. If only she could blink away the next minutes and move on. But it has to be faced. Now.

'Yes, I was just sixteen. I wanted to keep you. I thought I could, but it wasn't possible. Aurora wouldn't hear of it.'

'Oh God, Jeanie. Of course not! You had your whole life ahead of you! But what about the guy? Did he support you? Did you care for him?'

She looks up. 'Your father was Michael. Michael Golding.'

'Are you shitting me?' He raises his voice. 'Mum's patron? But he was so much older—'

'Yes.' Jean clenches her jaw. 'It was a difficult situation. There were extenuating circumstances—'

'What? Like he was a bloody child molester? Shit, Jeanie, I can't deal with this. I just *can't!*' He runs his hand through his hair and looks more shrinking violet than force of nature.

She steps forward, reaching for his hands. 'I'm so sorry, Rick. I never wanted to hurt you. That's why I stayed away, stayed out of your life. I avoided anything or anyone that reminded me of my past. I was hurt, angry, lost. Sometimes I don't know how I survived. But I love you Rick, as a brother *and* as a son. I only hope in time you can find a way to forgive me.'

Rick bats her hands away. 'I need time to process this. It makes a lie of everything I've believed in—of all I know of my past. Who I am. I thought my parents were fantastic. Perfect. But they lied to me! They both bloody lied through their teeth!'

The pain on his face makes her stomach turn.

'They *were* your parents. They loved you and gave you everything. Who you are, and the man you've become, is because of their love for you. They were more amazing than I ever gave them credit for. And they cherished you, Rick.'

'I can't.' He holds his hands up in surrender and leaves the room.

Jean crawls onto her bed into foetal position, tucking her knees in tight. Then heartfelt sobbing—relief that the conversation is done and sorrow at the hurt she has caused--heaves from her body until she has no more tears left to cry.

TATIANA

37

Petrograd, 1916

After more than twelve months of bandaging wounds and spoon-feeding dying soldiers, I'm tired of this war. I cannot shake the invasive stench of mud and blood nor the feeling of suffocation. Grit and grime work beneath my fingernails; no matter how hard I scrub, the reek of death and despair festers beneath the surface.

The wounded and maimed flow through the hospital doors faster than ice melts in the spring. Some have injuries so debilitating they will never work again, let alone return to face the enemy. I'm surrounded by men more accustomed to wielding scythes and sickles and ploughing fields than wreaking havoc on a battlefield with swords and guns. While women replace the factory workers conscripted into service, others are starving and arrive with their children on foot, presenting themselves for aid. Guns and cannons have destroyed our crops and farming land, and since the prohibition was enforced on alcohol at the beginning of the war, grain has become the best form of currency. Hungry peasants are now hoarding it.

The Tsar has dismissed his military commander and taken control. But he ignores the recommendations of his generals in the War Ministry and fails to heed the concerns of foreign diplomats. I live in a constant state of worry. The people grow restless, angered by the absence of the Tsar, the lack of victory, and the shortage—or reluctance—of capable men. Our defence is left to inexperienced youth, our women, and the elderly.

The underlying scent of danger is everywhere. Not only physical danger, but the threat to the pillars of our society; concern that the centuries-old structures that have existed in the Russian Empire will come tumbling down around us. The people have become wary, suspicious about the fate of our future. Some even whisper we might be better off in the hands of the Kaiser. Then there are those who would report such treasonous disloyalty for the payment of a *kopek* or two. *Where is the might and power of the Russian Empire? What will become of us?*

The wise woman in Crimea forewarned war and blood. Death for one who cannot escape his past. What more did she see ahead of me?

Daily it becomes clearer that my husband spoke the truth.

While reading by candlelight one night, I hear footsteps in the hallway. I gather a shawl over my slip, expecting Marthe. But when I open the bedroom door Ilya Petrovich stands before me, carrying a bottle and two lead crystal glasses procured from goodness knows where.

'What are you doing here?'

'Will you take pity on your husband and invite him in?' He appears nonchalant, yet I wrestle both thrill and relief. *He is alive.* He fills my room in such a masculine way that I am immediately at odds.

I clasp my shawl closer, conscious of my diaphanous night attire when he invites me to join him on the sofa. 'I wasn't aware of your return...'

'I can leave if you prefer?' He pours the brandy with his eyebrow raised.

'No, but of course, I would never turn you from your home. It has been quite some time.'

'I had business in the city to attend to and hoped you might welcome my company. Or perhaps, like to celebrate.'

'Celebrate? What have we to celebrate?'

At his ardent stare, I hold my breath. Time stands still. The tension between us sets a candle flickering.

'Us, *Tatushka*. We are alive. This war and the great losses make me realise there is no time to waste. Surely you cannot fail to admit what we know in our hearts.' His burning gaze meets mine and then lingers on my lips.

'I thought we agreed—'

While I may have insisted it was my decision, it seems he is the one to show a change of heart. My heartbeat thrums in my ears.

'Did we, indeed?' His beautiful eyes light with mirth. 'I am foolish enough to believe you feel something for me—aside from contempt. But if it is not the case, then let us celebrate that we are both here in flesh and blood—and drink to my patience, shall we?'

I clench my jaw. What does he know of my feelings? I've had no word from him, yet in truth, I have prayed for his safety. The mix of relief and anger discomfort me. 'Do you dare to presume to know what I feel?'

'Do I *dare*?' His voice lowers, like a rumble of thunder through my core. 'Do I dare to presume—what? To care for you?' He leans forward and takes my hands. 'Dare to want to protect you?'

I wriggle free.

'God knows, Tatushka, I have dared you to let me love you, but instead you make me beg. I confess to many things, but I am no beggar.' He's so close I can feel his chest rise and fall with each short breath.

This declaration has come from nowhere. Or has it? I've been so intent on my son and this wretched war that I have stealthily avoided addressing my feelings for him.

'I've stood by while you smiled and curtsied to the Tsar and Tsarina and held my tongue at the poor treatment given you and your son. Although, I can imagine many reasons for the Tsarina's jealousy.'

He is foolish to speak in this way. 'Hush, Ilya. You mustn't.' I point to the walls and the door.

'Indeed, there is much I *mustn't* do or say. But the world is changing. Russia must change too. You, with your noble heart and misguided loyalty, drive me to distraction. I cannot stand by and watch you follow the ways of the imperial family if it threatens to bring about your downfall.' His fingers untangle my braid, and he loops them into my loosened hair.

'I'm crazed, Tatushka. Day and night you haunt me. I've desired you since I first saw you. You are beautiful, and yet so much more. The war sets me on a path that may well see to my end. I ask you, am I wrong to hope you care for me too?'

His declaration flashes and tumbles inside my head. I do not doubt the desire in his eyes nor the flame of warmth lit beneath them. He is as decisive in his words as his deeds. I understand his steadfast loyalty belies what he sees as best for Russia. I see it in his concern for the rule of the country, and for the fears and concerns he holds regarding all we must build on once this war is over.

I have been starved of his presence. Indeed, I long for him; this man offers me hope for the future. But still, I am coy in my reply.

'I cannot say...'

'Cannot or will not? Come. Let us stop the ruse.' He brushes a kiss across my knuckles, his eyes bright with passion. 'Grant me one kiss, and if you feel nothing, I will walk away. I swear on my life, I would never force you against your will. But if this is not what you want—if you care nothing for me, say the word and I will not persist.'

Through the fabric of my robe, the heat of his hand burns my flesh. 'Your hair is the colour of sunlight.' He twirls a lock around his fingers. 'As though you glow from within.'

'Please...' I am at a loss.

His face levels with mine. 'I admire your strength. You are a contradiction—both defiant and evasive. But I see the fire inside you, waiting for the flint.' His words are murmured in a husky breath. My body aches—aches to be held, aches for his arms, his mouth.

'I love you, Tatushka, and by God, I want you.'

A gasp escapes my lips. His heartfelt confession shocks me. I waver like a tower of jelly toppled from its mould, and my heartbeat pounds in my ears.

Eager for his kiss, it is me who takes the plunge. Heady with the scent of his breath, the sweetness of warm spices and brandy envelop me. I long for his hard body against mine. I sink deep into his full lips and cradle his face, drawing him closer. His arms wrap around me like iron bands, and the need of him is hard against the film of my nightdress.

'I did not know you felt this way.' I pull back.

'How could I make you understand?' He rests his forehead against mine. 'You, the proud, twice-widowed Romanov princess. But I dare not go a day longer without declaring it. Tomorrow I leave the city. I cannot promise what lies ahead, but I must make you understand what you mean to me.'

I take him by the hand to draw him into my bed, but he stops and holds me from him with a groan so primal it stuns me.

'I have desired you from the beginning, but I must have all of you, Tatushka, your body, your heart, your love—'

I stare into eyes full of love and sadness. He is a mixture of fire and ice, humour and scepticism. A man who will stand for what is right and fight against all that is wrong. I see truth and honesty swimming in amber eyes.

My heart. I once thought it locked and clasped shut forever. He loves me. The sense that I have been fighting in his presence, my uncertainty in his company—I recognise it now for what it is. Fear. Fear of love, of loss, and the greatest fear of all—fear of opening my heart to a man who might break it.

But I will risk it. I will risk all of my heart to love him. Life is too short.

'Yes, you have my love.'

He lifts me to him, and his strong arms hold me tight. I straddle my legs around his waist and feel his heart beat in time with mine.

'I'm not certain when I will return. But I love you, and I will find you, Tatushka. I will do everything in my power to come back to you wherever you are. That I promise you, my love.'

38

Ilya's extended absences are dotted with brief moments of return. The longer we are parted, the harder each departure is to bear. Yet the brevity of our reunions makes me long for his touch. I send my letters to his garrison with no idea if he receives them. The long months we are parted are more of a torture than I imagined possible.

As I seal today's letter with a kiss, Marthe announces a visitor in my parlour.

'Olga, *ma chérie!*' I kiss her cheeks warmly and offer her tea. She shakes her head. 'I thought you were in Kiev?'

'No, I had business to attend to here.' Her smile is forced. 'Nicky has finally agreed to have my marriage annulled. I can hardly believe my good fortune.'

'I am delighted dear, congratulations. You deserve every happiness.'

She inclines her head, but her expression is of concern. 'That is not all. I came as soon as I heard. I'm afraid there is more news for you...'

My immediate thoughts are for Misha.

'It is regarding your cousin, Oleg, and has only now been reported. Nicky informed me he was killed at the Front in the first weeks of the advance—*tragically and heroically* was the tribute he used.'

'Oleg is dead?' I lower my head and ease in a breath to stifle my tears.

My dear, gentle cousin. That explains why I had not heard from him since the war began.

'Nicky asked me to pass on his condolences.'

I see Oleg's bright smile in my mind. His nonchalance, his casual gaiety. The memory reminds me of Georgiy, too.

Olga goes on to explain how he had volunteered to lead a reconnaissance patrol ahead of his regiment at the south-western front. My cousin was never reckless. I find it hard to imagine him willingly sacrificing his life for the cause. He was better suited to business matters and his role in the manufacture of armaments. He was a man full of life and happiness. It is indeed a tragedy. I despair for his young widow and small child.

Rosalind will mourn him too. The years have not diminished her regard for him despite his marriage to another.

'Tatya, I fear for Russia's future. I had a terrible row with Nicky when I voiced my concerns. And Alix relies more and more on Rasputin to ease the Tsarevich's pain. He alone offers her comfort and support in her prayers. She refused to even speak with me. But prayers alone will not help heal the dear boy.'

I shiver and draw my shawl across my shoulders at the mere mention of the monk's name. At the implications of losing the Tsarevich.

'Nicky insists they have faith in Rasputin's ability to heal him. He said he is a man of piety, and that he alone recognises the imperial family's difficulties and those who are against them. You cannot imagine the intent on my brother's face. I'm concerned he is as beholden to the monk as Alix!'

Olga's eyes are wide and teary. 'I pleaded with Nicky to listen, but he dismissed me with such the cold look of stone in his eyes. I am bereft. Now he refuses to attend my wedding ceremony.'

'Oh, Olga.' I clasp her hand. These are trying times for us all. 'I'm sure he understands that you meant well.'

Olga sniffs. 'Mama is desperately concerned too. Nicky told her that he now seeks the monk's council in all matters. I ask you this: what does he know of war and battle and ruling an empire?'

That man has too much power. Rasputin is dangerous. Shocked, I listen without comment.

'Their conversation also mentioned Rasputin's alarming visions.'

'What kind of visions?'

'He has foreseen that he will not live into the New Year and that his death will be due to unnatural circumstances,' she whispers. 'He said that following his death, the imperial family would not exist beyond two years—'

'That is preposterous!'

But Olga's eyes are wide with dread. 'Mama was apoplectic on her return home. What's to become of us, Tatya? What of Russia?'

Unsettled by the news of dear Oleg's death, my alarm is further tempered by fears regarding the power and influence of the monk. Who gives the orders in this country? Russia appears gripped in that man's thrall. If only the Empress would heed the warnings of the court—or at the very least, listen to the concerns of the family.

It is only the next morning that a memory comes to me.

I recall lying in bed after lovemaking, watching my husband pull on his boots and sling a gun across his shoulder. He called me 'twice-widowed.'

The one witness to my marriage to Georgiy is no longer alive. I daren't question the circumstances of Oleg's death, but in the following days, I can't help but suspect there is more to it.

If Ilya knows of both marriages, does he know the truth about Misha too?

British expatriates have set up a food station near the hospital, offering soup and meagre rations of bread to feed those on the streets. My heart breaks to see the suffering. I'm grateful they do what they can to combat the destruction the Kaiser inflicts on our lives. The losses from this war are in numbers greater than at any time in Russia's history.

When not handing out food, Rosalind works alongside me in the hospital. Over the years she has thrown herself into any role she can to ease her grief for the man who broke her heart. Cousin Oleg is a great loss to us all. I pray one day my British friend will find the love of a kind gentleman, as she deserves. Meanwhile, her once ivory hands are red and wrinkled from washing wounds and tending patients.

One morning, she passes me between the wards. She lowers her lovely eyes. 'Foreign diplomats are hovering in the hallways, today. Buzzing like bees around a hive.'

'They seek decisive action,' I shrug in answer.

I dare not repeat my thoughts: our ruler's father, Alexander III, was an inspirational military leader, but Nicholas II is no match for him. We can do no more than stand silently and watch. While ministers argue and shuffle papers across desks, far too many men have died while defending our borders in Belorussia. Sadly, civilians too are falling victim to this war while the Tsar prevaricates.

'Papa's hands are tied. All he can do is support the Tsar in his decisions. However, when it comes to Russia's future, it appears he doesn't take the input of foreigners lightly.' A frown wrinkles her forehead.

'Russia's rule is as it should be. Perhaps things will change now the Tsar is at the front with his troops—'

'Tatiana Vladimirovna! Bring more bandages.' The matron, Lady Callaghan, interrupts from the doorway. She wipes an arm across her forehead as strands of grey hair escape her headscarf.

The Nicholas Hall houses men recovering from head injuries and amputations. We never have enough bandages.

We rush through our daily routine, surrounded by the constant drone of voices interspersed with moans and cries of pain. The halls of the Winter Palace are unrecognisable. Much of the valuable art collection has been removed from the walls or covered for protection. Linoleum is spread over the floors and boards are fixed over the Jordan staircase to enable medical staff to wheel their patients. The beautiful main staircase now conveys a constant stream of sombre faces working to save poor souls.

As I hurry back to the ward to fulfil Matron's requirements, I'm confronted by a small child hiding behind a pilaster like a frightened bird. She may well have seen death before, but I doubt she has ever seen a scene such as this. She takes in the rows of canvas beds and frowns at the sound of the men's moans and cries.

Surprisingly, it is not the wounded that most alarm her. Her gaze is fixed on the only painting that remains; da Vinci's *Madonna Litta* hangs at the end of the room with the benign and loving smile of the Virgin Mary and the Christ Child attached to her breast.

'*Rybka*,' I address her gently. Little fish. 'Where have you come from?'

Her dirty face is streaked with the trail of dried tears when she turns to face me. I encourage her with a smile, but she frowns, staring at my covered hair. My white apron is speckled with blood and one fine arc is sprayed across my chest.

'Come, I will not hurt you.' I hold out my hand and use the voice that had soothed Misha when he was young. 'Let us find your mother—'

'Mama is gone.'

'Where did she go?'

'The man took her on a cart. I could not wake her. She was so very cold....'

My heart breaks for her. How will this poor child survive alone? I imagine Misha, lost and hungry.

'Please, can you spare bread?'

I nod and take her hand. It's like a slab of marble inside mine. 'Come. Let us find you food, and clean clothes. What is your name, *rybka*?'

'Anya Ivanovna.' She shows me six fingers.

'A beautiful name. It means gracious and merciful. Did you know?'

I ease her along the halls with a friendly tone, seeking Rosalind. This morning, she was charged with distributing bundles of clothing to the needy of Petrograd; there are many abandoned or orphaned children like Anya with no one to care for them. With the weather turning, they will need warm clothing too.

Rosalind has begun talks with the Red Cross to relocate the children to an orphanage in the farther provinces where it is safer. I pray that their parents will find them when this is over.

'This is Anya,' I say in English. The child frowns and looks between us, wary and confused. 'The poor child's mother is dead. Can we find her something to eat?'

Rosalind rises from her chair and takes her hands. She shoots me a knowing look. 'Of course, Tatya. Come, child.'

'There is warm water here.' I turn to Anya, reverting to Russian. 'Let us wash your lovely long hair, and Mademoiselle Rosalind can find you clean clothing and some food.'

At the conclusion of my shift, I return to find Anya seated beside Rosalind. Her head is lowered, and hair the colour of glowing embers curls about her shoulders. She is deep in focus with a needle and thread held between deft fingers, copying an embroidery sampler.

A crooked smile reveals a toothy gap in her gums. 'Look what I have made!' She lifts her work and proudly exhibits shaky stitches in coarse red thread.

'Bravo, my *rybka*. You have done all this?'

She meets my gaze proudly. 'I am a quick learner. Do you know how to do this work too?'

I laugh and smile at her. Anya is such a sweet little thing; far too slight for her years, but with the face of an angel.

'Tatiana,' Rosalind stands and takes my arm. 'I'm afraid I have nowhere to place her at present. Protocol prevents me housing a national within the walls of the consulate. What shall we do?'

I see by the tremor of her lips exactly what she expects.

'I will care for her until you find somewhere suitable. I insist.'

'What a wonderful idea. Did you hear, Anya darling. Tatiana Vladimirovna will take you home with her tonight. You will be her guest for the evening and keep her company. How does that sound?'

Rosalind's Russian is stilted, but Anya looks up and smiles. 'Thank you, Mademoiselle Rosalind. And you too, Madame.' Soulful eyes the colour of bluebells in springtime watch me earnestly.

'You are most welcome, Miss Anya. I am delighted to make your acquaintance.' Taking her hand, I give a little bow and feel the warmth as her tiny palm presses into mine.

39

I collect my coat at the end of my shift and hurry through the streets with Misha's latest letter in my pocket. I can't wait to read it to Anya. The child is eager for news of her 'big brother,' so used to the stories I share about him that she believes she knows him well. It's been weeks since he visited, but he promises to stay for tea with us when next on leave.

'Marthe! Can you draw a bath for my *rybka*, please?' I call out as I open the door to my apartments. 'Anya! Anya, your mama is home.'

'Your *mama?*' His voice raises the hair on the back of my neck and sends a shiver right through me. 'It appears I have not been missed at all, my position in the household usurped by a child.'

My empty stomach tumults with butterflies. *My Ilya.*

'An enchanting child, nevertheless,' he grins.

'What are you doing here?'

'Although it has been some time, my love, unless there's been a law written to overturn it, we are still very much married.'

Our marriage was not by choice, yet I am shocked by the intensity of my love for him. It has grown, like a contagion, an ache, an irritation that creeps and burns so slowly that it throbs beneath my skin. I am overcome with a heartfelt fever.

'Is he *really* my papa?' Anya's face is alight with excitement, her hair a riot of strawberry curls. 'I turned him into a horse and rode on his back. We made a charge at Marthe and now she's hiding from us.'

'Rode on his back?' I turn to face him. Though Ilya's face is gaunt, his size has not withered. Instead, his muscular body looks quite menacing. 'Anya Ivanovna has no one and we have room here.'

'A generous offer,' he nods, as Marthe appears to take the child to bathe, 'but I do hope there remains room in your bed for me?'

I meet his gaze with a smile and fire builds inside me. 'How long are you here?'

'Tired of me already?'

'No, that's not what I meant at all—' I feel like a foolish schoolgirl. It's been months since his last return. My cheeks flush remembering our last farewell. 'Is the war at an end?'

'Not yet. And sadly, it is not my only concern. The recent strikes suggest there are too many idle and hungry men who might be tempted to take up weapons against us. We need recruits. I am here for a night and then I must return.'

I nod sombrely, thinking of the casualties I nurse each day.

'I hear Misha is doing well. He is safe with the Pages, at least. I am well-informed of his progress.'

I purse my lips. Misha is my responsibility.

'Just one night?' I ignore further comment.

He raises his eyebrows and golden eyes flash at me. 'I regret I cannot stay longer. But there is only one place I would choose to lay my head tonight...'

His meaning is clear, and his eyes cloud with emotion. But I am nervous.

'I will not interfere with your routine or the child's. I imagine she has already seen more than one her age needs to. But you must take care. The war is far from over, and I expect this unrest to continue for some time.'

My mouth opens and closes like a trapdoor.

'I also need to tell you that whilst I appreciate your letters, I must ask you to stop writing.' He looks away.

'Why? Whatever for?'

'The city is dangerous, and you must take care. There are matters in play that I prefer to keep private. Let us say, it is in your best interests to remain ignorant of my whereabouts. Your letters, charming as they are—may provide enemies with reasons to incite trouble.'

'That is absurd!'

'It's not you alone I am concerned for.' He looks towards the door that Anya exited. 'I cannot say more than this. But it is better you—and Misha--have no knowledge of my movements.'

I cross my arms over my chest. *Dear God!* Is it possible he is a radical, a Socialist after all? Can I trust him? I wrestle with my thoughts.

A fist pounds on the door and Ilya waves me away, opening the door with a pistol in his hand. I hear the rumble of fast speech and irritation in Ilya's low tone.

The door closes and he returns. 'I regret, there has been a change of plan. I must leave immediately.'

'No! Surely you can stay for one night!' I grip his hand with my earlier fears forgotten, instantly feeling the loss of him. I do not want him to leave.

'I am needed, Tatushka. But I implore you,' His eyes are warm and intense once more. 'In the event it becomes unsafe for you here, I ask that you listen to Lord Brassington or seek his help. You may need to leave Russia—'

'Why would I? Russia is my home.' It is only Anya's giggles echoing down the hallway that stop me from raising my voice.

'Please do not argue, and for once, do as I ask. For your safety. Take care, my love.' He steps forward and kisses me deeply then presses his lips to my palm.

He reaches the door. 'Remember, my love, I will find you, wherever you are.'

Too late, I reach for him, but he is gone.

40

Petrograd, January 1917

Marthe has taken Anya with her to queue for provisions. We share the household duties now, and I take pride in all I do for my daughter. I return to my needlework; a dress remade into one for her, in a shade of violet that is a perfect foil for her eyes and Titian locks. She and Misha are the joy that keeps me from despair.

Footsteps approach my door and I hold my breath. My husband appears and pulls me to him. 'How delightful to find my wife here alone.'

'Ilya! Is it safe for you—'

I read the unspoken meaning in his eyes. Our lips meet eagerly, and I savour the taste of him.

He soon pulls away. 'I came to tell you the news.'

'Not more treasonous gossip—'

'It may well be a balm to Russia.'

He smiles and runs his thumb across my lip. His eyes are lit with desire and mischief. He is handsome, and he knows it. I feel a traitorous twinge in my body—a flicker of heat sparks from the pit of my stomach to my toes.

'The war is over?'

'No. The mad monk is dead—'

'Rasputin?' Surely, I misheard.

I can't distinguish relief from angst as a rush of emotion drains through me. A cry catches in my throat.

'Yes, my Tatushka, it *is* true. And while the Empress is locked in her rooms, bereft and grief stricken as she mourns Father Grigori, the city of Petrograd is celebrating the news of his death and people are chanting in the streets. The murderers have confessed.'

'Murderers?' Even a man as distasteful as Grigori Rasputin does not deserve murder. 'Who would do such a thing?'

'A great many would have liked the honour. But I believe they thought to save us from autocratic rulers who took advice from the wild religious preaching of an illiterate and self-serving peasant. One who was repeatedly proven a whoremonger and false prophet.'

'Please do not speak this way.' His words make my stomach churn. 'It is dangerous talk. But the Empress relied on him—'

Ilya ignores me. Self-importance radiates from him like the glow of a white night blazing the sky. His masculine scent surrounds me. In the warmth of his arms, I'm like a tiny starling cradled in a nest.

'The police will investigate, but Felix Yusupov has admitted killing him.'

'Felix?' No, surely not. The handsome prince is one of the court favourites and his wife is the Tsar's niece. They once entertained guests at the best parties and indulged in a life of pleasure. As we all did. I can barely imagine Felix hurting a beetle, let alone a man twice his size.

'Rasputin's body was dragged from the river yesterday, frozen solid and held down by chains. He had taken a bullet to the head.' Ilya continues. 'It appears he proved difficult to dispose of, even in death. I admit, no animal deserves to die like that. However, the generals and politicians will celebrate the monk's demise. The man was like a plague. I, for one, think Prince Yusupov did us a great favour. Though I'd never have believed the young prince capable of it.' He appears greatly impressed.

'Our Empress has banished Yusupov from the city. Or rather, she has instructed the Tsar to demand it.' He raises his eyebrows.

'The imperial family will mourn their holy man.' Alix must be distraught. While they will pray for his soul, I'm ashamed to say I feel no great loss.

Friends and family who counselled against Rasputin have for months been refused entry to Alexander Palace. Alix would hear no talk of Rasputin's departure from her inner circle.

'Now the Empress hides like a hermit in a cave—Saint Seraphim himself. But there is much at stake. The *Duma* requests a greater voice, one representative of the people. The marches, the protests, move us towards this. Rasputin was no friend to Russia. Perhaps this will be for the best.' He takes my hands. 'I'm sorry, it is time to go.'

He stands. 'Without Rasputin's influence over our ruler, the war might finally end. I only hope it has not come too late. With luck, it will be sufficient to hold back the tide of growing tensions and prevent a revolution.'

'Revolution? But only three years ago the tercentenary of Romanov rule was celebrated. The Russian people came out on the streets to rejoice—'

'The Imperial heads do not see what is happening outside their walls. You have witnessed the unrest of our people. My concern is for you, for our future. Life for the *dvoryanstvo* has changed, Tatushka. Take care.'

As the door closes behind him, I place a finger to my lips and savour his parting kisses. Then I lower onto a chair and like the ripple of waves across the water, my body begins to shake. What will become of us?

And what hope is there now of healing the Tsarevich?

JEAN

41

Verity House

Jean checks her watch again. She's sure Summer said she'd be here at eleven.

She picks up her handbag and makes her way to the orange pay phone.

'Jean!' Summer answers on the third ring. 'I was just looking up the number—'

'You haven't left yet?'

'Sorry, Debbie, called in. She was up for a chat. That Mrs Di Maggio —boy does she have an axe to grind!'

'I still have no idea what I did to upset her.' Jean rolls her eyes.

'Never mind,' Summer answers. 'Now she's gloating about how important she is to have a member of the executive management meet with her. Look, I'll fill you in later, but Rick's on his way now.'

'Rick?' Her heart beats quickly. It has been torture not speaking to him since telling him the truth, but Summer insisted that giving him space was best.

'Jean, he was pretty shaken by what you told him. You must have expected it.'

'I'm glad you know too. I would have told you myself, but I had to explain it to him first—'

'Of course, you did! Don't you worry. Everything will work out. Leave it to me. Anyhow, I'll see you tomorrow. Pete said it was fine with him.'

Jean blushes. Her relationship with Pete is now well known. He even suggested she stay with him after leaving rehab, but she will settle back into her cottage first.

'I'd love to see you...both.'

'Bye, Jean.'

Not long after she hangs up, Rick rushes in with a frown crinkled across his forehead. He avoids eye contact for an agonising few minutes as the doctor approaches to shake his hand.

Jean's stomach flip-flops when she reads the embarrassment on his face. He barely glances at her while he engages with the doctor. She stands nearby like a statue, waiting patiently.

They farewell the staff, and Jean leads the way along the cool linoleum-floored corridor and into the sunlight.

As the door shuts behind them, Rick finally addresses her. 'You're looking much better, Jeanie.'

'Thank you.' Grateful he has found his voice, she waits for him to open the car and store her suitcase. 'Summer told me she's coming to Pete's tomorrow.'

'Yes. I'm grateful he's watching out for you. He's been wonderful, hasn't he?'

Jean nods cautiously.

He heaves a sigh. 'Look, I'm really sorry about my reaction. I've been a bit of a dick. I just needed to process what you told me. But seriously, I couldn't be happier. Mother, sister, it doesn't matter to me so long as you're in my life.' He opens his arms and looks at her expectantly. 'Are we okay?'

Jean's smile beams into the sunlight as she steps into his hug.

'Before we head off, I have something to tell you—'

'What is it?' Jean steps back.

'Summer has helped me through all of this. She's been great. And I know it might seem fast, but, well, when you know, you know. I'm going to ask her to marry me.' His hair flops over his eyes, and he looks like a schoolboy. 'What do you think?'

Jean hugs him. 'I'm happy for you, Rick. That's wonderful.'

'The thing is, I'd love her to have Mum's—Aurora's—engagement ring.' Rick looks away. 'It should be yours by rights, but is that okay?'

Jean smiles and kisses him. Her heart feels too big for her chest. Is this what it's like to be a mother? 'Rick, I'm happy for you both. You have my blessing.'

Rick blinks. 'You don't think it's too soppy?'

'Don't be ridiculous. It's perfect. Giving her Mum's ring is a gorgeous sentiment.'

Jean feels the chasm in her heart slowly closing. With a bit of luck, it will be whole again soon.

During her rehabilitation, the psych and her peers in the group sessions encouraged her to address the patterns and habits that have previously tripped her up. There will always be challenges, but she is now surrounded by plenty of people who love her and will support her recovery.

She doesn't miss David Jones, not for one second. It's a relief not to have to return to a workplace where misogynist and chauvinistic attitudes are so entrenched. *I won't dance to that tune again.* After years of hiding her past and concealing her addiction, she's had enough of pretending and playing games.

TATIANA

42

I'm shocked by the change in the ambassador when I visit Rosalind at the British Legation. Lord Brassington appears considerably smaller in stature. He excuses himself and spends the afternoon locked in his study.

Rosalind whispers, 'Papa is writing letters of petition to the King, requesting exile for the imperial family in Britain.'

I sit up straight.

'Papa has also sent the Tsar telegrams urging him to consider the offer, but he continues to ignore all entreaties. He fears he has lost the Tsar's favour and is at pains to know what more he can do to help the imperial family.'

I contemplate her words and take a generous sip of tea. Surely it is dangerous for Lord Brassington to suggest what Russia should do? I'm not certain I have the stomach for such a discussion today.

'I expect the Empress is the only one who can get through to the Tsar.'

'Papa tried to speak to her too. He was distraught when he returned from the Alexander Palace yesterday. He said she gave him the most horrid look of distaste, accused him of interference, and the British government of dictating terms. She insists Russia refuses to be placed in British subservience by following his instructions. Her words were, "The Emperor of All the Russias is the ruler of the largest land in the world, and the most powerful by its sheer number of people." What more can Papa do?'

'We have lost so many men. The people are angry. How can she not see it?' I sigh.

'The failure to sufficiently arm the men during the war has been the downfall of the Russian military and the monarchy. All we can do is wait for word that Britain agrees to offer the family sanctuary.' Rosalind's eyes widen.

'Can Alix not understand that the crowned heads of all countries are in danger? The people are marching for change. They seek democracy. A government who gives them a voice!'

'Papa tried to explain it, but she practically had her man throw him out the door. He said he had never felt so much the wrath of hatred, nor an enemy, in all his years of diplomatic service.' Rosalind nods. 'Papa cares. He is only trying to do what he thinks best for them.'

'Yes of course. I know from experience that the Empress is at all times stubborn. She loves the Tsar unquestionably, and it makes her blind to the fate of the people outside the palace walls. She has never acknowledged a future beyond autocratic rule believing it the Romanov's God-given right. No matter how hard you try, I fear you will not change her mind.'

'Unfortunately, Papa fears it *is* too late. Russia needs to move with the times and accept the offer of forming a Provisional Government.' Rosalind shakes her head. 'They might offer them exile in Livadia or Galicia, but I expect it will not be considered prudent. Papa's deepest fear is for the Emperor's safety.'

'Are those close to the family in danger too?'

'The nobility poses a threat to any new government. I expect it is dangerous for us all.'

'Ilya warned me that the threat of factions of power who want to either restore the monarchy, or oppose a counter-revolution are ever-prevalent. All they would seek is one leader to stand up....'

Rosalind's eyes fill with tears.

Indeed, it is a chilling thought. Misha is almost at adulthood. For years I have feared that if his birthright was exposed, a time would come when he was forced to rule Russia as tsar. What scares me now is that if the current tsar is overthrown, my son could well be the man an alternative government seeks to lead them.

43

Petrograd, 1918

It was only a matter of time.

The boom of cannons muffles the thunder of hooves as people are fired upon in the streets of Petrograd and innocent lives are lost. The newly revived Petrograd Soviets declare that all troops are to ignore the Tsar's generals and submit to their directives. Military forces are quickly overrun; tanks and cannons commandeered by the people are fired down the streets. When the Tsar instructs his troops to maintain the peace and fire on the rioters, his Volynsky Regiment refuse and instead point their rifles into the air. By the next day his troops have joined the revolutionaries.

Within weeks, Tsar Nicholas II has no option but to abdicate.

Word that the Corps des Pages has been disbanded and ordered to assist in the protection of the foreign embassies gives me some small comfort; troops guarding the foreign legations offer a safer refuge than patrolling the streets. My son is not yet eighteen. I pray he uses his good sense and steers clear of trouble. When Rosalind advises that Misha will be stationed at the British legation, little Anya mops my tears of relief with her pinafore.

The Tsar and Tsarina are now imprisoned in the Alexander Palace. But while people in the street cry with excitement and celebrate freedom with a newborn sense of hope, I fret for the imperial children who will be shocked by the reaction of the people they believed love them.

I pen a note to Alix with my regards, acknowledging how afeared she must be for her family's safety. But then, realising the risk of reminding anyone of my relationship to the family, I burn the missive instead.

My thoughts turn to the Dowager Empress who bravely attempted to speak sense to the Tsar. She must be appalled at the turn of events. By the time she intercepted him, he had already signed away the end to Romanov rule. With Olga far away in Kiev, I decide to pay her a call, concerned for her welfare.

My nurse's uniform is my best protection as I make my way to Anichkov Palace. When I enter the drawing room, the dowager is pacing the floor and dabbing at tears. Throughout the hallways carved Novgorod trunks are open and maids are packing and unpacking her belongings.

'Why did Nicky agree, Tatiana Vladimirovna?' She takes my hands and leads me to the settee. 'And then, to sign away Alexei's crown too.'

My heart is in my throat as the gravity of her words sink in.

'I tried to reach Nicky on the telephone, and by telegram, and missed him by mere hours. He was given no choice. The Provisional Government sent him home from the frontline to suffer the shame of losing the throne after three hundred years of Romanov rule. *Three hundred years, Tatiana!* If only he had listened to me.

'Now Soviet Red Guards surround Alexander Palace. They are the supporters and soldiers of this new worker's state.' She tilts her nose in distaste. 'The imperial family is under house arrest.'

'Your Imperial Majesty, I am so sorry. What will you do?'

'I can no longer remain here. I leave for Crimea immediately. But no new regime will welcome interference from a deposed tsar or his family. I imagine they will remove Nicky too. As soon as the new Provisional Government exile him from Tsarskoye Selo, then with God's blessing, all will be well.'

'I sincerely regret it has come to this....' I take the dowager's hand.

'You, my dear, must think of your son as well as yourself!' She leans in and kisses my forehead. 'Come with me! Come to my summerhouse. Bring Misha and leave the city.' She lowers her voice. 'You will be safe there.'

I shrug her concern away with a feigned smile. I cannot expect her to provide sanctuary for us in Crimea. I have Anya to think about, and Marthe too. The dowager would not consider them her responsibility. But they are mine. I assure her of our safety.

Her words remain with me long after I leave. The streets are chaotic. Men and women pillage goods from shopfronts where doors and windows are smashed, and gunfire rings out while inebriated men wave pistols in the air as though they are playthings. I dart like a fox from corner to corner until I reach the front of the palace, and the entrance used by the medical staff. But men bar my way. I indicate my uniform and they wave me on; given the dangerous combination of loaded guns and wine purloined from the cellars of vacated palaces, I do not argue.

A car turns into the street with the flag of the British Embassy flapping. I wave my arms to signal it to stop, relieved to see Rosalind inside.

'The streets are not safe, Tatya!' she exclaims.

'Might I ride with you to the legation? It is essential I speak to Misha.'

At the Embassy, Rosalind kindly leaves us in private as I hug my son, almost a man, to my breast. 'Misha, the Dowager Empress is leaving for Crimea. There may come a time soon, when we too, must consider leaving the city—'

'Leave, Mama? I have no interest in fleeing the city. I have a duty here, as a cadet, and as well as that, there is change afoot for this country.'

He stands defiantly, and I am shocked. I listen to him champion the rights of workers and the need for government reform. When did my son become so strong, so principled?

While to an extent I agree with his sentiments, how can I explain what that might mean for him? 'My darling, that may be so, but it is for our safety. People like us—'

'Mama, we are in no danger. My father was a sailor, an ordinary man, and you are a worker now.'

My stomach turns as I realise how ardently he supports change. How has this happened during his years at the Corps des Pages—an institute with age-old traditions in service to the Emperor?

'Besides, I must remain and follow orders. Then once the embassies no longer need me, I will follow the way of the future. Educated men like me have the opportunity to progress and rise in this new system of government. It is important for all voices to be heard, Mama. I am keen to be part of it.'

It appears his discussions with Ilya Petrovich have very much influenced his view of the world. Of course, he has no knowledge of his position; perhaps it is time to tell him?

No. It will be impossible to make Misha leave, and I refuse to go without him. Desperate for a way forward, I return my thoughts to the two people who also need my protection. Without news from Ilya, I know not what to do.

By the time I reach the rear entrance of my building, tears are streaming down my face. My heart races as I take the servants staircase, listening for signs of trouble. Marthe opens the door and flings herself into my arms. Dear Anya clings to my legs like a wet skirt on a windy day. We three are safer together.

That night I beg Marthe to follow her sister and brother-in-law who are ready to flee the city, taking their possessions to begin a new life. But she vows to remain with me. Her loyalty is a gift indeed.

Within months, even the new Provisional Government has lost control, with little authority over marauders who besiege the streets. The news that property and possessions are to be divided and shared equally has thousands of people descending on the city and taking whatever they see as their egalitarian right. Windows smash as they storm the shops, looting, fighting, attacking, and assaulting anyone who crosses their path. Transport is blocked, and the power is out. With no way to bring in supplies and the telephone lines cut, the city is under complete and utter anarchy.

I, who avoided talk of politics and dissent, now recognise the shifting sands between the opposing radical factions. No one expected Lenin to return from exile, or for his Bolshevik party to rise to power. As Party leader, he demands a Soviet government consisting of soldiers, peasants and workers. There is no room in his plan for the former ruling classes. Lenin's Reds now fight the socialist Whites—represented by the remaining allied forces that support democratic socialism, along with monarchists and the capitalists of the city.

First the people abandon the monarchy, and then they overthrow the Provisional Government. Finally, the garrison troops give up their posts and join the Bolshevik Reds as well.

Red flags are the new insignia and hang from windows and walls of every building in the city. The streets become unsafe for men in any uniform other than a Red. They gather in numbers like mud sticking to a dry wheel.

Any man with a red band on his arm sees it as an opportunity to 'appropriate' whatever they see of value. People are paid for lies, for reports, to spy, or worse still, for the lies and propaganda they invent. There is no law, no order, and no policing. 'Former people' are seized, led away, and disappear without a trace.

We live in constant fear and danger, locked inside my apartments. Marthe and Anya cower behind me as another frenzied attack begins outside.

'Mama, I am so afraid!' Anya closes her eyes and rests her head in my lap. With no electricity, we sit in the shadows, our rooms lit by the amber glow of candlelight.

'Hush now, *Anushka*.' I force the quaver from my voice and whisper in her ear to hide the sound of fury outside as I stroke her hair.

Marthe moves to close the curtains. 'Stay away from the windows,' I urge. We have removed the few remaining ornaments we have left to avoid breakage.

Outside, the screams and shouting reach a deafening crescendo; the mob moves closer, pounding on doors and demanding entry. Boots echo through the hallways and within minutes they reach mine. I dare not consider the damage they might provoke. Or what they will do to us. It is terrifying.

'Take what food we have and place it on the table. With luck it will be enough to deter them,' I tell Marthe.

I retrieve the pistol Ilya left with me from a cavity secured in a false floor beneath my bureau. I pray I will not need to fire it.

A resounding crash echoes from below and heavy footsteps move closer, thundering up the marble staircase. Ilya warned of revolution. With luck, he will return to me soon, but in the meantime, I'm responsible for those I hold dear. I turn to Marthe.

'Take Anya, lock the door to your room and remain silent.'

Anya's eyes fill with tears. 'Please, Mama! I want to stay with you.' She clings to me like a second skin.

'Hush, my *rybka*, be brave. Come.' My voice is braver than I feel as I rock her in my arms and nod to Marthe to leave us. I'm trembling so hard that hugging my daughter close is all that gives me strength.

I slide with my back against the wall to the opposite side of the room; if only we could sink into the floor and disappear without bearing witness to this moment. My breath catches in my throat. I whisper a prayer, though I have suspected for some time that God is not listening to us here in Russia. How could he, with all that is happening?

A group of men crash inside and their stares dart around the room. Thankfully, few are armed, apart from the bricks they used to break down the door. Their faces redden when they notice me alone with Anya clinging to my skirts. I'm astonished as several men remove their caps, as though unsure what to do next.

'Give me your guns,' one bullish voice barks from the pack. 'Your weapons. Where do you keep them?' His eyes are wilder than the rest.

I force control into my voice. 'What need do I have for guns?'

He takes in the furnishings. My sitting room is a woman's world, devoid of hunting trophies or vestiges of masculine power. I shake my head, doing my best to assume I am innocent of whatever they suspect.

'What *boyar* lives here?'

I do not wish to appear highly born and glance to the mending on a chair with my sewing basket beside it. The man's gaze follows mine. His associates shuffle nervously, uneasy in this overtly feminine parlour. I imagine it is quite unlike anything they are used to.

'I've worked at the hospital since they fled to their estates. But there is food here. Please. Take it.' I beckon to the table, feeling the weight of the pistol deep in my skirt.

They rush like wolves, filling their mouths and stuffing pockets with whatever they can manage. Suddenly a cannon booms. Panes of glass rattle and the walls tremble from the deafening blast that appears to have come from the port. My heart beats fast as the leader looks to his men and calls them to action.

'That's the signal! We must go! Take to the streets!'

I pull Anya close and cover her head with kisses as the stench of dirt and sweat fades with them through the open door. My legs shake, and we drop to the floor. I rock back and forth, my hold so tight on her that eventually she squeals and wriggles free.

'I was frightened, Mama,' she nods. 'They are very bad men.'

'You are a brave, brave girl, my *rybka*. But they are not bad—just hungry and tired. Life is hard for them. Hush now, I will always keep you safe.'

We barricade the doors, and I lie awake all night, listening as groups of drunken soldiers and sailors join in the rampage. The city is in chaos. *Revolution.*

Officious voices call at my door, and two men barge inside wearing the red armbands of the Soviet state. They coldly demand to see our papers. 'Whose child is this?' One flicks his head from Anya to Marthe and then to me.

'She is an orphan, in my care.'

'Where are her papers?'

I shake my head.

'Register her immediately. In the Council of People's Commissar State, it is essential every Russian citizen has the correct documentation.'

'Yes, yes, I will arrange it.' My senses are heightened and in the confines of the entrance, his odour is overpowering. 'Is that all?'

They take inventory of my apartments, noting the so-called 'vacant' rooms and listing the size and height of all 'immovable' objects in my possession, such as the pianoforte. Then they write me an order and insist I am under obligation to be taxed on these objects and require payment immediately.

The two return a few days later. Although, I cannot be sure—the Reds all look the same to me.

'The surplus rooms have been registered. You, too, must register for work. All apartments have been requisitioned by the State. *Bourgeoisie* and *dvoryanstvo* buildings are for the use of *proletariat* workers—not for capitalists and former people. You three are assigned one room. The new housing superintendent will make the necessary arrangements.'

'I *am* a worker,' I hold my head up, 'at the hospital.'

'Soon, there will be no need for a hospital. You must obtain new documents and sign on for other work.'

'But what of the men injured in the war...'

'The Tsar's war is over. We refuse to waste the lives of workers for capitalist gain. Workers are required in our factories. We all must contribute to make the state great.' With that, he turns. 'You have three days to register for work. Move your belongings immediately. Register your details with the housing commandant. The expropriation order to rehouse workers and allocate surplus rooms of bourgeois and noble property is in place.'

Within days, the hospital is disbanded, and a floor of the Winter Palace is taken over by Bolshevik officials.

'What will we do?' Marthe asks.

I look around and, in the midst of a room that once held valuable objects, a wide-eyed child stares up at me in trust. I shrug. Marthe and my family are what is important.

'We make room.'

44

My husband emerges from the shadows, dressed in the tunic and trousers of a factory worker. I weep in relief. His eyes are ragged and red-rimmed with tiredness.

'You have grown so thin. Here, Tatushka, eat this.' Ilya reaches for a tin in his overcoat and my stomach growls as the smell of pickled cabbage rises around me. Like a magician he then produces a chunk of blackened bread and a wedge of dried cheese. I divide it into portions to save for Marthe and Anya when they wake.

'I'm sorry. It was all I could find. There are too many soldiers...'

I shiver and Ilya pulls me close. I breathe in his masculine scent; he's been hiding deep in the woodlands. He is real and alive, and I love him, fiercely. I feel safe in his arms, as though nothing can hurt me. I give thanks to every moment spent in his company.

'My darling, thank God you are safe! What word is there...?'

'Hush, Tatushka. Save your energy.' He takes me by the hand to our bed and cradles me in his arms. Tears of relief wet his chest. With few words to share to explain away our fears, we convey our feelings through the touch of naked skin against skin, and in the love and refuge we share in each other's arms.

His kisses are tender, and his lips awaken passion in me, as always.

My body yearns for him. The heart of my womanhood throbs in anticipation and my breathing quickens. He quickly divests us of our clothes and lifts me as though I am a feather in the breeze to straddle his body. Ilya stares into my eyes while pleasuring me with masterful strokes, and beams with satisfaction when I can no longer stand it, and I shudder in delight. The spark in his eyes inflames me; I ride him deeper, until with the weight of my breasts in his hands, he takes me swiftly and utters a jagged groan with his mouth pressed to mine.

Afterwards, I lay across his lap tracing a finger along the sharp line of his jaw, the hard lines etched on his face. When I speak of the future, his eyes cloud with a sign I cannot read.

'Is there word of the Tsar? The family's exile?'

Ilya shakes his head. 'I expect they will tell us in their own time.' His voice is strained. I rest my head on his chest.

Since the Bolsheviks opened the prison gates, vagrants and the poverty-stricken walk alongside thieves and murderers who were punished for crimes under tsarist rule. Now, men of the most despicable kind are free while there are reports the bourgeoisie and nobility have been dragged away and detained for questioning. Most of the aristocracy have fled the city, but others receive no justice and are paying the price with their lives.

'Leaving Russia is the Tsar's only hope now.'

'Will the Reds allow it? I don't know which is worse—the Germans or the Bolsheviks.'

'I tend to agree.'

'Rosalind said the British would help them. But why are they taking so long? And what of the rest of us? Olga, the grand dukes and duchesses, the Yusupovs? With the world still at war, where will we all go?'

I try to picture life in another country. Will we ever be a family, with Ilya and I at the head and the children safely in our care?

'As allies, France should be open to us; many have settled there already. But the French are distrustful of Germany, and if Lenin and Trotsky make a German alliance, we will have little hope of exile there.'

Ilya takes my hand pressing his lips to my knuckles, my fingertip, then turns it over and kisses my palm. Goose bumps trail the back of my neck. It is the sign he uses in parting. Tears prick my eyes. 'No, my darling, you've just returned!' I cling to his chest.

He kisses my hair and curls a strand around his fingers. 'Tatushka—if I never had to arise from your bed, I would be a fortunate man. But I must leave at dawn. I have a duty to my family, as you have—'

'Your family?'

'It appears my brother seeks to meet with me, and I am at liberty to speak to him. I received word today he is on his way to Petrograd. It is best I meet him alone.'

Ilya's smile doesn't reach his eyes and I see him picking through his thoughts for the right words. I cannot imagine how he must feel, to be without his brother, and then for him to miraculously reappear.

But then I notice the tightness in his lips, the strain furrowed between his brows.

'Is he dangerous?'

Ilya avoids my stare as he gently pushes away from our entanglement to stand. He reaches for his coarse worker's shirt, and straps beneath it the armaments as much a part of him as life itself.

'I love you, Tatushka, but I will not lie. If my brother finds me first, or determines our connection—well, let us say, it will not end well. I've heard he rises in power through the ranks of the Reds. I cannot guarantee how changed he is since his imprisonment. He was always one to expect remuneration in return for his actions. I imagine he wants no more than to avenge those in the tsarist regime who locked him away. But I will not risk him near you.'

'So, I am a threat to you? What will happen when he learns about us?'

Ilya holds my hands between his. Then he cups my face and lowers his lips, gently kissing my eyes, my nose and then my mouth, saying nothing more. Amongst all the fear and uncertainty in this world, his love is the only certainty I can believe in.

But Ilya cannot start anew until he resolves his quarrel with his brother. There's no other way for him, not for a man with such a high moral code of personal honour. I know nothing of their animosity, but I suspect it is mutual. They are different men who have shared no more than blood for their entire lives.

'Hush, my darling. Do not concern yourself. If there were another way, I would take it. First, I must win my brother's trust and once I gauge the situation, I will deal with him. But with him free and baying for blood, you are in danger. You need to leave. Take the child and seek help from the Brassingtons. Send Marthe to her relatives.'

'And what of Misha?' I bite my lip.

'He is almost a man. Misha is safer at the legation. The tide is turning, and we must continue to fight for what is right.'

'Fight? What do you mean?' My hands fly to my mouth. 'Do you expect my son to turn over to the Reds? To oppose MY family? Is this what you suggest?'

'The imperial family cannot protect you now.'

I am at a loss at how to make him understand. 'My darling,' I employ my most soothing tone, 'I cannot allow Misha to remain.'

'You are right to protect Anya, but Misha and I can take care of ourselves. Leave as soon as you can. Once order is restored, we will follow you through Finland. Give me time, Tatushka. I will find a way back to you. Please don't make this harder than it is.'

'But my son! Please, Ilya. With the socialist factions rising—'

'Tatiana Vladimirovna, enough!' Ilya stands with hands on hips. I'm reminded of his proud heritage. Snow runs through his veins while passion burns in his heart. 'Your safety is my concern,' he hisses. 'Trust me, Tatushka.'

With a heavy sigh I turn away, tormented by the secret I keep from my husband and my guilt at not trusting him enough with the truth.

JEAN

45

Castlemaine

'It's good to be home.'

Jean smiles as she brings a tea tray down to the garden. Pete has been checking her veggies and watering the dahlia seedlings she planted before her relapse. He runs his hands under the tap and joins her on the garden bench.

'It's terrific news about Rick and Summer.' Pete smiles down at her like the giant in *Jack and the Beanstalk* emerging from the clouds. 'I'm happy they found a way back to each other. Perhaps when they first met, they were just too young.'

'Summer is such a steadying influence.' Jean stirs sugar into her tea, 'and a great fit for Rick. She's certainly helped ease the way forward in our relationship too. My revelation came as a complete shock. He adored Aurora—'

Pete takes her hand. 'It was a huge burden for you to carry all your life, but your mother had good reason to do what she did. He'll come around.'

'You're right, of course. Though I'm sure there'll be some resentment.'

'He will understand.' He smiles, 'When I found out I was adopted I was angry at first, but in time I saw it was for the best. Rick will too.'

'You never told me you were adopted!'

He shrugs and takes a sip of his tea. 'Tell me why you came back to Castlemaine if this is where Rick was born? It was brave of you...'

'I needed to face it. The trauma of our separation was the start of my battle with alcohol. It's been strangely cathartic.'

'There's no doubt confronting a difficult past is hard, but you're doing all the right things, Jean.' He draws her into the crook of his arm.

'You know, rehab uncovered certain memories I must have blocked. Some came back to me, but there are other things I just can't remember; little things, like the woman who helped me when I was in labour.'

'Was she a local woman? I bet Merle would have known her,' he laughs, 'or Baba—'

'Baba?'

'My mother. I called her Baba.'

'Wasn't she English?'

'I was born in England, but no, she was Russian.'

Jean shakes her head. 'The woman who assisted me spoke with an accent and quite a heavy one.'

'Really? Do you remember anything else about her?'

Jean gazes into the garden. 'I remember hearing voices, but I couldn't make out the conversation. It's coming back to me now...'

She frowns and rests her hands under her chin. *Nyet*! *Nyet*! She pictures a woman holding up her hand while Aurora swore and paced the room.

'My eyes were closed for most of the time. I was so frightened. I sensed that Aurora wanted me to go to the hospital, but it seemed as though the woman wouldn't agree. I wonder who she was?'

Jean smiles encouraged by Pete's intent focus.

'As far as I know, Harriet Sorokin was the only person Aurora knew here. She was the subject in the portrait that won the Archibald. Maybe the woman was a friend of Harriet's?'

Jean stares into the garden. It's peaceful, the only sound the melodic harmony of chirping crickets. The approach of summer is heralded by bands of mauve and rosy pink in the twilight sky and the prospect of warm days ahead.

Pete rubs his chin thoughtfully. 'My aunt was a housekeeper for the Sorokin family at one time. Baba used to help her out if she took on extra cleaning work. She *might* have cleaned the house—'

'Well, it's not every day you help a girl give birth. I'm sure she would have mentioned it if she had.'

'I always thought Baba lived a quiet life.' Pete squeezes her hand. 'But after she died, I found a chocolate box pushed into the back of a wardrobe filled with letters written in Russian. Over the years I translated them—'

'Translated them? You *are* a man of many talents.' The more she knows about Pete, the more endearing he becomes.

'I recognised my name in the first lines of a letter and assumed they were from a relative. I could tell by the familiarity that the correspondents were dear friends and that Baba wasn't as educated as the one writing to her. They were postmarked from the early 1920s to the start of 1940, but Baba had never mentioned them.

'That's how I discovered she wasn't my birth mother.' He takes a deep breath. 'I understand how Rick might feel. Although she wasn't my mother by blood, in my heart Baba will always hold that honour.'

'And did you learn anything more about your parents?'

'By then it was too late.'

As the sun slides slowly to the horizon, he explains that his birth mother had suffered a stroke following his birth and was unable to care for him. Baba nursed him and his mother while she rehabilitated. When complications set in, it appeared Baba continued.

'While she didn't have much, Baba was a loving mother, and I'm grateful. I always knew she adored me. Life wasn't the same without her.'

The evening grows darker.

'Time to go inside.' Pete draws her to her feet. 'I'll dig the letters out to show you another time. That's enough about me, for now.'

TATIANA

46

Petrograd, 1919

I carry hope and life inside me. Crouched by candlelight, I'm placing the finishing stitches on a bonnet for my child. I feel the signs now—a flutter of sweeping wings inside me like a dragonfly's kiss on a summer's day. Marthe and Anya have been asleep for some time when angry fists pound at my door.

Already weakened by previous intruders, a few swift kicks and the lock gives way. A man storms inside. Dark-eyed and raven-haired, he stinks of vodka. My stomach clenches as I rise from my chair.

'Where is he?' He roughly pushes me aside and marches around the room, picking up the items of clothing drying and then dropping them. I glance to the bureau that houses my pistol, but it is out of reach.

'Who? What do you want?'

'Where is your husband?'

'My husband?' I step back slowly, but he keeps on approaching. 'Who are you?'

He reaches for the wooden box on the mantelpiece. It holds only a few *kopeks*. 'You might have heard of me. Yuri Vorontov.'

He slips the money into his pocket. There is little family resemblance except for the dark hair and the deep tone of his voice, far more menacing than his brother's.

'He was always one for beautiful women. Such a fine lady wife. Where is the traitor hiding?' His snarl reveals the cavernous gap of a missing front tooth.

I edge away, my thoughts for Marthe and Anya's safety. I pray they stay on the other side of the curtain. 'I have not seen him.'

'Is that so? Be sure to tell me when you do. I'll be back, sister.' He circles. I clench my fists and freeze, cursing my lack of fight.

'I see why he kept you a secret. I have spies too—' His laughter is not pleasant. 'My little brother has angered enough people to get himself killed. That's what happens to traitors who side with former people...'

Former people. My stomach turns. The term that denigrates those of imperial blood. Pressing my lips together, I hold my fists by my sides.

'What I want to know, is what secret has him playing both sides? What is he hiding?'

I see it immediately. The covert visits, the secretive missions Ilya is involved in. Is it to do with Misha? Has he known all along?

'My brother is far from a saint. He's playing the assassin.'

He moves forward and backs me against the wall. I feel his hands on my shoulders and hold my breath.

'Did he tell you about your husband? Ask him how he died—what he did—that is, unless the traitor is already dead. I am tasked with bringing him to justice.'

'He's your flesh and blood!' I push my fists hard into his chest. He staggers, surprised by the strength of my fear. Then he steps forward and slaps me across the face with such force I land on the ground at his feet.

My head aches as he pins me to the floor, with the weight of his body crushing me and an elbow across my throat. I ignore the curl of fear in my stomach and try to push him away, but his hand lifts my skirt, and he wrestles with his trousers. 'I'll show you what it's like to have a real man between your legs—'

'No!' I cry as his head blocks my sight, and I brace my body for his attack. Suddenly a shot rings out. Yuri shudders and then convulses on top of me. It takes a moment to realise the primal scream I hear is mine. Then I push his stilled body aside and wriggle free.

Marthe cries out and reaches for me.

And there before us is my dear, sweet Anya, her eyes wide and full of tears. The ten-year-old drops the pistol to the floor and runs into my open arms.

JEAN

47

Aurora Estate, Red Hill, 1984

Jean turns a page of the newspaper and Summer's haunting eyes stare back at her for the second time this week. Photos in the elegant poses that made her name as a supermodel have re-emerged following news that 'Australia's own Summer Harrington' is engaged to the son of renowned artist, Aurora Champion. Local newspapers, magazines and radio stations have flooded them with requests for interviews and turned the pair into an overnight sensation. As a result, enquiries regarding Aurora Champion's portrait collection and the upcoming gallery opening are through the roof–– it will be a sell-out.

Rick and Summer are the current 'it' couple. They don't have quite the celebrity acclaim of Mick Jagger and Summer's old modelling pal, Jerry Hall, but as Melbourne's own, people are curious to know all about them. (Jerry had commissioned an Antonio Lopez original as a gift for the couple's engagement—an illustration of one of Summer's most famous Vogue covers).

It was hard to not be caught up in the enthusiasm of the loved-up pair. Rick was strutting around and beaming like the Cheshire Cat.

Meanwhile, the more measured Summer, heartily assured Jean that she was honoured to wear Aurora's ring. 'The sentiment means so much to both of us, Jean, but your blessing makes it all the more special.'

My blessing. Jean shifts her gaze to the vineyard where Pete is assisting Rick in checking the vines. How truly blessed she is.

Summer joins her on the verandah and fans out her hand, her eyes as sparkly as the diamonds in her ring. She's never looked more beautiful. No glossy cover could do her justice. Jean is delighted they are so happy. Only a fool would be hard pressed not to notice how crazy they are about each other.

Speaking of fools. Ross Milton made the mistake of pinching Summer on the bum after a staff meeting. She resigned on the spot. She told Jean that when she slapped Milton's face, in full view of the general manager, it was an automatic reaction. The lawsuit she threatened him with, and throwaway line suggesting the press would love to hear her side of the story, sealed his immediate departure from the store.

If only Jean had been there to witness it! Milton must be squirming. Summer's picture is everywhere.

Witnessing her inner strength transform into power is a thing of pure beauty. Summer is in her element. To top it off, she has rolled up her sleeves and is helping Jean organise the forthcoming gallery event as if she was born to it.

'I'd best get back to the display.' There is lots to do before Evie arrives.

'I'm rapt Pete is lending us his mother's beautiful samovar,' Summer nods at the sideboard. 'It's like a Grecian urn, don't you think?' She rests one hand on the cool metal.

The beautiful silverware stands about half a metre tall. Ornately curved handles and decorative engraving give the piece its old-world decadence, and the elaborate filigree spout echoes an age long ago.

'It will look much better with a good polish.' Jean takes it into the kitchen.

'Did you say tea?' Pete calls from the doorway a short time later.

Rick is behind him. 'I'd love one too. And some of Pete's apple cake,' he grins.

'Let's make tea in the *samovar*,' Summer points to the now

gleaming *pièce de résistance* on the kitchen bench. 'How do we do it, Pete?'

'I have no idea.' He scratches his head. 'Baba always made tea the "English way" as she used to call it. She said it was more economical.'

'Really?' Rick says. 'I thought samovars were in constant use in Russian households?'

'I guess she preferred a teapot after her time in England,' he shrugs.

While the kettle whistles steadily in the background Jean tilts the samovar on its side. 'Well, we can't use it anyway. I think there's something stuck in the spout. Can you pass me a knitting needle from my bag, Rick?'

A few minutes later, she retrieves a tiny pouch. 'Oh my God! It's the brooch!'

It's smaller than she recalled, less menacing, but the ladybird is exquisite. Sunlight flows through the glass and shines a sparkle over the white stones Jean now recognises as diamonds.

'Pete,' she shakes her head in disbelief. 'Your mother *must* have known Aurora. But how?'

Pete shakes his head. 'Baba insisted the samovar was the most valuable thing she owned. In fact, on her deathbed, she made me promise not to sell it. I never thought to question her.'

'It's been there all this time.' Jean rolls the brooch between her fingers. 'I don't understand....'

Rick returns from his office with a magnifying glass and Jean studies the details under the lamp by the telephone.

'Can I take a look?'

She swallows a lump in her throat, knowing the gift was intended for him.

'This really should be authenticated.' Rick turns it over and marvels at the tiny gold legs underneath.

'Authenticated or valued?'

'Both, I expect. There are initials here.' Rick looks up at Jean. 'And a maker's mark too.'

'May I see?' Summer takes the glass and peers closely; a frown nestles between two perfectly arched brows. 'I'm almost certain this is from the House of Fabergé.'

'Fabergé? How do you know?'

'I did shoots for them. One of the head jewellers took an interest in me and insisted on showing me behind the scenes. He explained the maker's marks. See here? What a shame it's been hidden away. It's a fabulous piece.'

'These initials look like GA and TV. There's a big swirling loop around it too—or another letter.'

Jean covers her mouth with her hand. *Michael's mother?*

'The House of Fabergé, as in Fabergé eggs, was connected to the Romanovs. Everyone knows their tragic story. But hey, I have an idea!' Summer turns to them. 'How about 'family' as the theme of the exhibition?'

'It sounds perfect given we'll all be together,' Jean nods.

'We can call the exhibition something catchy, like, you know, royal family, Champion family. We'll think of something.' Summer's eyes spark with excitement.

'The way your mind works.' Rick slaps a hand to his forehead and then hooks her into a hug.

'Your bird trios will work too, Pete.' Summer is on a roll.

During Jean's recovery, Pete returned to a project he had begun as a sideline to his furniture. His miniature bird carvings are exquisite, proving him as adept in fine carving as he was with cabinetry. He explained that many Russian surnames were derived from birds and animals.

'The Champion family flying back to the nest...'

'Now *that* is lame,' Rick rolls his eyes and the four of them laugh together.

He touches Jean's arm. 'Didn't you say that Hazel might have some early photos of Mum? It would be great to get our hands on any old mementoes.'

'I'll speak to her.' Jean nods thoughtfully. She still has questions. 'Now, let's get cracking, we have heaps to do before Evie arrives.'

Jean can't wait to see her twin. Soon the whole Champion family will be together.

When she contacts a jeweller in the city to ask how best to authenticate the ladybird piece, Jean is advised that Fabergé have a register that catalogues all custom jewellery pieces. She immediately sends a fax to the company requesting further information and then eagerly awaits a reply.

Next, Jean calls on Hazel to see if she can fill in the gaps. They had been in contact since she left Verity House. The misunderstanding about Jean's birth had been touched upon, and once Evie arrived and was told the truth, Jean planned to explain about Rick too.

'How wonderful, to see you, dear. Now what can I help you with?' Hazel appears a little frailer than the last time they met.

'I was hoping you might have photographs of Aurora for our exhibition; perhaps some of her as a child in England.'

Hazel gives a little cough. 'A lovely tribute. I've been going through Mother's personal effects since you were last here. They've been boxed up for years. I'm afraid I don't have many photographs, but I did find Mother's diary. I had a flick through it, but I'm not much of a reader. You're welcome to it. You might find something in it for inspiration. They all kept one in those days. I never had the patience, myself. Mother was quite prolific…'

'That sounds lovely. Thank you.'

'I'll check my albums too. Tell me, what else do you have prepared?'

'Pete has offered us a gorgeous samovar. It's like the one in the beautiful still life painting in your room.'

Hazel's painting is of a table set with fine china on a lace tablecloth with a samovar placed beside a basket of cherries. The clear light is reminiscent of Manet.

'That was painted by a Romanov, you know, the Grand Duchess Olga, the last Tsar's sister. I bought it from an antiquarian in London.'

'Really?' *A Romanov.*

'Apparently, she was a keen artist and even held an exhibition back in the 1950s. She settled in Canada after the revolution, but the painting made its way to London at some stage between the wars. I found it in a shop that belonged to an antique dealer, a Russian émigré who was an old friend of Mother's from her youth. I gather they met when my grandfather was the British ambassador in St Petersburg.'

Jean's stomach somersaults.

'I happened to be in London just before Hitler bombed it to rubble, and it was my first visit back after Mother had died. I was suffering her loss greatly and popped in to have a gander at the dear little shop. I knew from her time in the legation that she had known the grand duchess and her family. When the antiquarian fellow told me who the artist was, I was fascinated. I couldn't resist. I guess it doesn't matter how old you are; your mother is always a great loss.'

'So, your mother knew the Grand Duchess Olga?'

'Yes, and the dealer, whose name escapes me now, was delighted to meet me. He referred to Mother with fondness. He began talking about the days of their youth and said they had lived very different lives back then. But he did say something quite strange, as I recall. He told me his family were extremely grateful to mine for their kindness. Something about how Mother provided safe passage for the children? I never understood what that was referring to.'

'Safe passage?'

Hazel hurries her on. 'I'll send you anything I find of interest, dear. I imagine you're far too busy to collect it, and there's a lovely man here who does deliveries. I insist—'

'If you're sure?'

'Yes, yes. Now off you go, dear, it's time for my bridge game.'

48

Jean laughs when Evie insists on making her own way to the vineyard, reminded of her twin's indomitable spirit. She's not expected in Melbourne until the day before the exhibition. Jean is counting down the days.

Pete is back in Castlemaine checking on their gardens and finishing a few orders for his customers. But he posed a delightful proposition before he left.

'There's plenty to do here at the vineyard to help out. Now your lease on the cottage is coming to an end, how about we find a place together, closer to Rick and Summer? We're not getting any younger, my love.'

His wink had filled Jean with an almost childlike delight.

She adores him. He's a kind and generous man. They've agreed to begin searching for a farmlet nearby as soon as Aurora Estate is up and running.

On the morning of Evie's arrival, Jean escapes the household before they awaken. The undulating fields glow with an amber light that kisses the earth while morning dew glistens on the leaves of the pathway of vines.

The parcel from Hazel arrived the day before as promised. And then late yesterday evening they received a reply from Fabergé, verifying the provenance of the ladybird brooch and name of the purchaser.

Bespoke piece created for G.D. Georgiy Alexandrovich Romanov. 1898.

Jean checked the encyclopaedias in Jack's study that had been on the shelves for as long as anyone could remember. While distinctly out of date regarding the names and division of European countries since WWII, for example, they were still useful for research on prior history. She searched for details of the Russian imperial family. It appears Grand Duke Georgiy Romanov was the brother of the last Tsar, Nicholas II. However, he had died the year following the brooch's commission.

The identity of TV, Michael's mother, remained a mystery.

Jean's knowledge of the Russian revolution is sketchy. Bolshevik extremists had murdered the tsar, and although their bodies have never been found, it is believed the tsarina and their five children may have been murdered too. Stories from the USSR in the early days of Soviet Russia were often garnished with anti-communist speculation. The truth might never be discovered.

Perhaps more information will be found in Hazel's belongings. She was correct in saying her mother, Rosalind Brassington, was a prolific correspondent. Rosalind's diary reads like a classic novel filled with extravagant descriptions of a lifestyle of opulence and service; of lightness and merriment but also a time of tragedy, courage and despair.

Hazel had also included a parcel of aged letters that proved as interesting as Grand Duchess Olga's painting, along with a short note:

I believe Mother intended writing her memoirs but never quite managed it. A record of a time long since passed. She despised the storming of the streets of St Petersburg by the Reds, now Leningrad. She once told me the ways of diplomatic service and ambassadorial life were lost in the wake of the changes that swept Europe in the early part of the century. She spoke fondly of the life she had known as a girl, and it broke her heart that people she had known well had come to a grisly end the way they did. There's a great deal in her correspondence about St Petersburg before the Great War. You should read it, Jeanie, to give you some perspective, though I'd rather it didn't go into the exhibition, if you don't mind, dear. It's private in parts and rather personal.

The brooch will not form part of the exhibition, either. It is far too precious to display to the public and too difficult to explain the connection. Rosalind's diary had sent Jean's mind spinning the previous evening as she read it and tried to connect the dots. Now she's eager to share what she has discovered with the others.

She resists the call of the deckchair on the verandah and returns to the gallery with Rosalind's diary in her hand. Jean contemplates her mother's self-portrait and re-examines the symbols in the painting. *What can you tell me?* Fabergé's authentication of the enamel *guilloché* ladybird poses several questions, most importantly, who is the mysterious TV?

She looks to Aurora every so often as she reads, as though willing her spirit to somehow point her to the right page for clarity. Suddenly, a flow of words appears with descriptions and information more disturbing than anything Jean has imagined.

References to Rosalind's friend, Tatiana, or Tatya, mention the pair's acquaintance with Grand Duke Georgiy Alexandrovich and his death during her years in St Petersburg. With the wisdom of hindsight, Jean gauges the lightness and youth in the letters with a sense of growing unease, reading of a time so far removed from now while also knowing retrospectively the fate that awaited those mentioned.

Some survived, but what difficulties had they endured?

Several years later, another man's name becomes dominant regarding Tatya—*Ilya Petrovich*, sometimes referred to as Count or Lieutenant Vorontov. The endearing habits of Tatiana's son, Misha, are described in detail too, and early in the war years, a younger child, Anya, is mentioned. Judging by the gratitude and thanks in the letters to Rosalind, it appears the Brassingtons had helped both children find exile in England.

Sent to safety in England. Jean feels a shiver, the superstition of a soul walking on her grave. She shrugs it away as thoughts run ahead of her. There is still something missing.

As soon as Evie comes through the door Jean recognises the impish grin splayed across her sister's face. The years simply fall away as she welcomes Jean into her arms. She is surprised to witness her twin's eagerness to accept her. While there are floods of tears, there is no sign of irritation or caution in their reunion.

Evie is blown away by the changes to the old orchard and quickly shakes off her jet lag by spending the morning fossicking outside in the fresh air. The twins walk to Evie's favourite pocket of the property, eager to revisit childhood memories.

'Even for me, coming home was difficult.' Evie nods for emphasis. 'It was because you weren't here. It wasn't the same without you.' Her hair is flicked neatly into a pixie bob that frames her dark eyes.

'Then life got in the way. After I married Fred, we moved overseas, and I didn't come home as often as I'd have liked to. It was sad for us all, Jeanie. Shirley missed you terribly. But it must have been so much harder for you, all alone.'

Jean glances at her sister and swallows a lump in her throat. How many years have passed? How many decades, wasted?

A tractor engine hums in the background. Rick is on the farthest hill, at the top of the track near the property's front gates. The pair watch him jump down and attend to a fencepost before resuming his seat and starting the machine up again.

Butterflies grip her stomach. Jean takes a deep breath.

'I have something to tell you, Evie...I need to explain.' She recalls once phoning home when she was at a low moment and longing to hear her sister's voice. She'd hung up as soon as she answered.

Evie turns away and pointedly meets Jean's gaze. 'Mum went away on that painting sabbatical with you, but you never returned. Or called or wrote—'

'I had no choice. I had to leave school and go with Aurora. But then—'

'Shirley and I were furious when Mum took you away and left us behind. You were gone for ages. We never understood why she singled you out. Or why you didn't return to Beaulieu. The girls all stopped asking after a while although a few of the nastier day girls made some pretty wild accusations—'

Jean cuts in. 'While I was at Verity House, I underwent therapy, and understandably, a lot of things came to the surface. I realise now that back then I was probably in shock, which made everything more difficult for me to deal with.'

Life is short and too many stones have been overturned. Jean is making ground but is aware she still has a long way to go. But with each conversation it becomes easier to unravel the past.

'Do you remember the day I went to meet Michael Golding, in the city? After I won the art prize and went to the gallery—'

'Vaguely.'

'He'd been extremely kind to me, and we discussed art and his work. He had quite the collection. He treated me like a friend, an adult. We had a lovely day at the gallery, and he amused me with stories about the cities he had seen. It was all very romantic, sitting in an apartment at the Paris end of Collins Street, talking about Europe. He was a very handsome man for his age, like a fair-haired Richard Gere, or Paul Newman. You must remember—'

'I recall him being quite full of himself,' Evie rolls her eyes. 'I certainly remember that. He had an affectation of superiority.'

Jean nods slowly. It's clear Evie hadn't seen him the same way.

'I assumed he was a social drinker—at least, he often had a drink in hand. Looking back, it was probably a mix of substances, to be honest. We went to the gallery and he made a huge fuss of me. He complimented my work and my appearance. I was flattered by his attention. It was just after our sixteenth birthday. He made me feel special, but he kept repeating how much I reminded him of Aurora...'

'Go on...,' Evie's tone rises.

'He offered me a cigarette and then...we drank champagne, and all of a sudden, I felt free and interesting. I felt like a woman. He put on a record, and we started dancing and laughing. But then he kissed me, quite passionately. It was the first time I'd been kissed. I felt dizzy, literally weak at the knees. It was a combination of drink and exhilaration. Now I realise that my body simply can't tolerate alcohol.'

Evie's mouth is shaped like a perfect 'O' as Jean continues.

'Yes, I'm an alcoholic. They know...,' she nods towards the homestead, 'but after the kissing, the rest is a blur and we ended up in his bed

—' Jean takes a deep breath. The ache of her guilt twists inside her, recalling her behaviour, and then the thumping headache the next day. 'Afterwards, I was a little teary, and he mopped my eyes and whispered to me in French. Then it was strange. He started to cry too.'

'How ghastly! But he'd taken advantage of you, Jeanie.' Evie holds Jean's hands. 'It was wrong.'

'It was. I fell pregnant, Evie. Rick isn't our brother. He's my son. Mine and Michael's.'

Evie's face blanches white, then glows pink.

Rick is cautiously approaching, holding two mugs of tea. 'Reinforcements?'

Jean takes them from him and eases out a breath. 'I'm sorry, Evie, I know this must be a shock for you.'

Rick squeezes Evie's shoulder. 'It has been for us all. But I guess we should have had our suspicions, given the age difference.'

'But you were a child, Jeanie. What a horrid man! Oh god, I'm so sorry!' She turns to Rick. 'I don't understand. If he was such a great friend to Mum, why would he have taken advantage of you? How could he?'

'We went away to Castlemaine, so I could have the baby there. That's why we couldn't tell you.'

'Jeanie. I don't know what to say.' Evie covers her mouth with her hands.

'Aurora realised Michael was the father when she found a brooch in my things. She was furious. I'd never seen her so angry. She said he mistook me for her.'

'Brooch? Sorry, what brooch?'

'You're a little behind.' Rick tries to make light of her dismay.

'I had no idea about any of this. All Shirley and I were told was that Mum was painting and you'd both be away for a while. Then, when we found out she'd had a baby, we were so excited we didn't think to ask anything more. She kept insisting you'd come back soon.'

So *that's* what Aurora had told them? Then Jean recalls Aurora stroking her hair, telling her she was sorry she had let him near her, that she promised he'd never see her or her sisters again.

Evie looks at Rick. 'Of course, we were delighted we had a new baby brother to play with, but we missed you terribly, Jeanie. I was afraid I might have said something nasty to you.' Her eyes shine with tears. 'I was so caught up with Fred at the time.'

'I couldn't face you.' Jean shakes her head.

'It sounds like Mum was protecting you from him.'

'Maybe it was because of something she knew about him?' Rick asks.

Jean rests her chin on her hand. 'Hazel suggested there was more to their relationship. That's why I contacted you, Evie. I thought they might have been having an affair.'

'Perhaps she thought he'd go to jail and that's why she behaved the way she did?'

'I was sixteen—'

'Lucky for him,' Evie's eyes darken in anger, 'but it doesn't fit. Mum and Dad loved each other, almost sickeningly so when I remember how Fred and I used to carry on. If there were problems between them, as you say, or if she was ever in love with Michael, well, they must have patched it up.'

Jean kneels and then sits, staring out to the vines.

'Jeanie?' Evie reaches out to her.

'I think she was protecting us. All of us. All my life I've thought Aurora hated me; that she wanted to keep Michael's child for herself. But she wanted to give me a chance. I couldn't see what was right in front of me.'

'What he did was wrong. Terribly, terribly wrong. It wasn't your fault! I'm sorry to say it, but he was an entitled jerk.'

Jean nods, swallowing the huge lump in her throat.

'Come on you two!' Rick holds out a hand to help Jean to her feet. 'Summer will have lunch ready for us. She's been trying out recipes from that new Pritikin Diet book everyone is raving about. Do me a favour and please don't tell her it tastes like crap!'

49

Jean asked Pete to bring Baba's chocolate box carton of letters with him when he returned from Castlemaine. He told her that following Baba's death, he had considered discarding them but retrieved the box at the last minute.

'I never thought there was anything particularly interesting about her,' he says as hands the letters to Jean. 'We lived a secluded existence. But to begin life in a foreign country as a single mother must have been terribly difficult. There is nothing to prove she ever had a husband, which explains her reliance on me. She could be claustrophobic at times with her expectations, but she was a loving mother.'

Jean sorts through the yellowed envelopes while Pete makes the tea. Her head is full of questions. Although she can't understand the Cyrillic alphabet, she admires the beautiful script that dances across the pages, and the flourishes of her handwriting. 'Do you think she left before the Russian revolution?'

'The only thing I know is the name of the ship.' He hands Jean her favourite Blue Willow pattern teacup and they settle on the sofa. 'I always laughed that it was called *Marlborough*, the same as the brand of cigarettes I first smoked as a kid behind the shelter sheds.' He grins.

'Me too!' Jean laughs.

'Smoking was all part of trying to fit in, for me,' Pete chuckles. 'In the fifties it became increasingly unpopular to have Eastern European links. People were alarmed by the Petrov Affair and all the communist propaganda. Any foreign-speaking person in Australia was presumed to have communist links.'

'I remember the photo of the Soviets dragging that poor woman onto the plane at Essendon airport with her shoe left on the tarmac.' Jean covers his hand with hers. 'It was shocking.'

'That was the start of the Cold War, the threats of spies and the Red Terror. I can assure you, it was drawing a long bow to suspect Baba of being a spy! But as a bi-lingual male, it was harder for me. I was *very* concerned about being accused of espionage. I tried to discourage Baba using her native tongue—you never knew who might dob you in for being a "commie." In the end, though, she was beyond caring and rarely spoke anything *but* Russian. She died, as she lived, with little complaint.'

'So, your birth mother, do you think she was a relative?'

He shrugs. 'I doubt it. Baba kept the past close to her chest but shared the traditions of her childhood in more practical ways. Sometimes she spoke about the beauty of the countryside, the grand buildings and the people she had met. I assume she worked in the household of a wealthy landowner as a young girl. She mentioned lavish parties—dancing and beautiful gowns and the music they played when the family entertained. But then, when she was a little melancholy, she'd wring her hands and whisper names over and over like she was chanting a prayer.

'War, and the Bolsheviks destroyed the life they knew. There was nothing left for her to go back to. We know about the revolution and the murder of the tsar and his family, but many families lost their fortunes or their lives.'

'Imagine the stories she could have told you!'

'Many. I'll never know the truth of. That's why your situation offers hope. You and Rick have the opportunity to explain the past and build on your relationship together.'

'I see now that Aurora did what she thought best.' *How wrong she had been about her mother.* The more time Jean spends considering it, the more she understands Aurora's actions were selfless. 'When did you leave England?'

'I was a toddler. I barely recall it. Baba must have found it difficult to support me there. Russian émigrés had a pretty hard time in England after the war, and my aunt was already in Australia. According to the letters, it was my birth mother's suggestion we join them here until she was well enough to follow.

'I must have had siblings too—the letters refer to *the children* quite often,' Pete smiles. 'There was mention of them coming to visit in the holidays, or words to that effect.'

'Oh, Pete. Imagine finding them.' Jean puts down her teacup.

Pete picks up two letters and checks the postmarks before taking one out of its envelope. 'Here my birth mother writes that she promises to follow once she is reunited with her husband. His name was Elliott. He's mentioned in every letter.'

'What happened to him?'

'It took ten years before he eventually made it to England. The joy is clear in her letter. She explains the delight when he arrived, having survived imprisonment in Siberia. Apparently, he escaped and made his way to England through Finland.'

Jean smiles. 'What an epic journey to reach her. United after so long.' She smiles at the commitment. 'Sounds like a beautiful love story.'

Pete looks pensive. 'I wish I didn't have to read between the lines. If only Baba had explained...'

Jean clasps her hand over his. 'Mothers do what they think best. I see that now. Baba did what any mother or surrogate mother would do for their child. It was done out of love for you.'

Pete tells Jean the letters continued right up until one mentioned sending his passage for him to return to England. The one that said it was time to tell him the truth of his birth.

'And then war broke out in Europe again. I missed meeting them by a few months.' Pete hands Jean another envelope from September 1940. 'This was the last one.'

A note from a neighbour explains the letter was found inside the diary Pete's mother was holding when she died.

'It says here, "the sky opened up over London in a rain of fire as the German Luftwasse bombed London".' Jean looks up to see tears brighten the golden light in Pete's eyes.

'"For fifty-three nights in a row."'

'Oh Pete! How terrible.' Jean moves closer and rests her head on his shoulder.

A newspaper clipping accompanies the note:

The bodies of Mr and Mrs Corbett were discovered lying under the rubble of their home. By all accounts, they kept to themselves but were polite and cultured. Mr Corbett's accent suggested they were not originally from these parts.

Mrs Corbett's body was cocooned protectively in her husband's arms, the pair entwined as one until the end.

'I'm sorry.' Jean leans in and kisses his cheek.

'That's why I'm glad you've managed to explain things to Rick.'

'Yes, it's a relief. I naively believed I could live at the orchard after he was born. I know it would have been hard as a single mother in the fifties. But the choice was taken from me. I wish Aurora had explained her decision.'

'But imagine the stigma you would have suffered, Jean. No matter the situation, a single woman with a child will always find it difficult. People can be incredibly unforgiving and ignorant. I think Baba was brave—perhaps not speaking the language well enough made it easier for her to ignore the gossip. I was the one who copped the scepticism and insinuations of being a bastard. No one believed I had a father.'

Pete moves closer and wraps his arms around her. She rests her head on his chest and breathes in the comforting scent of sandalwood and beeswax. It's not too late for her to be the best mother she can be. Rick is an adult now, but she has the chance to build on their relationship and be a part of his life. Of his future.

'Baba called my mother Tatya. That's how she signed her letters too.'

Jean jumps, and her teacup clatters into the saucer.

TATIANA

50

London, 1919

I am summoned by the Dowager Empress to her apartments at Marlborough House, the residence of her sister, Alexandra, the Queen Mother. While grateful for her aid when leaving our homeland, I pray she has news of my husband. I immediately recall the last time I arrived at her door....

I was ashamed to arrive in Crimea alongside patients transported to the hospital in the relative comfort of the Red Cross vehicle. The poor men we inched past *en route* were like worn out shells, trudging on foot with shoulders stooped and heads hung low. After long years of fighting and lost productivity, boots were scarce. Some wore *lapti*, the traditional plaited shoes made from the bark of linden trees.

When we reached Yalta, British naval ships were awaiting orders and anchored out at sea some distance from the port. Meanwhile, German soldiers with hardened faces marched the dock in a brisk and menacing fashion.

I swallowed down the lump in my throat. 'What if they ask for our documents?'

'We will be fine, Tatya,' Matron Callaghan smiled, but her eyes were wary, and her lips stretched tight. 'We three are nurses and display the Red Cross flag. They will see that we come in peace.'

Finally, Marthe and I stood at the dowager's gates. Her country estate was overrun with officious Germans who showed great disrespect for her age and standing and made a much of the fact that we Russians were their captives.

'They are instructed to guard us and to deter the Reds,' the dowager nodded as she informed me of her plans for exile. 'Even the Germans don't trust them!'

'The Bolsheviks are moving closer to the peninsula each day. My supporters report trouble between the Reds and Whites in Odessa. Our Whites have held them back, but for how much longer I cannot imagine. The navy are ready to escort us, but I refuse to leave without news of Nicky and the children. I must know they are safe!'

'Are there any reports of Ilya Petrovich?' I lowered my eyes.

'Indeed, I hold grave fears for him, but pray to the Lord he will find his way to us.'

I stared at my feet. Ilya knew nothing of my plans beyond the possibility of leaving St Petersburg with the Brassingtons. Tears pricked my eyes. I hoped the children and Rosalind had arrived in England safely. I needed to reach them soon.

'Once I make the decision, we will leave immediately. You will come whether your husband is here or not, Tatiana. Lives depend on you, as they are likewise relying on me.'

Over the next few days, we discreetly packed our trunks, ready to load into the carriages with the briefest of notice.

Evening fell on our last day and masked the autumnal sunshine. When the Reds took the village, we made haste to leave. With a heavy heart I boarded the ship, hovering and stalling until I was the last on deck, scanning the roads and the port for Ilya.

'Weigh anchor!' The sailor's call was strong against the breeze. Tears pricked my eyes and the wind picked up from the shore as though the elements insisted on blowing us as far away from Russia in the shortest of times.

We had no need for sails to aid our journey as the *Marlborough* was a steamship—a military vessel with superior mechanics designed for speed and with the endurance of performance the British Navy were renowned for.

I was tormented. Carried off on the wings of a puff of wind and cast adrift on unchartered and tempestuous seas. What would my new life bring without him?

I stood rigidly on the deck, searching the shoreline with my hands firmly on the handrail. The White Ensign flag was raised, flapping in the breeze above me.

Suddenly, the boom of a cannon sounded in the distance and gunshots fired.

'A skirmish at the docks,' nodded an officer with a telescope glued firmly to his eyes.

'Full steam ahead! Don't be concerned. We'll soon outrun them,' another uniformed man reassured me with a frown. 'The Bolsheviks have reached the port, but the Whites have them cornered. Good timing, I'd say! Perhaps it's best to take to your cabin, Imperial Highness.' He gave a small cough as though my title had stuck in his throat. *And no longer mine since we Romanovs had fallen...*

'Look there, Jones,' the first officer shouted. 'See? That fellow is mowing them down hand-to-hand! They're dropping like flies.'

My heart raced as I looked to the coastline. Gunfire peppered the shore like firecrackers and puffs of smoke rose in the air.

Then I saw him, recognising my husband's loping gait as he stepped over fallen Reds and picked up speed, running towards the dock.

'Wait! You must stop. My husband!'

Ilya's commanding presence was apparent. He signalled to us with his arms thrust in the air, circling them like windmills.

'I'm sorry, Imperial Highness. I truly am. We have our orders.'

I held up my handkerchief in a feeble attempt. *He was too late.* The ship was powering away.

Dropping to my knees on the deck, I cradled my girth, aware in the commotion around me of the dowager's stern disapproval and the admiral's insistence that he was following the orders of his British king.

The *Marlborough* sailed towards the horizon. The last I saw of Ilya was him cupping hands to his mouth; his words lost as the wind swept the sea and the expanse between us grew wider.

How would he ever find me now?

I push the memory aside and meet the steely dowager's gaze.

'Is there word of my husband, Imperial Majesty?'

'Be patient, my dear,' she pats my hand. 'I hold grave fears for Ilya Petrovich, but he is a hardened combatant. That man has saved we Romanovs more times than I care to count—'

Fear pulls deep in my stomach.

'—and worth his weight in gold when you consider the way he has protected you and Misha.'

Eyes as dark as coal study me strangely. 'You look as though you have swallowed a fishhook.'

Saved we Romanovs? 'I apologise, Imperial Majesty. I'm afraid I don't understand.'

'For years, Ilya has been my most faithful servant. It was he who extricated darling Georgiy from the mess he was embroiled in with that wretched adjutant...'

Yuri had suggested Ilya was to blame for Georgiy's death. I fan my napkin furiously, overheated by talk of his great loyalty. Whatever can she mean?

'That wretched Borsky had evidence, photographs of the most revealing kind. He threatened to use them to destroy the imperial family. It was he who was most inconvenienced by the strength of your relationship with Georgiy. The vile man said he *loved* him,' the dowager raises her eyes to the ceiling. 'I had to task Ilya to step in and cover up the...indiscretions.'

I sway in my seat. Borsky? *In love* with Georgiy? I cannot speak, but it appears the dowager is at pains to relieve herself of this burden and continues her diatribe.

'Of course, no one was aware of Georgiy's illness, and we dare not reveal it while he remained Tsarevich. Consumption would have killed my son far too early as it was, but in the end, it was that foolish automobile that saw to his demise.'

My hands briefly cover my face as I try to take a breath. I sit back in my chair. 'I was unaware—'

'Indeed. But after Georgiy died, the damning evidence of your marriage remained a threat. Ilya came to the rescue. I sent him to Abbas-

Tuman to secure the official documentation before Borsky used it against my family. From all accounts he put up a fierce struggle, but Ilya dealt with him efficiently, as always. Borsky was threatened with exile, but given his immoral proclivities, I imagine the thought of living out his life in the mines of the Ural Mountains did not appeal.'

I daren't voice the thoughts in my head, but I had to know. 'Did Ilya...kill him?'

'Of course not!' She frowned. 'But then we found out that you were carrying Georgiy's child, and a suitable husband for a woman of your station had to be found. I suggested Ilya immediately. The only man I could entrust with my grandson's safety.

'However, Alix interfered and tempted Nicky with plan after plan to remove you from Russia. I was furious, but in any case, the documents were held safe.

'Naturally, we expected Alix to give us an heir, and when Alexei was born it should have all gone smoothly.'

I stare into the distance. I see the light in Ilya's eyes, shining with his love for me. *How had I ever doubted him?*

'Imperial Majesty. Will you please let me know as soon as you hear from my husband? I'm eager to return to my son...and my daughter.'

'You mean the orphan girl you sent with the British in your place?' the dowager gives a slight toss of her head. 'Lord Brassington agreed it was a rash and foolish decision. Selfless, assuredly. However, like your mother, you have always been one for reckless choices.'

Although the dowager might call it reckless, my need to protect my family outweighed my fear.

I think back to the morning after Yuri's death when I went to the British Legation to seek an audience with the ambassador.

'Surely, we can help Tatya exile, Papa?' Rosalind had urged upon hearing my plea.

'I wish it were that simple. There are protocols...' Lord Brassington looked away. I had no British lineage to endorse my case and the word of a deposed tsar under house arrest no longer held weight. 'I will do my best, Your Highness.'

'Since the abdication, Papa has had little communication from the Tsar,' Rosalind whispered as his door closed. 'Nor has he received indication from our King regarding assistance. He has been left to deal with the new regime, but ever since the Bolsheviks' attempts to align with Germany, they have shown little interest in speaking to the British. Many foreign ambassadors have already left the city.'

Rosalind squeezed my fingers. 'Let me speak to him again.' She followed her father into his study.

My friend's lack of a poker face made the truth clear on her return. 'I'm deeply sorry, Tatya. We cannot guarantee a safe passage. You must arrange papers and be ready to leave immediately. But we can only take two. He cannot risk more.'

I hurried past boarded-up shops on the embankment that had been ripped apart as people stormed the streets, ransacking anything of value to sell or trade. Madame Chechenka's familiar façade was decidedly shabby but surprisingly unscathed.

The seamstress was barely visible behind a roll of rough brown-grey fabric and the pile of worker state uniforms stacked beside her. She shrugged in her affected manner and raised an eyebrow.

'Tovarisch,' I noted caution as she flicked a glance towards a man collecting a brown paper parcel. 'How might I assist?'

I hoped the seamstress was all I believed her to be. 'I have outgrown my skirt and seek your skills to make the necessary adjustments. This child grows beyond all expectations.' The man uttered a grunt of disinterest and continued his collection.

'For the right price, of course. You will need extra fabric. You have your ration book?' She blinked twice to see I understood. 'Go through to the dressing room,' she pointed me past a screen, 'I'll be in to take your measurements.'

A doorway was concealed behind the curtain. I held my breath and turned the handle, walking along the narrow corridor and down a set of stairs. I hesitated between two doors that opened off to the left, and my heartbeat quickened in the stillness.

Suddenly, one opened, and a man who barely reached my shoulders ushered me inside, a finger poised to his lips. He locked it behind me.

Inside, oddly-sized pieces of paper were laid on a cutting table with pens, ink and stamps set beside them.

'Your payment first,' he whispered, 'and details...names, dates of birth.' I swallowed down nausea and sourness filled my mouth. I prayed this wasn't a trap.

The name, Zolotovsky comes from the Russian word for gold. When I finally convinced Misha that he could best fight for Russia from afar, we agreed on Michael Golding as his British *nom de plume*. Then it was he, who suggested Anya's new identity.

'She will be Anne, of course.' It made sense.

'No, Mama,' his eyes lit with mischief. 'It was the ship, the Aurora, that fired the cannon shot into the walls of the palace at the commencement of the revolution. It's a way to remember Russia forever.'

Did my son understand the politics of this discussion? But speaking with such freedom had become a popular narrative for ordinary men within the worker state.

'It's perfect, Mama! Our Aurora will be reborn in England like the dawn of a new day.'

How could I resist when the dear child loved her new name too although I suspect, more so, because Misha had chosen it.

The counterfeiter committed the details to memory and burned my note on the candle flame nearby. When he stated the amount of his fee, the life inside me shifted as though sensing I was ill at ease.

I was at his mercy. I touched a finger to Georgiy's brooch and then gathered the pouch beneath my blouse. 'I have these...' I regretfully parted with my mother's string of pearls and a ring with a cabochon ruby encircled by diamonds.

'Jewels are more difficult to move, but these are... sufficient.' Then he opened the door, and I braced for the cold air.

What a relief it was to have my children safely on British soil.

Returning to the present, I meet the dowager's piercing stare. 'Not always reckless choices, Imperial Majesty. The two men I have loved, I loved with all my heart.'

She looks away. I swear I notice a tear.

'I implore you to keep my grandson safe. I believe he will do well at Cambridge, and I will continue to account for his education. Arranging his place was *the least* my sister could do.'

'You have been most kind, Imperial Majesty.'

'You deserve a great deal more, dear girl. I apologise for the animosity you have suffered under Alix's eternal piety.'

She takes a deep breath and holds a handkerchief to her chest. 'But I refuse to give up hope for my family.'

I understand the pain of loss, a pain so visceral you cannot imagine ever surviving it. I felt it in the months parted from my children. My husband.

'I cannot contemplate dear Nicky's death and will not believe it until the Bolsheviks produce evidence and I witness his body lying in the Cathedral of St Peter and St Paul with my own eyes.'

'Do you know where the revolutionaries have sent Alix and the children?'

'Our poor Alexei,' she interrupts with a cry, 'with his wretched health! You *do* understand that if he—if anything happens to him—then it means, Misha—'

'I understand,' I clasp her hand and squeeze it gently, 'but the best way to protect Misha is for my family to blend in as British citizens.'

The dowager picks up her handkerchief and dabs at her nose. 'The British were guarded and cautious in their dealings with Nicky. They have always been suspicious of we Russians. Envious, I imagine. Perhaps it is wiser he is regarded as an Englishman.'

Though I do not require her permission, I am grateful she agrees.

'In my darkest times, I never imagined that *my* family would be the ones to lose the Romanov throne. But I give thanks that dear Olga and her husband are safe, and the line continues through you, Tatiana, albeit with no crown to place upon our heads. For the time being...'

I feel the wave of fear turn inward and then rise in me like confidence. I cannot allow the nobility of Russia to retain any seed of hope; for White Russians to believe that Misha is the means to restoring the Russian monarchy. I have no wish for him to be ensnared in the trap of those who seek greater influence.

'Your Imperial Majesty, I will never acknowledge any part of Misha's bloodline. I beg of you to do the same. For the love of his father, please do not expose him. There will always be men vying for power and seeking Russian rule for personal gain.'

'If need be, Misha must do his duty.' Her voice is firm.

'I will not allow it.' I hold up my head. 'Nor will I ask him to side with the Bolsheviks or see him caught in the subversive plots of counter revolutionaries.'

'Of course, there are documents attesting to the truth—'

'Misha need never be told. He doesn't deserve to have to live in hiding or in fear for his life! As an Englishman he will have the opportunity to live a normal life. Let us leave him free to make his own way in this new world.'

The dowager sighs. 'You are wise, Tatiana Vladimirovna, with the heart of a lioness to match. I wish you well, child.' She inclines her head. 'I will miss you.'

'You are leaving?'

'Indeed, I am. I cannot abide these draughty English palaces. And I've had enough of politics during my stay. I see now there has been a grave lack of regard for my son's safety and that of his family.

'My sister was interminably slow to act when I requested her help to aid Nicky to exile. I shall return to Denmark and await news of his family with my nephew, the Danish King. I wish you good health and a life of happiness, Tatya.'

With a kiss on each cheek, and then one more, I am greeted for the last time in the Russian way.

And so, my duties as a Romanov are complete.

JEAN

51

Aurora Estate, Red Hill

The gallery looks magnificent ahead of the opening of *Empire —The House of Champion*. Aurora's portraits are installed on the freshly painted walls under centralised tracked lighting with displays of personal items and handicrafts interspersed throughout. Her self-portrait is centre stage.

Summer has arranged the samovar beneath the Grand Duchess Olga's still life painting, cleverly matching the fabric of the tablecloth. Beside it is a brightly embroidered traditional headscarf and a quirky arrangement of Pete's wooden birds: a miniature carving in the shape of an eagle with wings raised in flight along with trios of crows, magpies and kookaburras.

Pete joins Evie and me in the gallery and leans in to inspect Aurora's self-portrait, displayed for the first time.

He points and peers through his glasses at the two blurred words. 'Jean, these words here are Russian. *Rybka* is a term of endearment, a pet name. Little fish. Baba called me that as a child. And Anya is a girl's name: Anne.'

Jean's mind has been working overtime, her thoughts racing as she pieces together the information from the letters and Rosalind's diary. Another piece of the puzzle...

'Anya is mentioned in Rosalind Brassington's diary,' Jean recalls. Pete has helped to translate passages from Tatya's letters, and she has cross-checked the information. *She almost has it.*

Evie frowns. 'I don't understand...'

'Rosalind mentions her dear friend, Tatya, and son, Misha, and daughter, Anya. Tanya is a Romanov—'

'Really? I'm sorry. I'm still not sure what you're getting at.' Evie's eyes widen behind her dark-framed glasses.

'Misha is sometimes called Prince Zolotovsky,' Jean opens a page. 'And then, in her later letters, she calls her friend, Tania. They also mention Martha.'

Pete interjects as he takes a seat by the window. 'That was Baba's name.'

Evie's eyes grow wider and her mouth opens.

'It took me a while to work it out, but Tatiana-Tatya-Tania was Michael's mother.'

'Michael's mother was a Romanov?' Evie screeches.

Jean now recognises the man in the background of Aurora's portrait —Misha—and the symbolism of the gold spires of St Petersburg, and the significance of the Fabergé ladybird. The portrait is a poignant reminder of a different time, a period when blood and birthright entitlement was a life and death affair.

'Tatya and her children went by English names after they fled Russia. Michael Golding is Grand Duchess Tatiana's son. But he wasn't the only one keeping a secret...'

Pete and Evie watch her closely.

Jean takes a deep breath. 'Our mother wasn't English. She was Russian too. The orphan Rosalind mentions in her diary, the one Grand Duchess Tatiana took under her wing. Aurora's name was Anya.'

'Oh my goodness!' Evie takes a seat and stares at the portrait with her hand covering her mouth. Pete returns with a glass of Rick's Aurora Estate shiraz for her, and, for Jean, a tall glass of soda with a squeeze of lemon.

'Hazel mentioned the collector who sold her the samovar painting,'

Jean says wistfully. 'If he knew Rosalind *and* Grand Duchess Olga from those days, he might have known Tatya too. Unfortunately, when Hazel went back to London after the war, the shop had closed, and no one knew what had happened to him.'

'How extraordinary.'

Jean flicks through Rosalind Brassington's diary again and points Evie to another page and a whole new understanding emerges.

'Talk about secrets!' Evie looks from one to the other. 'That's unbelievable!'

'We know the ladybird was commissioned by the Grand Duke Georgiy Romanov for *T.V.*— Grand Duchess Tatiana Vladimirovna Romanova of Russia. This is Tatiana's brooch.'

Jean clears her throat. 'It seems Aurora was keeping a huge secret. She was looking out for Michael—protecting him from someone or something—'

In her self-portrait, Aurora preserved the links to her past in a way she could never reveal aloud. But at the time it was painted, there was so much pain and trauma that she must have considered it best to hide it away.

Pete interrupts. 'Aurora must have given Baba the brooch after Rick's birth. Perhaps in thanks for her loyalty—or her secrecy?'

'I agree,' Jean nods, 'and if Misha was Georgiy and Tatiana's child, some might say that as the last male in the direct line, he had a legitimate claim to the Imperial Russian throne.'

'Wait!' Evie's eyes are like owls behind her glasses. 'If Michael is a Romanov, then that means Rick—'

'Yes.' They look from one to the other as the significance dawns.

'And Pete, if Martha brought you up, then your birth mother was...?' Evie blinks rapidly.

Jean reaches for Pete's hand and squeezes. His connection to Tatiana is probably too much to address for one day.

The opening of the Aurora Estate Gallery is a glittering affair. Bright sequined cocktail dresses of taffeta and silk give life to the gallery as tracked lighting pinpoints vivid splashes of colour and men in dinner suits mingle in the crowd. Photographers prowl the room and circle the guests hunting for a story.

Everyone has helped, but no one could fail to be impressed by Jean's great eye for detail and Summer's command of promotion. Naturally, it's a success. With Jean in charge, the whole operation has been super-efficient. She hasn't lost her cool once. Excitement fizzes around her like sparks catching a flame. Jean is in her element, in tune with the artwork, her family and her surroundings.

She takes a sip of sparkling water and catches Evie's attention across the room. Evie smiles and signals she will join her soon.

An elderly woman in a splendid swathe of olive-green silk approaches Jean. As recognition dawns, lines around the woman's eyes wrinkle. She squints into the glowing light.

'You're the artist's daughter, aren't you? You're the image of her. I must say, I do love that gown. Is it couture?'

'Thank you.' Jean's smile is perfected and second nature after years of social functions. Then the woman spots a camera and quickly moves towards it.

Resisting the urge to check the time again, Jean places her empty glass on a passing waiter's tray. The pretty white gold bangle band of her watch glints under the lighting. Her jewellery is understated, nothing gaudy or chunky. Costume jewellery is in vogue these days—every second woman here is sporting bright resin beads or gold painted shells around their neck. But Jean is a classic kind of girl. Aurora was too.

Her tension eases as she revisits a portrait of her father as the elderly man she never witnessed. People are grouped around her with their heads close together in conversation. She recognises a few executive types in high-powered corporation suits with their wives (or mistresses) in tow. And several celebrities. Summer and Evie move to join a new group enjoying the social activity now that the catering staff have the refreshments flowing.

A man behind a pillar catches her attention. Abe Stephens is the head of a multi-national advertising agency. Jean met him years ago and has no interest in reacquainting. His stooped profile reminds her of the wolf hovering over Red Riding Hood. Fortunately, he's deep in discussion with Rick. She hopes he's brought his chequebook.

Hazel leaves a group of women to join her. They haven't had a chance to speak in private. Jean noticed her regaling guests with stories on the background of some of Aurora's earlier works. She's in good form tonight. But when she leans in to kiss Hazel's cheek, Jean reels back. The bitter smell of death lingers on her breath, stale and potent like mothballs. Jean takes her wrinkled hand and squeezes it. Hazel has put on a brave front, but she is far less healthy than she'd have them believe.

'What do you think?' Jean smiles brightly, but Hazel's resting face is serene.

'It's wonderful, dear. Simply wonderful. You've done a marvellous job. Aurora would have been delighted. I'm so glad to have made it.'

'We are too.'

Then Hazel frowns, the lines on her face wrinkling deeper into the peach-coloured pancake powder that is her trademark.

'You know, I'm surprised she never painted Michael, especially given what happened. I thought she might have, after he died. It was such a tragedy.'

'A tragedy?'

'The hit and run that killed him. And quite the mystery at the time. No witnesses, and so close to his apartment in Collins Street. The man from that lovely Italian café downstairs mentioned something about a black car, but when the police questioned him later, he insisted he was mistaken. I was shattered, of course...'

Jean turns to face her. Michael had swiftly disappeared from her life, so she had no idea of the circumstances of his death. 'When did it happen?'

'Oh, I imagine, not long after you disappeared, dear. You would have been in Sydney.' She squints in thought. 'The mid-fifties? Right when there was all that scaremongering about Soviets and the Red Terror...and the Cambridge spies. Do you remember?'

Jean holds a hand to her diaphragm.

'Of course, I'd fallen from favour by that time. I was out of the loop, so to speak.'

'I'm so sorry, Hazel.' Jean is lost for words. Her chest feels tight.

Tears glisten in the older woman's eyes. 'I'm just so happy to see you all again and to be here with Aurora's fabulous masterpieces. To see them one last time.'

Hazel takes out her handkerchief and checks her watch. 'Now, like Cinderella on the stroke of midnight I must go. My man will be outside to collect me.'

Jean signals to Pete to walk Hazel out to the car and moves to the balcony for a breath of fresh air. She leans on the handrail. She can't face another goodbye.

Her skin tingles in the warm air as the hint of rose wafts from the garden beds, as though Aurora has paid them a visit too. The night is clear, and the sky is dotted with a fine array of stars; cicadas chirp like a backing track crooning an insect concerto to the vines.

She has almost survived her first social event and is pleased she hasn't been tempted to drink once—despite the many compliments to Rick on his first vintage of Aurora Estate shiraz, the Heritage.

'If you stay hidden out here for too long, you'll be missed.' Pete rests his hand on her back. 'Happy? It's been a great night.'

'Yes. It's fabulous.' She smiles into the darkness. 'I can't tell you what it means to be here again and to see all her work displayed and admired.'

He turns her to him. 'And I can't tell you, how much you mean to me. More than words can say. You are a diamond in the rough, my love. A marvel...'

'Oh, stop it!' Jean closes her eyes, but her heart is full of love for him. She has everything she needs right here; everyone she loves is in this building, in the home she loved so dearly as a child.

Pete lowers his head and kisses her. His kiss deepens and renders her helpless; it stirs her body and awakens her response as nothing before. They have much to look forward to.

A few minutes later, they enter the room, and a series of flashes go off in their faces. Jean keeps hold of Pete's elbow until they have finished. The formalities are almost done.

Rick calls her to the microphone to close the proceedings. Artists and art critics, along with long-time supporters of Aurora's work, have turned up to view the self-portrait, which is pronounced one of the artist's finest works. Several reporters have interviewed Rick regarding his plans for the future of the vineyard and photographed the family together beneath Aurora's portrait. It's been a huge success.

As Jean's sashays across the floor with willowy grace, the beads on the bodice of her silver evening dress swish in time to Tchaikovsky's joyful '*Valzer dei fiori*'. Tonight, she has stepped into the past.

EPILOGUE

Aurora Estate, Red Hill 1988

Jean takes Rick's coffee to him amongst the vines and returns to the verandah. A warm breeze scented with freshly watered soil rustles the pages of the newspaper spread on the table. As she flattens the upturned page with her hand, a ladybird settles on the print and crawls across the heading:

> Secret Child of Grand Duke Georgiy Alexandrovich

The article goes on to explain that the archives of Rosarchiv, the Federal Archival Agency in Russia, have been opened for the first time. The journalist interviewed two American historians who had visited the Soviet Archival Research Centre in Moscow and inspected the personal papers of the imperial Romanov family and were the first outside of the Soviet Union to view the archives.

> An entry written in the diary of Tsar Nicholas II of Russia records his despair on learning of the death of his brother, Grand Duke Georgiy, who died tragically in 1899. The entry discusses his

concern over Georgiy's request for marriage to Grand Duchess Tatiana Vladimirovna Romanova. Henceforth, tactful negotiations were necessary to keep peace between the two nations who had previously agreed to a political marriage involving Grand Duke Georgiy.

The historians were unaware of any documentation regarding this marriage, and further searches neglected to disclose or confirm the information. There was, however, reference to an agreement regarding the forthcoming union between Grand Duke Georgiy and Duchess von Brandt of Bavaria which never took place.

The article refers to an entry stating that Grand Duchess Tatiana was expecting a child when Georgiy died. The Tsar noted it was appropriate to see to her future security whilst necessary plans should also be addressed for the future of Georgiy's child.

Jean gently sweeps the ladybird away with her hand as she reads down the page.

Tsar Nicholas II was the last Emperor of Russia. Bolshevik factions brutally murdered Nicholas II, and, allegedly, the Empress, together with the Tsarevich and his four sisters in Yekaterinburg in 1918. Documentation proving specific Soviet involvement was not available to view.

Grand Duchess Tatiana, an acclaimed beauty of the imperial court, was a favourite cousin of the Romanov family and was often in their company. For reasons that remain unexplained, she was never formally acknowledged or publicly proclaimed as Grand Duke Georgiy's wife. Documents, however, were discovered relating to her marriage to naval captain, Nikolai Zolotov, and, later, to Count Ilya Vorontov, a former lieutenant of Her Imperial Majesty's Life Guards. Beyond that, the records disappear.

Interest now lies in the identity of the child. Given recent *glasnost*, or political openness, regarding the release of cultural information leading up to the Soviet revolution.

Remaining members of the extended Romanov family, and supporters throughout the Russian émigré community, would no doubt be interested to know if there is a direct male line descendant in the event the monarchy should ever be restored.

Jean hears a shuffle behind her in the pram. The baby gurgles and opens his eyes. Jean coos as her grandson's tiny fingers grip hers securely. 'Who's my handsome boy?'

'Mummy!' a shrill voice interrupts from inside, 'can we pick the grapes now?'

'Please, Mummy, is it time?' echoes another as Summer and Rick's identical blonde–haired daughters appear, wearing fluoro tutus and matching rainbow gumboots.

Jean laughs. 'There's no stopping those two! Go on, he's fine with me...'

Summer nods. 'Come on, girls. Let's see if Daddy needs our help.' She follows them into the fields.

Jean returns to the article.

> The possibility of a child is pure speculation. Grand Duchess Tatiana exiled to England along with the Dowager Empress Maria Feodorovna and extended members of the family in 1918. There are no further records regarding her whereabouts.
>
> Given that any child of Tatiana and Georgiy would now be eighty-five years old, at best, the likelihood of a direct living descendant to the last tsar is relatively slim. While primogeniture laws preclude females from inheriting, a male child would unreservedly be the rightful successor and proclaimed the head of the Romanov family.

In the distance, Rick waves as his daughters reach him and roll on the grass at his feet. He finishes twirling a vine back to its post and lifts the girls over his head, circling them one by one. The sound of their laughter echoes through the valley.

'Here we go.' Pete appears and hands Jean a beautiful *matryoshka*, freshly glossed with a light coat of varnish. Her traditional diadem is covered in pearls; she has hair the colour of golden honey and sapphire eyes which glow in the sunlight.

The nesting dolls have become a signature of Aurora Estate. Jean and Pete create them together, a combination of his meticulous woodwork and her fine artwork.

He uncurls his palm.

'More painting for me,' Jean laughs at the tiny carved doll. 'He's perfect.'

The ladybird spreads her wings. A breath of wind gently lifts her airborne and she glides over the pram, hovering on the stitches of the blanket Jean knitted.

The newest Champion looks up, his rosebud lips parted in a milky smile.

And Jean's love is mirrored in topaz eyes that shine bright with trust as the ladybird flies away home.

THE END

AUTHOR'S NOTES

When a letter came into my possession from a dear schoolfriend several years ago, written on filmy notepaper bearing our old school letterhead, and found in archives quite a distance from its origins, it inspired the first threads of this story. The mention of a pin led me to Fabergé, and by association, to the Romanovs.

It is widely known the last Tsar of Russia, Nicholas II and members of the entire Romanov family were murdered in cold blood by Bolsheviks in 1918. The gruesome tale has both haunted and fascinated me; family portraits show the four beautiful Grand Duchesses in white dresses, the sickly haemophilic Tsarevich, and the Tsar and Tsarina serenely posed in images that endure. It is unfathomable to conceive that anyone deserved to be executed in such an abhorrent manner.

As a mother, what horrified me most was not only the sheer brutality of the act but also the senseless and despicable murder of the children. Tragically, we are still faced with the slaughter of innocent children in far too many parts of our world today. With that said, in the early stages of the story, their history prompted the question: to what lengths would a mother go to protect her child?

With the combination of my letter and an Australian article about

AUTHOR'S NOTES

the death of the great-grandson of Olga Romanov, sister to the Tsar, the contemporary narrative started to take shape.

While the characters of Tatiana, Misha and several others are pure fabrication, the names of many in my story will be familiar to you as their characters are drawn from Russian history. I have pinpointed certain significant events leading to the revolution and the overthrow of imperial rule, but for the sake of the plot, there were times when it was not possible to include every detail. Any mistakes in the reportage of history, though not intentional, are mine.

I remind readers that this is a story of fiction—and while not party to exact conversations and events, I was deeply immersed in research that included several thought-provoking texts and records and contemporary accounts and diaries of the imperial family and those in their inner circle. My research on Fabergé sent me down a huge rabbit hole of procrastination! I found pre-revolutionary Russia fascinating to research, and because of this, wrote far too many tangents and scenes that did not make it into the final draft. My sincere thanks, too, to a certain lecturer in Russian history and diaspora studies for his research assistance; I hope he recognises (and approves of) the character named after him.

Other wonderful resources were the collected works and incredibly informative autobiography of a real ambassador's daughter, Meriel Buchanan, daughter of the British ambassador. Her poignant recollections of her life and experiences in a diplomatic family in St Petersburg and across Europe proved inspiration for Tatiana's friend, Rosalind Brassington.

Verification of the deaths of the Romanov family came in stages over several decades. While Bolsheviks initially reported the Tsar's execution at Yekaterinburg in 1918, it wasn't until 1991, after the fall of the Soviet Union, that the Romanov family's deaths were finally confirmed, and their remains exhumed. Soviets kept the sites secret, but amateur historians had uncovered the site containing the remains of the Tsar, Tsarina and three of their five children as early as 1979. In 1998 the remains were reinterred but without the presence of the Russian Orthodox Church who to this day have not acknowledged them as the Romanov family. Conspiracy theories abound.

AUTHOR'S NOTES

In 2007 a second burial site revealed the remains of Anastasia and Alexei, and after DNA analysis was completed later that year, confirmation that the entire family had been executed put rumours of a remaining Anastasia to rest.

For further reading, Dr Helen Rappaport has written several fabulous books on the Romanovs. Also of interest is the following article from Town and Country by historian Simon Sebag Montefiore; https://www.townandcountrymag.com/socicty/tradition/a8072/russian-tsar-execution/ taken from his book, *The Romanovs 1613-1918*.

I have attempted to portray the Romanovs as a loving family, living in the manner and style that I believed they lived. All accounts suggest that Alix and Nicky were madly in love and entirely devoted to each other, and in turn, adored their five children. The close-knit family unit relished their privacy, and as both my story and history attest, perhaps to their detriment and in turn instigated cataclysmic repercussions for Russia and her people.

ACKNOWLEDGMENTS

As with all stories that come to fruition, there are many people to thank for this final production. First of all, I'd like to thank you, dear reader, for choosing my book and for investing the time to read it. I am truly grateful for your support. It is my pleasure to be able to write what I love, and all the more heartwarming to be able to share my stories with you. A thousand thank yous.

As always, my sincere appreciation to my amazing family for giving me the time and space to create. I love you all to the moon and back and especially appreciate your hugs when I resurface again from the depths of my story and into the real world.

From the first draft to the final product, and over several years, I have been fortunate to receive advice, mentorship and encouragement from many wonderful authors and editors for this book, including Pamela Freeman, Nicola O'Shea, Kylie Mason and Laura Boon. I would sincerely like to thank early readers Tania, Deborah, Tracy and Robyn for their time, patience and feedback. Also, the fabulous Pamela Cook and Lisa Ireland for their generous support and endorsements. The result is all wrapped up in this lovely cover from Hazel Lam.

My final thank you is for the enduring optimism of my dear friend, the eternally effervescent Debbie, who provided me with the spark to light the flame for this story. From the beginning of our friendship, writing furtive notes in the back row of Mr Pyke's English Literature classes, she has supported and encouraged me with love and kindness at every step of the way. Thank you, dear heart.

READER REVIEWS

Thank you for reading *The Romanov Secret*. I hope you enjoyed getting to know my characters as much as I did.

Reviews are the lifeblood of an author. If you enjoyed reading this book, please consider leaving a review on the retailer's website or a peer review site such as Good Reads to help other readers discover it.

If you would like to keep up-to-date with my news, you can sign up to receive my newsletter: https://substack.com/@chrissiebellbrae.

Printed in Dunstable, United Kingdom

76934686R00211